THIS COOL GREEN EARTH

THIS
COOL
GREEN
EARTH

A Novel

Don McBurney

NEW YORK

LONDON • NASHVILLE • MELBOURNE • VANCOUVER

THIS COOL GREEN EARTH
A NOVEL

© 2022 DON MCBURNEY

Published in New York, New York, by Morgan James Publishing. Morgan James is a trademark of Morgan James, LLC. www.MorganJamesPublishing.com

Publisher's Note: This novel is a work of fiction. Names, characters, places, and incidents are either products of the author's imagination or used fictitiously. All characters are fictional, and any similarity to people living or dead is purely coincidental.

The majority of Scriptures are taken from the Holy Bible, New International Version®, NIV®. Copyright © 1973, 1978, 1984, 2011 by Biblica, Inc.™ Used by permission of Zondervan. All rights reserved worldwide. www.zondervan.com The "NIV" and "New International Version" are trademarks registered in the United States Patent and Trademark Office by Biblica, Inc.™

Some Scripture quotations are from The ESV® Bible (The Holy Bible, English Standard Version®), copyright © 2001 by Crossway, a publishing ministry of Good News Publishers. Used by permission. All rights reserved.

Some Scripture taken from the New King James Version®. Copyright © 1982 by Thomas Nelson. Used by permission. All rights reserved.

Some Scripture taken from the King James Version, public domain.

Some Scripture quotations taken from the (NASB®) New American Standard Bible®, Copyright © 1960, 1971, 1977, 1995, 2020 by The Lockman Foundation. Used by permission. All rights reserved. www. lockman.org.

Some Scripture quotations take from JPS Hebrew-English TANAKH. Philadelphia: Jewish Publication Society, bilingual edition, 2003.

One Scripture quotation taken from the *Holy Bible*, New Living Translation, copyright © 1996, 2004, 2015 by Tyndale House Foundation. Used by permission of Tyndale House Publishers, Inc., Carol Stream, Illinois 60188. All rights reserved.

One Scripture quotation taken from the Contemporary English Version (CEV) Copyright © 1991, 1992, 1995 by American Bible Society. Used by Permission.

Morgan James BOGO™

A **FREE** ebook edition is available for you or a friend with the purchase of this print book.

CLEARLY SIGN YOUR NAME ABOVE

Instructions to claim your free ebook edition:
1. Visit MorganJamesBOGO.com
2. Sign your name CLEARLY in the space above
3. Complete the form and submit a photo of this entire page
4. You or your friend can download the ebook to your preferred device

ISBN 978-1-63195-598-3 paperback
ISBN 978-1-63195-599-0 ebook
Library of Congress Control Number: 2021906813

Morgan James PUBLISHING Builds with... Habitat for Humanity® Peninsula and Greater Williamsburg

Morgan James is a proud partner of Habitat for Humanity Peninsula and Greater Williamsburg. Partners in building since 2006.

Get involved today! Visit MorganJamesPublishing.com/giving-back

DEDICATION

For Marilyn, my best friend and wife of more than fifty-two years: Thank you. Thank you for your patient participation in this lengthy writing process, for allowing me the requisite quiet time with God for gathering my thoughts and setting them down on paper, for seeing them grow beyond the merest fragment of an outline into a coherent narrative. I cannot imagine my life without you in it. I could not wish for a greater gift than you are and have been. You are *more than all [I] can ask or imagine,* as Ephesians 3:20 so elegantly puts it. You're a blessing—not only to me but also to all those whom you love so well!

And for my family: I'm thinking about you and desperately wanting each of you to know and love God with all your heart, mind, soul and strength. I hope and pray that when you read this, even years from now, you will gain wisdom from my mistakes and experiences. You don't have to learn everything the hard way.

ACKNOWLEDGMENTS

Two couples, Nick and Rose Bubnash and Tom and Carol Bangs, hosted and showed us across their farm and ranch land. They were generous with their time, impressed us with the quality of their local museums and provided valuable historical background on their lands. Thank you for your time and for sharing with us. Marv and Debbie Bethea gave us an insider's tour of St. Marie like few others could have done. We enjoyed a wonderful evening of good food and Christian fellowship. Thank you for your inspiration.

Kristin Hagg read an early portion of my manuscript. She gave valuable and thoughtful feed-back to me that I heeded. Thank you, Kristin. To Doren Renfrow, an early reader of this book in its initial stage of completion, I offer my heartfelt thanks. Your encouragement meant a lot to me, not only on this project but on many others as well.

Likewise, thank you, Rich Closson. You read this manuscript when I thought it might have been finished. I appreciated your comments, both for their correction and affirmation.

And to Michele Chynoweth, the editor I had to have, the one knowledgeable and brave enough to deconstruct what I had written. The finished product is all the better because of your work and professional input. Your suggestions on how to improve my narrative flow were vital to the completion of this project. You had a big job. Thank you for your diligence in seeing it through.

To Noah Lewis, your ability to understand the personal computer software world and solve its myriad issues was a God-send. Above all, I appreciated your helpful attitude. Without your expert guidance, I didn't have a chance of navigating the unfamiliar terrain of electronic programs.

Finally, I was fortunate to have expert input from Wayne Franklin, an experienced and highly regarded engineer. He kept me on track and graciously guided me with technical information and mathematics. Many thanks, my friend. I also read many books and articles and watched on-topic teaching sessions from credentialed professors and astrophysicists. I'm grateful for all of you. Big thanks from me to you, to one and all. You helped me tell my story accurately but if there are mistakes in the telling, they belong to me. Terry Whalin, acquisitions editor with Morgan James Publishing, read my early manuscript and went to bat for me. My work would not have seen the light of day without his help. Margo Toulouse was a wonderful coordinator who juggled the various departments for me at Morgan James. I would have wandered, lost and confused, without her holding my hand. Cortney Donelson was the final proofreader who checked for and eliminated any final errors. Thanks to both of you lovely ladies. It's been a privilege to work with Morgan James because of you.

PART 1
MONTANA ON MY MIND

Be fruitful and increase in number and fill the earth.
(Genesis 9:1)

CHAPTER 1

GIL, 2006

A new year would begin at midnight. In some ways, it would be a harbinger of a coming apocalypse. But people were as yet ignorant of that fact. On this particular New Year's Day, the sun would come up over their Iowa farm the way it did when Gil Webster had been young. That hadn't changed. But now he was married: had a wife, Gail, and a baby girl, Maisie Joy.

The sun hadn't changed, nor had this house and land—but Gil had. His skin was still brown and his eyes were still large, round and dark but he was no longer a Middle Eastern orphan; he had been adopted and brought to America. He was an American.

Gil was loved, educated and grateful for so much in his life. He had been a boy growing up on this farm; now he was a grown man, visiting his parents. It was their farm, not his. But in this new year, he had a renewed commitment to search for his own land and his place in the world. This fresh new year contained three hundred and sixty-five days of golden opportunity that was as yet unspoiled and unsoiled. By God's grace, he would find his own land this year, put down his own roots and make his own forever home.

The days were short in January in Iowa but the first faint hint of dawn greeted Gil as he got out of bed to welcome this new year. As it grew lighter, he looked out over familiar postcard perfection after a night of calm, soft, winter snowfall. There was no wind, no sound at that hour in the country. All was quiet.

Gail came up behind him at the living room's front window near the fireplace. She had a cup of hot coffee for him. They enjoyed a muted glimmer of the newly jeweled morning, the pure white snow as yet untracked on the driveway. They knew the ephemeral beauty of snow goes as quickly as it comes, but at that moment, these snowflakes painted a pastoral picture.

After enjoying a few leisurely minutes together, Gil kissed his wife then put on his coat and boots to go outside and breathe deeply the crisp air with its subtle fragrance of wood smoke from his parents' chimney.

He went to greet his father Duane, who was just stepping out of the barn. How he loved that man, watching him standing there with his battered old hat in his hand, for the great gift of saving faith in God he had shared with him. How he loved this man, this land, this place—his heritage. Here it was he had learned about redemption, experienced love, dared to dream, found out that God knew his name. He went to stand with the older man in silence for a while, then together, they turned for the house and breakfast.

Maisie stirred. Gail heard the mewling sounds of her infant daughter and went to change, feed and dress her. Gil's mother, Ethel, had already been up, as was the habit of farmers' wives all over the world. She was putting the finishing touches on breakfast as the two men came in, stomping the snow off their boots. They gathered around the table as Duane opened in prayer, "Heavenly Father, thank you for the beauty of this fresh new year, for work to do and for food on the table. We praise You and give thanks especially for our son and his family who have joined us for the beginning of this new year and helped brighten this day. Thank you for the life they bring into our house. We pray these things in Jesus' name, amen."

Maisie couldn't yet sit up but she could roll over, coo and blow bubbles. She enjoyed being with them on her blanket on the floor by the kitchen stove's warmth.

"Mom, I surely do like to wake up, go outside, then return to come in to your cooking." Gil smelled the biscuits with white gravy, sausage made from the neighbor's farm, and fresh eggs from his mother Ethel's own chickens.

Gail added, "This is a lazy treat for me. I feel like you're doing all the work."

"Not a word of that!" Ethel chided with a smile. "The pleasure is all mine. I love cooking for you. And a new mother who nurses her first baby in the middle of the night deserves to be treated well."

Duane asked his daughter-in-law, "Gail, when do you think your parents will arrive? You think they can make it for lunch?"

"No, my brother Clyde can handle chores by himself but my father won't want to leave until that work is done. So they won't leave ahead of sunrise."

Gil interrupted, "Plus the deer on the roads."

"Right, they've got to watch out for deer during early morning hours." Gail spooned some gravy over a biscuit on her plate. "They're probably eating breakfast right now like we are but I'll bet Mother's already packed and ready to hit the road as soon as she gets the dishes done and put away. It's too far for them to drive and be able to get here until mid-afternoon, though. It was nice of you to invite them for New Year's and I'm sure they won't be late. Mother will have already made sure Daddy didn't dawdle at the barn."

"I'm looking forward to seeing them again. We haven't seen them since our paths overlapped at Maisie's birth when you were still in the Army at that NATO base in Turkey," Duane said. "I hope they stay a while and don't leave too soon."

———

Gil went back outside after breakfast and fired up the tractor to spread hay for the cattle. He could picture Dad relaxing with baby Maisie by the fire. Sometimes those two took naps together but this time they were quiet and just watched one another, taking turns smiling at each other.

After a little while, he saw Gail put on her coat and boots and walk down the driveway to the mailbox so she could fetch the newspaper. She shoveled the mailbox clear so their rural carrier had easy access to it. She brought the paper back inside and Gil could picture her handing the cartoons to her father-in-law, the crossword to her mother-in-law and then taking a minute to glance through the rest of the local paper before handing it over to both.

Gil finished feeding the cattle. He brought the tractor up from the barn to plow the driveway and keep it clear of snow. He came back inside the kitchen just in time to see his wife poke the fire in the adjoining family room, put another log on it and hear her fondly say, "Gil used to tell me he felt ready for winter when he had the woodpile under cover and ready to go. He has fond memories of gathering wood and clearing brush from fence rows with you in the autumn, thinning timber and watching sparks fly up out of the burning brush piles in the evenings at the end of the day's work. He was always amazed that you could return to the ashes up to a week later and stir up a fresh fire out of them."

He quietly removed his dripping boots on the kitchen tile floor, watched his father nod his head in agreement and overheard him say, "It's good to work outside, side by side. Physical labor, father and son. Those times are good memories for me, too." Gil smiled to himself.

Ethel added, "I heard you men say a hundred times: 'wood is good—it heats you twice, once when you cut it up and once when you burn it up'."

Duane chuckled, "Now, Ethel, if I've told you once I've told you a million times, don't exaggerate."

Idyllic a scene as it was, Gil felt a flash of melancholia because he suspected, deep inside himself, that he was in the process of saying goodbye to it. For some reason, he had Montana on his mind. He realized he might be taking Gail a long way from their childhood homes in Iowa. *But why?* He knew deep down this new year was a harbinger . . . *of what, exactly?* He would have to pray and study on it.

CHAPTER 2

SING, 1942

It's a long story—how I got from there to here. My name is Sing Liu, and I am a third-generation Chinese man in America. As a child I grew up at Grandfather's side, listening to his stories.

Many times, while fishing, I've heard Grandfather tell of how our family's story began in the rural area near the seacoast north of Shanghai. His hip bothered him when trying to sit at our campfire. He had lines on his face and old wisdom in his eyes. As his white beard would move in the breeze out on our big fishing lake, he could seem otherworldly, yet to me, he and his wisdom were always well-grounded.

It all began with World War II. Yes, China was a part of it. China had a role to play in it.

Japan, known to be an aggressor nation, had already invaded China before 1940. Their soldiers' aggressions were often violent and radical, wicked to the extreme, evil without reason. Yet Grandfather knew that Genghis Khan, centuries before, had inspired terror in people. He wanted people to fear him and what he could do to them. In cities that didn't surrender to him, he dripped molten silver into the eyes of their leaders to send a message of warning to other cities. Since Khan was Chinese, Grandfather knew it was not only the Japanese who were brutal. The Chinese could be cruel and aggressive as well.

But the Americans didn't feel threatened by the Japanese invasion of China. They thought it had nothing to do with them. And besides, Japan was half a world away from the North American continent, beyond range of her aircraft and navy. So the Japanese attack on Pearl Harbor on December 7, 1941 took the Americans by surprise.

As a result, the American Congress declared war on Japan but the United States armed forces had already been severely damaged by the time Congress acted; they were ill-prepared for open hostilities. Cruisers, destroyers and eight battleships had been either damaged or sunk at Pearl, aircraft had been strafed and over thirty-five hundred people had been killed or wounded.

American armed forces suffered setback after setback as they tried to get on a solid operational footing. Morale was low. Military commanders didn't know what Axis powers in the Pacific planned to do. It might not have made much difference but U.S. Secretary of War Henry Stimson had shut down the State Department's cryptanalytic office as he said, "Gentlemen don't read each other's mail."

The U.S. Army Chief of Staff, General George C. Marshall, was concerned about this sad state of affairs in military intelligence preparedness so, ironically, he had scheduled a high-level Pentagon conference on the topic for December 8. Of course, it was canceled because it ended up being one day after the fact and the question was no longer whether intelligence training was necessary, but rather, how quickly could it begin. As it turned out, six months later, on June 19, 1942, the Army leased Camp Ritchie from Maryland for a dollar a year and opened the first facility for centralized intelligence training in the history of the United States military.

One of America's many problems was that Japan was outside the range of almost all her bomber aircraft. To meet this challenge, a daring plot was hatched—daring in that nothing like it had ever been attempted before.

An enterprising soldier got the wild idea that perhaps, just maybe, a heavy Army bomber could be launched off a Navy aircraft carrier. One can imagine him thinking, *the Japanese sneak attack damaged many of our ships at Pearl Harbor—but not a single aircraft carrier was there in port. They all happened to be out delivering planes to Midway and Wake Islands. So none of them were sunk. They all escaped. And they are available for us to use in revenge in a strike-back. Could we use one of our carriers to get some of our bomber aircraft within striking distance of Tokyo?*

And thus, Special Aviation Project #1 came about. B-25 Mitchell bombers were selected as the planes best suited for this special project. They could carry 2,000 pounds of bombs. Extra fuel tanks were installed, which increased their capacity by more than 76 percent to 1,141 gallons and extended their range from 1,200 to almost 2,000 miles. The Army went so far as to put one rubber fuel bladder in the lower gun turret while another was inserted into a portion of the bomb bay itself. As a result, gussets to cradle the bombs had to be repositioned and wooden broomstick handles were substituted to mimic the look of the missing gun barrels. Weight was a problem so radios and other equipment that would typically be considered essential were removed as extreme weight-saving measures.

Sixteen of these modified B-25s flew to Alameda Naval Air Station on April Fool's Day of 1942 under Lieutenant Colonel James H. Doolittle's command and were hoisted onto the *USS Hornet*. The take-off distance had to be cut by two-thirds for the bombers. They would simply have to pray they made it into the air . . . and find pilots who were willing to take the risk.

Jimmy Doolittle was a military test pilot with a doctoral degree in aeronautical engineering. He had set air race records and was the first to fly coast to coast across the United States in less than twenty-four hours. His training, experience and name recognition qualified him to lead this hazardous mission, even though he was an elderly forty-five years of age at the time. The various aircrews for this mission later came to be known to the American public as "Doolittle's Raiders."

After being loaded, the planes were stacked so closely and so tightly on the carrier's deck that the sixteenth and last plane's tail hung off the rear of the carrier and its right wing cleared the *Hornet's* command and control island by only six feet. The convoy of one carrier, two cruisers, four destroyers and one oiler put out to sea the next morning and sailed under the Golden Gate Bridge at 0900 hours in broad daylight despite the fact they were on a Top Secret mission.

Colonel Doolittle told his men, "Think of it this way, boys. Some of you will be coming back here as heroes and some of you as angels." Even if survivors of the take-offs and bombing runs were so fortunate as to be able to complete their mission, they would not be able to return to and land on the carrier's deck. They might barely be able to take off but there would be no way those Army bombers and Army pilots would be able to return to and land on a Navy carrier rolling and pitching at sea.

In short, America was losing the war in the Pacific because she was at such a disadvantage from the very beginning. Japan felt secure in the belief that the United States could not reach out and touch them. And America's military commanders knew that even if the Raiders' mission was successful, it, by itself, would not be enough to secure victory.

Therefore, the idea behind the Raiders' mission was primarily psychological—if they could inflict damage on major cities on Japan's mainland, that action would shock and humiliate the Japanese as well as deprive them of their presumption of immunity, and it would boost American morale and her will to win. The idea was not that U.S. forces would bomb Japan into submission with a single mission but that they would force the Japanese to divert troops for their own national defense while, at the same time, American troops would be encouraged to redouble their efforts to initiate many more successful military endeavors or, in other words, build momentum and troop confidence.

The plan was to attack five cities: Yokohama, Nagoya, Tokyo, Kobe and Osaka. These sixteen planes were to lift off from the *Hornet* four hundred miles from the coast of Japan, fly at low levels of fifty to one hundred feet to avoid radar detection, rapidly climb to fifteen hundred feet to release their bomb loads, return to low level, and alter course to continue an additional thousand miles to mainland China. There they would refuel and return to a carefully selected American-held Pacific island.

Serious problems scuttled those plans, however. Japanese picket ships disguised as fishing vessels discovered the American naval convoy. Those little picket ships were sunk but not before they had radioed their discovery to Japanese headquarters in Tokyo.

Colonel Doolittle, because of this, believed he had no other choice. He was forced to make the decision to launch early—twelve hours and two-hundred-fifty miles ahead of schedule.

Thus, it came to pass that April 18 became the day he and his crew took off first in the line of sixteen heavily modified B-25 bombers . . . and they made it! There were loud cheers from those who watched him soar into the air. What had never been done before had now been done.

In the excitement and confusion of the morning, the pilot of one plane forgot to lower his flaps and disappeared below deck level as he ran out of runway. Still, even he managed to stagger along just above the waves as he continued to gain airspeed.

All the planes launched without issue until the sixteenth and last plane maneuvered into position for its take-off. A sudden gust of wind swirled up and one of its propellers scissored into the left arm of a member of the naval ground crew. A spurt of blood splattered across the uniform of that plane's bombardier, Jacob DeShazer, who sucked in a quick breath as he jerked his head up from his work to see a sailor lying under the prop with his arm hanging by a slender thread of skin.

DeShazer, the bombardier, would be captured and taken prisoner by the Japanese just two days later. The Plexiglas nose cone in which he sat now had a jagged hole the size of a dinner plate smashed into it and a strong wind swirled inside. He hadn't seen the accident but surmised that the nose of his craft must have come in violent contact with the tail of the fifteenth plane when the wind caused its tail to buck around.

DeShazer's plane finally lifted off. It had taken an hour to get all sixteen planes airborne so this last plane's flight engineer used his extra time to scrounge as many five-gallon fuel cans as he could. He pitched them inside the hatch with him. En route to Tokyo, he poured this extra av-gas into his plane's primary fuel tank, punched holes into the empty cans and threw them outside the aircraft where they would sink to the bottom of the ocean.

It took these flight crews and airplanes another four hours to reach the main Japanese island of Honshu at mid-day, which was unfortunate. Their original schedule had them flying over Japan in the middle of the night but the twelve-hour bump in schedule meant they were flying over Japan in the middle of the day—not a good thing for what was supposed to have been a secret approach. Theirs was now a totally exposed bombing run.

Colonel Doolittle and the first planes over their targets enjoyed the element of surprise such that they were not shot at but planes that followed had artillery and anti-aircraft guns to contend with. None were shot down but several took hits as they flew through the shrapnel. That was the good news. The bad news: Barring a miracle, none of the sixteen planes was going to be able to make it to their destination a thousand miles away in China before running out of fuel.

Somehow, though, they got their miracle. A freak storm gave them a tailwind that pushed them the extra one-hundred-fifty miles they needed. But miracle or not, the tailwind didn't completely solve their problem. Homing beacons in China were never turned on for them. And, because of the twelve-hour alteration to their original schedule, instead of arriving in China in daylight they arrived at night in a storm.

None of the sixteen crews had ever bailed out before so it happened that their first jumps into near oblivion were quite an adventure: They were ten thousand miles from home jumping out at night from dying airplanes into a storm over unknown, possibly hostile terrain. After all, Mao Zedong and Chiang Kai-shek had plunged Grandfather's China into civil war at the same time as portions of her territory were occupied and held by Japanese invaders. Chaos and animosity were everywhere, which multiplied the danger to these Raiders ten-fold.

Beating the odds, while seven men were injured only three of the eighty crew members died during their parachute jumps. Eight were captured immediately and treated cruelly by the Japanese as prisoners of war. DeShazer was one of the eight, Doolittle was not. So where was he?

CHAPTER 3
GIL, 2006

Gail's parents, Harvey and Emma Gomerdinger, arrived mid-afternoon. This was their first visit to the Webster's farm, so they toured the house as their luggage was carried in and deposited in the guest bedroom in the upstairs loft. This guest room was a tad bit on the cool side but not chilly since the heat from the fire downstairs wafted up through its open door.

Ethel said, "I hope this is okay and the stairs don't give you trouble. I put a quilt on the bed. If you need more there's a down comforter here in the cedar chest."

"It's perfect," Emma replied. "We have a farmhouse a lot like this one and Gail grew up in a room like this. We feel right at home and couldn't ask for anything more."

Harvey was ready to stretch his legs and Duane was eager to show off his place so the two of them readied themselves to survey the farm. The two women watched as their men walked out, one in his bib overalls and the other in faded jeans with a flannel shirt and suspenders. "Fashion plates, both." Emma grinned, gazing out the window.

"They're lovable," Ethel replied, turning to put some clothes away. "I guess we'll probably keep them a few more years, don't you think?"

Outside, Duane surveyed his property alongside Harvey. "Our little creek is frozen over now. We can loop around through the bean field, walk up the creek to the barn and you can get the lay of the land. I don't have big acreage but it's about all I can handle."

Harvey had declined an offer of snowshoes, said his Paks were all he needed, and after they had been out a half-hour or so he said, "This feels good— just the right amount of exercise. Your place looks good. You should be proud of it."

"Thanks, I am. Slopes on some of the steeper hills are better suited to pasture and hay ground than row crops so I'm able to run a few head of cattle."

By this time Duane was a little out of breath as he pointed slightly off to his left, "We're getting on up toward the barn. If you don't mind, I'd take it as a favor if you'd look at a cow for me. She's one of our favorites. Ethel and I keep her on as our personal milker."

"Lead the way. Does she have a problem?"

"Naw, I don't think so but she's four months ahead of calving cycle, due 'most any day now. I fixed up a spot for her but it's not the same as wide open pasture in springtime. It'd help me rest easier if you'd give me your expert opinion."

They left the creek behind, came up to the backside of the barn, climbed over the corral fence and went inside. The loft was still over half-filled with alfalfa bales but all the animals were below. Duane had straw already laid in plus feed and water for the heavily pregnant cow. He said, "Her name is Mollie. This will be her third calf. She's done fine before; we've not had any trouble with her."

Harvey nodded. "She looks comfortable. In fact, so much so I don't think you need to have her singled out; she'll let you know when her time is near and she wants to be alone. Let her be with the herd 'til then. She's familiar with this stall so you can just leave its door open and she'll wander in when she wants. Since you've named her and she's a pet, she prob'ly won't kick. Can I go up to her and feel for the calf?"

"Sure, she's fine with that, but just to make double-sure, I'll go to her head and talk to her. Then you can inspect her." Duane approached the cow, rubbed her around the ears and patted her on her neck. "There, there, that's a good girl."

Harvey felt for the calf's nose and hoofs along and behind Mollie's belly. He said, "There's no reason for me to glove up. The calf's positioned correctly for an easy delivery. The hooves are to the rear and the nose is above. Everything's perfect. I wouldn't worry about a thing."

After the New Year's festivities and breakfast together with both sets of parents, Gil approached his father. "Dad, the weather's not bad. May I borrow your truck to go to the library and do some research? I've got something on my mind. I won't be long."

"Of course, son. Take all the time you want. Harvey and I've got nowhere to go and all day to get there."

"Thanks. Is there anything you need from town?"

"Well, a new hip if you find one on sale—otherwise, I'm good."

"I'll keep a lookout but I doubt they have that particular item at the feed store." Gil put the truck in four-wheel to punch through a couple of small drifts out on the county's roadway but it was no trick to get to the library, his destination in town. First, he pulled out a United States atlas to verify what he already knew, then he went online for population statistics from the 2000 Census figures.

He used his common sense to select fifteen states, knowing there was no need for him to research all fifty. From those fifteen, he selected what he wanted according to his criteria. He did a few simple calculations and filtered the data, ranking each state's size, the number of square miles under non-federal or private ownership, population, and in the last column, the state's average density in persons per square mile.

Gil arrayed his data from least to most dense. He studied the short list of states from top to bottom: Alaska, Montana, North Dakota, Wyoming, South Dakota, New Mexico, Idaho.

Hmmm . . . Montana, Wyoming and Idaho were possibilities . . .

CHAPTER 4

SING, 1942

I've heard my grandfather tell his story many times.

"I helped a white man once, long ago," Grandfather would say, stoking the campfire. "It put me in much trouble. But he was worth it. As I tell my tale, see if you do not agree. The white man had a name—John Birch. Knowing him for the short time I traveled with him changed my life and the lives of my family members. He himself single-handedly changed the course of history by his actions in World War II.

"My friend John was born of Presbyterian missionary parents in India on May 28, 1918. His physical life ended just twenty-seven years later on August 25, 1945. He was killed near my house in Shandong Province after he was shot then stabbed with bayonets by Chairman Mao's communist soldiers. His body was thrown into a ditch by the side of a country road. I found and carried it onto my ancestral land for an honorable burial. He gave himself fully and completely to us as not only an American soldier but also as a missionary to my Chinese people.

"My friend whom I honored was unmarried and left no children. How could this young man, a decade younger than myself, with his lack of legacy and ignominious end, have altered the course of world history? I had some hard days but my end was easier than his . . ." And here he would pause, deep in reflection. "My life had no effect on world events so far as I know. His did and here's how . . ."

John Birch grew up poor, went to school poor and graduated from seminary with few possessions, except for a one-way ticket aboard a freighter from Seattle. He was both intelligent and industrious. He graduated as valedictorian from high school in Georgia in 1934 and then magna cum laude from Mercer University in Fort Worth, Texas five years later in 1939—again first in his class. God called him to be a Christian missionary to southeastern China, so he then went to Bible school there and graduated first in his class in half that program's allotted time.

Arriving in Shanghai in 1940, John was gifted in learning the Chinese language as he became fluent in the Mandarin, Gan and Wu dialects in just two years. As quickly as he could, he began venturing out from the city into rural areas to evangelize and spread the gospel of Jesus Christ.

He had to be careful—traveling by night and sleeping by day because Japan had invaded this portion of China some years earlier. Risk, however, was nothing new to him and God continued to bless his fruitful ministry during the next two years.

Then conditions worsened because Japanese forces had issued an arrest warrant for him the day after their sneak attack on Pearl Harbor. John Birch became a fugitive as far as the invading Japanese forces were concerned.

He was hard to capture, though, and was adept at blending into the native population. He could get away with this since he was short for an American but the same height as many of us Chinese. He spoke the language, dressed like a native, dyed his reddish-brown hair black and wore a hat to hide the shape of his eyes. Aside from the obvious and quite visible activity of preaching and witnessing, he did nothing to attract undue attention when not with friends or acquaintances.

During one of his many mission trips, while traveling as a working passenger on a local fishing boat, John Birch, in his disguise, stopped to eat at a small, native restaurant on the low bank of a river in a kind of no-man's land between territory occupied and controlled by invaders and that still held by the native, non-Communist Chinese. He ordered his fish and rice in the native dialect and sat down to eat his meal with chopsticks as all the others were doing. Nevertheless, while he was eating, an older, crippled native brushed by him and whispered, "If you are American, follow me." It was my grandfather, of course.

After finishing his meal to satisfy his hunger and so as not to attract attention, Birch left the restaurant. Grandfather was waiting for him and directed him onto a covered boat that was docked adjacent. It was not a trap. To Birch's pleasant surprise, he came face-to-face with another short American whom he recognized as the famous Jimmy Doolittle. He had heard nothing about Doolittle's bombing raid so he wanted to ask, "What are you doing here?" but didn't. Doolittle introduced himself and the rest of his beleaguered flight crew.

Grandfather whispered to Birch, "I have heard you are a white man who can be trusted. These flyers fell out of the sky onto me in the middle of the night. I don't know what they are doing or have done but I know they are fighting my enemies, those cursed Japanese invaders. So I smuggled these flyers this far. I can't do any more. I don't know English to even be able to talk with them. May I hand them over to you?"

John Birch had circumstantially wandered into a humble eating establishment by the side of the same river along which Grandfather had ferried Doolittle and his men. Accepting this unexpected hand-off, Birch undertook to finish the task on the condition that Grandfather remained with him.

Grandfather agreed. The two then delivered Doolittle and his crew out of enemy territory and into friendly protection. Their trip to safety took four days and was not without its narrow escapes. Grandfather and this missionary bonded during those four days.

The first day, Grandfather trained Doolittle's crew in simple tasks fishermen do in order for them to blend in better with the other boats. Two at a time, they would come out into the open and kneel down, bend over and mend nets while the others hid in the covered part of the boat. This paid off on the second day when a Japanese patrol boat hailed them and pulled alongside. Grandfather was, of course, exactly what he was pretending to be and Birch looked and spoke the part. The other two pretenders completed the crew of the fishing boat, and bending over intent on their tasks, could remain silent without arousing suspicion.

On the last day, the four who were visible were drawing in the net that had several fish in it. A patrol boat again started to come near but saw the four hard at work, so it cruised off on its way. Doolittle whistled out his breath and looked at Birch, who smiled at Grandfather and said in a loud voice, "Master, we will have a profitable catch when we dock." They laughed at each other over their clever joke.

John Birch, a Christian missionary, loved God, but he also loved his native American country and wanted to serve it in this, its critical hour of need. To that end, he had volunteered to enlist in the U.S. Army on April 13, 1942—which just happened to be during the seventeen days Doolittle and his B-25 Raiders were sailing to their destiny and five days before they lifted off and became airborne on the final leg of their journey to Tokyo and the other four cities. Birch's offer was not accepted since he was a missionary—trained as a Christian soldier in love and compassion, not as a military soldier who wears a uniform and carries a gun, perhaps to shoot somebody.

Neither he nor Doolittle was aware of the other's presence or activity, but I believe God arranged their schedules to rendezvous with each other at an appropriate and specific time and place.

Grandfather was fond of saying, "John and I became friends as we traveled together with Doolittle. He answered my questions about the cruelties of life and convinced me his God of love was real during those four days. His kind words and Christian witness changed my life. And his heroic actions changed world history because of God's providence and his obedience to it. John taught me by his example in both word and deed. He had given his life so completely to his ideals that I decided to trust his witness.

"After the successful completion of our mission, I took my fishing boat and returned home." Grandfather continued his story. "Just a little while later, I was taken prisoner by some Japanese when they found a crashed airplane nearby and overwhelmed our poor village in retaliation for Doolittle's bombing runs. It was then I would have to put John's witness to the test. . . ."

Chapter 5

GIL, 2006

Back home that afternoon, Gil sat at the farmhouse's big kitchen table where he could spread out his papers and show the results of his library research to Dad and Mom, Harvey and Emma, Gail and Maisie—although Maisie wasn't at all interested so those two excused themselves for nap time after about ten minutes. Gil said to the two sets of parents, "Naturally, I've been thinking and praying about the future and wondering what God has for us to do next. I was blessed by my Army training and posting but to tell you the truth, I've had Montana on my mind. Up to now, though, I couldn't tell you why."

Gail's father Harvey interrupted, "Montana? Where'd that notion come from? This is the first I've heard of it."

"I just wanted to find out a few things about Montana because it's been on my mind the last couple of years," Gil resumed. "That's why I went to town this morning."

"So . . . ?" Gil's mother Emma left her question dangling with hesitation and worry.

Gil stared at his chart. He picked up his coffee cup, started to bring it to his lips but thought better of it, set it down and cleared his throat. "Every state has less populated and more crowded areas. I thought I might make a scouting trip with Gail and Maisie after the winter . . . when spring breaks in a couple months. I don't know what we might find—in terms of anything—but I wanted to keep you informed, hear myself thinking out loud and ask your advice on this subject.

"Dad, we talked before just a little bit about Montana. That's when I first heard you say you'd been there as a young man on wheat cutting crews. What's your opinion?"

"Well, son, that was a long time ago, years ago. It's big, beautiful country. It's called Big Sky Country for good reason. Mountains and forests are mostly on the western side of the state while the huge wheat fields are mostly on the eastern side. The Continental Divide separates west from east but mountain ranges and wide valleys are scattered all around on both sides of the Divide. Being on a combine crew, I didn't sightsee over the whole state. I don't know what to say more than that."

At this point, Emma broke in: "What are you trying to tell us, Gil. A scouting trip for what?"

"Well, I want to investigate moving to Montana. There has to be a reason it's on my mind. One of my instructors on the airbase in Turkey mentioned she was from Montana and my heart sang as soon as she said the word. I think that was about the first time I had thought about Montana. The fact that the mention of its name rang in my heart means something but I'm not sure exactly what. I'm trying to find out. I'm trying to figure out if perhaps God is leading us to locate there."

"Oh, my. I see," sighed his mother as the two older women looked at each other.

"You know, your mom and I would love to have you live in our back yard," his dad interjected. "We'd give you land to build a new house on and I'd spend time with Maisie every day."

"I know, Dad, I know. And you're very generous . . ."

"You're our only child." Duane's voice started to break. "I can't tell you what to do nor do I want to. I think I knew you wouldn't actually live in our backyard so I'm not surprised by your wanting to explore but this news actually hits us pretty hard—right now, this moment. You know, if you'll forgive us, your mother and I just couldn't help daydreaming."

Gil had no words. He was at a loss. The table was silent. Gail had come back to join the group while Maisie continued to nap. She got herself a cup of coffee during the quiet interlude.

Duane took a breath, then let it out slowly as he continued, "I can rejoice for you if you find and experience a clear call of God on your life. Not many people are fortunate that way. You have to make your own decision as to what God has in store for you and what He would have you do but I pray He blesses you with a supernatural, divine call on your life, wherever that might lead. If that happens, Mom and I would much rather have you in Montana in the center of His will than in our backyard missing His call on your life."

"I agree but I don't really get why you're thinking about moving to a place none of us has ever been." Harvey said, looking at his daughter warily. "There's no family or anything in Montana. I'm glad my son Clyde, his wife and two children live on our farm. We see them every day and it's great to watch how he runs things. I'm not jealous that he's more experienced and better educated than I was when I began. I'm glad he's improving on my ideas and that I'm there every day to help him do it." He gave a little laugh to lighten the mood and looked across the table to his daughter. "And I'm glad Gail's not still in Turkey. I'm glad you're not wanting to move to Hawaii or Alaska but again, like you said, Duane, we hoped our daughter and granddaughter would stay closer to home. I've got a nice fish pond and would love to hike out to it with Maisie and spend time there with her and have her play with her older cousins. What's the matter with here in the center of the country? What's the matter with Iowa?"

Gil responded, "Nothing's the matter with here. I'm sorry if I've given you the wrong impression. This place is great. Gail grew up here; I grew up here. We've still got Iowa dirt under our fingernails I'm sure. We would love to live in your backyards because we love you both. We love our families. We love sharing Maisie with you and watching you hold her. We're both proud of our heritage. No matter what happens or where we go, that won't stop.

"Harvey, we cherish the thought of you teaching our little girl how to dig worms and fish for bluegill that are the perfect size for her to practice on. It's a privilege to be here with you at the beginning of this new year—exactly here, precisely now. But . . ."

Gail chimed in, more softly, "Dad, we want you and Mother to help raise our children. We will make sure they spend time with you, wherever we end up."

Harvey muttered, "It won't be the same. You know it won't be the same."

Gil nodded and spoke softly. "I know. Let me put it this way: You remember Gail and I had only been married a couple months by 9/11 when Moslem terrorists perpetrated their atrocities on the Pentagon and New York City's Twin Towers. That proved the impetus for my joining the Army . . ."

Harvey didn't give in. He grumbled under his breath, "Yeah, I remember."

". . . I had been fascinated by big and tall buildings before—and they can be *very* beautiful, breath-taking in their design and scope—but the 9/11 tragedy caused me to think about the world's tallest buildings in an entirely different way. I have come to view them as evil, not in and of themselves, of course, but as being representative of rebellion against God and what He told mankind to do."

"You lost me there, Son," Mom interjected. "How are tall buildings evil?"

"Not themselves, Mom. They're just things, not sentient beings. Here's what I mean. The words I settled on that summarize my conclusion are *concentration* versus *dispersion* with the former put negatively and the latter, positively.

"Early in history, God told Abram to 'go out' but, even long before then, He said to Noah, '. . . fill the earth,' the implication being that Noah and his descendants were to 'go out,' multiply in number and disperse across the earth."

"I know you're right but will you cite chapter and verse for me?" asked Mom.

"Of course, I'm glad to. Let's look it up. Genesis 9:1 refers to the time after the flood when Noah is departing the ark. It records God as saying to Noah, *'Be fruitful and increase in number and fill the earth.'* Scattering and dispersing aren't specifically mentioned but the logical implication is that to fill the earth you need to spread out over it.

"Then only two chapters later in 11:4, *men* said, *'Come, let us build ourselves a city, with a tower that reaches to the heavens, so that we may make a name for ourselves and* not *be scattered over the face of the whole earth.'* That seems to me to be a clear indication of rebellion against God's instructions—men chose to concentrate together in cities and build tall buildings. They specifically said they did *not* want to disperse or scatter; they wanted to concentrate and cluster together in big groups.

"If somebody reads Scripture differently than I or draws a different conclusion, it's okay but, generally speaking, this is why I drew up population density statistics. Iowa doesn't have a particularly high density and I don't mean to imply that it's wrong to gather together in families or enjoy holiday fellowship—nothing like that at all. But it's true that if given the choice, I would rather not move to New York City or any other area that has high, urban density and lots of tall buildings. And it's equally true that, for me and my family, for some reason, I have Montana on my mind."

Emma asked, "Out of curiosity, where does Iowa rank? How does it show up in your research?"

"Good question. It's twenty-third in size so it's right at the mid-point of the fifty states but it has nearly three million people such that its average density is the same as the number of weeks in a year, fifty-two persons per square mile."

Emma's eyes opened wide and her brows went up, "Well, I declare! I had no idea. Iowa doesn't seem crowded to me but its density is ten times what you showed us Montana's is. Maybe Montana doesn't have enough people—maybe you're right. Maybe it needs a few more. But, I don't know, do you 'spose you'd get a mite lonely? Like I said, Iowa doesn't seem crowded to me."

Gil appreciated her support—and her concern. He said, "I'm investigating, not moving. You might be right so we'll proceed one step at a time." He looked across the table at his father-in-law and asked, "Does this answer your question, Harvey? I understand that your backyard or my parents' backyard doesn't look out to tall buildings, but is your backyard where God would have us live? Density isn't the main reason I'm attracted to Montana but it helps explain why I'm interested in exploring that admittedly far-off state.

"Please know this: we don't think of moving as going away *from* something but as going *to* something. We don't think of any move we might make as leaving you, we think of it as walking into God's plan for our lives. We pray for God's clear leading and that He makes it abundantly clear to us what He would have us do and where He would have us go."

"Well, yes, now that you put it that way, I see your point. And I'm with you all the way in not wanting to move to New York City," answered Harvey. "That city's got way too many people for me. I don't feel crowded on my farm but there are places, lots of them, I suppose, where I'm sure I would feel hemmed in. My son, Clyde, learned in college that full-time farmers now make up less than two percent of the American labor force and that we have more inmates in jails and prisons than there are full-time farmers. It didn't used to be that way and I remember when it wasn't. If you can find good land in Big Sky Country then I might get on board with your notion of going so far away."

"The crowding of people into great cities is happening like never before," Dad agreed. "I'm sure we've all noticed that demographic shift. Ours is one of the few small farms left around here. Other folks like me have sold out to kids who have to get more acreage to stay competitive."

Mom nodded, "Our church struggles against loss in membership, and our town lost one of its grocery stores last year. People are both dying off and moving away."

"We lost three stores in the last two years and our high school graduates fewer seniors than it did ten years ago," Emma added.

Dad continued, "Movement to big cities isn't conducive to individualism. It can and does encourage folks to hide in anonymity. And now that you mention it, I can see that anonymity might promote godlessness."

"Cities had a bad founder," Gil continued. "Nimrod was a hunter of people, a killer and murderer. Cities easily become places of broken sidewalks and broken dreams where human tumbleweeds drift across the streets and predators hide in a concrete jungle."

"Our politicians are doing their darnedest to move us toward globalization, which is unscriptural." Dad sighed, his head bent in reflection. "The Bible hints at nationalism in positive terms without quite ever using that word—but never globalism. I agree with what you're saying, son. Not that the good ol' days were perfect but two hundred and more years ago—before the industrial revolution—people tended to live in really small towns and rural areas where social needs were taken care of by neighbors, family members and churches. Later, when people migrated and crowded together in new and strange places, they lost their safety nets as public health issues, juvenile delinquency, housing shortages and a host of other social ills began to predominate. Society was transformed, but not all in good ways."

Ethel chimed in, reminiscing. "I was never alone growing up. I might think I was but little towns have many eyes. If I fell down, a neighbor would come out of her door and comfort me. If I tripped and skinned my knee, someone would bandage me up and send me on my way. It was a comforting feeling. I felt secure."

Emma agreed. "A girl who spent her childhood in the country loved her native hills, the fields that lay in sight of her parents' house. She formed deep attachments with her familiar countryside. Trees, shrubs and fencerows were each connected with pleasant memories."

"Son, as you said, the key point is not to run away— not to run away *from* cities, tall buildings and high-density population but *go to* where God would have you fulfill your ministry and His calling on your lives." Duane's eyes were still misty but he smiled at his son now. "We all agree that we prefer country living to big city crowds but that's not really the point of this conversation, is it?"

Gil agreed, smiling back at his father. "No, it isn't."

"It's one thing to talk about country versus city and God's calling on our lives but we're also talking about family," Ethel said, doubt in her voice.

Emma became increasingly upset, agitated at Ethel's words. "Family, yes! It's close-knit and self-contained. It's its own shelter from storms, a school in which we learn life's basic lessons, a church where God is honored, a place of enjoyment with wholesome recreation and simple pleasures, even a factory where life's necessities are made. Family. That's what life should be about.

"When you moved to Georgia, it shocked us badly enough but we all knew it was temporary; California, temporary; D.C., temporary; even halfway around the world to Turkey, temporary. But this has a whole different ring to it—it sounds permanent. You said so yourself. I've gone on overload with this news and I need more time to process all this."

Ethel looked across the table to her husband and then to her son sympathetically, "I love you; we love Iowa. You've given us a lot to process but I guess Dad and I knew your visit with us was only temporary. I've had a little more time to get ready for what I suspected was coming so my emotions aren't on overload but I want to make sure you know what you're doing. You love Gail and think you might love Montana." She looked at Harvey. "And you love Mollie the milk cow, you love Emma, you love having your son around to carry on your farming operation, you love cake and ice cream."

"Well, amen to that," Harvey said.

"So—love has different meanings and I think we're talking about more than one definition. Am I right? I think I remember our preacher talking about different Greek words for 'love,' with one of them having something to do with family. Am I wrong? I don't know statistics from a hole in the head or people-density from the price of tea in China but Emma and I are thinking about family, especially at this time of year with all of us gathered together under this roof around my table.

"Dad and I didn't have children until God blessed us with you, Gil, in our later years. We love this country, our state, Mollie the milk cow, cake and ice cream but they don't compare to our love for you and Gail. And, of course, there's nothing like holding Maisie in our arms and looking into her eyes as they flutter closed in the relaxed hush of the easy crush before sleep. Dad and I are willing to let you go to Montana if it involves love for God but not if it's anything less than that. What is it exactly that we're talking about here?"

Duane teased his wife, "I saw steam earlier but thought it was coming from the tea kettle. I guess if you were thinking too hard it might be that you overheated your brain. Should I take your temperature to see if you're back to normal?"

She gave him a cross look but relented and grinned. Emma smiled, too, and reached out to take Ethel's hand, "Thank you for clarifying my emotional overload." Then she added. "The old joke is, 'If we had known how much fun grandkids are we'd have skipped over the kids and gone straight to the grandkids. Harvey and I enjoyed holding our little babies but we enjoy holding our grand-babies at least as much and maybe even more." As if on cue, Gail heard Maisie stir and make a squeak. She started to get up but Emma said, "You stay. I'll go take care of her." Before she left the room she turned back around to the table. "Gil, you've emphasized Montana but are you planning to tour the other four states you narrowed your list down to?"

Gil answered, "My plan is vague—it's hardly a plan—but I'd like to, as we say in military combat, put 'boots on the ground' to make the process more real. Perhaps we could make a giant circle, going west through South Dakota into Wyoming's Yellowstone National Park then up to Montana and head back east through North Dakota. Gail and I will try to hear God's voice above looking at scenery; we pray to be sensitive to His Spirit's prompting—and we ask you to join with us in that same prayer. I anticipate that we shall pay closest attention to Montana."

Harvey looked at his daughter and asked, "How do you feel about this?"

Gail had remained quiet to this point, but now it was her turn to vocalize her thoughts. "I trust Gil to hear God's voice and know His leading. Like Ruth said to Naomi and like I echoed in my wedding vows to Gil, *'Where you go, I will go.'* Which is not to say I haven't done some of my own research—as I did before following him to Incirlik. I've been pleased so far. I found more that made me nervous about Turkey than I have about Montana. I'm looking forward to, as they say, a voyage of discovery."

Ethel suddenly said, "Look at the time! I need to get up and fix supper."

The two older men agreed it was time to get a move on and decided it was high time for them to go out and check on the livestock, especially the very pregnant Mollie.

CHAPTER 6

SING, 1945

Grandfather told me, "My young wife and I loved each other. We sprinted through our first two years of marriage, not knowing better than to slow down and enjoy it. We smiled and squinted under a sun so bright we could not see clouds gathering just over the horizon. Like most young couples, I suppose, we were ready for anything—except what actually happened to us. When reality happened, we felt like we had been pushed into the middle of a minefield wearing clown shoes."

As he described those years to me, I formed a picture in my mind of farmworkers bent double under sacks of rice, walking through paddies to store the grain in their sheds. Clothing was dusty brown, sheds were red-brown, fields were golden brown, weathered faces were wrinkled brown, even the sun shone through layers of sepia brown. Vivid color didn't intrude in my whimsey until splotches of red exploded into it at random intervals.

He continued, "My forebears paid a heavy price during the three months following Doolittle's Raid. Peasants suffered at the hands of the Japanese invaders in retaliation for rendering aid to those raiders. Japanese motivation was revenge for America's bombing of their homeland and we Chinese were weak, vulnerable, easy targets upon whom they could vent their rage. The tortures that ensued could be likened to someone pulling wings off a butterfly, only we were the butterfly. It was a carnival of vengeance, sick and depraved."

Grandfather's tale continued. "The Japanese didn't kill everybody they rounded up for so-called questioning and interrogation. But they killed a lot, an awful lot of us. They killed two-hundred-fifty thousand. Think of it! Break these numbers down. That's an average of almost three thousand people killed each day for three months, Sundays included.

"I'm sorry to say the killings included my wife, your grandmother, after they raped and tried their worst to degrade her." At this, Grandfather's face crumpled and he wept.

"I was tortured to within an inch of my life," he continued, taking a deep breath after his sobs subsided. "It was bad—those were dark days. I was able to save my five-year-old son, your father, only by hiding him with elderly relatives at the last minute."

I hate to say it but my Grandfather had become obsessed with a study of atrocities committed by various cultures through time. His bitterness had been tempered by the time I was born but he told me about these atrocities as I grew up . . . how the Romanian military governor, Vlad the Impaler of Transylvania, drove the bodies of his enemies down onto spikes and then, in their presence, ate bread dipped in their blood. His action deterred his enemies but it was also cruelty in action for its own sake.

He told of how, in Rome, crowds in amphitheaters were reported to have watched Christians fed to lions after they were strapped onto iron chairs with flames burning underneath. The wild beasts would not kill and eat them, of course, until after the fires had died away. And beyond belief, blood-thirsty crowds would shout for more.

I hated to hear Grandfather tell of these tales but he said it was important for him to come to grips with the sad fact that all have sinned, that cultures through the ages have had a bent toward the dark side.

How can mobs be so cruel? I've often wondered.

Maidens on the east end of the Mediterranean were stripped naked for public spectacle, then their heads were shaved and their torsos were split open and filled with slop for pigs to eat. There, men were beaten bloody, stuffed into wicker baskets, then anointed with honey to draw hornets and wasps to make their final hours as unpleasant as possible.

Assyrians killed Jews and hammered iron hooks through noses and lower lips of survivors so they could more easily lead them away in chains as slaves. The most recent genocide was when Nazis made a science of killing six million Jews in less than six years—ten times the rate of death Grandfather experienced.

I was reminded of others who were stoned, sawn asunder, driven out to live in goatskins in deserts, caves and holes in the ground. I had heard it said of those Christian saints that they were people 'of whom the world was not worthy.' On the one hand, I was proud of martyrs who were true to their ideals, but on the other, I didn't know which ideals were worthy of such beliefs.

"But the cruelest thing I saw was when idealistic children were forced to watch dreams die," Grandfather said. "Children soon enough learn all is not well with the world; but to mock their tender spirits, shock their sensibilities and snatch their childhoods away from them before it is time is breathtaking in its depravity. Little ones don't have a choice whether or not they want to be martyrs; they don't even have a chance to form their own core beliefs."

Grandfather didn't ruin my childhood by speaking of these tortures when I was too young to hear of them. We simply enjoyed each other's company in fishing boats and tents around his campfires. We bonded during our excursions, some of the few times I was allowed to stay up late.

It wasn't until much later in my adult years that I was able to piece these terrifying stories together and come to understand that my grandfather had searched for deep meaning in the events of his life. I loved him for what he didn't burden me with in my youth as well as for what he taught me as an adult.

"Japanese soldiers were also enthusiastic in their sadistic retribution," he said to me on one occasion. "They didn't ask questions. They just screamed, pointed fingers and made accusations." Grandfather concluded his story, "Somebody had to pay for their humiliation and loss of face. We were the chosen ones. They starved me 'til my stomach thought my throat had been cut; it got so empty it felt like it was glued to my backbone. They beat me over those terrible three months. They kicked me over and over in the ribs and broke several—again and again. I could only breathe in shallow, raggedy breaths. They broke my lower left leg with an ax and smashed my right hip with a sledgehammer so I could no longer walk or work my fields. I didn't have a cane, couldn't find a proper stick.

"In their cunning minds, they thought I would die a lingering death from lack of mobility, food and medical care. They didn't want quick death for me; they wanted my death to be slow to prolong the torture as much as possible.

"When they at last released me, relatives rescued me. Later, I rejoiced when atom bombs fell on those brutes. I rejoiced a second time when they were humiliated further by their surrender to Allied forces. I am sad to say I didn't know better than to hate them. I hated them all.

"Later, I realized that anger, brutality and depravity live in me exactly as they do in the Japanese, Romanians, Romans and all cultures of all ages. In other words, in my younger years I knew the problem but not the answer. I lived inside the problem and didn't know how to get out of it."

———————

Grandfather then told me what happened three years after his release from the Japanese prison camp and the circumstances that led up to it.

At an airfield outside the town of Kweilin on June 10, six weeks after escorting Doolittle to safety, Grandfather's friend John Birch met one of the most legendary commanders in China, Brigadier General Claire Lee Chennault and his Flying Tigers. He had been ordered to appear before the general because of his growing reputation and the successes he had via his daring escapades as an itinerant missionary preaching the gospel of Christ. Birch's influence stood on its own merits but it was also helped along by Jimmy Doolittle, who had passed the word around of how Birch and some native Chinese had rescued him.

Remember, at first nobody knew how Doolittle managed to escape—he and his flight crew had no radios. China wasn't a declared enemy but it was hardly an enthusiastic ally. The whereabouts of these heroes had been unknown. The Japanese knew they didn't have them in custody, but American commanders didn't know whether Doolittle had ditched and drowned at sea or crashed over land and been captured, if he was dead or in hiding, if he had been taken by Chinese Communists or protected by Chinese Nationalists. And later, after initial reports filtered in that most of the other crews were safe and at large, many still wondered where Doolittle was and how he was able to ultimately find sanctuary in Free China and return home to the United States. Grandfather explained that it was in Doolittle's disappearance, craftiness and reappearance that he himself was able to ultimately find freedom as well—when the most famous Raider of all helped him escape China's civil war.

But John Birch, the missionary-soldier who connected Grandfather and Doolittle, did not fare as well in the end . . .

Chennault had been informed and was so impressed by Birch's intervention that at the beginning of July, his application for induction into the military was accepted.

John Birch put on a uniform and was recognized as a second lieutenant and an intelligence officer in the armed forces of the United States of America. After receiving several commendations, he was promoted to first lieutenant, and for the first time in history, an American lived and worked in the field with Chinese soldiers behind enemy lines on secret missions. He established a precedent for radio communications and intelligence gathering. When Chennault pinned the Legion of Merit on Birch's chest, he spoke words of unusual praise: "In a war theater where courage is commonplace, that of John Birch has proved exceptional."

John was sent out to live behind enemy lines across the strait from Formosa (now Taiwan). He assumed his former disguise as a poor countryman, dyeing his hair black and keeping his round brown eyes hidden by wearing a hat.

He employed coolies to help him carry his radio equipment in rented boats. Once, he was alone and was forced to hide his equipment inside a farmer's straw basket that was normally used for manure. When he passed Japanese soldiers, they recognized the basket and held their noses, letting him go by without question. After arriving at an appropriate village on the coast where he could see ship traffic, he set up his radio station. He hired two Christian fishermen, taught them his radio codes and left them in charge to transmit back to headquarters concerning troop movements and ship traffic.

Another time, he traveled more than a hundred miles by foot and horseback to set up radio equipment on a hilltop. He called in coordinates for attacking aircraft and stayed on-site to fine-tune bomb drops as required. Of course, he was always on the move to avoid detection. This successful operation lasted six weeks. Upon the conclusion of this mission, Birch was promoted to captain and again received commendations.

Meanwhile, although the Allied landing at Normandy occurred on June 6, 1944, things weren't going well in China. Germany surrendered on May 7, 1945 but Japan continued to fight against the Allies, though not with the same vengeance. Three months later, on August 6 and 9, the United States dropped atomic bombs on Hiroshima and Nagasaki. On August 15, Japan surrendered unconditionally, although the formal ceremony aboard the USS battleship *Missouri* didn't take place for another two weeks on September 2, 1945. World War II was over, including Japan's invasion and war with China.

But that didn't mean China's civil war was over. On the contrary, communist forces under Mao seized this as an opportunity to make a land grab and strengthen their positions. It was vital for American troops to reach military bases abandoned by Japanese forces in China before communist troops could arrive to commandeer armaments. Birch was ordered to go about one hundred miles northeast to an abandoned Japanese headquarters. On August 20, he commanded a party of ten who departed for that destination. They traveled by train through various small villages as far as the tracks allowed. He was approaching Grandfather's village though he had no way of knowing that.

After encountering a break in the tracks, Birch secured a handcar onto which he loaded their equipment. He and his party of ten took turns pushing the loaded handcar but around noon the next day they met up with a force of several hundred Chinese Communists who were engaged in tearing down telephone communication lines. After a few tense moments, Birch and his troops were allowed to pass but a few more miles up the line they came upon a second group who disarmed them and took them prisoner.

When Captain Birch demanded to know by what right they could disarm an American officer, he and his Chinese Nationalist lieutenant were shot in both legs, stabbed repeatedly with bayonets and their bodies were unceremoniously thrown into an open ditch.

"My leg had healed by then," Grandfather said. "It was crooked but I could put weight on it, so when I heard the sounds of commotion from my house, I ventured out as fast as I could to see what was happening. I hid behind some bushes because I knew we didn't control the train. Its tracks had been cut and there shouldn't have been any activity on them. I didn't know who might be making that noise or why. I spied on those noisemakers and saw two small groups of men wearing two different uniforms, in obvious conflict. I saw one group isolate two people from the other group and stab them with bayonets. Then I heard shots from their rifles. I watched as those two bodies were tossed into the ditch. Then I saw the other soldiers captured and taken away.

"I went down to investigate after all the soldiers left and I thought it was safe. Imagine my shock when I discovered one of the bodies was that of my friend, John Birch, who led me to saving faith in Jesus those long three years earlier when we escorted Colonel Doolittle to safety. I loved that man, not only for who he was but also for what he had given to me. I did all I could to honor him and his memory.

"I never forgot John Birch or what he taught me about his God. My neighbors acknowledged my respect for him and sorrow in losing my wife. They helped me care for my son but they never understood my faith in God. Yet I knew it was through John and his witness that God saved me."

Grandfather told me how survivors in the work party later described Birch's final hours. They said, "He stood like a man and did not die by inches. As peasant farmers and simple fishermen, we know that living fish rarely drift with the stream but dead ones always do. There are plenty of people who drift, drift, drift with the current like dead fish, twisting round and round if the stream is running in an eddy. John Birch did not drift! He did not twist round and round! He was more alive in his final moments than the communist brutes who killed him."

Villagers rallied around Grandfather and helped him bury the captain's body in the field next to his house, next to an unknown, peasant woman who had died that same day in childbirth. He who was not married, he who had sired no children, was given the honor of holding a newborn infant in his arms, the child of that neighbor of Grandfather's, as they slept together in death. His grave was safe because it was hidden. The marker did not name his name but three had died that day, two of natural causes in childbirth and the other of unnatural—war after peace had been declared. They put a simple, wooden cross on this single grave—though plain, it was nonetheless mythic in Grandfather's mind.

CHAPTER 7

GIL, 2006

On the fifth of January, a couple of days after Gail's parents had returned to their home, Gil awakened early, opened his Bible to check things out, read quietly for a half-hour or so then said to his wife as she began to stir, "Listen to this. This is exciting stuff! God downloaded an idea into my mind during the night that solved a real puzzle for me. Sit with me. Let's do some Bible study before breakfast and flesh out this revelation. Okay?"

Gail had been up in the night to nurse Maisie but she agreed and whispered, "Wouldn't it be quieter and more comfortable downstairs in the living room by the fire with a cup of coffee? I'll fix it while you build the fire. We could ask your mother to be on baby duty if Maisie begins to make noise."

"Of course. That's a good idea. Are you ready to stir? Did you get enough sleep?"

"It's alright. I'm mostly awake now. I'm glad you're excited," she mumbled. "Actually, I've got a surprise for you, too."

Gil didn't need to start a fire because Duane had already been up to stoke it. He had just gone out to the barn to feed and check on his livestock. And Gail didn't need to make coffee because Ethel was already fussing around in the kitchen and the coffee was hot. She was happy to be Granny-Nanny for an hour or so. So Gil and Gail had a warm, leisurely time to open their Bibles and develop his fresh revelation from God. They sat for a few minutes and watched the flames with steaming cups in their hands.

Then Gil began. "You and I have previously settled on Matthew 24:34 as one of our foundational verses regarding our study of prophecy. *'I tell you the truth, this generation will certainly not pass away until all these things have happened.'* Jesus is foretelling significant events that will occur shortly before He comes back the second time to usher in His kingdom in greater fullness. And the most obvious interpretation is that those who were alive to witness the fig tree bud, or, viewed in light of current events, Israel reinstated as a nation in 1948, will not all have died before Jesus comes back. We hope we're correct in our interpretation."

"You're right. It's common sense—*and* the most obvious interpretation by the plain meaning of the words but there's more to it." Gail sipped her coffee.

"How do you mean? How is there more?" Gil closed his Bible.

"You began by saying you had fresh revelation. I'm glad to report I've got the same—fresh revelation during my quiet time last night. It looks like God spoke to both of us through His word at the same time. I was pondering the events of Passion Week—I don't know why, it's Christmas and New Year's, after all, not Easter—so I turned to and was reading through Matthew 23. I took note of the fact Jesus was excoriating the 'teachers of the law and Pharisees.'"

"Yes, He pronounced eight 'woes' on them, if I remember correctly."

"Right. But what did He say at the end?" Gail challenged her husband.

"I don't recall any specific thing. He just finished, I think."

"No, look at it. He made a prediction. Read verses 35 and 36."

"Okay. He said 'Woe to you' eight times. Then He pronounces judgment on them, 'How will you escape?'. Then those two verses read, *'And so will come upon you all the righteous blood that has been shed on earth, from the blood of righteous Abel to the blood of Zechariah son of Berakiah, whom you murdered between the temple and the altar. I tell you the truth, all this will come upon this generation.'"* Gil finished quoting the verses.

"Do you see?" Gail asked.

"Yes, I think I do. It's almost exactly the same words we chose from our foundational verse that follows in Chapter 24."

"Precisely. So here's the simple arithmetic. According to most scholarly opinion, when was Jesus born?"

"Four B.C.—give or take. When our calendar was set, His birth was set at the zero year, of course, but scholars now think that initial reckoning was off a few years."

"Yes, except I think you mean to say Jesus' birth was set at year number one," Gail corrected her husband. "Our system has a base year but not a zero year. And about how old was Jesus during Passion Week when He was crucified?"

"Thirty-three or thereabouts." Gil answered her, finishing his coffee.

"So what year would that have been on our calendar?"

"Twenty-nine A.D." Gil frowned, still not knowing where his wife was headed with her math.

"And when did the Roman general Titus ravage the land and destroy the temple or, in other words, in what year did Jesus' words of prophecy come true?" she asked.

"Seventy A.D. and there's no doubt concerning that date."

"So what's the time differential between twenty-nine and seventy?"

"Forty-one years, give-or-take perhaps one or two years," Gil answered.

"Alright, let's keep going. What was the event that drew so many to Jerusalem during Passion Week?"

"Passover. Torah during the time of Moses commanded the Hebrew people to congregate three times a year to observe God's 'appointed times,' one of which was Passover."

"Jesus was specifically lecturing the 'teachers of the law and Pharisees' but the crowd hearing His words was much more inclusive. Those hearing Him would surely have included people in their fifties and sixties but just as surely many between the ages of thirteen to twenty. So here's the bottom-line: Assuming dozens, perhaps hundreds of His listeners were no more than twenty years of age when they heard this prophecy pronounced, how old would they have been when it was fulfilled?"

"Wow, I see," Gil stood, excited. "Adding forty-one years would make them sixty-one and many of them still would have been alive, literally breathing and physically living as we define it, when 'all this' came upon 'this generation.' The verb tense changed from 'will come' to 'came' because it happened as foretold. They witnessed the literal fulfillment of Jesus' prophecy 'in their generation.'"

Gail continued, "The verse in Matthew 23 sets precedent for your literal interpretation of practically an identical verse in Matthew 24. The generation that witnessed the giving of the prophecy in Matthew 23 also witnessed its fulfillment. We can and should expect the same to be true in Matthew 24.

"And this is where the rubber hits the road. We are living in exciting times! Those who were born, say, between 1940 and 1948 can be logically described as that specific generation referenced in Matthew 24:34—those who witnessed the blooming of the fig tree, the legal formation of the modern State of Israel in May 1948. They will also witness the fulfillment of 'all these things.' If they were thirteen to twenty years old in 1948, they would be seventy-one to seventy-eight years old right now, today." Gail beamed a triumphant smile at her husband.

"Fantastic! Amazing!" Gil paced the room now. "Some, likely several, of that final generation will live to be ninety or even one hundred years old such that we can anticipate Jesus will have returned on or before 2030 to 2048—in other words, our world as we know it might only have another twenty-five years or so before *all these things have happened*. Time is short. You and I probably will not die of natural causes in old age. We have a good chance of being alive to witness Jesus' return."

"An exciting thought," Gail said. "And sobering. And intimidating. But most of all, exciting. We will see things other generations longed for but did not see. Of all the generations, ours is the one, the one and only, that will witness this prophetic fulfillment. But this review so far only includes *my* fresh revelation," Gail added, frowning. "You said *you* had something new? What is it? What fresh revelation did God give you last night?"

Just then Duane rushed in from the barn with a red flush in his cheeks and interrupted their conversation. "Mollie's calving. I'm not as strong or agile as I used to be so, Gil, will you come out and help me?"

"Of course. Has the vet seen her?" Gil grabbed his jacket off the coat hook.

"Yes, two months ago, on his regular schedule. He wasn't concerned. Harvey also looked at her for me and gave his opinion there was nothing to worry about. Mollie has delivered fine in the past. But I'm nervous, I don't why. I'd like you to be there with me."

Gil put his coat on and headed toward the door. "Let's go. I'll do what I can. It makes sense to save a vet bill."

Mollie was in her stall and restless. Her time was near. She had circled two or three times before laying down. Duane had gunny sacks handy. He set a bucket of water by her nose for a drink if and when she wanted one. The animals generated enough heat in the night that the barn was warm and dry and all had been done for Mollie that could be done.

Gil enjoyed companionable silence with his father. They went up to the loft and got some hay bales for the evening's feeding before coming back down and resuming their post. Contractions began. It was easy to see the muscular waves move through the cow. The sac and front hooves of the calf showed in only fifteen to twenty minutes then its nose poked through.

The head was out in another five minutes and Duane broke the sac to make sure the calf could breathe. The rest of the calf slid out and the birth itself was complete in less than half an hour. Duane cleared the calf's nostrils and Mollie got up and started licking it all over. He opened his eyes. It wasn't long before he stood and nursed.

The two men marveled at this new life and the miracle of birth; they had seen it before but that made no difference—it was a miracle each time. They went up to the house for breakfast and to share the good news.

A few hours later the men checked on Mollie and her calf. Both were doing fine. Gail came out to pet the calf for a few minutes. She said, "Would you just look at this little one's innocent exuberance. Only a few hours old yet bursting to kick up his heels. I'll be inside with your mother whenever you're ready to finish our conversation."

CHAPTER 8

SING, 1946

"My only child, my son, was now eight years old and without a mother," Grandfather continued his sad tale. "He asked me, 'Will I always miss her so much like this?' I told him, 'I miss her, too. I wish she could come back to us but she can't. Someday we will go to her in heaven, but she can't come back here.'

"I couldn't bear to tell him, 'So long as we are in this place of civil war and political turmoil, soldiers will continue to march past our one-paddy rice field farm by these railroad tracks and they could snatch you away at any moment and make you fight their fight.' I just couldn't speak those words to him. He still had innocent eyes. He remained a gentle soul. How could I take that away from him?

"I began to wonder, *Could I move to a better place to give him a better future?* I began to think his future might be somewhere else, not here."

Captain John M. Birch's body was exhumed and buried in a mausoleum in Hsuchow, China with full military honors. Grandfather said, "This presented me with a rare opportunity but it was also an ironic commentary on the nature of warfare that this decorated hero was killed ten days after World War II was over and official hostilities had ceased. How tragic. How sad. Death is especially unnecessary when it is caused by so-called 'friendlies' after peace has been declared and sworn combatants have laid down their arms."

Grandfather continued his narrative. "I had no advance notice, but I thought as my white friend's body was being exhumed for relocation, *I should go to his native country, the United States of America. I can give my rice field to my kind neighbors.* After all, they had helped me plow behind my ox when my hip was hurting. I had become less attached to my field of rice in my mind and emotions. China no longer seemed like home.

"Such a wild, unexpected thought staggered me. But at the same time, it seemed like the guidance I had been praying for, an answer to my prayer for my son. It seemed I had been holding my breath, waiting for this moment to settle in my consciousness.

"My best chance to go to a better place lay with the American soldiers who were laboring and digging in my yard. I had to act quickly. It was a moment pregnant with possibility; moments like that come but seldom and they don't last long. I had to decide on the spur of the moment.

"I accompanied them and my friend John's body to Hsuchow for the ceremony honoring him. In order not to arouse suspicion, I didn't pack more than overnight supplies and a few precious belongings. I wrapped them up in two little bundles, gave one to my son and carried the other myself. I left a note for my neighbors, telling them of my intentions, thanking them and giving them all I had.

"Colonel Doolittle was in Hsuchow for John's ceremony. I asked the colonel if I could participate in my friend's memorial and if he might perhaps help me with sponsorship for emigration. To my immense relief, he agreed! He said it was the least he could do since I had risked my life to save his. Thus, the miracle came into being. I prepared to emigrate from China and take my son to America.

"I didn't know it at the time, but America had only just begun allowing limited Chinese immigration. At that, they were forced into it. Their Congress previously had enacted legislation called the Chinese Exclusion Act, which totally prohibited Chinese immigration. Japanese propaganda made full use of this exclusion for political reasons. So . . . repeal in late 1943 was via what was called the Magnuson Act.

"Colonel Doolittle sped our clearances through San Francisco as two of only one hundred and five Chinese allowed into the United States that year, which was the maximum legal quota permitted to our country of more than a billion people. We would not have been able to leave China at all apart from God's miraculous timing."

Grandfather knew I would never challenge him but sometimes I would ask at this point in his reflection, "Are you sure? Did you and Father occupy two out of only one hundred and five slots for one billion people?"

"Yes, Grandson, I am sure. But remember: One hundred and five is greater than zero, which is what it had been. It was only in God's providence that such a thing was now possible. Never forget that. And Colonel Doolittle dropped down on my head out of a night sky when I didn't know who he was. I didn't seek after him. He almost literally fell on top of me. And my friend John Birch arrived to eat at the water shop before me. I didn't seek out a rendezvous with him. I knew neither of those men but God sent them to me as opportunities. I simply responded to what He supplied. He chose me, and by extension, your father. And by further extension, you. Never forget, Grandson—you are chosen."

Grandfather's story as he told it to me continued. "I would have been stuck in a laundry in San Francisco's Chinatown were it not for Colonel Doolittle's connections and continued help. Despite my grateful heart, I don't think I would have been comfortable living in that big city. But I never dreamed I'd end up in one of the most remote places in the world.

"My experience as a rice farmer helped me get temporary work east in the big valley near Modesto and north of there around Sacramento but I knew little to nothing about lettuce fields or almond orchards or orange groves. Other migrants had bodies younger and less broken than mine so government officials found non-agricultural sponsorship for me in a place called Glasgow, Montana. It was a long journey and the winter weather was much colder than I was accustomed to but I learned to call it home."

Indeed, Grandfather was most impressed by topography and climate since he had never before experienced wind-swept prairies, minus-sixty-degree temperatures in winter and one-hundred-ten-degree summers. He had grown up with coastal humidity, lots of water and small-scale flood irrigation in rice paddies. The weather couldn't be more opposite in eastern Montana—there was very low humidity and a massive flood control/irrigation project called Fort Peck Dam.

Glasgow had two claims to fame—its remote location and the earthen dam across the Missouri River a short distance south of town. The Canadian border crossing and huge wheat fields were north of town and Indian reservations were east and west. Glasgow held three thousand eight hundred people but the nearest population centers in any direction were about six hours away in good weather. It was isolated and as unlike what he had known in China as anything he could imagine.

Neither Grandfather nor Father knew about it at the time, but citizens of the United States had gone through what they described as the Great Depression in the years prior to Germany's and Japan's aggressive, military invasions that caused World War II. It was hard for Grandfather to accept the notion that millions of people in the most prosperous nation on earth, this place of dreams called America, had been hungry and desperately looking for work during the early-1930s. Nevertheless, it was true.

Except I was too young to know what it was, so I asked and he replied, "The Great Depression was when drought and wind blew farmers off their land and a stock market crash robbed city people of their cash savings. Banks failed. City people lost jobs and had to stand for hours in bread lines for handouts of food. Country people had food except many of them lost their farms. Families moved from place to place. Familiar connections were broken by desperation."

I learned that so-called rich Americans had been tortured as he had been—except for them it was because of unemployment and weather conditions, not armed, foreign invaders. Grandfather's body was broken but he gradually came to realize that many Americans were equally broken and traumatized—in spirit.

Even a cursory study of history reveals that man's inhumanity to man is not new. We can imagine terrible things from people we've heard about in history, like Genghis Khan and Attila the Hun and the violent acts they did. But some of us don't have to imagine. Modern-day instances abound. Grandfather's torture in China was not isolated in either time or space. His pain and loneliness in Glasgow were not uncommon but were shared by millions.

He said to me, "I learned that loneliness, persecutions and tortures were nothing new. I acquired a Bible in my native language and, as I studied it over the years, I found that it said, *Beloved, do not be surprised at the fiery ordeal among you, which comes upon you for your testing, as though some strange thing were happening to you; but to the degree that you share the sufferings of Christ, keep on rejoicing.*'

"I also found that I was not alone in my sufferings. Jesus Himself suffered. *Although He was a Son, He learned obedience from the things which He suffered.*' And He identified with deprivation and loneliness, *Foxes have holes and birds of the air have nests, but the Son of Man has no place to lay his head.*' The Bible goes so far as to say there is a benefit to deprivation, to suffering, to loneliness: It helps us *know Him, and the power of His resurrection, and the fellowship of His sufferings, being made conformable unto His death . . .*'"

Grandfather continued, "I wasn't sure about this concept at first, but to my delight, I found that I became better, not bitter. I became more reflective and came to understand I had a soul, a thing within me that was beautiful. Suffering actually helped my soul flower. Heaven's holy seed grew in my heart and I no longer lived as a shell with an interior wasteland. These trials were producing a great depth of patience and maturity in me."

***

Glasgow is in the Milk River Valley. The Milk River flows into the Missouri River about twenty miles southeast of town. The Missouri is the nation's longest river. It flooded regularly during spring thaws. For a variety of reasons that included flood control, a project was approved in October 1933 to build an earthen dam across the Missouri near Glasgow. It would provide jobs at a time when they were needed desperately.

President Franklin Roosevelt gave this project such high priority in his New Deal politics that he visited twice, once in 1934 and again in 1937. The dam was five times the size of any other earthen dam ever constructed. Slapdash boom towns sprang up to accommodate more than ten thousand workers by the summer of 1936. They were places where bad whiskey and poor tobacco were sold to single men at unreasonable prices. Named the Fort Peck Reservoir, it was the largest Depression-era project in the United States.

The dam capsized during construction in 1938. Sixty were killed over the life of the project, six of whom are still buried in the dam somewhere. In 1938, a heavy equipment operator who jumped off his dozer and survived the capsizing tragedy wrote, "I hit the ground running. I wasn't running fast but I passed some people that were!" In spite of serious setbacks like this, construction resumed and the dam was topped off in 1940, six years before Grandfather and Father arrived in Glasgow.

The Fort Peck Reservoir eventually extended one hundred thirty-four miles to the west, had more coastline than the entire State of California and was the greatest alteration mankind ever made to Montana's landscape.

Homesteaders were forced to sell because of "eminent domain" at a time when prices were at historic lows so most had nothing to show for their years of back-breaking, spirit-sapping labor. Yet, most of them had already given up on their dreams of rural prosperity and were glad to trade them in for opportunities to work on this huge New Deal government project with its guaranteed, regular paychecks.

Grandfather wasn't familiar with aircraft. He was surprised to learn that B-17 Flying Fortress bombers, larger than the B-25 Mitchells that Jimmy Doolittle's Raiders flew, were based at the Army Airfield in Glasgow. A prisoner of war camp for captured Germans had been added to the base in 1944 but both had closed prior to his arrival in 1946. Nothing remained except empty buildings out on the prairie. It was bleak.

There were few pastels in Glasgow in 1946. Most colors were shades of brown. This was the environment that welcomed Grandfather to Glasgow.

He told me, "It was different for me in San Francisco's Chinatown and in California's central valley at Modesto but Glasgow, Montana was *really* strange. It made me miss my wife more than ever. When you're lying there in the dark of night it's hard not to feel lonely. But in all fairness, adjusting to life here wasn't much harder than it would have been on any other distant planet. I knew it was up to me to adapt my attitude. I hoped that the 'winter of my discontent' would be 'made glorious summer' if I persevered, that the great wind of winter that made the earth cold and bleak in Glasgow would yield to the silver trumpet of spring, the golden plenty of summer and the cornucopia of autumn in those wheat fields. Life in my adopted country was hard and tried my patience, but in the long run, it produced hope in my heart, hope that did not disappoint.

"My sponsor was kind and provided employment my broken body could manage but still I asked myself, *have I improved my son's future?* There was no one else like me, who looked like me, talked like me, in all those square miles of open grassland. Loneliness was personal, ever-present. The English language was foreign to my tongue. I tried not to show a face of discouragement to your father but there was no one else like him in all those empty miles of cold and snow, either."

CHAPTER 9

GIL, 2006

Since Gil didn't want to be a burden to his parents or inconvenience them, and since he and Gail were planning a long scouting trip in the relatively near future, he said to his wife as he put on his pajamas, "Don't you think it's time we purchase a vehicle? If so, do you have a preference? A two-seater sports car is out of the question since there are now three of us. But should this vehicle be our primary family car or should it be specifically targeted for our upcoming trip? Should it be a truck, an SUV or a mid-size sedan? Or do you have an opinion?"

"I vote for bigger rather than smaller." Gail climbed under the heavy quilt on the bed. "At some point, you'll want to get a truck but some sort of sedan should be better for this trip, don't you think? On the other hand, I might like to sit up higher in a van or SUV where I can see the road more easily."

"Ah, Queen of the Road." Gil winked at her. "Why don't you go shopping with my mother while I go on duty with Maisie tomorrow? You have some milk stored up for her and I can put her down for her nap. We can look in on Mollie with her new calf and have all sorts of adventures. It's not far to the county seat but take whatever time you need and choose the vehicle that suits you best. Pick your favorite color as long as you don't embarrass me with violet, purple or pink. Dad and I can fix lunch. You don't even have to be back before supper. We'll be happy here."

Gail agreed that Maisie could handle one morning and afternoon apart from her. "Okay. A day out sounds like fun. I'll probably find something in a dealer's inventory. After all, we've seen auto dealerships around here grow from having a few cars on a couple of city lots to carrying huge inventories on twenty-acre sites. We'll see how Maisie does for one day, if you think you're man enough for such a big job."

He laughed. "I'm game and good to go!" They both fell asleep with a smile, dreaming of their plans for the next day.

Gail enjoyed her day off from motherhood, which surprised her. Instead of worrying about her baby as she had thought she would, she returned to carefree days before adult responsibilities. And it was the first time in her life she had cash enough to actually shop for a new car.

Her first impulse was to go for one of the major American nameplates, but she saw a sign for a Hyundai dealership and remembered Mr. Hyundai had been a North Korean refugee in his childhood. She pulled into that lot because of her sympathy for the plights of Middle Eastern refugees she, Gil and their dear friend Tuo had worked with during their Army time in Turkey.

She and her mother-in-law selected a front-drive, four-door sedan for testing, then enjoyed a leisurely lunch before visiting a second dealership for comparison purposes.

Over dessert, she asked Ethel her opinion. Her mother-in-law was wisely non-committal and didn't say much one way or the other. The deciding factor for Gail ended up being uncertainty as to dealership locations for maintenance and service for a Korean Hyundai in the sparsely populated areas of Montana she and Gil had researched, although she didn't worry her mother-in-law with that detail. She chose an American-made SUV that should have a dealership location near them, no matter where their new home might prove to be.

The next day, with Mollie, her calf, their parents and Maisie all taking naps, Gil and Gail had their Bibles open again sitting in their same places in the living room when Gil had mentioned his revelation. Now he elaborated further. "God put these words in my mind: '*Read about Noah.*' I did that first thing two mornings ago. Let me show you. Just like God quickened a Scripture to your heart that required simple arithmetic, He opened my eyes to Scripture and simple arithmetic that I'd never noticed before. Let's start with Genesis 7:11. Will you read it please?"

"Of course," she replied. She looked at her husband with a spark in her dark brown, doe-like eyes and Gil felt his heart warm. "*In the six hundredth year of Noah's life, on the seventeenth day of the second month—on that day all the springs of the great deep burst forth, and the floodgates of the heavens were opened.*' Okay, Noah's an old man when the flood began but there's nothing new in that thought."

"No, not in what you mentioned. But notice how specific this verse is. I wondered why it was so specific." Gil smiled. "Why did God take pains to prompt Moses to write that the flood began on the seventeenth day of the month? I didn't know of anything special about the seventeenth but my attention was drawn to it. So I continued reading and in just a short while I came to Chapter 8, verses 3 and 4. Will you read those two verses, please?"

She did. "*The water receded steadily from the earth. At the end of the hundred and fifty days the water had gone down, and on the seventeenth day of the seventh month the ark came to rest on the mountains of Ararat.*'"

"Bingo! See? There's the word *seventeenth* again. My eyes were immediately drawn to it. Chapter 7 said the flood began on the seventeenth day of the second month, and Chapter 8 said the ark came to rest on the seventeenth day of the seventh month; in other words, the text tells us there was a difference of five months between those events. An exact specific day was cited for the beginning and ending of those two events such that the time period from beginning to ending was not roughly or approximately or more-or-less-than five months, but exactly and precisely five months."

Gil continued, his voice rising in excitement. "Both Chapters 7 and 8 also define the precise time period another way: *one hundred and fifty days.* Simple arithmetic again comes into play: one hundred fifty days divided by five months equals thirty days per month. My conclusion: the months in the time of Noah's flood were exactly and precisely thirty days long."

"Got it," Gail said immediately. "You've spent years trying to solve what was to you a vexing puzzle from Revelation. Thirty days per month times twelve months equals three hundred and sixty days per year. But we have three hundred and sixty-*five* days in a year . . ."

"Exactly. Both Daniel and Revelation write of times in the future and they are specific in speaking of forty-two months, three-and-one-half years, and one-thousand-two-hundred-sixty days. The common denominator to this number series is thirty days per month and three hundred and sixty days per year. But that's not our reality.

"We had hoped that the Hebraic, lunar calendar would have resolved the discrepancy but it didn't. We were so disappointed when that hope fizzled out for us."

"I remember," she said. "We discovered that the typical lunar year is three hundred and fifty-four days. It produces a roughly identical deviation from three hundred and sixty days as does the solar calendar's three hundred and sixty-five days. So, whether or not a person is stuck with the Gregorian or Hebraic calendar, eventually he would be celebrating Christmas on the Fourth of July. Except in the one case, he would have gradually crept up on it and in the other, he would have slid back to it."

Gil nodded, "Everybody recognizes these deviations and that's why the solar calendar adds an extra day to February every four years and the lunar calendar adds an extra month five times every nineteen years."

Gail said thoughtfully. "At no time in the past few thousand years has Earth experienced a year that was three hundred and sixty literal days in duration, no matter which calendar was used."

"There's the problem: reality and the Bible don't seem to agree but they *must* agree because the Bible *is* reality," Gil said. "And now we can explain the apparent discrepancy: once upon a time in ancient history, Earth's year was three hundred and sixty days in duration and at some future time it will again have that same number of days. Something happened in the past that caused a deviation in one direction and something will happen in the future that will cause a similar deviation in the opposite direction. It seems likely that some catastrophe is associated with Noah's flood that is itself a catastrophe. But what? And what's going to happen in the future? And when?"

CHAPTER 10

SING, 1946–1956

F ather started school in Glasgow. He was three years older than other students but he had to learn English. It was hard for him. He caught up to his class by fourth grade but slipped back a year in seventh.

He fit in at church, though. Families shared their Christian hospitality with him. He attended Sunday School and sang in the children's choir. He had his own form of mild loneliness but was ignorant of Grandfather's more serious type.

Father was timid, gentle and ever so slightly confused, partly because of his minority status in this new land but mostly because of his personality. He was bookish, not particularly athletic and kept to himself quite a bit. I think the only joke I ever heard him say, and not until later in his life was, "Don't screw the inscrutable."

My father enjoyed solitude. In that regard, he fit right into the wide brown spaces and big blue skies of Montana. As the saying goes, 'he kept his peace.'

He wasn't a good dancer, not in high school and not even in grade school when some children wiggle with wild abandon. One of Grandfather's family stories was of watching Father try to dance. He said, "We were still fairly new to Glasgow when the grade school's annual spring program was scheduled. Every child in every class had a part of one sort or another. There must have been twelve or fifteen, maybe even twenty, different acts. The show was long and boring except nobody left—parents were interested for their children's sake. Like everyone else, I waited for my child's five minutes on stage with his class.

"When he came on, I remember smiling, looking at him and feeling pure joy. He couldn't dance a lick but his face was all serious and scrunched up because he didn't want to make a mistake. His steps were wooden but they were exact and precise, in time with the music and the other children. I was almost bursting with pride.

"I'm sitting there with tears of joy in my eyes, thinking of how my wife would be so proud and then—and this is the most amazing thing—I looked around the auditorium and saw all the other parents reacting the same as I was. We were all different yet we were all the same. They loved their kids the same as I loved mine. Our kids were all the stars of the show, whether they could dance a lick or not.

"This wave of love wasn't mine alone. I shared it with the Swedish and Irish parents as they shared it with the German and Italian parents, as we shared it together with the Japanese parents. I saw the wet eyes and the smiles and I was awed. This shared emotion was common to us all.

"So I learned anew, but with a clarity I hadn't seen before, that if I sought revenge, holding on to hatred would make me let go of everything else—all the good things in life. Hatred is its own enemy. In that clarity of vision, I resolved to love my new home and my new neighbors."

Grandfather told me he eventually found that other minorities lived nearby. Montana had seven Indian reservations and the Fort Peck Reservation began only eight miles east of Glasgow. Father was the only child of Chinese descent in his class at school but he was not the only minority student. There were many others. For various reasons, including the railroad and the lure of mining and agriculture, Montana had drawn families from around the world in prior decades. For instance, the names of the starting players on my father's high school football team were Jones, Red Cloud, Cohen, Andersson, Kona, Gonzalez, Schmidt, Koyama, Norinski, MacTavish and Jaborini. If Father had been bigger and more athletic, he might have added a Chinese name to those eleven, but he wasn't, so he didn't. However, he did what he could to socialize and participate in school spirit: he served as an assistant trainer and water boy for the team. He made friends with several of the players, especially Koyama—with whom he shared Asian ethnicity. Grandfather was fine with this friendship because he had long since come to realize that not all Chinese were good and not all Japanese were bad.

Reservation children attended school with Father in Glasgow. They were often more timid than Father and at least as poor. But Grandfather had made the big break from his culture and country so Father was not tempted or pressured to cling to his Chinese heritage whereas Native children lacked that freedom. In certain ways, they were shackled to their past because their parents hadn't made a clean break from their culture and country. They were here first and they hadn't left and yet they were still being forced to change. Grandfather chose assimilation when he emigrated but Native American Indians had never emigrated so, logically, they resented forced relocation and assimilation.

I know all of this because my mother is a Native American, a Dakota Sioux. Her American name was Mary Ann Lightfoot. Her mother was in grade school when the Dawes Act was passed in 1886. It had a significant effect on Montana. This act may have been well-intentioned or it may have been destructively subversive but its long-term impact was clear. It regulated land rights on tribal territories and subdivided Native American communal landholdings into individual allotments, which was in and of itself a foreign concept to them. It forced First Peoples into an American way of life they didn't want.

Many tribes were relocated and smaller tracts of from forty to one hundred sixty acres in size were parceled out to these relocated individuals who didn't necessarily understand or want to understand the concept of individual ownership on non-ancestral land. So they didn't claim all the land that was offered to them. The balance of unclaimed land was offered for sale to the highest non-Indian bidders who, of course, *did* embrace and grasp this concept of individual ownership.

Native peoples had no history of private ownership, and having been recently relocated, many felt no kinship or link to what they were told was their new homeland. Where were the buffalo? Where was their old way of life? Those who accepted title to this new and strange land were but little interested in keeping it. Consequently, non-Native ownerships on reservation land proliferated and expanded. Federal government officials observed this but it took them a half-hearted fifty years to put a stop to it. By then, as you can imagine, it was far too late. The harm, whether intended or not, was done. From 1887 to 1934 the amount of land owned by Indians decreased from one hundred thirty-eight million to forty-eight million acres, a sixty-eight percent reduction. Little wonder that so many live in poverty.

President Andrew Jackson, the hero of the battle of New Orleans and the Louisiana Purchase, was a vocal advocate of what he called "Indian removal." He urged Congress and later signed their Indian Removal Act of 1830 into law that authorized the federal government to exchange tribal land for land west of the Mississippi River in what is now Oklahoma—land that had been recently acquired in the Louisiana Purchase and designated Indian Territory.

The Choctaw Indians were the first to be evicted from their homelands. They were made to walk to what to them was foreign countryside. Some of the more troublesome ones who resisted were bound in chains. They were not given food, supplies or aid from those who expelled them from Alabama to Oklahoma. Thousands died along the way.

Action against Creek Indians followed. About thirty-five hundred out of fifteen thousand did not survive their own version of the Bataan Death March. The Shawnee, Delaware and Wyandot tribes were forced to relocate from Ohio to Kansas City, Missouri.

Only about two thousand Cherokee had begun their long, painful walk by 1838 so President Martin Van Buren sent General Winfield Scott and seven thousand soldiers to expedite the process. His troops prodded these unfortunate Indian souls at bayonet point into stockades while settlers looted their belongings and burned their houses. Five thousand Cherokee perished from disease and deprivation during their journey to foreign land west of the Mississippi River.

All survivors along what later became known as the "Trail of Tears" had been promised that their new land would stay forever unmolested but as white settlements pushed inexorably westward, this so-called Indian Territory shrank again and again. Oklahoma gained statehood in 1907 and thus it came to be that the Indian Territory was no more.

Grandmother was from the Dakota Black Hills, where a similar situation of land and money played out. Though Grandfather and Father were ignorant of Indian histories during their first years in Glasgow, Mother was not.

Settlers continued to push west into Dakota Sioux Territory just as they did into Alabama and Oklahoma. Westward movement occurred for a variety of reasons but the discovery of gold was one of the biggest. Prospectors struck rich deposits in Deadwood Gulch in 1875 and others in the Dakota Territory's Black Hills the following year in 1876. Gold fever took over and ruled the day.

Sioux were high plains Indians whose lives revolved around buffalo. Because they claimed the Black Hills as sacred ground for sacred journeys, they had previously signed a treaty promising that these sacred grounds were to be set aside for their "absolute and undisturbed use." As skeptics in good standing might guess, that didn't matter to the prospectors and gold seekers who didn't honor the treaty's provision. Neither was it enforced by the United States government so the treaty itself was shamefully abrogated. The Sioux and their lands were violated.

My mother's ancestral family was forced to move to Glasgow, Montana. Father came later. They met at Glasgow High School—a timid Chinese boy and an equally shy Dakota Sioux fell in love in geography class, a town boy and a Reservation girl.

One night after high school graduation, Mother sat me down at our kitchen table to have a talk. "Sing, no one in Glasgow has spit in your face and called you a half-breed but when you leave here someone might. I am full-blood Sioux and your father is full-blood Chinese. I am nervous for what you may encounter as you venture into the wider world beyond your hometown. Will you listen if I tell you a bit of history I was taught on the Reservation but that you were not taught in your high school?"

I gave her my full attention.

"Pilgrims landed on Plymouth Rock in 1620. They had a hard time. Most died. All would probably have died if the Wampanoag Chief Massasoit hadn't shown kindness to them at the first Thanksgiving. That's what you were taught."

I told her I remembered. Except I didn't know the name of the Indian tribe.

"Of course, and that's the point of my story. You know only its beginning, not its ending. The tribe no longer exists. Metacom, the son of Chief Massasoit, became the next chief. The Pilgrims flourished and many, many other English settlers came to the area such that Metacom and his people were hemmed in by them. Settlers crowded out Indians in Virginia and Massachusetts the same as they did in Alabama and Oklahoma. Tension grew into conflict until both sides committed shameful atrocities."

I told her how sorry I was to hear of another sad recounting of unfair treatment of her ancestral people.

"As am I. In 1675, war broke out in open hostilities that is named in the history books, if it's named at all, Prince Philip's War. In 1676, fifty-six years after the first Thanksgiving, Metacom was captured, beheaded, drawn and quartered with his head hoisted high on a spike in the town square where it was left on display for the next twenty-five years."

"Mother, twenty-five years? Are you sure?"

"So I was taught. Metacom's son was sold into slavery in Barbados."

"So that is the end of the story?"

"Yes—and the end of the Wampanoag tribe. It took only three generations for this situation to progress from kindness on the part of my ancestors to brutality on the part of the people to whom we had been kind to extinction of an entire Indian tribe. So I just wanted to say I am happy for your high school graduation achievement but nervous for your future. You're going places outside Glasgow I've not been. And history is not on your side."

"Mother, don't worry. I'm nervous, too, but I'll be careful."

My family always tried to impart what they knew deep in their psyches, their bones, their innermost beings—that it wasn't just the Japanese who forced people to walk death marches. As Pogo, a character from the popular Sunday comic strip of the time, said, "We have met the enemy and he is us."

CHAPTER 11

GIL, 2006

In Iowa, the three generations took pleasure in each other's company over the next five months. And not to be excluded, Mollie cared for her calf. Gail's parents and family weren't forgotten. Gil and Gail packed Maisie and her paraphernalia into their new vehicle so they all could make a couple of trips to visit her parents and brother on their farm as well. Time passed quickly during the interlude, but the day came when spring fully arrived and it was time for the young couple's journey of exploration to Montana.

They took their leave of Iowa and both sets of parents on the seventeenth, a date that had taken on Genesis meaning for them, for what they thought would be no more than a month. Gail's itinerary took them to their first stop at the Corn Palace in Mitchell, South Dakota. Gil hadn't heard of it.

It turned out to be quite the place with quite the history. Lawrence Welk, of all people, played concerts there in years gone by. The young couple knew he had been popular but they hadn't thought of his touring the country so extensively outside major cities with his large entourage. And South Dakota was about as far as one could get outside of New York or Miami or Dallas or Los Angeles or San Francisco.

The Corn Palace was a big gymnasium where state basketball tournaments had been held but it took its name from the tradition of decorating the outside of the building with murals of natural, organic plants from around the local area—corn, obviously and most notably. The murals changed each year. They were professional in presentation and similar to those seen at Pasadena's Rose Parade except there was no parade to speak of and its colors were not bright from flowers but muted from corn and other natural, organic upper-midwestern seeds. "Maisie must feel right at home with all of this maize in the mural," Gail said, and Gil laughed at her silliness.

Gail thought it appropriate they spend a day or two outside Rapid City in the Black Hills to tour Mount Rushmore, looking at the four presidents whose carvings were long finished—plus Crazy Horse, whose monumental, slowly-in-progress carving dwarfed those of the presidents. They enjoyed seeing new country, all the while little knowing they were on sacred Indian ground, the ancestral home of the Sioux.

They got off the interstate to view Devil's Tower in northeast Wyoming. Neither had traveled through this area before. All they knew of it was what Richard Dreyfuss had dreamed and drawn in his mashed-potato fever for the *Close Encounters* movie. In real life, it was quite tall, imposing and impressive. The Park's paved road circled around and up to it, showing its different facets with vertical channels going up and up and up toward its flat top. Eroded rubble was strewn around its base, which terrified Gail as she thought about climbers who had been so foolhardy as to attempt various assents. Devil's Tower didn't stand by itself in a high prairie wheat field, by any means, but there wasn't anything else remotely like it nearby—or that they had ever seen before. It was striking in its singularity.

They continued west to Gillette, where they spent the night in a local motel. It surprised them to learn that Wyoming supplied forty percent of the nation's coal and that eighty percent of Wyoming's coal came from around Gillette. They also toured a couple of the area's dozen strip mines. The size of the equipment was impressive, yet these huge machines appeared small when compared to the coalfields, which covered hundreds of thousands of acres at up to two hundred feet in depth. Every day, coal train after coal train after coal train departed Gillette for parts unknown.

Interstate 90 turned north at Buffalo and ran through Sheridan into Montana, where Gil and Gail began their traverse of America's fourth-largest state. Gail was surprised to learn that Montana's motto was actually in a foreign language—

Spanish (*Oro y Plata*) that translated to *Gold and Silver*—so she wondered if mining might have been part of Montana's history. They enjoyed themselves and took time meandering but were surprised by one or two unexpected yet over-arching impressions.

One was the Bear Tooth Highway that Charles Kuralt made famous in his description as the most beautiful and magnificent road in America, ascending to eleven thousand feet in elevation. The descent down into Cooke City at Montana's southern boundary produced another surprise. They decided, without question, that it was the most isolated community they'd ever seen or visited. They read in a guide they had in the car that not only did it require miles and miles of driving in summer months to get to towns hardly larger than a thousand people but the roads themselves were all totally impassable and snow-packed during winter months. Cooke City had a few year-round residents but they were cut off from civilization during a significant portion of the year.

Gil said, "I'd hate to be here on December tenth . . . that would stretch to January tenth to February tenth to who knows when. We were barely able to get here today and it's late spring back home."

Gail answered, "Much as I enjoy your company, I don't think I could live in this extremely remote and isolated location, either."

They both enjoyed the scenery but discovered there was more to the picture than majestic mountain ranges with wide, fertile valleys and crystal clear rivers with world-class fishing, canyons, caverns and breathtaking big game wildlife herds of elk and Yellowstone buffalo. They knew there could also most likely be lonely independence that bred Godless despair.

Montana was widely thought to have more cattle than people. Sixty percent of its population claimed no religious affiliation. It consistently ranked high in suicide, often first or second among teenagers. Still, Gail told Gil that she felt drawn to the state as a place rife with potential for Christian ministry. Although taverns, not church buildings, were on every corner, Gail suggested the Big Sky state would provide ample opportunity to shine the light of Jesus into its mountains.

Gil agreed. He remembered a boxer saying, "People play baseball, basketball, football, tennis and golf but no one plays boxing. It's unforgiving, brutal." He used that sports analogy to say that harsh conditions in Montana produced opportunity as well as loneliness and depression. "In other words, people living on the edge of existence know they can't succeed on their own," he concluded.

Their second surprising realization bolstered the first. While looking down on an old, manual typewriter in Choteau's little museum, they saw the first draft of the first page of A. B. Guthrie's 1949 Pulitzer Prize-winning novel, *The Way West*, complete with strike-throughs. It was a delightful museum, but their primary and foremost impression was that Guthrie's huge talent came out of such a small town. Literature around the museum declared that Guthrie was raised there, and his father had at various times been editor of the local newspaper and the high school's principal. Guthrie himself stayed put in this town and died there in Choteau at the age of ninety in 1991.

This impression so inspired them that Gil, Gail and Maisie continued up the East Front to Dupuyer where an equally famous author, Ivan Doig, had lived. Dupuyer was a town of fewer than a hundred people. They learned that Doig grew up the motherless son of a sheepherder in those unfenced acreages on the mountain slopes outside of town. Gazing out of the windshield, they noticed pastures were lush from spring moisture. It was beautiful.

Doig graduated from high school in the "big city" of Valier in 1957 as one of twenty-one students. His were truly humble beginnings but he was the only living author having both a fiction and a non-fiction book voted in the top twelve of all books written in the Twentieth Century. With obvious justification, he described himself as coming from "the lariat proletariat, the working-class point of view."

What were the odds? Gil wondered as he stood in the town's park and rest area reflecting on what they'd learned. *Two authors of this caliber, living so close together yet apparently not knowing or associating with each other? Depression and suicide coexisting with solitude and excellence. Truly, Montana was a paradox.*

Gil and Gail smiled at each other, nodding. They decided they loved it and couldn't wait to buy some land and call it home.

CHAPTER 12

SING, 1977

F ather was nineteen years old when he graduated from high school in 1956. He married and stayed put in Glasgow. He and Mother live in a modest dwelling inside the city limits. I was born to my parents as their first and only child in 1959 on, of all days on America's calendar, the Fourth of July.

Glasgow had languished after 1940 when Fort Peck Dam was topped off. As a result, Grandfather struggled to support Father when they moved there in 1946. After nine lean years, things picked up for them in 1955 when construction began on the new Glasgow Air Force Base. Father began working there part-time while he was still in high school and upgraded to full-time employment after graduation. The base opened in 1957 and the town grew. Father stayed at the base as a civilian contractor in the maintenance department. Buildings on the air base included a grade school, gymnasium, bowling alley, general store, hospital and church besides married housing, dormitories for single airmen, hangars and administrative offices.

Hard times were over. Everybody had work and steady paychecks.

The base's mission changed in 1960 to heavy bombers. Its runway length was increased to thirteen thousand five hundred feet. With all that activity and military personnel (more people lived on base than in town), people were optimistic. They shouldn't have been.

Good times don't last forever, especially when more than half the town's vitality came from a single source. Glasgow Air Force Base closed in 1968 and by 1970 the town's emigration rate was thirty-three percent. Father lost his job. All those buildings out on the prairie suddenly looked sad and forlorn without people in them, noise around them and activity among them.

Sixteen thousand people left the area. The town's population was quickly cut by half. Pessimism became the order of the day. Still, my father was able to put and keep a roof over our heads by starting his own maintenance business.

Grandfather's house had one bedroom; Father's was a two-bedroom house. Grandfather never had a car, nor did he learn to drive; Father bought an older-model car to drive to work. Growing up, Father slept on a cot in the kitchen; growing up, I had my own bedroom. In our younger years, both Father and I were assured that we had two good legs which could and would carry us safely to and from school. I learned to run from an early age.

One day I asked, "Grandfather, how did you get to work?"

"My immigration sponsor was thoughtful, kind and faithful to drive me in those early days to the job he'd secured for me. He picked me up in the mornings and brought me back in the evenings to the home they had found for me and your father. I owe him much."

Grandfather attended my parents' wedding, witnessed my birth and spent precious time with me as I grew—time he had as he aged and his workload lessened. He came to nearly all my extracurricular school functions. I mowed his lawn and ran errands for him. The two of us were best friends. I was comfortable sharing thoughts, feelings and teenage angst with him and he was comfortable listening. He didn't criticize or judge but would offer counsel if and when I asked for it.

Among other things, we fished together in Fort Peck Lake. Grandfather took time to teach me life lessons while bobbing out in his little boat. Once he said, "Sing, businessmen say that if you're not moving forward, you're falling behind. Even in China it was true but I hadn't thought about it. But I finally realized that even there, if I decided not to fish for a couple days or tend my rice paddy for a couple weeks, I was actually falling behind, not standing still."

That was hard for me to understand because I knew there was such a thing as standing still. So I asked, "How can that be, Grandfather? If you're doing nothing, you're doing nothing."

"True, but my stomach is doing something. The weeds are doing something. My stomach is growling at me in hunger, saying, 'Feed me.' And weeds are growing, choking my rice. While I'm doing nothing, they're doing something. Even in my simple life there, the world around me was not standing still.

"And it's the same for you in school, you see. If you decide to go fishing with me again tomorrow instead of studying in school, your teacher won't let all your classmates come along with you. They'll be moving ahead with their lessons. So you would either be moving ahead with them—or falling behind them. If you're standing still while they're moving forward, you're falling behind them.

"It's a relative deal. Capitalists know about deals. Most children born and raised here in this country are ambitious and competitive by nature. That's not all good—but neither is it all bad. They love to compete against each other. 'May the best man win,' they say. My kind neighbors in China weren't ambitious or competitive partly because they saw no opportunity to 'get ahead.' Still, we knew our stomachs and the weeds in our fields were opportunists.

"My stomach was greedy. It wanted food every day. Weeds were competitive *and* greedy. They wanted *all* the sunlight and water. If I wasn't pulling weeds or feeding my stomach I was falling behind their demands. So, Grandson, as much as I enjoy spending time with you, we can't fish all day every day and I can't let you come with me if you're doing nothing at school." He paused to pull in his fishing rod, then turned to me in the boat. "Now, tell me why I say that—let me know you understand what I taught you."

"Yes, Grandfather. There's no standing still because other people are moving forward all the time. If I think I'm standing still, I'm actually falling behind them."

"Very good. You're a smart boy. Remember the lesson. Now, are you brave enough, smart enough, to take this lesson a step further?"

"Oookay, I . . . I guess so."

"What is true physically is also true spiritually." Grandfather pointed at a few bright white cumulus clouds that were crossing the sun in the bright blue sky. "Things above," he said.

"I don't understand."

"What is true in the world you can see is also true in the world you cannot see. It might seem like you don't have to do something about God in the same way it might seem like you don't have to deal with your schoolwork but both thoughts are false. You said you understood about the schoolwork. Right?"

"Yes."

"You *must* deal with your schoolwork. Also, you *must* deal with God. God has an adversary who grows like a weed and wants to consume all the sunlight and water like a weed. Have you learned about this adversary in church?"

"Yes, his name is the devil, ha-satan, the deceiver, the accuser, the liar."

"Both God and this devil want your soul. But only one of them can have it. Here's a question. What's the goal of your faith?"

"The goal?" I hadn't thought of it like that but after scratching my head for a minute, I said, "A goal line is like a finish line so I suppose it's to cross the finish line and make it into heaven someday."

"That's a good answer. But you can't make it there by yourself. You must choose people or other entities to help you. Many choose the devil, but again as you say, he's a liar—he says he can help you but he really can't. By the way, did you know he has a plan for your life? Do you know what it is?"

"No. I guess I just thought if I left him alone, he'd leave me alone."

"I wish. But he's a pest. As a pest, he'll pester you. He won't leave you alone. The Bible also describes him as a thief. John 10:10 says he will try to steal from you, kill you if he can get away with it, and destroy everything around you if he can. That's his plan for your life, so you see, he won't leave you alone. And the bad news is that he's bigger and more powerful than you.

"But the good news is that God is bigger and more powerful than the devil. God also has a plan for your life and the same verse that explains the devil's plan for your life explains God's plan. Jesus, the good shepherd, offers life, abundant life, to you.

"So you must choose. There is no such thing as being neutral in spiritual things. It's either God or the devil, the Truth-teller or the liar, life or death. Both God and the devil are actively involved in your life. And that's why I say if you're not walking with God, you're falling behind Him and you need His protection to keep you safe from the devil and the lies of the deceiver.

"Spiritual weeds grow just like physical weeds grow. If you're not pulling and uprooting them, they're getting bigger and choking out the good fruit of the Spirit, the things of God. When you're not pulling them, they're growing."

We had caught our limit of fish by this time and the sun was beginning to beat hot off the water so we headed toward the dock. Grandfather wanted to finish his lesson, though, so he said, "You have a future, Grandson Sing, a bright one. Remember, it's only an illusion to think you can stand still and not lose your future. Keep moving forward, spiritually as well as emotionally as a man, and intellectually as a student."

That was hard for me to swallow—not that I rebelled against Grandfather or what he taught. I understood about visible reality, physical things I touched, smelled and walked on every day. I dealt with emotional and intellectual realities at school, interacting with teachers and classmates. I heard about invisible reality at Sunday School and church but the concept that it was as real as the visible was something I hadn't thought much about. Listening to Grandfather, though, made me realize I had been taking schoolwork more seriously than Bible reading and prayer. I believed in God, somehow, but I hadn't spent time thinking about Him or, as Grandfather put it, walking forward on a daily basis with Him.

When he spoke of living life to its fullest he sometimes described it this way—"Each part of you, Grandson, can and should be permeated with life—life for your understanding that it might not be preyed upon by pernicious error, life for your imagination that it might quench any stifling doubt from mundane thoughts, life for your memory that it might not be haunted by wrecks of past sins or spectral visions of evil, life for your affections that they will pour out the full wealth of your soul, and life for your destiny that it might not be darkened by the shadow of death." He would conclude with this: "I pray the light of an everlasting day will dawn in your heart and rise with ever-increasing luster into your mind, strength and emotions."

Whoo! But Grandfather wasn't always serious. He made fun of his diet and memory. Once, he poked me in the ribs and said, "At my age, forget health food. I need all the preservatives I can get. I'm so old I no longer have memories—just memories of my memories."

Grandfather had worked hard to learn English and had been diligent to expand his vocabulary but it was still a second language for him so I learned to speak Mandarin with him and Father. I thought nothing of it but it came in handy later.

Another time, when Grandfather was eating supper with us in our house, he said, "After all these years, I'm still amazed at America and the differences between this country and China. I grew up working seventy hours a week in rice paddies, walking on dirt paths, eating noodles and rice, struggling for basic necessities of life, lacking luxuries, not even having hobbies or leisure pursuits of happiness."

Father said, "My world expanded greatly from early childhood in China to my teenage years in the United States. My horizons broadened beyond dirt paths and noodles. All I had to do was look around me, even in Glasgow, to see huge tractors, fancy cars and big houses. Things existed and were available that were grander than an ox in a rice paddy, far beyond a crowded dormitory and an old, worn-out city bus. At first, I was satisfied simply to see them, to know they were there, but now I work so you can actually have them someday, Sing. I am content to earn a steady paycheck in a land of plenty but I want more for you than I have known."

I was happy in Father's house with Grandfather's company. Looking back, I could have felt pushed by their ambition for me but I didn't—I felt supported, a good feeling. My family wanted good things for me; they wanted better for me.

I never thought I was too cool for school. I took it seriously and did well enough that guidance counselors thought I had college potential. They said my cognitive capabilities were above average then gave me applications and helped me fill them out. They also said my athletic accomplishments as a quarter-miler made me attractive to college recruiters. I graduated from high school in the spring of 1977 with the number one, all-class track time in the state of 48.3 seconds. I enjoyed running—both its discipline and the freedom it gave me. I admit I was and still am proud of that accomplishment, given my size of 5'8" and 172 pounds.

One day we had a family conference about my upcoming plans for the future. Grandfather began, "I am proud of you, Grandson. I watched you grow to become a fine young man here in Glasgow, America."

Father echoed the sentiment and added, "I never did well in school. I started off late, caught up but then had to repeat seventh grade. I'm sorry to tell you I barely graduated high school. When people ask, I sometimes say my worst subject in school was school itself. You've done much better. I, too, am proud of your accomplishment."

My father gave me a rare smile. "Remember that when you come to a fork in the road, take it. Have you chosen the best fork for you now? What are your plans? We will help you, no matter what. My maintenance and handyman business has grown and flourished so I have been able to save some money. We'll pay what we can and borrow if we have to."

"Oh, I don't know. I'd like to try college and see how it works—for a little while, maybe. But I wouldn't feel right about you borrowing money."

"We might not have to—depending. Where do you want to go?"

"Glasgow is so smack dab in the middle of the surrounding territory that I've got to move to find a college," I said. I had given it some thought. "If I go far, far away it'll probably be expensive and I won't be able to come back to visit you. That's kind of scary for me. I think I'd like to go to Montana State University in Bozeman. It's closer than most and, I hope, less expensive. My high school counselor helped me fill out paperwork to apply there. I don't know if they will accept me, but I should have an answer soon. As I understand it, their answer may or may not include a financial assistance offer."

Grandfather sat quietly for a moment then cleared his throat and began, "I've not told this story before but now is the time. I'm mature enough to tell it without bitterness. Son, you're old enough to hear it and, Sing, you need to hear it before you go away.

"After the Doolittle raid when the Japanese killed so many of us and threw my wife and me into a squalid prison where some were kept in steel cages, some in drainage culverts and others in pits in the ground, I dealt with the smashing of my hip partly because it wasn't the worst thing I ever witnessed. I saw people broken in their spirits. I watched them give up, lose hope and die without being killed.

"Sometimes torture was simply for torture's sake but not always. Sometimes the point was to humiliate us and take away our dignity as human beings. One day the guards hauled me out, bound me to a post and brought my wife to witness my execution.

"Obviously, they didn't execute me that day but they did unspeakable things to her. They tried to humiliate her in front of me. While it was hard to watch, she maintained a special dignity.

"They failed. Their attempt at humiliation was in vain. She triumphed. At that moment, she demonstrated that it is possible to be stripped naked, jeered at, spat upon and raped, yet keep your dignity. She proved herself human; they showed themselves as nothing more than brutes, beasts who only knew to tear and rend as beasts do by brutish nature. She was more human than they—by far. I've never forgotten her example. When I'm tempted to hang my head, I remember her triumph in that trial. I want to be like her and unlike them.

"And that's my point. The world is unregenerate. Don't be like it! Certain people in it will try to humiliate you in one way or another, some more subtly than others. Having watched my dear wife triumph in that horrible situation, I tell you with confidence that you don't have to *be* humiliated. But it takes strength of character. I also tell you not to be naive as you go into new environments and situations. Remember that Jesus warned us, *'If the people of this world hate you, just remember that they hated me first.'* Not all men want to do the right thing; the fact is, an isolated few, extremely wicked people want to do the wrong thing as efficiently and ruthlessly as they can.

"I say 'Go' to you with my blessing. Read your Bible. Seek out Christian fellowship. Be filled with the Spirit. Pray for daily guidance. Live a life worthy of the God you serve. Don't be afraid. God is with you. But be alert. Don't think you won't be tested in some hard ways. Not everyone will be your friend."

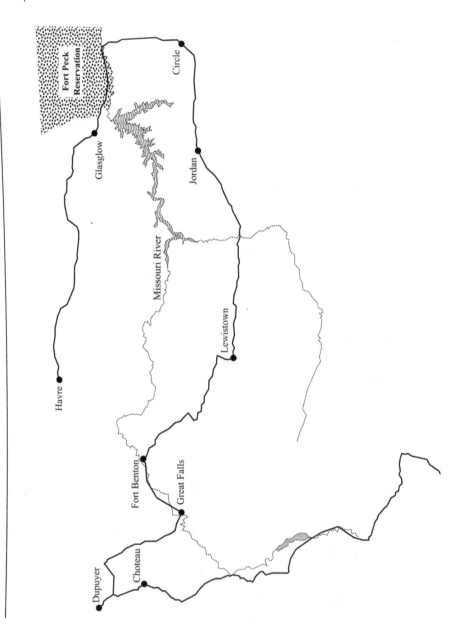

CHAPTER 13

GIL, 2006

G il, Gail and Maisie rolled into town, explored Fort Benton for a day or two and asked questions. Based on the feedback they got, they entered Jamie Ferguson's office the third morning and met Helen, who greeted them warmly and welcomed them to town. She buzzed Jamie, who asked how he could help them.

Jamie was a real estate broker in Fort Benton on the Missouri River whose office specialized in ranch land. His daily attire was boots, blue jeans and belts with big buckles. The look fit him because he was six feet tall and a solid two hundred pounds. Of course, he drove a pick-up truck. He cast a wide net because of the nature of his business, working east in the Golden Triangle, the Missouri Breaks, along the High Line and into Charlie Russell country around Fort Peck Lake. This territory included various Indian Reservations and National Wildlife Refuge areas.

Land quality and productivity varied in this huge region, of course. Some land was more valuable and some less so. It required knowledge and experience, as well as important contacts, to grasp the range of differences between the two and operate a successful enterprise. Water and its availability also was a significant consideration. Jamie understood these factors. He was personable and was one of the best land agents in the state. He truly enjoyed his work.

After the realtor and receptionist offered their "good mornin's" and a chair and cup of coffee to their new prospective clients, Gil said, "We're looking to buy land and relocate to Montana." Gail nodded.

Jamie sat back in his swivel chair, ran his hand through his full head of blond hair and asked, "In town? Ranch acreage? Crops or cattle? Water frontage?"

"We hate to admit our ignorance, but this is our first visit to Montana. Both of us were raised on farms in Iowa. We came here with the idea of purchasing land that's rural but not isolated. Crop land with room for cattle and horses."

Gail added, "We've been sight-seeing through southern portions of the state over the past couple of weeks. We drove north along the Front Range outside Great Falls. Valleys and mountains were beautiful but we weren't impressed to settle down and buy in any of those locations. We're thinking perhaps north-central or northeast holds the greatest promise for us."

Gil agreed and said, "But we don't know why. We'd like to tour with an eye to purchase but, truth be told, we haven't put boots on the ground yet."

"I understand. Ordinarily, I would recommend you explore first, but as it happens, I need to check in with a client near Lewistown then move on to visit a rancher near Jordan about listing his property. We could caravan that far if you'd like and I could give you a head start with your research in that part of our state."

"That sounds great! Thank you so much. What's your schedule?" Gail's eyes were shining with excitement.

"I planned to go tomorrow morning. Out and back the same day."

"Perfect. We'll spend another night here in Fort Benton and see you tomorrow. All ears and eyes." Gil smiled, stood and shook Jamie's big rugged hand. *I think we can trust this guy,* he thought.

"Alright. See you at seven in the morning, if that's agreeable."

"You bet. See you then, 'God willin' and the creek don't rise,' as we say back in the Midwest."

"I get it, but folks here, we pronounce it *crick*. Better to sound local, you know." Then Jamie added, "Say, I just had a thought. Let me check on reservations for you to tour Bear Gulch Pictographs southeast of Lewistown. It's a unique, off-the-beaten-path excursion. Instead of staying here, you could spend tonight at Lewistown's Yogo Inn at Montana's geographic center and soak up some of their history. That is, if you're ready to move on from here today so you could explore further tomorrow."

He gave them directions and said, "Tickets are on me. I'll rendezvous with you tomorrow around noon and escort you to Jordan. I think you're going to enjoy Bear Gulch."

Gil looked at Gail and she nodded in approval so he jumped on the offer. "Thank you. That's generous and very thoughtful. We'd love an adventure on the road less traveled."

Their journey that afternoon began by crossing the Missouri River on the east edge of Fort Benton. It was hard to believe that steamboats had once come this far inland from New Orleans and St. Louis to ferry goods and passengers but such, indeed, was the town's history and claim to fame. They stopped for a break in Geraldine. Jamie had explained that the area held some of the more productive agricultural land in Montana. Gil and Gail were surprised to learn that honeybees in their hives were trucked in by the millions when alfalfa fields (and other hay crops) were flowering. Bees were necessary for pollination in the fields for those crops but the by-product of honey was an added bonus for the local economy. It was too early in the season for fresh honey but a local told them they might want to come back in early summer for the view over the fields in full flower.

They entered Lewistown from the north except they were lured to detour to an old mining camp's remains not far off the highway. On the way, they encountered a cattle herd that was being moved from one pasture to another. Cowboys were at the front and rear of the herd while a man on a four-wheeler was available to escort traffic that chanced along the road.

Life offers serendipitous pleasures, as that one proved. The man on the four-wheeler told them to stay close on his bumper and follow him through the herd. They did, cattle touching both sides of their vehicle—then continued up the mountain road on their way.

It was obvious when they arrived at the mining camp. Three or four original buildings remained, one of which was a log cabin saloon long out of business. Two burly, bearded young men, lounging in the front yard of the house next door, came over to chat. They asked, "Would you like to see inside the saloon?"

It proved to be a going-back-in-time experience. A stream ran alongside, with a willow tree giving shade. The composition of the image made an idyllic picture in their minds. All in all, it was quite pleasant and they were glad for the side-trip.

The young men told Gil and Gail they could travel up the mountainside road, take a turn-off to the left and continue three miles up a forest service road to the tippy-top of Judith Peak, the highest point for miles around—if they wished.

Gail said, "We've got time. Let's do it."

Gil asked, "You guys see our SUV. Can it make it up the road?"

The guys repeated the road was primitive but maintained. So Gil thanked them and agreed to give it a try. The rocky road was washboard but not rutted so he went slow and their vehicle made it just fine. After arriving as described at the tippy-top they pulled out their binoculars and enjoyed scanning the panorama. They watched traffic along the paved road. They could only see two or three ranch steads in their field of vision, which were tucked away in sheltered locations with trees around them. But what made the open vista fiercely pastoral and scary at the same time were the building cloud banks being blown in. They saw rain squalls in half a dozen places. They didn't want to act frightened but they were intimidated. Gail looked at Gil, her eyes huge with awe. "I have a feeling we're not in Kansas anymore."

Maisie had awakened at the mining camp. Gail nursed her at the top of Judith Peak and she fell back asleep on the slow descent of the mountain. The bumps and washboard turned out to be the perfect frequency to rock her into dreamland. The storm squalls were at the lower elevations so they didn't drive through any wind or rain at all; in fact, they enjoyed intermittent sunshine.

They checked into their motel and learned that the area was world-famous for its sapphires, so much so that the gems were given their own names, Yogo Sapphires. Though Gail wasn't a huge jewelry fan, Gil bought one for her to commemorate their trip into this country.

All three of them slept well that night.

The next morning, Gail would have described the drive to Forestgrove, an abandoned shell of a country town, as breathtaking except she had experienced so many breathtaking vistas she had given up using the word. The gravel road between Lewistown and Forestgrove wasn't mountainous but it was elevated in places such that she felt as if she were riding along the top of the world. Views across rolling fields stretched for miles. Pastures were green and gorgeous. Contrary to the pasture land they'd seen yesterday, it seemed like these fields could grow a bounty of almost anything. A county road crew was grading and repairing winter's damage.

Two miles south of Forestgrove, she and Gil, with Maisie in tow, arrived at a farmhouse with modest out-buildings, one of which served as an office of sorts. A hand-painted sign was the only indication that they had found the correct destination. The owner's son escorted them a short distance off-road and, sure enough, Bear Gulch opened up in front of them. They were the only people on the tour not only because of the early season but also because the site was so many miles off the main roads.

They walked down to the hundred-foot cliff wall to observe one pictograph after another—over four thousand of this ancient form of picture writing. Their guide told them he had grown up and played in this place so he hadn't thought of it as unusual but word had somehow gotten out and circulated in academic circles. Archaeologists visited and had declared it to be the world's number one site for this sort of thing. The type of rock cliff existed in only five places in the world. It was truly unique and thus had development potential for research and as a museum center. The guide told them his three-generation family needed money so were doing their amateur's best to make a business out of this archaeological wonder, which they no longer took for granted.

The late-morning sun shown on them in the gulch and reflected back on them from the wall. It was hot. They hadn't prepared for the heat or anticipated it, though their guide had given them each a bottle of water as they left the truck and began their descent into the pictograph gulch. Gail almost didn't make it without fainting. She had to find shade and sit down to wait while their guide kindly brought his four-wheel-drive truck down to her. Gil took this as his cue and did his best to cover Maisie and shield her from the sun and the heat build-up.

At their tour's conclusion Gil said, "Every one of the visuals you showed us is fascinating but I'm most amazed by the white man's land ownership record written in pencil on a rock at eye level in the cliff face. It goes back over one hundred years yet it hasn't weathered or faded away. It is as readable as the day it was written. Those pencil marks are somehow made to be permanent. I wouldn't have believed it if I hadn't seen it with my own eyes."

Gail said to their guide, "This was a great tour. I appreciated your showing us the pictures etched in and under pictures. I saw them when you pointed them out and highlighted them with your special camera, but otherwise, I wouldn't have noticed or understood them. This excursion is something I won't soon, if ever, forget. Thank you so much for giving us this experience."

She meant every word but by the time they got back to their car, she and Maisie were ready to sit quietly in air-conditioned comfort. Driving out, they stopped at one of Forestgrove's abandoned buildings, a church, and had an early picnic on the springtime grass between it and its picturesque cemetery. It was a tranquil setting. Not a soul bothered them.

Then they had to hustle to rendezvous with Jamie at the appointed time and place. He escorted them as they continued east from Lewistown on Highway 200 toward Jordan. After they had traveled a hundred twenty miles, Gail exclaimed, "We've hardly met any traffic at all, we've barely gone through any towns at all, we haven't gotten to Jordan and I need a break. How much farther is it? How much farther can it possibly be? This vista is gorgeous but almost too big."

Gil replied, "I understand now why Montana was said to not have speed limits on its roads in earlier years, that Highway Patrolmen would only pull drivers over if they were clocked at greater than a hundred miles an hour. At that, they would write you up for a five-dollar ticket and you could pay the fine to the patrolmen right there on the spot and continue on your way."

Gail said, "Iowa's only two hundred miles north to south. If we were in Iowa, we'd have driven more than halfway across it. And think how much traffic we'd have met and how many towns we'd have gone through. This is starting to feel a little spooky to me. It's not until we're actually doing this that it gets real how big Montana is and how sparsely populated parts of it are."

"I agree with you. I don't think we'll be buying land in Jordan or raising Maisie in it. It's worthwhile having this first-hand experience, though, because otherwise, we wouldn't have had the emotional impact of driving through its wide-open spaces."

It turned out that Jordan was the county seat and the biggest town in Garfield County. The County itself was almost the size of the State of Connecticut but Jordan's population of three hundred people was a fifth of the county's population and not even close to being in the same ballpark as Connecticut's.

They stopped for a final conversation with Jamie at the courthouse, a metal building smaller than many convenience stores. Gail said, "This area of the country is too remote and isolated. A town of three hundred is fine if it's near larger towns . . . I'm glad we saw it but we're not comfortable here."

Jamie said, "I agree. I'm in love with almost every inch of Montana but I wouldn't have made this trip unless my business had brought me here today. This country is remote. Jordan is the most remote and isolated county seat in the United States—eighty-five miles to the closest bus line, a hundred fifteen miles to the nearest train station and one hundred seventy-five miles from the nearest airport. A dormitory for ranch kids of high school age was used until about 1980. It's still standing and you can see it just over there." Jamie pointed to a building in the distance. "Do you see it? The school graduates ten, maybe twelve, seniors each year, that's it. It's good country but it's not for everyone.

"I understand this is too isolated and you prefer to move on. If you make a big loop going another sixty-five miles east of here to Circle then fifty miles north to Wolf Point then fifty miles west to Glasgow along Highway 2 and what we call the High Line, you can see a lot more of northeast Montana.

"Here's a list of for-sale properties I've prepared for you. I won't interfere if you contact another agent and purchase something off this list from him. But I'd count it a privilege to meet with you again if you come full-circle back to my office in Fort Benton. It's been my pleasure to meet you. God be with you as you explore. Until we meet again." And he tipped his well-worn cowboy hat in a good-bye gesture.

Gil fantasized about driving a hundred miles an hour but he reminded himself that they weren't in a hurry so his temptation was only a fleeting fantasy. Their purpose was to soak in the *feel* of the landscape, after all. But then, oddly enough, two high school girls in a boat of a station wagon passed them at a terrific road speed as they left Jordan heading east. He sped up to one hundred ten miles per hour but they left him in their dust. He and Gail got a good laugh out of that and said to each other, "Wow, the stories are true."

As they neared Circle, they entered irrigation country. Water made the land look greener and more attractive but they still had it in their minds that this region was too remote for them. They turned left at Circle as Jamie suggested and headed north for Wolf Point. They crossed over the Missouri River immediately prior to arriving at Wolf Point and noticed an old bridge left in place from earlier days that was at a much higher elevation than the new highway bridge. They wondered if their observation was a measure of an engineer's flood control effectiveness. Gil exclaimed, "Would you look at that! Get a load of how those old on-ramps are built up! I bet the difference in height of these bridge decks is at least twenty feet."

Gail, who was more tired at this point than she let on, responded, "There must be some sort of massive flood control upstream from here. Maybe we should stop soon and take a day to investigate, see what we might find out."

They then turned left to travel west toward Glasgow. For some reason, they felt more comfortable and the countryside appeared more welcoming and inviting to them on this last leg of their day's journey. They weren't able to identify the reason but they both felt it.

They had driven over three hundred miles by the time they arrived at Glasgow. "We're planning to stop here, right?" Gail asked tiredly. "I'm worn out. This has been a long day, a very long day."

"Yes, it's time to break for the night. Maisie's been good but we're ready to stop. Besides, it's time to literally put boots on the ground. Not only do we need to walk and exercise; we also need to walk on the dirt, not just drive over it."

Thus it came to pass they spent their first night in Glasgow.

CHAPTER 14

SING, 1977–1984

God smiled on me and I was accepted to Montana State University as an MSU Bobcat with a generous but partial track scholarship. Father, Mother and Grandfather drove me down to Bozeman. None of us had been there before. It seemed a big place. An upperclassman was assigned to welcome and show me around on that first day. He helped us carry my few belongings up to the fifth floor to my room in my dormitory.

My roommate said he was from Belfry. He had just moved in and taken the lower bunk in our two-man room. I introduced myself and my family; he did the same. "Hi, I'm Wyatt Haskins. These are my parents, my brother who's one year younger and my two sisters—Sue, a sophomore, and Amy, an eighth-grader. Where are you from?"

"Glasgow. Grandfather, here, moved there from China with Father in 1946. I'm sorry but I don't know where Belfry is."

"It's a small Montana town with a couple hundred people that's south of Billings near the Wyoming border. We do have a claim to fame, though. We won the Class C state basketball championship three years in a row. Our school mascot is the bat. We're the Belfry Bats. Maybe you've heard?"

"Noooo . . . how could I have missed that? Apparently, my life's been *way* too sheltered. The Fort Peck Dam and Reservoir are just outside Glasgow. Maybe you've been up to where I live to do some fishing?"

"No. Looks like neither one of us has traveled much. All I've heard about northeastern Montana is that it's like a small town with extra-long streets."

I had no idea then how much Wyatt and contact with his family were going to impact my life. This, our first meeting, was pleasant but inauspicious. His family excused themselves for their goodbyes.

Mother made my bed while I unpacked, then we walked down to say goodbye at our car. My family wanted to drive home before dark. It was a long drive and would be a long day for them.

After I waved farewell, my upperclassman guide-for-the-day took me to the campus bookstore and gave me a map so I could find the locations for my classes. He explained the freshman orientation schedule and asked if I had questions. I thanked him, said I hardly knew enough to have questions but asked him to point out the track and athletic department offices. He left me with his name and phone number in case I needed further help.

———

Later, as Wyatt and I were getting better acquainted in our dorm room, I said, "You bragged on your school as being a basketball powerhouse. Do you play? Are you a baller?"

"Show up for tryouts at a school the size of Belfry and you've got a good chance of making the team. I played but as our coach said, 'Boys, we may be short but at least we're slow.' It was fun but my playing days are over. And our powerhouse days are over, as well. Our team had a winning record but just barely. What did you do in high school?"

"I was more family than sports-oriented. I studied hard and went fishing a lot with my grandfather that you met today. I played French horn in concert band but didn't march at football games. I wasn't singled out for special honors in anything. Except I ran track and have been recruited to try out for the mile relay team here."

"Good for you. I admire athletes with the discipline it takes to run well." Wyatt told me that his family owned a lot of farmland, and he planned to major in agronomy, animal husbandry or other similar subjects so he could go back to his family's ranch and take it over when his father retired. That made sense to me since he was the oldest male child in his family. He talked me into signing up for some classes with him so we could study together. I asked, "What about the business side of running a ranch? Are you ready to do that?"

"I don't know," he said. "Probably not. My father's taken care of all the management on our ranch. It seems like a good thing to learn, though. Thanks for the tip. I'll be on the lookout for business classes on ranch management."

I said, "It's nothing fancy but Father taught me not to spend more than I make, to tithe to God out of my earnings and save money. I think I'll try to up my game with a business class or two myself. Our family's managed what God's given us but we don't own land or a ranch or cattle or wheat or machinery or anything like that. Maybe someday."

Wyatt was a vibrant sort of guy, full of life, with energy and infectious joy radiating from him. I felt like a methodical plodder next to him, which is not to say I felt bad or Wyatt put me down; on the contrary, he made me feel included and I was attracted to his dynamism. He was much taller than I but he didn't make me feel short. His confidence encouraged me and opened my eyes to realms of possibility.

"What clubs could we join?" Wyatt had brought a basketball with him and was spinning it on his finger as he sat sandwiched in on his bunk. His sandy brown hair wasn't long enough to get in his eyes. "Let's get involved. I hear there's a Campus Crusade here that rocks. You wanna try it out?"

"Crusade for what? I've never heard of it."

"Its full name is Campus Crusade for Christ. I suppose there's preaching and Bible study, maybe some witnessing, but the main thing I'd be interested in is Christian fellowship. Are you a Christian? Do you know about Jesus?"

"I went to Sunday School in Glasgow. Grandfather's a Christian. He talks about Jesus."

"What I meant was, do you have a personal relationship with Jesus?"

"I think so. Maybe. Grandfather and I spent a lot of time together but I have to admit I didn't understand everything he said to me. He sent me out with his blessing, told me not to be afraid but also not to be gullible. He said that not everyone would be my friend, that I should make good friends I can trust." I

looked at him and folded my arms. "Of course, somehow I got stuck with you."
I grinned.

Wyatt unfolded himself out of his bunk and threw the ball at me, his blue
eyes sparkling mischievously. I managed to catch it without looking too clumsy.
He smiled back.

I said, "Just joking. I'd be willing to check Campus Crusade out. Do you
think we might find friends we could trust at that place?"

"I hope so. Let's try it."

"Okay," I agreed.

So it happened that Wyatt helped me honor Grandfather's advice and the
first extracurricular activity I tried was Campus Crusade for Christ. It had Bible
study. There was preaching but not too much. People mainly interacted and
told personal stories, what they called their testimonies. I found it all to be quite
refreshing. I liked it. And it turned out that the friend I made was Wyatt. I
believed he wouldn't betray or hurt me, that he was indeed trustworthy.

The leader was a young man with a family. He wasn't a student. He led this
club because he cared for us. He called us his ministry.

School kept us busy, especially with my commitment to daily track practice,
but we still had free time. Belfry was closer to Bozeman than Glasgow so one
Friday Wyatt said, "Let's stay for the football game this Saturday and then go
visit my family afterward. Come with me and I'll take you horseback riding.
How's that? You can be a Bat the same day you're a Bobcat. Wild, huh?"

Wyatt had a car (an old farm truck, actually) so I rode with him to Belfry
that October weekend. A tree-shaded creek ran through their ranch. Their land
was well-tended and the barn fit into the homestead. It was a very pretty place
for me to work in a relaxed five-mile run.

Wyatt's sister, Sue, was excited and wanted to take me to meet their horses.
I agreed to go along with her because she was cute and I didn't want to be rude.
She was almost a twin to Wyatt, only shorter . . . with longer hair and, well, a
girl's figure.

I hadn't told Wyatt but I had never been on a horse in my life—hadn't even been up close to touch one before. Sue saw that I was a total novice but she didn't poke fun at me. She gave me an apple and showed me how to open my hand and hold it up for the horse to eat. I was nervous around such big animals at first but she was patient and the horses weren't skittish so I got over it.

Supper was a lot more boisterous than I was used to with Mother, Father and Grandfather. I guess the stereotype about the calm, inscrutable Chinese has a little bit of truth to it—maybe. Anyway, supper at Wyatt's house was lively and a lot of fun with seven of us around the table.

The next morning we dressed up in what they called their 'Sunday best' and we all went to church. The little white building with a steeple on it wasn't in the middle of nowhere but I was surprised when so many vehicles gathered to fill its grassy yard at their appointed start time. They had loud singing—and if I thought supper had been boisterous, it didn't hold a candle to the raised hands and dancing in that church building. I'd not experienced anything like it ever before. Its exuberant joy scared me more than the horses had! Those people had gratitude in their attitude.

It was a great weekend in Belfry. I enjoyed it thoroughly, despite my timidity.

———————

Weekends back in Bozeman were crammed full with activities but in November, so many students planned to abandon campus over Thanksgiving that I asked Wyatt, "I'm headed home for the holiday. Would you like to come to Glasgow with me? I'd buy your ticket and we could take the bus. It meanders a bit but you could discover new scenery on the ride north."

I didn't know what his response would be but to my relief he wasn't offended. He said, "Sure, I haven't ridden a bus. Let's do it. I'd like to see new country and get to know your folks. But I'll get my own ticket. That's not a problem."

The day came and we went. I sat on the right side window seat one row in front of the rear axle. People were mostly quiet but I watched a young couple's occasional conversation and an older gentleman whose head bobbed as he dozed. Wyatt sat nearer the front. As people got off at various stops, we changed seats so we could sit together. The trip was only a couple of hours longer than if we had taken his old farm truck. And it was okay visiting with other people.

Father was waiting for us at the depot. Mother had a light supper on the table and Grandfather was keeping her company in the kitchen. We washed up and sat down for the meal—which was much quieter than at Wyatt's house. He didn't seem to mind; actually, he seemed fascinated by Grandfather and his stories.

We ate slowly and told jokes. We caught up with each other's lives, which was easy on their end since not that much was happening for them in Glasgow. At one point, Father made up a tall tale on me for Wyatt's benefit. He said, "In his younger years, Sing had a spell of running and hanging with an unsavory friend who had built a reputation for small-time theft. I took them both by the ears and hauled them off to our pastor for counseling. He left Sing on a bench in the hall and began with the other youngster in his office. He asked him, 'Son, do you know where God is right now?' The boy answered, 'No.' Our pastor didn't much care for that so he repeated himself—louder, 'I'll ask you again. Do you know where God is?' The boy said, 'I done told you, no.' This made our preacher madder than it should have so he raised his voice and said, 'Don't you speak to me in that tone of voice.' At which the boy jumped up, ran out of the office, grabbed Sing and took off down the road runnin' wide open. Sing, between breaths, asked, 'What happened? What happened in there?' The boy told him, 'God's missin' and they's a-blamin' us!'"

I felt my face flush because that didn't really happen to me so, amid the laughter and finger-pointing, I protested. But actually, I was proud that my family was showing Wyatt such a fun time even if it was at my expense.

I told a joke but admitted it was only a joke. It would have been fun to name its main characters Father and Mother and pretend it was true but I resisted that temptation. Instead, I named them Hillbilly Jed and his wife, Judy. "Jed began to worry about his age, that he was headed downhill and gaining speed. One night, he watched Judy take a pill and asked, 'What-cha takin', Honey?' 'Oh, just somethin' to make me feel young in the mornin'.' She went on to bed but Jed hung around and took the whole bottle before he went to bed. The next morning, Judy couldn't find Jed. He wasn't in the kitchen or anywhere in the house. Finally, she spotted him outside all dressed up and sitting on the curb, jes' a-sittin' on the curb. She hollered out, 'Jed, what-cha doin' out there?' He yelled back in a little-boy voice, 'I'm jus' a-waitin' on thuh school bus.'"

We adjourned to the living room and the warmth of its fireplace for dessert and coffee, except Grandfather still preferred tea. Wyatt had questions. He was so open and his interest so sincere that it seemed natural when he said, "Sing tells me you knew Jimmy Doolittle and helped him escape China after his bombing raid over Japan. You must have a whopper of a story to tell. What is it?"

I think those two could have talked all night. As much as Grandfather and I enjoyed each other's company, Grandfather and Wyatt *relished* each other's. I was awestruck. It was magical. Father reminisced over some of his memories too. Stories I'd heard so many times were fresh again for all of us. There was even a new one I didn't remember hearing before.

"I had a little dog that trailed around after me," Grandfather started. "One day on the dirt path between rice paddies I surprised a cobra that had been sunning itself. It startled me. I tried to jump out of the way but fell in the water and the snake acted like it wanted to come in after me. My little dog barked and barked to draw off its attention so I could kill it with my hoe. He saved my life. I'm sure of it."

Wyatt pictured the scene and went quiet. He said, "Sing."

"What?"

"Your grandfather gets it."

"What?"

"Our pet animals. Sometimes they become more than pets to us. Here's my own little joke. Lock your dog and your girlfriend in your car trunk. Go away. Leave them there for a couple hours or so. Come back. Open the trunk. Which one is happy to see you?" We all laughed but Grandfather chuckled the loudest. Wyatt continued, "Your grandfather gets it. You know, man's best friend and all that."

"Oh, yeah. Well, since you put it that way, I guess you're right. I read a prayer somewhere that said, 'Lord, make me the man my dog thinks I am.'"

Grandfather smiled at the thought, then told us another tale. "God created Dog and said to him, 'Sit all day by the door of your house and bark at anyone who walks past. For this, I will give you a life span of twenty years.'

"Dog replied, 'That's a long time to be barking. How about only ten years and I'll give You back the other ten.' And God saw that it was good.

"Immediately after, God created Monkey and said to him, 'Entertain people, do tricks and make them laugh. For this, I will give you a twenty-year life span.'

"Monkey replied, 'Do monkey tricks for twenty years? That's a long time to jump around, scratch myself and perform. How about I give ten back to You like Dog did? Again God saw that it was good.

"Then God created Cow and said to her, 'You must go into the field with the farmer all day long and suffer under the hot sun, have calves and give milk to support the farmer's family. For this, I will give you a life span of sixty years.

"Cow replied, 'That's a tough life You want me to live. How about twenty and I'll give You back the other forty years?' God agreed for He saw that it was good.

"Last, God created Adam and Eve and said to them, 'Have a pleasant life. Eat, sleep, play, marry and enjoy your lives. For this, I'll give you twenty years.'

"But these humans replied, 'Only twenty years? Won't You please add for us Cow's forty years she gave back, Monkey's ten he gave back and Dog's ten he gave back? That makes eighty years. Okay?' God nodded in agreement but added, 'Remember, you asked for it.'

"So that is why we eat, sleep, play and enjoy ourselves for our first twenty years. Then for our next forty years we slave in the hot sun to support our family, during the next ten years we do monkey tricks to entertain our grandchildren and for our last ten years we sit on the porch and bark at everyone.

"Now, it's late so if you'll excuse me I'll go out to sit on our porch, look at the stars and bark at the neighbors. Good night to all of you." We laughed with him.

Time flew by. I'm pretty sure we didn't get to bed before midnight.

CHAPTER 15

GIL, 2006

Gil and Gail rested well and ate a leisurely breakfast the next morning. They studied Jamie's list of properties for sale and saw he had a few of his own listings included on it. Gail said, "I bet there's a Chamber of Commerce here that has a publication advertising real estate for sale. It's cool outside so let's get directions, wrap up, get Maisie ready and walk, if it's not too far, to the Chamber's office and pick up brochures. That way, we wouldn't have to commit ourselves to any one salesman or real estate office."

Gil agreed, "That's a good idea. Let's do that but add to your notion. Our motel has connectivity so let's extend our stay one night and search online too. If we don't find anything we like, we can call Jamie and ask him for detailed maps of his listings."

"Deal. I like it."

They secured and flipped through slick-paper, full-color brochures and studied Jamie's list. They made marks on their map then spent the afternoon driving in the countryside northwest of Glasgow. Land near various small rivers as they flowed south out of Canada caught their attention.

Gil declared, "This trip is worthwhile. We have confirmation. Who knows? We might even stumble across the perfect place for us. Here feels like home, don't you think? Does this part of Montana seem like home to you?"

Gail replied, "It does. But I'd rather pray God's perfect place be perfectly revealed to us ahead of time instead of our stumbling over it."

"Of course. All I meant was I don't always know His leading ahead of time. Sometimes but not always. Right now, I admit to wondering if this obsession will end in mastery, mockery—or madness."

"Or miracle," Gail added. "Don't sell God short. He gave you the vision. You didn't just conjure it up like in a Walter Mitty daydream."

"Thank you. I needed that word of encouragement. I was beginning to fear our trip, delightful though it has been, is hopeless hooey. Here, take my hand. Let's pray."

She did. Gil's prayer was short, "Lord, as Gail has taken my hand, I pray You take our hands and guide us. We don't know where we're going. Please, show us the way. And make it plain so we won't have any doubts."

She sensed Gil was struggling so she prayed too. "Father, this is a life-changing move we're contemplating. It'd be great if You supernaturally revealed Your will to us before we plunge into a deal and made a commitment we might later come to regret. We don't want to wander in the wilderness as the Israelites did but what I'm asking is the same assurance of guidance they had while they were in their remote place. They didn't move until they saw Your glory cloud move. Show us Your glory cloud. Let us see it move so we know when and where to move. Give us vision, grant us revelation. So far, we've been trying to work a giant jigsaw puzzle, piece by piece without knowing what the picture looks like. Please show us at least some of the picture to give us confidence in what we're doing."

To which Gil said, "Amen."

They agreed it would be a wonderful bonus—icing on the cake, so to speak— if God revealed Himself to them in a glory cloud.

They continued the search for a couple more days but knew they hadn't found their perfect place yet. Gil said, "I almost hate to drive west away from Iowa but it seems like we should because it seems like we should check in with Jamie. Let's set an appointment with him, get up tomorrow morning, head west along Highway 2 then swing south to Fort Benton. We can visit with him face-to-face before pointing our noses toward Iowa and our parents' home turf."

"Alright. Maybe. I don't know. We've done part of what we set out to do. We have general confirmation; that's good. But my heart aches that we don't have more than that. It feels like we're giving up on specific confirmation, giving up on finding our perfect place.

"Can't we investigate rentals in Glasgow? We might even look at two or three. That way, if we move here this summer, we wouldn't be blind when we come and it wouldn't feel so much to me like we're giving up."

"Great idea. I'll set it up while you take care of Maisie."

"Don't forget to call Jamie, too. Try to make an appointment with him for day after tomorrow."

"Sure thing. I'm on it."

When he called, Helen put Gil through to Jamie, who said, "Great to hear from you. How's your trip been?"

"Wonderful. We're in Glasgow, spending a few days but we haven't found our perfect place. We're investigating temporary housing today. Can we schedule time with you day after tomorrow in Fort Benton before we head back east?"

"Sure, you bet. In Havre, I suggest you tour their underground city. It's fun and educational. A two-hour stop would give you a driving break. Then swing down Highway 87 through Box Elder and Rocky Boy.

"One of Montana's two senators is a farmer from Rocky Boy. He's advertised as the only working farmer/rancher in the United States Senate. As if that weren't distinctive enough, I judge him to have the best flat-top haircut, the fewest number of fingers on his hands and the biggest belly of any senator. Check it out. Find a picture and tell me if I'm not right. And travel well. Be safe. I look forward to seeing you when you get here."

They found plenty of available rental housing at reasonable prices in or near Glasgow. It was nice to know temporary housing, if required, wasn't a problem. On their way to Fort Benton, they followed Jamie's advice and toured the part of Havre's history having to do with cold weather, fire and an underground city. They also looked up Senator Tester's photo and agreed with Jamie's assessment.

They were surprised though when Helen greeted them at Jamie's office. She was fidgety—and so was Jamie. He paced the office and barely waited until after Helen fixed coffee for them before he blurted out, "You'll never believe it! I don't believe it. In all my years working out of this office nothing like this has happened with me. I got a call this morning—less than an hour ago—from a well-to-do rancher northeast of Glasgow near Scobey. He wants to retire, his daughter doesn't want to take over his operation and he had a dream. God woke him and told him to call me.

"Naturally, I was skeptical but I know of him by reputation. He's a real person, he exists, he's six-foot-eight, three hundred pounds and everybody knows him as 'Big John' Jackson around Scobey and Glasgow. I looked up land ownership records, called his daughter, spoke with his attorney—and his story seems legitimate. I don't think this is a joke. I don't think I'm being pranked. It's pretty far outside my normal service territory but, for some reason, I think this deal has your names writ large all over it—if you can afford it.

"We haven't mentioned your price range but let me describe the deal the way this seller outlined and described it to me. I gather that everything's big about him, including his ranch's price tag—it's expensive, a whole pot-load of dollars. His ranch has trees, water, arable land, a lot of pastured acres and elevated views. If you're curious, have the time and money, we'll fly up and look at it together. It's weird that I'm asking you to turn around and go back to where you came from—but there you have it. I'm passing on to you what I just learned."

Gail responded, "I prayed that God would give us supernatural revelation. He's done it before and He can do it again. I hope He will. I hope He is—now."

Gil turned to Jamie and added, "I think I mentioned to you that while I was in the army at the NATO base in Turkey, God worked in our lives such that money is not an issue for us. We're blessed financially but we don't want to misuse this privilege of plenty. We don't want to make a 'splash' just because we can. There have been instances when God gives influence to people but they pander to self-aggrandizement. There have been occasions when God gifts young athletes or musicians with talent and they prostitute it with personal ambition. Sometimes God blesses people with wealth and riches, only to watch them lay it on a foreign altar and indulge a formerly hidden covetousness. In humility, we say we don't want to be those people.

"But you definitely have our attention. You bet we're curious. We're also cautious. We're also excited. We've been expecting supernatural guidance. Except we didn't know you have an airplane."

"I don't. But a friend of mine has a turbo-twin in his charter business. I use him for special occasions as weather permits."

Gil and Gail looked at each other and winked. Gil said to his wife, "Let's do it. Saddle up, cowgirl—for the plane ride, I mean. But first," he turned to the real estate agent, "Jamie, we need to talk about an item that bothers me before we burrow too deeply into this."

"Alright. Have I done anything that gives you heartburn?"

"No, you've been nothing but generous and kind. My hesitation concerns dual agency. To take it out of its immediate context, the Bible has a verse that reads, *'No one can serve two masters.'*

"This man obviously wants you to represent his interest. That's why he called you. If you sign to represent this man, your fiduciary responsibility is with him, not us. On the other hand, if we sign paperwork with you that you represent us as a buyers' broker, he might refuse to sign with you.

"Some people are comfortable signing papers agreeing to dual agency but I'm not. I just don't see how it's possible to have divided loyalties."

"I understand." Jamie rubbed his chin thoughtfully. "You raise a good point. How about we do this the old-fashioned way—nobody signs papers before we proceed. I can introduce the two of you to him and listen as you talk with each other. But I will still be available if either of you asks questions of me."

Gil said, "I like it. Sounds good."

"We don't want to cheat you. If we negotiate a deal with this man, how would you get paid?" Gail asked.

Jamie responded, "I appreciate your question, as you can imagine. If all goes well and you strike a deal, perhaps a flat fee from both parties could be included in it."

Gil said, "I'm comfortable with that. It would involve a level of trust on your part. Are you comfortable with that scenario?"

"With you, yes." Jamie gave them a huge grin and tipped his cowboy hat. "Thank you. Here's my hand on it."

"You got it, my friend. One last thing. I like to take my German shepherd with me on forays out into the vast unknown with people I've not met before. My dog has flown before. He's obedient, trained and gentle but he doubles as a security blanket for my wife's peace of mind. Is that alright with you?"

"By all means, feel free. We've both grown up around animals. We're not allergic or afraid. We're partial to shepherds as a matter of fact."

They were back in Glasgow by noon with a baby and a dog in tow and a real estate broker on a handshake deal embarking on a mysterious adventure.

Mr. Jackson met them at the airstrip in his pickup that sagged a little bit on its left side. His height reminded Gil of a certain commander, Colonel James from his military time in Turkey. Except the colonel, at six-foot-five, was three inches shorter, and being younger, was lean and wiry from his collegiate basketball days, while the seller was heftier—lean and wiry was in his rearview mirror. Gil imagined Mr. Jackson wrestling steers at branding time without breaking a sweat. He seemed like a straight shooter in a cowboy motif of big hat, boots and a bolo tie. His firm handshake was robust, as was his demeanor and bearing. But he was not overbearing . . . gruff but not overbearing.

Gil liked him. Gail did, too. So did Jamie's dog apparently. Mr. Jackson had his big dog with him too. Even the two dogs liked each other—after they sniffed each other, of course. It took them a minute but they eventually wagged their tails.

Jamie introduced himself and explained the situation.

The big rancher swept his hand to one side and said, "Whatever. We're suffocating under an avalanche of big city lawyers and lawsuits so I'm glad to do business the old-fashioned way as long as I get good results." He looked at Gil and said, "Young man, you'd better be what you say you are. I'll give you all the time you need as long as you're straight with me." He took them to a local eating place where everybody knew him and said, "Hey, Big John" and slapped him on the back. It took a while to work their way through the crowd and find a seat but they eventually got a bite to eat before leaving for the drive out to his ranch.

It was over an hour away. Gail teared up at her first sight of the homestead, of the big valley framed by cliffs on one side and a river on the other. She yet again used the word "breathtaking." Gil thought, *there really isn't a better word to describe it.*

This was it. They saw the glory cloud move. It hovered over this perfect place.

Later, when they were alone, Gail said, "This is all happening very fast."

"I know, my head's spinning," Gil agreed. "I'm almost afraid it's too perfect, too easy. My parents resisted the urge to sell when land prices were bid up to three hundred dollars per acre in the 1970s. Farmers were expanding like crazy, then when foreclosure auctions happened those same farmers realized too late they had, in fact, been crazy."

"My parents didn't resist," Gail said. "They were buyers. They expanded during that time."

"How did they avoid foreclosure?"

"Easy, they paid cash for their purchases. Not entirely but they didn't leverage to the max. They avoided debt. That's why they didn't get into trouble. We're long past the 1970s and three hundred dollars per acre but the principle is the same for us. We're dealing with bigger numbers but so what? We can pay cash, avoid debt and stay out of trouble. This deal's not foolish from that perspective."

"It puts me in over my head in terms of experience and management ability. It's perfectly clear that this is God's miraculous provision but the sheer scope of the deal frightens me."

"Agreed—on both counts. But do you remember what you said to me when I was pregnant with Maisie, after our Middle Eastern dinar had revalued?"

"No, I don't know what you're driving at."

"You told me there were two kinds of people, paper and dirt."

"You're right. And I'm a dirt guy."

"There you go. So—we've got money and you're a dirt guy. We've given money away to assist in God's kingdom work but He continues to bless such that our remainder has multiplied back to us. The question is, would you rather invest in pieces of paper or clods of dirt—the stock market or farmland?"

"But this is so fast!" Gil's black eyebrows gathered in concentration.

"Agreed. It makes me want to use the word 'breathtaking' in a spiritual way. How about this? In an abundance of caution and so as not to be foolish in a rash, over-excited sort of way, let's take the weekend to bring both sets of parents plus my brother and his family here to include them in this adventure, get their opinions and have a day or two simply to catch our breath. This is God's perfect provision—unless they see something we're blind to. Let's buy this ranch unless they talk us out of it."

Gil said, "Do you suppose they can?"

"Yes, the size of this place might scare them to death."

"No kidding! It's got me scared, for sure."

CHAPTER 16

SING, 1977–1999

Thursday morning Grandfather went with us as I drove Wyatt down to Fort Peck Dam and Lake. Since it was Thanksgiving Day, the museum and visitor center were closed but we filled our time wondering at the magnitude of that project from a by-gone era. I waved my hand as I pointed over to the remains of a few of the boom towns that had filled the area. The show house was still there and in good condition, of course, since it performed lots of sold-out shows for tourists during the summer months. Wyatt said he'd like to come back before haying season in late June for a show and to go through the visitor center. Grandfather offered to take him fishing if he did—and said he hoped he would come back.

Mother and Father had done a great job with their Thanksgiving feast. We lolled about that afternoon as we rested and slept off too much turkey, stuffing and pumpkin pie. I wasn't too motivated but nonetheless spent a couple of hours over a textbook I carried with me. We grazed at leftovers through the evening and had pecan pie piled with ice cream and whipped cream for dessert.

The next morning Father said to Wyatt, "May I show you where I work?"

Wyatt replied, "You bet. I'd love to see it."

So Father drove to St. Marie to show Wyatt the spectacle of the abandoned air base and the ghost town it had become. The five of us were together so we made a day of it and continued north to Opheim on Montana's northern

97

frontier at the Canadian border. Father pulled into the cafe at its more-or-less abandoned hotel for a rest stop. He said, "Believe it or not, three years before St. Marie came into existence by the opening of the Glasgow Air Force Base, the population of this small town boomed as well. The Opheim Air Force Station four miles west of where we now sit opened in 1952 as a Gap-Filler radar site. It brought twenty-three civilian workers like me plus one hundred thirty-five active-duty military personnel to this town. Crowds gathered here every weekend at Opheim's new bowling alley and its three taverns. But as came to pass in Glasgow, good times didn't last because the installation closed in 1979 after twenty-seven years, and Opheim's population fell from over five hundred to less than one hundred fifty.

"But the point of my little story is that I came to know the daughter of the owners of this two-story property in which we now sit. Back then, it was known as 'The EZ Rest Hotel—Opheim's Finest.' A big chandelier was here in this lobby and the state liquor store was right across this aisle. There were four apartments upstairs. Both levels were well furnished with some pretty classy antiques.

"While the good times were still booming but not long before they came to an end, the long-term owners here sold out—lock, stock and barrel, as the saying goes. The buyer claimed not to have a lot of excess cash money so the sellers agreed to a minimal down payment with generous terms. Their daughter married an Air Force guy and moved away; the sellers also relocated since they had no other family in town. They trusted the buyer to keep his word and honor his obligation.

"Unbeknownst to them, after making less than a year's contract payments, this buyer scheduled an auction and sold off all the furnishings. He then skipped town, leaving the sellers and their daughter with nothing but an empty shell of a building in a town that, as you can see, was abandoned pretty much like St. Marie had been eleven years before in 1968. He made money but my friend's parents lost everything."

Wyatt whistled and said, "Wow, that's a bitter pill to swallow."

Father summarized, "People say they're honest but they also say they have to look out for themselves and protect their own best interests. Particularly during hard times, when push comes to shove, honesty flies away like a bird as people scramble to survive."

After emptying their coffee cups and taking a last look around, Father drove us six miles north to look at the Port of Entry at the Canadian border. Heading back home to Glasgow, we meandered east to Scobey then south through the Fort Peck Indian Reservation.

I was accustomed to the look and feel of this country but Wyatt exclaimed, "I live in Montana but Belfry is nothing like Glasgow or Opheim or Scobey. There are no trees here! The sky looks big—truly big. I live in what is called Big Sky Country—but this right here is the real deal. It's awesome and intimidating at the same time, wild and woolly."

Father said, "We don't have big mountains, our terrain looks flat and our sky is overwhelming but we're used to it. A lot of this, I think, is because we don't have many trees, as you noticed. This land is and has been since anyone can remember, prairie. The High Line, as we call it, is about four hundred fifty miles long and it's all prairie with occasional trees along rivers and such. Some people feel exposed in this land. It's true you can see for miles but it's also true it's not really flat—it has ups and downs, coulees and buttes.

"Scobey has always had cattle but at one time it was the largest shipping point for grain in the whole world, believe it or not. Those days are long gone but it still has about a thousand people. Farmers are prosperous and the town is well kept and attractive, more so in some ways than Glasgow."

As we headed home through the Reservation, Mother pointed out the tumble-down shack where she had been raised. She was factual, not embarrassed, but Wyatt was ashamed to see how the people who were here first now lived on such a subsistence level. He said he felt like he didn't know who to blame, if anybody, but he knew what he was viewing was a world apart from his life as a Bat in Belfry.

Overall, I had a great Thanksgiving back home in Glasgow with my family but Wyatt and I had to get down to Bozeman before classes resumed. Break was over. As the cowboys say, we had to get back in the saddle.

Our sophomore year flew by in a blur except for one thing. I began to notice Wyatt's sister, Sue, who had now matured as a high school junior. Had she been Indian like Mother she would have had long black hair in a braid; instead, her hair was shorter and lighter. Her curves were nice but it was mostly the sparkle in her eyes that attracted me. She was spunky!

We visited each other's homes a few times; Wyatt continued to get along famously with Grandfather, and I continued to enjoy the rowdy company of his entire family.

Each trip to Belfry, Sue would ask me to ride with her and I would agree. She taught me how to curry and care for the animals afterward. However, among the chickens, cattle and horses I noticed a dog because of its peculiar behavior. I asked about it. "What's up with this dog?"

"He's deaf, totally deaf, hasn't ever heard a sound in his life."

"Wow, there must be a story behind that. How is it you have a deaf dog?"

"Daddy says that after decades with dogs of dubious pedigree and unknown backgrounds with idiosyncratic behavior but only accidental usefulness, he took the plunge to spend money for one that was actually bred to herd cattle. He got a mix of border collie with something called Hanging Tree Cattle Dog. He was adorable like all puppies but we noticed he never looked at us when we called or talked to him. He was oblivious."

"You hadn't noticed before?"

"No."

"The breeder didn't tell you?"

"He didn't know. When we got back to him and told him, he offered a full refund or exchange, whichever we preferred. He clarified that this unusual Hanging Tree breed carried a rare genetic defect of total deafness. It hadn't ever shown up in his litters, so he hadn't thought to mention it to us. He apologized, but for our part, we had already grown attached to the puppy. We kept it."

"Was it a good decision or have you regretted it?"

"No regrets. We love the little guy but there's no question about usefulness—he isn't. But he doesn't have to be useful to be loved."

I thought about this situation and its broader application. This little dog didn't know other dogs could hear. It didn't know sound existed. How about me? Were there things in my life I was missing out on? Was there something I had been deaf to? It hit me pretty hard to realize I hadn't identified with all the spiritual things Grandfather had tried to teach me. God was real to him in a way He wasn't to me. I hadn't rejected Him but neither had I embraced Him with open arms. I had been deaf.

I enjoyed Campus Crusade in Bozeman but the exuberant worship in Sue's church made the greatest impression on me. Grandfather's faith was real but that was the problem: I regarded it as his faith, not mine. Sunday School in Glasgow involved stories that were interesting but didn't inspire me to claim them as my own. I would never criticize my heritage, but it was Sue and her church fellowship that drew me in. It was watching Sue's little dog being ignorant of the fact other animals were hearing sounds he didn't know existed that convicted me. I wanted to be deaf no longer. I wanted to hear new sounds and sing new songs.

I guess I'd never realized it but I was hungry for my own spiritual experience. I wanted God to be personal for me the same as He was for Grandfather and those who testified to personal relationships in Campus Crusade and Wyatt's church. I had known *of* God—that's how I'd been raised—but now I wanted more. I wanted to *know Him*, to have heart knowledge instead of just head knowledge. I wanted Him. I wanted my own testimony instead of being satisfied with listening to what others had to say about Him.

Without being melodramatic about it, I acted on that desire, stood in front of the Belfry congregation and made exactly that personal declaration one Sunday morning during a visit with Wyatt's family. I asked Jesus into my heart. I asked Him to be my Lord and Savior and I experienced that He is, in fact, the way to the Father, the only way to God the Father.

And Grandfather's faith became mine. Sunday School stories came alive, suddenly I knew they were much more than stories. My name was written in the Lamb's book of life. And I raised my hands and danced with those Pentecostal Christians in Belfry with all my heart. I was no longer deaf.

Wyatt's sister developed into just about the prettiest girl I ever laid eyes on. She had a great smile, her face was radiant and her attitude, in general, was filled with life. I already mentioned how much I liked the sparkle in her big blue eyes. My trips with Wyatt to Belfry began to be more about her than horses. Sue wasn't just the life of the party, she was the party. And I guess she thought I was sort of interesting because we began making plans for our future together.

Wyatt's father was the patriarch in his family, as Grandfather was in mine. It was important for family to know and approve of family. Grandfather made arrangements and invited Sue and her family to Glasgow for a visit the summer after my sophomore year in college. In return, Sue's and Wyatt's father invited my Grandfather, Father and Mother to Belfry for a visit that same summer. Sue had just completed her junior year of high school and was preparing for her senior year.

It was amazing to me how our disparate families meshed so well together. It was like they had known each other many, many years.

I asked Sue to marry me. She said "Yes," fell into my arms and we shared our first kiss. I asked her father if I could have her hand in marriage and he said "Yes," as well, but with one reservation. He said, "My daughter is too young. She needs to finish high school—at least—before I agree to a wedding.

He continued, "You don't have to know how to spell the word 'commitment' to have it. In my way of thinking, commitment has to do with a personal set of rules you make for yourself that keeps your mind right and your life in order. It's a code you set up for yourself where honor means everything. You, like any man, will be loyal to your code. You, like any man, will serve your personal rules. You're committed to running track. I commend you in that but a life well lived involves a higher calling than running.

"That's why I was so glad to watch you commit to a personal relationship with Jesus as your Lord and Savior. You adopted our historic Christian code to keep your mind right and your life in order. God's rules are the best. Be loyal to those.

"So what I'm saying is I want you to honor and be loyal to the personal rules you made with God. Be true to your code of conduct. When you do that, you'll also be true to my daughter, your future wife. You and I might be ordinary guys but we can have extraordinary commitments. And that's what I expect from you. That's how I expect you to treat Sue. Be true to her as you're true to yourself, as you're true to God. As I heard a fella say one time, when you have a setback, don't take a step back because God is already preparing your comeback.

"Is that a fair enough deal? Do we understand each other?"

I answered that I hadn't thought about it that way but said, "Yes, sir. I've got a code of conduct, an internal set of rules. To violate them would be to violate my conscience and I would lose self-respect. So as I stand in front of God here with you, I commit to honor God, myself, Sue and our relationship with each other."

Sue loved her horses. As she shared that love with me, my appreciation for horses and all the other animals grew. We enjoyed riding together. It occurred to us as we planned our future that working with animals as a veterinarian was a profession we should consider. Montana didn't have a School of Veterinary Medicine, but Washington did. Perhaps I could finish my agronomy degree at Montana State and apply to vet school at Washington State University in Pullman, I thought. It was an established and highly regarded School of Veterinary Medicine.

Sue was set to begin her senior year in high school and I was set to begin my junior year in college. If she applied to matriculate to Washington State's four-year bachelor's degree program and was accepted, and if I applied to its three-year School of Veterinary Medicine and was accepted, our ultimate graduation dates would synchronize. The kicker, of course, was that her first year in Pullman would coincide with my last year in Bozeman—meaning we would be separated by hundreds of miles instead of dozens.

But it was a plan. We talked. Our families did the same. We finally agreed to a lengthy engagement period. All agreed that Sue and I shouldn't be separated during our honeymoon year of marriage but should wait two years until she finished her first year of college and I graduated with a bachelor's degree to set our wedding date for early summer, 1981. Both of us would be in Pullman.

Two things were certain: waiting would be difficult and it would be beneficial.

We waited. Things worked out as planned and, yes, waiting was both difficult and beneficial. We matured. We learned patience. Our separation gave added impetus for me to run track and go out in the proverbial blaze of glory: I was part of the relay team that set a new school record of 3:13.12—an achievement of which I was justifiably proud.

Sue's high school graduation day was great; my college graduation day was wonderful. Our wedding was a perfect extravaganza. I should mention, though, that it wasn't until we wrote and ordered our wedding invitations that we saw, in print, Sue's new name—Sue Liu. After the shock wore off, we couldn't help but laugh about it. Her college graduation and my vet school graduation coincided exactly in 1984 and we were ready to face life head-on together as a married couple.

Meanwhile, Wyatt was transitioning with his father on their ranch and their next-generation plan was working. And I had arranged to buy the practice of an older vet clinic in Glasgow on terms since the owner wasn't ready to retire, and I hadn't yet earned any income. Our arrangement served as a guarantee that I would take over his established practice at a definite price and future date. We were satisfied with the security our transition agreement provided for both of us, seller and buyer, veteran and novice.

Moving to Glasgow was going home for me; Sue had visited many times so it was familiar to her too. We lived in Grandfather's house starting out. It was vacant because he moved in with Father and Mother in preparation for our coming. Our first baby, a perfect, beautiful girl we named Sallie, was born in that house in the early part of 1985. I resisted the temptation of giving her the middle name, Lou, because my wife thought it was too "over the top" for me to introduce my family by saying, "We are Sing, Sue and Sallie Lou Liu."

We delighted in watching Sallie, just looking at her in those first days of her life. I knew about calves, colts and kittens but very little about 'people' babies. Animals get up on shaky legs in a couple of hours but not so with our babies.

Baby Sallie's arms would flail in the air and occasionally bonk her on her head. She was always surprised so it gradually dawned on me that she didn't realize those things flailing in the air were connected to her, that they belonged to her and were part of her. I was surprised that she was surprised. It was a wonder just to watch her, sometimes Sue on one side of the crib and me on the other, sometimes both of us together, Sue in front and me behind.

So there were four generations in close proximity. Sue had all the help she needed with Sallie. We had room for her mother to come spend time with us as well. All in all, the situation was perfect. It was winter outside but warm and cozy inside.

Years passed. We had three more babies, all boys. We eventually bought our own house since we needed more bedroom and living space. Grandfather stayed on with Father and Mother so he sold his little house and aged gracefully. I took over the vet practice as scheduled. We had a comfortable life.

As the millennium approached, Grandfather was in good health, still enjoying school activities and fishing with my children in the same way he enjoyed them with me. Nobody was quite sure, but consensus was that he was at least eighty years old.

Think of it—he began life in China before Mao came to power. He was tending his rice paddy before Japan bombed Pearl Harbor and Jimmy Doolittle fell out of the sky on his head. He made friends with John Birch, whose witness led him to saving faith in Jesus as his Lord. He actually knew these people!

He never went to school, barely learned to read his Bible in English. Yet by God's grace, he was one of only a hundred and five Chinese permitted to enter the United States in 1946. He raised his son, my father, here. He helped raise me here. He was still helping raise his four great-grandchildren here. In spite of deprivation and extreme hardship, in spite of losing his wife, he knew God is good. His life was a living witness to that glorious fact. I am thankful for my heritage.

CHAPTER 17

GIL, 2006

Gil and Gail told Jamie to relay their request for a second visit to Mr. Jackson's property for sale outside Glasgow, Montana that coming Saturday. Big John agreed. He said, "That's reasonable."

The couple wanted their immediate family members to see it before they made their final decision so they made arrangements and bought airplane tickets to Great Falls for Gil's parents, Duane and Ethel, and Gail's parents, Harvey and Emma, to fly out that Thursday. Gail's brother, Clyde and his family, didn't want to come until Friday out of consideration for their children.

All four parents flew on Thursday so they could have a day to rest overnight in Great Falls. Gil also arranged a rental vehicle for them and said their real estate broker recommended an easy excursion to the Visitor Center there.

Clyde and his family planned to fly early Friday, secure their rental vehicle, join with the two sets of parents and continue together the two hundred fifty miles from Great Falls to Glasgow. They hoped to arrive by nightfall. Gil also made room reservations for them at the motel in which they were staying. It would be a long trip but they wanted to drive over the land on the last leg instead of flying over it.

All was fine except neither Gil nor Gail knew what to do with their extra time since it was only Tuesday. Jamie took care of that. He sent the charter back to Fort Benton, checked himself into their motel, rented a vehicle large enough for the four of them plus his dog and Maisie's paraphernalia, and then escorted them around Fort Peck Dam and Reservoir the first day and the abandoned town of St. Marie the next. Gil and Gail looked at each other at Fort Peck and said, "This is the flood control we wondered about when we crossed the Missouri River and saw the old bridge outside Wolf Point.

Jamie had become much more than a real estate agent to Gil and Gail. He had become a friend.

———

The whole family arrived safely as scheduled Friday night. They remarked on the scenery. Duane said, "We really enjoyed the Visitor Center at Great Falls."

"And now we can say we've seen the world's shortest river," Ethel said.

Emma added, "I was impressed by the size of that log canoe-thing Lewis and Clark's expedition used. It was huge. This is an unexpected and wonderful adventure for us."

Neither Gil nor Gail knew what they were talking about but they kept quiet and filed the comment in their mind for something to do on a future trip.

Jamie joined the four families with their three generations for breakfast Saturday morning in the motel's lobby. He circulated a map around and said, "It's been my privilege to meet your children. You should be proud of the fine people they are. If you approve, I'll lead the caravan along the route I've marked on these maps. It's over an hour's drive to this ranch. We'll go to the homestead first and meet the seller, who will show various out-buildings to you. Then we'll spend most of the rest of the day going over the land itself."

Clyde spoke up, "I'd like to ride with you if that's possible."

"Of course," Jamie said. At the last minute, the older men, Duane and Harvey, piled in with Clyde, Jamie and his dog. Gail rode with her sister-in-law in the SUV with all the children. Gil escorted the older ladies, Ethel and Emma, as the tail-end of the caravan.

Gil was quiet as the women talked. Their talk was interrupted, however, as they gasped when they crested the hill just as he and his wife had done the first time and caught sight of the farmstead with its rolling wheat fields clothed in their spring finery of cool green. One could almost say it was love at first sight for them as it had been for him and Gail.

The seller impressed the group as he had Gil. Thumbs tucked in his belt loops, Big John Jackson stood against one of the porch pillars while the family sat in rockers sipping lemonade. He answered all their questions. His tanned face was weathered from wind and winter; as always, he wore his faded, worn leather boots, cowboy hat and plaid flannel shirt even though it was seventy-five degrees that afternoon. Without the bolo tie, Gil suddenly realized he was like an older and larger carbon copy of Jamie. He and Gail were inside a fantastic scene of big life with big people in Big Sky Country. They were dealing with forthright, honest people. For the umpteenth time, he marveled at how privileged he was.

Harvey asked, "Do you have Amish or Hutterite farm colonies near you?"

"Funny you should ask," Mr. Jackson answered. "Hutterites have four hundred fifty colonies in the United States, of which at least twenty-five are in Montana. None are near my ranch; that is, none are within seventy or so miles of me on the United States side of the border. I'm glad. In my opinion, they're not good neighbors."

Harvey responded, "I understand and agree. We've got colonies in our part of Iowa and those Hutterites are stand-offish. They keep to themselves and aren't involved in our community activities. In a sense, I don't object to their presence, but they drive land prices up and are tough competition for farmers like Clyde and myself."

To which Clyde added, "They get financial support from other colonies so that they pay cash for properties that come up for sale and are better able to survive instances of drought or flood than many of us. My hat's off to them because they help each other avoid debt and deprivation but the fact is that we're at a competitive disadvantage with their communal style of farming enterprise."

"I try not to be prejudiced but it rubbed me the wrong way when my son was killed while in uniform in Afghanistan and they were home asleep in their own beds because of pacifist exemption." Mr. Jackson shifted his stance and his smile faded into a grimace. "Not only did I lose a son, I also lost his labor. They lost neither.

"Neighbors told me they couldn't afford my ranch and my most probable buyer was a Hutterite colony, but I just didn't want to go that route. A lot of folks don't want to say that out loud but I guarantee you they think it!"

At the end of the day, after the men had walked and driven over miles of land, the consensus was unanimous that this was the deal of a lifetime.

Mr. Jackson stated his price for the property, which included machinery but no livestock, Jamie offered his opinion that it was fair, and Gil and Gail shook hands with him on the deal. Each side of the transaction paid Jamie a flat fee and all were satisfied.

Gil and Gail had a new home.

It had been a long day for the two older couples. Maisie's nap had been eliminated because of the boisterous activity from travel, dogs and older cousins so she needed quiet time. After parting company with Mr. Jackson, Gil's group drove back to Glasgow but decided they could go no further. Jamie was responsible for Gil's, Gail's and Maisie's transportation. Since he had sent his charter plane back to Fort Benton, he needed to spend one additional night at their motel as well. He would drive them back to their vehicle in Fort Benton the next morning as part of their family caravan.

The only unfortunate incident involved Jamie's dog, Toby, the next morning. As obedient as he was, Toby was fascinated by yesterday's smells: dirty clothes, cigarette butts and garbage cans with their various unsavory contents. Gil would later think back to wonder at one of life's many mysteries—how animals with such a keen sense of smell weren't able to distinguish between *good* and *bad*. Drug dogs and ordnance dogs could sniff distinctive odors with a sensitivity thousands of times greater than humans' ability, yet what gagged a human simply made a dog tilt its head and think, *How interesting. I want to get my nose closer.* They lost all sense of propriety.

Jamie was exercising his dog before loading him for the drive back to Fort Benton. He had let Toby off leash to fetch and run in a grassy area near the motel. A garbage truck entered the alley behind the motel's kitchen to make its weekly pick-up. As lids were lifted off the metal cans so they could be emptied, the banging and smelling were too tempting for Toby and he went to investigate. As he ran out of the park and across the street toward the alley, the big German shepherd ran in front of a car. The collision was low-speed but sent the dog flying.

He yelped as Jamie ran over to him. The car's driver stopped to apologize but Jamie knew the accident wasn't his fault. The driver said his vehicle wasn't damaged but Jamie gave him his card with his name, address and phone number just in case. Jamie's attention was fixed primarily on his dog. Toby was limping but at least was alive. Jamie asked the driver for directions to a veterinarian and called for Gil to come drive them to the vet's office in the rental vehicle so he could hold Toby on the way.

Gil followed the directions to the Glasgow Animal Hospital. He let Jamie out, parked the SUV, then joined Jamie, who was finishing the required paperwork. The vet came to greet them and they left the reception area for the clinical area to get X-rays.

The vet was friendly and competent. He asked if he could pray over the dog before he touched and began working over him. Jamie readily agreed.

As concerned as he was about his friend and the dog, Gil couldn't help but notice the similarity between the vet's and his own body type, height and weight. He thought, *If it weren't for the shape of our eyes and the shade of our skin, we could be twins.*

The vet inspected the X-ray films, massaged the dog's sore spots and said there should not be any lasting damage. No bones were broken. He pronounced the dog "okay" and said he should enjoy a wealth of health but scolded him about jumping in front of cars. The dog looked at the vet with his big brown eyes as if promising never to do it again.

Gil noticed that the vet looked Asian, perhaps Chinese. He thought that was odd for he hadn't seen other Asians the whole time he'd been in Montana and wasn't aware of an Asian community in any parts of the state he and Gail had visited. He introduced himself.

The veterinarian said, "My name is Sing Liu. I'm glad to have been of service."

Gil thought, *I bet this fella has a whale of a story to tell. I would like to meet him again and get to know him better.*

PART 2
SKY LAND

. . . this generation will certainly not pass away . . .
(Matthew 24:34)

CHAPTER 18

2006

A brass plaque set into a boulder near the basketball hoop by the entrance to their home property was engraved with these words—*Welcome to Sky Land.* The hoop was just a hoop nailed to a pole. The half-court was just grass and dirt but it had seen plenty of action. There was nothing fancy about the boulder, the hoop or the court but Gil and Gail agreed that the plaque captured the essence of their new place. Sky Land was its name.

Winter wheat was greening. Spring wheat had been seeded. The seller had accomplished a great amount before Gil and Gail bought his ranch, which is not to say work was finished. Much remained to be done—which was good because *work gives a man internal satisfaction,* Gil thought. *In the final analysis, work isn't so much about what we do or how much we're paid as it is about satisfaction.*

Gil was excited and paced back and forth in the barn, kicking up tufts of hay and whooping and hollering as Gail and Maisie petted one of the cows. "I'm chomping at the bit, ready to roll—'git 'er done, boy.' There's work to do!"

"Whoa, hold on, cowboy. Maisie and I can't have you running around in circles like a chicken with its head cut off. You can start the tractor and practice driving it just to get used to it but then you'll have to ask yourself, '*what's the point?*' You'll need to point that tractor in a straight line in a particular direction." Gail continued, "Things have happened fast, maybe too fast. So let's slow down for a minute. Focus. Calm down. Take a breath. Harness your testosterone for a purpose. Do the right thing at the right time for the right reason."

Gil sat down on a hay bale, taking slow deep breaths. Gail and Maisie joined him, inhaling the fragrant scents of fresh hay tinged with cow manure. "You're right—right, right, right. The Bible says, '. . . one thing I do, forgetting those things which are behind and reaching forward to those things which are ahead, I press toward the goal for the prize of the upward call of God in Christ Jesus.' We've got to keep our priorities in order. From an earthly perspective, what's our *one thing*? What's our *goal*? Why did we buy Sky Land?"

"You're a dirt guy but Sky Land is more than an investment in dirt. We both know that God's call on our lives *isn't* to be farmers or ranchers, laudable as those occupations are. Our calling is to invest in God's kingdom. Our calling involves Sky Land's dirt, but dirt isn't the focus. We are here to invest in people, to offer redemption and hope to those in desperate need of it."

"As my situation was once upon a time," Gil said, leaning over and circling his hand through the dirt floor of the barn, lost in reflection.

"Of course, we can't neglect the wheat fields or the pasture land." Maisie hadn't yet learned to toddle on soft, uneven surfaces like hay bales but she was moving as best she could on her hands and knees so Gail got up to keep a close eye on her infant daughter as she continued to lecture her husband. "We have to be responsible managers of what God has given us, but we must keep our priorities straight. Keep our eyes on the one thing, the goal."

Gil didn't have to see his wife's face to know it was filled with compassion and dedication to their mission. Although it had curbed his enthusiasm, he was grateful for her wise reminder: they hadn't come this far to forget their purpose, which had become a mantra for them that they repeated to each other in times like this. Other than being good parents, a good son and daughter and husband and wife, it was their purpose now.

He took a breath and repeated it out loud. "We are to provide a safe harbor for Middle Eastern displaced persons, especially those refugees who are persecuted for their Christian faith. That's our one thing. After that, give safe harbor to disadvantaged youth from this country."

"Be a light for the least, the last and, in some cases, the lost."

"Minister to that person who has a limp in his life, a headache in his heart. Touch the emptiness he's full of."

"Honor our pact with Tuo after Kamal's death."

Gil thought back to his time as a "triplet" in Turkey, a name he had coined for the brotherhood he shared in uniform with Kamal, an Iraqi, and Tuo, from a Vietnamese family. He remembered the explosion in Baghdad that resulted in Kamal's death, holding him in his arms as Kamal whispered *Thank you, my friend, I'm ready* and breathed his last. He remembered Tuo's subsequent agony of conviction in Gail's kitchen that produced his being born again as a new creation in Christ Jesus.

Gil grew thoughtful, became introspective and finished, "Borrowing poetic language from a preacher of yore, I walked among the open graves but by God's grace I didn't stumble into them. Fierce and fatal maladies lurked in my path but they were not permitted to devour me. Bullets of death whistled by my ears, yet I stand—alive—for those bullets had no billet in my heart."

Gail whispered, "You were there. You'll never forget Kamal's sacrifice."

"No, ma'am, I will not. Nor will Tuo."

"Nor shall I. We will always honor it and assign it first priority in our plans."

"I agree. Now that we've completed our purchase of Sky Land, now that you've put your hand on my shoulder and told me to focus, it's time to contact my Army buddy and remaining triplet, Tuo Trang. We knew we'd see him again. Before I fire up the tractor I need to compare notes with him to see what he's done, as together we make a way forward for those starved for hope and healing."

They called their friend at the NATO base at Incirlik, Turkey and updated him on their relocation from Iowa and land purchase in Montana. He brought them up to speed on his contact with refugees in Lebanese camps. Together, they made plans for the immediate future.

Gail settled in with Maisie and turned their new house into a home. On a bit of a whim, Gil put in a phone call to Teen Challenge headquarters. After being connected with a director there he said, "I understand you have experience as a Christian ministry that deals successfully with troubled, disadvantaged youth. My wife and I minister to Christian refugees from Middle Eastern countries. We have a ranch facility with ag land and animals in rural, northeast Montana. If you might be interested in sending staff and students here, we would be honored for you to visit and inspect our facility and its location to see if it would work out for both of us." The Teen Challenge leaders agreed to visit Sky Land as soon as they could make arrangements.

Sunday was rapidly coming up on the calendar. Gail did a bit of research as to childcare then chose a church for them to attend. Maisie was still at the trusting age where everyone was a friend so there were no issues the following Sunday. Maisie accepted her drop-off at the church nursery without complaint as her parents went into the sanctuary for worship and preaching.

It tugged at Gail's heart to leave her baby in someone else's care—out of her sight, at that. It was a comfort that she had been given an electronic beeper in case of emergency. Gil reached out to hold her hand. He, too, was fighting back tears that threatened to sting his eyes as he thought, *we've taken our first-born baby on lots of adventures with us but this may be the first time we've not been the ones holding her.*

They were made to feel welcome by other adults, without exception. Gil was especially pleased and surprised when, in the congregation, he spotted the Chinese veterinarian who had worked on Jamie's dog during their emergency clinic visit.

Afterward, Gil introduced Gail to Sing and said, "You may not remember but a month or so ago you helped a friend of mine from Fort Benton whose dog had been hit by a car. His name was Jamie Ferguson. I was impressed that you asked if you could pray over the dog before you worked on him. Jamie was pleased with the compassionate care you exhibited."

Sing replied, "I remember. It was my privilege. I'm glad it was not a serious injury."

Gil said, "We've recently purchased land and moved to this area. We're visiting today because one of our first priorities is to seek out a church where we can worship God and have fellowship with like-minded believers."

Sing motioned his wife over, "Sue, meet these first-time visitors, Gil and Gail Webster, who are in the process of relocating to land outside of town."

Sue extended her hand and said, "It's wonderful to meet you. Let's get better acquainted. We'd love to have you for Sunday dinner today. Please come."

"Oh, we couldn't impose. Our daughter is just a baby," Gail politely objected.

"Nonsense. We have four children, an older girl and three boys still at home. Sing's parents join us on these afternoons so I'm used to a crowd. It's no imposition at all. Here, I'll help you collect your baby then you can follow us home. It's no trouble at all."

Gail capitulated but joked with Gil on the short drive to their host's house, "I hope they're not ax murderers."

Gil laughed, "I noticed she said they'd have us for dinner. Hopefully, it was just poor grammar and she's not planning to carve us up and put us on the menu."

"I'm almost ashamed to admit it but when I accepted Sue's invitation I was thinking, *Okay, I'll bite.* But she didn't mean any harm and my smarty-pants joke almost certainly would have hurt her feelings."

"Some things are better left unsaid. It's best for this to be just our private joke."

"Agreed. They seem like a fine couple. And I don't want to be a smart-aleck."

Gil said, "You know, this may be God's providence. Seriously, when I drove Jamie with his injured dog and saw Sing at his vet clinic I thought, *I want to meet this guy. I wonder how he ended up in Glasgow, Montana. I bet he has a fascinating story.*"

Dinner proved to be an eclectic gathering. Gil was twenty-eight and an ex-Air Force officer of Middle Eastern origin; Gail was a year younger and a farm girl from Iowa. Sing was forty-seven years old and of Chinese lineage, while his wife Sue was forty-four; both were native Montanans. Their grown daughter lived away from home but their three sons, Tommy, Billy and Bobby, were all present at the dinner table. The boys were all teenagers in high school and all three looked just like their father. Sing's parents were there as well; his father was sixty-eight, an immigrant from China and his mother was Dakota Sioux from the adjacent Fort Peck Reservation.

To Gil's surprise, as they sat down at the dinner table, Sing introduced his grandfather, who had come down from his nap upstairs to join them. Gil could see he was crippled and elderly but had his wits about him and could hear reasonably well.

It was an intergenerational, multi-ethnic dinner party. Yet somehow they clicked and enjoyed each other's company during the meal.

Sue was her usual outgoing, life-of-the-party self. Over apple pie a la mode for dessert, after the teens were excused, Sing and his family proceeded to tell Gil and Gail about how they came to locate in Glasgow.

"In case you're wondering, Grandfather emigrated from China in 1946. I was born and raised here and met Sue during my freshman year at Montana State University in Bozeman," Sing said.

His father said, "I was eight years old when I arrived in Glasgow with my father. Because he knew Jimmy Doolittle, we were fortunate to be able to flee China."

"My childhood home is in the Fort Peck Reservation." Sing's mother added.

Gil smiled at his hosts around the table, feeling warmly welcomed and at ease to fill them in on his backstory. "I was adopted by missionaries out of a Jordanian orphanage as a twelve-year-old so I know what it means to enter into a strange, new culture. I also know what it means to be redeemed and rescued out of a bad situation."

Sue asked, "But what brings you here? I'm guessing you've traveled a lot more than I've ever dreamed about. You no doubt have a lot of stories to tell just like Grandfather here." She fondly put an arm around her father-in-law's frail shoulders and he smiled up at her, wrinkles fanning out from the corners of his eyes.

Gil answered, "We want to be ranchers, but at the same time, we want to be more than farmers or ranchers. We believe that God has us here for a unique purpose."

Gail added, "It's a long story but last year we ministered in refugee camps in Iraq and Syria. Gil, because of his background and training, is fluent in Arabic so we were able to communicate. Conditions were squalid, as you might imagine. Christians especially are being displaced and persecuted all over the world, more severely in certain places than others—Iraq, for instance. We believe God has called us and will use us to aid and alleviate their suffering."

"You mean—here?" Sue asked, sitting down and eating her ice cream before it completely melted. "How is that? Sorry to be so full of questions. What were you doing in Syrian refugee camps?"

Gil realized Sue wasn't being nosy but was truly interested, so he went on to tell his story—how he was born to nomadic Arab parents, had lost his father in Lebanon's so-called civil war, then lost his mother as she had wandered with him in Jordan. He told them how he was taken into a Christian orphanage where he learned a smattering of English and was adopted by missionary parents upon their return to Iowa.

Gail picked up the narrative as she told of their meeting in college and marrying shortly before the 9-11 atrocity that prompted Gil to join America's armed forces as an Army intelligence officer. She used the occasion to brag on his accomplishments at Fort Bragg, his language studies at the school in Monterey, California and his posting at the Pentagon.

Gil was less effusive as he related their time at the large NATO base in Turkey and their coming to forge bonds of friendship with an Iraqi national named Kamal and Tuo, a fellow officer of Vietnamese extraction.

Again, Gail spoke up concerning her husband's discovering key evidence that broke up and interdicted a drug supply chain from Afghanistan's poppy fields for which he was awarded a special citation. She finished by saying they had been privileged to lead their two friends to salvation in Jesus as Lord and Savior, the true basis of their close friendship.

All, including Grandfather, listened with rapt attention. Sing asked, "Where are these two friends now?"

Gil answered, "One was killed by an IED in Baghdad. The other is on active duty at the same military base in Turkey where we met and served together."

"Excuse my ignorance," Sue said, "but what is an IED?"

"That's an acronym for 'improvised explosive device.' They are most typically planted by insurgents in buildings or along roadsides in highly trafficked areas. When triggered, they kill or maim indiscriminately—civilians as well as soldiers in uniform, women and children in addition to young men."

This sharing prompted Grandfather to tell his story of rescuing the Doolittle Raiders out of China and coming to know John Birch, who led him to Christ.

He said, "I'm sorry for your trauma and the tragedy you suffered even as I am sorry for the evil in my life. But I rejoice that good came out of it for you as it also did for my son and myself. As Joseph said to his brothers in Egypt who had treated him with such cruelty, *'You meant evil against me; but God meant it for good, in order to bring it about as it is this day, to save many people alive.'*"

Gil was excited about the reference to John Birch. He'd heard his father-in-law talk about the "John Birch Society" when he'd visited at New Year's but was so engrossed in his studies of where to move that he'd forgotten all about it until now. *Coincidence? Or divine providence?* He wondered, smiling to himself. "Wow, I first heard the name John Birch just this past January. The few people I've asked since then have heard the name but haven't known anything at all about the man. And now here I'm breaking bread with you, Grandfather, who actually lived with him. He sounds like he was a missionary saint . . . and a good friend. Thank you so much for sharing your testimony. I'll not soon forget it."

The afternoon flew by. Gil and Gail thanked their hosts for being so kind and assured them they would be returning to worship in church with them. Sing led in prayer as they parted company and Sue extended another invitation for dinner the following Sunday. Gail accepted on the condition that all would come to Sky Land on the third Sunday. She said it would motivate her to finish unpacking their things, buy other furnishings and arrange their belongings. "This will help me. I need a deadline to push me to get that job done."

CHAPTER 19

2006

The next Sunday after dinner Sue asked, "How can you contact these Middle Eastern Christian refugees?"

Gil and Gail had told over dinner about their plans to host troubled youth and displaced Christian families from refugee camps to Sky Land to work there and transition into productive living, whatever that might entail.

"Our military friend over there spends off-duty time with them. He's our contact." Gail sipped her after-dinner coffee, keeping a motherly eye on Maisie, who played a game of peek-a-boo in the adjoining room with the boys who seemed to delight in entertaining her.

Gil added, "Tuo Trang is his name; it's spelled T-u-o but is pronounced 'Too.' He helps distribute food and water supplies and arranges medical care via U.S. personnel whenever possible. One reason he has such a heart for the people is because his parents were forced to abandon everything when they fled for their lives after South Vietnam fell to the communists."

Sing followed up with more questions. "What will you do after you contact your friend? Do you have any idea how many people will be involved? Are there limits or quota caps?"

"First, we'll provide sponsorship, including ranch employment of various types." Gil and Gail had talked late into many nights while unpacking boxes to come up with their plan. "We'll offer a safe haven in a Christian environment. We don't want to start a large influx of foreigners that local residents would resent but we can rescue a select group of families, lift them out of their dire situations and give them hope and a future. Over time, the group should build up."

Sue asked, "Do you have experience running a ranch?"

"We have access to hand's-on advice," Gail answered. "Gil's parents operate a small farm in Iowa. I was raised on an Iowa farm as well. My brother went to college, studied agricultural science and runs my parents' farm now. That gives us a certain level of confidence."

"But we're still neophytes. We don't ooze with confidence." Gil fidgeted with his fork.

Gail continued, "Our families aren't knowledgeable with Montana, the vagaries of its weather or the scale of ranching required here. There's no question but that we'd like to solicit local help, be it informal advice from neighbors or hiring a ranch manager or such. We've only just arrived here. Neighbors are friendly enough but they're busy with their own lives and aren't overly helpful. We'll have to wait and see."

Sue said, "I was raised on a ranch in Montana. My brother, Wyatt, studied in college and has taken over our ranch's daily operation, as your brother has done. I'll talk to him. He and Sing were college roommates and formed a lasting friendship. Perhaps he can be the guy to offer local advice and perspective. Either Sing or myself can talk with him if you'd like."

As Sing's father refreshed peoples' drinks he added, "I began working in maintenance while I was still in high school. I gained experience and now I am humbled at how God has blessed me with my own business. It would be my pleasure to help you with mechanical or household repair issues, if I can."

He put the drink pitchers back in their place and continued, "I don't have advanced education." He paused. "But I have experience enough to know I'm not smart enough to make things work out as well as they have in my life. God caused good things to happen, so many good things that I could never have arranged them. In fact, this meeting may be one of those good things."

Sue got up to bring more ice cubes. "Well said, Father. I agree with you: this is the humble beginning of something big. The Bible says not to despise the day of small beginnings. And I don't. Our time together can blossom into something beautiful. These dinners we've had are God-ordained. 'Far out,' as hippies used to say. And I love it!"

Sing looked at his family members. "Father, Mother, Sue, we need to do all we can to help these young people fulfill God's call on their lives. We can give them a good start; let's help them do lots of little things well. Let's ask ourselves what we can do and how we can get involved. It seems as if we've had a ministry opportunity fall in our laps. It would be a serious blunder on our parts if we ignored it or didn't take it seriously."

Sue didn't hesitate. "My rascal brother needs an excuse to visit us anyway. I'll make it happen. Let me get him and Daddy up here. If you don't mind, we'll all come to your ranch and see what they've got to say about it. How's that sound for starters?"

"I already said we would come for Sunday dinner today on the condition you would come to our ranch next Sunday, so it's already a done deal," Gail reminded them. "So of course, bring your brother. Your whole family is welcome."

"Just let us know a headcount," Gil winked at his wife."

On their way home and while Maisie was asleep in her car seat, Gail said to Gil, "It seems like it was only a day or two ago I said things were happening so fast it was making our heads spin. Jamie introduced us to a seller who had our perfect spot, Sky Land, reserved and waiting for us. I told you to slow down, focus and take a deep breath. You agreed that we needed to slow down. And now our heads are spinning again about what has fallen in front of us, directly in our path . . . so I guess if we somehow miss what God wants, by His grace, we'll still stumble over it.

"If by some miracle Sue persuades her family members, if she comes through with them and they come through for her, let's ask our own families to make a second trip too. We'll get all these disparate families together and see what happens. To echo what she said and as a pastor friend of mine said several years ago, 'Always believe your beliefs and doubt your doubts; don't make the skeptic's mistake of believing your doubts and doubting your beliefs.' We don't want to act rashly or prematurely but we do want to be proactive and move when God moves. We don't want Him to leave us behind in the dust."

"Amen, sister. Preach it. God is on the move."

Sue persuaded her parents, her brother Wyatt and his family to drive the five-and-a-half hours and visit their new friends in Glasgow. They would attend church together then eat Sunday dinner at their new friends' ranch. Persuasion wasn't difficult. School was out for the summer so the idea was to spend a couple of days together before Sunday.

Gil had relayed the news to Sing that they had family members coming from Iowa who would also be in attendance for church and Sunday dinner. Weather permitting, it would be a cookout and picnic affair.

But at the last minute Sing had to relay sad news: Grandfather wouldn't be joining them. He said, "Wyatt and I are still long-time friends from college so when I invited him to your ranch, he eagerly accepted. It promised to be a new adventure plus he always looked forward to seeing Grandfather. We enjoyed Friday evening together, but Grandfather was a bit subdued, said he wasn't feeling well and excused himself to go to bed earlier than usual.

"After an hour or so he called Father and said to him, 'Son, my time is near. Bring my great-grandchildren in so I can say goodnight to them, remind them God loves them and they should live for Him. Then ask Sue and Sing in. And Wyatt. If you please, I'd like for you to sit with me—maybe hold my hand. I'm not afraid but I've never died before. I'd like you to be with me as I pass from here to eternity.'

"We filed in, one and two at a time, as requested. It was a solemn, intimate and quiet time as we expressed love for each other. One lamp remained lit. Father stayed in the room. Grandfather said to him, 'Weep not for me. Look at the condition of my broken body, so drained by time, affliction and toil. I am an unmanly old man, ready for new life.'

"Conversation was finished. Grandfather was peaceful but his breathing was a bit labored. Sometime after midnight, we had re-entered his room for a silent vigil. Grandfather sat up with sudden strength, spoke clearly and said, 'Oh, look. They're here. Oh, how bright they are!' He smiled, lay back down and took his last breath on this earth as his spirit was carried into God's presence.

"We all knew we had been privileged to witness a holy moment."

Gil's and Gail's parents, her brother Clyde and his family, nine in all, had been scheduled to arrive Saturday noon in Great Falls, the morning of Grandfather's graduation to heaven and into God's presence. They had planned to drive up from the airport to Glasgow, where they would spend the night in the motel with Gil and Gail as they had done previously. It was too late to change those plans but with Grandfather's passing, Sunday's picnic was postponed.

Funeral arrangements were made. Family and friends were mostly local so burial was not delayed. It was set for Monday. Sunday announcements broadcast the news. A big crowd was anticipated to attend to say goodbye to Grandfather.

So it came to pass that a contingent from Iowa attended Grandfather's funeral and joined the procession to the cemetery for his interment. Thus, these families bonded in a way no one could have anticipated.

The preacher eulogized Glasgow's elderly statesman from China. He said, "Our friend of many years knew heroes from World War II: John Birch and Jimmy Doolittle. He himself was a hero, though he was quiet about his exploits. He was tortured in a prison camp and his wife was killed. He lived through extreme hardship but he bore it with grace and dignity.

"His first years in Glasgow were lonely but no one knew it because he didn't complain. He is now at peace and at rest. His body that was so violated for so long in so many ways awaits the day of its glorification. The man we knew and loved will no longer limp or be crippled nor will scars from unjust torture remain—not even in his memory. For that, we are grateful. His spirit of love and compassion gave living witness to his saving faith in our Lord and Savior Jesus Christ. Angels bore him to heaven waving palms of victory in robes of beauty, with crowns of glory and songs of triumph.

"We were fortunate to have known Grandfather. He blessed us by his very presence. Greatness lived in our midst. Amen."

The postponed day of introducing Sue's family to Gil's and Gail's property was reset from Sunday afternoon to Tuesday, which dawned bright and clear at Sky Land. That day, Sing stayed behind in Glasgow with his parents for a time of solitude and quiet mourning of their loss, but Sue journeyed to the ranch with her three high school boys and the rest of the troop.

Wyatt told Gil that he liked what he saw at the ranch, but more importantly, he and Clyde discovered they shared many of the same interests. Their age difference was such a minor thing that it was not an issue at all. They truly seemed to like each other and decided they could easily work together.

Gil and Gail had Sue on their side and Clyde had already committed to participating in Sky Land's operation so persuading Wyatt to get on board with their ministry concept was easy. The day passed quickly.

As the sun set orange and red on the horizon, Gil spoke to the group gathered on the porch. "God surprised us with a financial windfall during our posting in Iraq. That's how we've been able to purchase this ranch. We plan to be generous and not take advantage of your kindness. Recognizing that we can't make a go of this operation without your education and experienced input, we insist on putting you on retainer. Clyde and Wyatt, we'll pay your travel expenses, as well. It's our prayer that everyone benefits from this enterprise. Fair enough?"

The two men nodded in agreement.

When Tuo answered the phone a few days later Gil said, "Things came together better and more quickly than expected." He paced the kitchen floor as he talked quickly out of excitement. "I can't make my poor words over a telephone do justice to the miracles God's performed in our lives here in Montana—and I think He's only just begun. So, since words don't suffice, please come visit. We believe that now is the time; in fact, we can't wait for you to walk this land with us so you can dig your fingers in the dirt and see our promised land with your own eyes.

"Then we'll introduce you to our new friends. Can you do it? I know it's a lot to ask but can you make the trip?" Gil held his breath, telephone in hand as Gail played with Maisie in the adjoining living room, gazing at him from time to time with questions in her eyes.

"Maybe," he heard Tuo say, static interspersed with his words. "I could probably hop on a military transport to Fairbanks and transfer to commercial from Alaska to Montana if I had to. What's your nearest airport?"

Gil pumped his fist into the air and Gail jumped up from the floor and hurried into the kitchen and grabbed the phone out of his hand, putting it on speaker.

"Hey, it only just now occurred to me—Montana's largest military installation is Malmstrom Air Force Base in Great Falls," she said into the phone. "That city also has the airport we've had our families fly into. Maybe you could catch a second military hop from Fairbanks on to Great Falls."

Gil got excited and said into the phone, "Isn't that the cat's meow! Check it out. Let us know."

Tuo agreed. "I'll do it, for sure. I need to know what things look like on your end before I think about beginning formal arrangements for rescuing any refugees out of here. I'll let you know what flights I find."

He called them back less than two hours later. "I can't believe it," he said into the phone. "The miracles you told me about aren't finished yet. I can make those two hops and be in Great Falls in less than thirty hours. I'll be off duty and won't even have to take leave time if I can make a quick turnaround inside four days. In case problems develop, I've made arrangements to be absent. Are you ready to see me day after tomorrow? You'd better be because you've got me excited for this trip."

"We're excited too," they both said at the same time, smiling at each other. "We'll be down to greet you and bring you up to Sky Land."

"No, don't do that. I can't guarantee the connections. Let me rent a car and drive up to you. You don't need to drag Maisie around like that."

Gil said, "Alright. Just remember, there are places in Montana where you have to drive two hours to get to the next town."

Gail added, "True, but don't let my husband scare you away. You've been in the Missouri and Arkansas Ozarks, for cryin' out loud. We've got paved roads the same way they do in 'them thar hills.' Besides, winter's over and most of our ten-foot snowdrifts have melted."

Tuo said, "Now you're scaring me. Not Gil—you."

Gil laughed. "Forget it. She's messin' with you. She hasn't even seen a six-foot snowdrift since we've been here. Grab a map, head north and northeast out of Great Falls toward Glasgow then call us and we'll meet you there."

"Now *you're* scaring me," their friend said. "But I'll screw up my courage and as the Nike commercial says, 'just do it!'"

———

Gil and Gail waited patiently by the phone the afternoon Tuo was to arrive. Finally, it rang. "According to my directions, I'm about an hour and a half outside Glasgow," he said loud and clear.

Gil whooped into the phone. "We'll load up right now and meet you in town. See you soon!"

An hour and a half later the three of them hugged, cried, prayed and rejoiced when they met on the sidewalk outside the little café on Main Street.

Gail said, "We knew we'd see you again—we just knew it. God bless you, my brother—my brother in Christ. Oh, how I love to say that. How very good it is to see you."

Maisie didn't remember Tuo but she went to him, as she had done with all the new people in her life. He hoisted her in the air. She put her little arms around his neck. As he held her, tears came to his eyes.

After they'd eaten a quick lunch, Gil gave Tuo his car keys. "Here. You've had enough time by yourself. I'll take your car and lead the way. You ride with Gail."

"If I don't miss my guess, I think Gil's going to take a detour. He's excited to introduce you to our new friends on our way out of town," she winked. "They're choice, God-sent people. They've blessed us tremendously by how they've shared their lives with us."

Sure enough, Gil turned on a residential street and they knocked on Sue's door. It was after lunchtime but she invited them in and, gracious hostess that she was, prepared to serve tea and cookies as she asked questions. Sing wasn't able to join them since he was making large-animal rounds at clients' ranches.

After a refreshing forty-five minutes, they resumed their journey to Sky Land and Gail offered that Tuo ride with Gil to get a break from driving and so that the two could catch up a bit.

On the ride to the ranch Tuo said to Gil, "What a delightful woman. With people like Sue in your life how can you not feel blessed?"

Gil agreed and filled Tuo in on how their two families had interacted. It was marvelous to tell how God was providing so many miracles of divine provision in their journey of relocation into Montana. He said, "If we had asked for all of this we would have been embarrassed to ask so much."

"How so?"

"It would have been too much. Not only would it have sounded impossible, it would have seemed selfish. God wants to bless His children with abundance but the abundance we've received is beyond anything we would have asked for."

Tuo remained quiet and surveyed the countryside for a moment as Gil drove. Then he said, "Of course. I compare my life now with what it once was, with what it could have been, with what it is for persecuted Iraqi and Syrian Christians and I think, *who am I to deserve the abundance and richness of these blessings?*"

"It's good to hear preachers define God's mercy as not giving us the punishment we do deserve and His grace as giving us blessings we don't deserve," Gil agreed. "But to experience it in real time makes the point more effectively than a sermon ever could. And we're so very humbled when it happens to us."

They both went quiet in the contentment and worship of that holy moment in time. Then Tuo offered, "It's like I'm learning that unless we make impossible prayers, we're insulting God. My tendency is to be timid but I'm learning to be audacious because He's the God of the impossible. Anything less than breathtaking audacity limits His sovereignty. I think, for me, it's sinful to be timid. And I'm so honored to know you and Gail, who are both teaching that to me."

"Thank you," he replied. "It means a lot to hear your testimony. It's an honor for us to be used by God. And we're learning to ask more and more that our impotence and His omnipotence intersect as we live out our lives. After all, the Bible says that *nothing is impossible with God.*"

Tuo added, "Put another way, it asks the question, *'Is anything too hard for the Lord?'* Of course, the answer is self-evident, as we're in the process of learning."

Gil crested the last hill. Tuo gasped at his first sight of the cliffs along the river and the ranch stead cradled nearby. The setting sun shone purple on the cool, green hills as they glistened with God's glory in the beauty of His creation. Heaven above seemed a softer blue, earth around, a sweeter green.

They parked at the house, exited the vehicles and Tuo exclaimed, "Gil, you were right. I see now what you meant when you said words weren't adequate, that I needed to come see this for myself. You have blessings piled on top of blessings."

"Welcome to Sky Land, my dear friend. Do you agree that it's named well?"

"No question about it at all. I thought I would lay down to rest—but not now. Let's get after it! Show me more. I'm just drinking it in. How did you ever find this place that couldn't be more perfect for you?"

Gail walked with them a few hundred yards beyond the barn as Gil told the tale of the seller and the broker, Big John Jackson and Jamie Ferguson, but then she turned back for the house to put Maisie down for her nap and start supper.

The two friends, both Americans but one of Middle Eastern origin and the other of Vietnamese extraction, continued stretching their legs and praising God as Gil told the story of His timing and provision.

"I've invited Teen Challenge to come look at the ranch," Gil explained. "Gail and I want to provide a safe haven for Iraqi refugee families persecuted merely for claiming Jesus' name. But we're also burdened by the need for intergenerational ministry. To that end, we decided we may add troubled American youth into the mix, those needing God's presence in their hearts and guidance in their young lives."

"I understand," Tuo replied. "Who knows better than I that poverty can be spiritual as well as physical. Have they been here yet?"

"No. You're the first to see it—besides Sue. I'm glad you came so quickly."

They walked and talked until supper time, then Tuo's jet lag caught up with him and Gail showed him to the guest room shortly after eating.

Questioning began again the first thing the next morning, before breakfast. Over coffee, Gail asked, "We're not sure how best to provide sanctuary for refugees. Given your history and work in the camps, what can you recommend for us, Tuo?"

"My family started with nothing in their assigned location just north of the Ozarks in Missouri. As you know, they began their own restaurant business. That probably won't work here because your location is so rural—plus it doesn't have a built-in cultural enclave like my family found in Springfield.

"Your local Montana economy is clearly built around agriculture, and just as clearly, you have more acreage than you can manage by yourselves here at Sky Land. Several refugees held professional positions before they were displaced so they are well educated and accustomed to management responsibilities. You know that as well as I do. My only advantage is that I have spent more time in their midst, being elbow to elbow with them. Most are self-disciplined and high achievers when given the opportunity. If you can give them hope I believe you can train them to help you right here on this ranch. In fact, because of your proficiency, language that ordinarily would be a barrier would be less so in this isolated environment.

"I must say, though, that names and faces of a father and son came to me in the night. I believe the Holy Spirit brought them to my attention—but the problem is that they don't fit your criteria."

Gil asked, "How do you mean?"

"In a couple significant ways. They're not a complete family. And they're not Iraqi so their primary language is Farsi, not Arabic. On the other hand, they are Christian and have suffered because of that; he has somewhat of an agricultural background but, as far as I know, it's limited."

Gail asked, "What do you know of their story? What is the father's training, if not nomadic agriculture? Why do you suppose God brought them to your mind? What are their names?"

"His name is Dariush, a traditionally Persian name. You might recognize its origin from King Darius from the Bible. Dariush is a follower of Jesus. His late wife's name was Ashti. Again, you might recognize it as a derivative from Queen Vashti in the Bible. Ironically, it means peace. She was raised as the daughter of strict Moslem parents who arranged marriages for their children. They met and fell in love with each other, despite their religious differences. Knowing her family would never allow them to marry, they separately crossed the border into Iraq and settled near a mission compound, where they took shelter. There she accepted Christ, was baptized, began a personal relationship with Jesus as her Lord and Savior and the couple married. They had a baby and lived in hiding for two years until her family tracked her down.

"Naturally, this alarmed them but her family assured them there was no animosity. Travel between the two countries is fairly open such that her parents made two or three trips and demonstrated affection for Farzad, their grandson. Despite their initial apprehension, all seemed well."

Gil had experience with situations like this so he said, "But I bet all wasn't as it seemed."

"Sadly, it wasn't. Her parents sent her brothers and uncles to avenge the dishonor of Ashti's marriage and conversion by what they term *honor killing*. Farzad was in the mission compound so they were unable to kidnap him but they found and strangled Ashti. She, whose name was *Peace*, had to pay a heavy price for the shame she had brought on the family by abandoning their Moslem faith, whose propaganda advertises it as a religion of peace. They found Dariush at work and were in the process of beating him to death when he was rescued.

"He lived under constant threat of death so he eventually fled with his son to Lebanon. These two, father and son, have been six years in the camp I visit. Dariush has been without employment or income. He and Farzad subsist on charity from aid workers. He's disheartened, as you can easily imagine. Of course, their situation isn't unusual. Out of so many people, I can't tell you why God brought their faces and names to my mind."

Gil said, "Thanks for your perspective. Working on the ranch might be just the ticket. Farsi is an entirely different language than Arabic, though. We'll have to pray about it and trust your judgment. Keep us informed and let us know who else you recommend. We might be able to start with one more family. You answered Gail's question about backstory but not about the father's training or occupation before his exile."

"You know. Now that I think about it, I can't remember ever asking him. I'll do that the very next chance I get."

Gail brought over a hot batch of blueberry pancakes and added, "Machinery came with our purchase. Naturally, it will have to be maintained and repaired. Our families can demonstrate and teach us how to use it plus Sing's father, whom you've not yet met, has his own maintenance and repair business so that issue has an easy solution.

"But one important item we don't have is animals. Especially if Teen Challenge brings in young people who need to learn responsibility, we should have animals—all kinds and sizes of them, from chickens and rabbits to sheep and goats to cows and horses. Nothing teaches responsibility like caring for animals. Younger kids could gather eggs and older ones could ride horses to herd cattle.

"Gil and I were both raised on farms but neither of us has experience with chickens or sheep or horses. You've met Sue. Her husband is a veterinarian. What do you think about animals? Do any of your people have experience with them? Is there someone who comes to your mind in that regard?"

"Generally, yes. The more highly educated, not so much—but others, yes. I'm embarrassed I can't answer your question about Dariush. I've got more gaps in my knowledge than I realized. I'll get to work finding out who's been trained in what. We might be surprised. Who knows?"

Gil said, "Sue's father and brother have come up here to look things over. She's excited and was raised with horses so it's a no-brainer that we should talk with her in more detail before taking action. Let me see if I can set up a meeting with Sue and her husband while you're here, if that's alright with you."

"Of course. You bet. I probably won't say much but I'd be privileged to meet her husband. If he's as impressive as she, it would be another reason to rejoice."

Gil called Sue in Glasgow, explained the reason for meeting and asked if it could be scheduled to include Tuo. Without hesitation, Sue agreed and said, "I'd love for Sing to meet Tuo. Let's do it tonight. Come for supper. I'll invite Sing's parents, as well, if that's okay with you. They need something else to think about besides their loss of Grandfather."

That evening, Tuo and Sing were introduced to each other. Tuo was as surprised as Gil had been when he caught his first glimpse of Sing. He said, "You and I look alike in some ways. My parents came over from Vietnam. Judging by your name, I'm guessing yours came from China. Am I right?

Sing explained, "Yes, my father was brought over by his father. They arrived in Glasgow in 1946." He reminisced as he looked at his wife, "In a way, horses brought us together. Sue's brother Wyatt was my college roommate. He took me with him for a weekend visit one Saturday after a football game. Sue was a sophomore in high school at that time. She wanted to show off her horses to me. She asked me to ride with her and that's how it all started.

He turned his attention to Gil, "I think Sue would be a good one to help you find and purchase livestock. I'd be glad to check their overall health before you actually bought them. Father can help you with maintenance of machinery and I can do the same with animals. This is a good deal for all of us."

Sue added, "I'd welcome the opportunity to train and ride horses again. Large animals can be expensive to purchase and keep but caring for them has off-setting benefits. That's a proven fact. One thing that might not have occurred to you in this age of big machines is using draft horses for farm work. Of course, machinery is more efficient in many ways. It's a thought, maybe not worth much, but it's a thought. Probably the greatest value to you from work horses would be psychological and emotional, not economic. Horses can help you with forty acres but not with thousands. But—who knows?"

CHAPTER 20

2006

G il telephoned his friend Wayne Heifetz from his days in the Pentagon and asked, "How's civilian life treating you? I hear you got an offer you couldn't refuse to go to sunny California."

Wayne was a former co-worker from Gil's Pentagon days who was now a world-renowned math and astrophysics professor at Cal Tech in Pasadena, California.

"Hey, glad to hear your voice and it's good to know the ol' grapevine is still such a well-oiled machine," Wayne replied. "I thought I was maxed out as a bird colonel and was getting a bug to teach so when I got the offer here I made the break from 'Uncle' and jumped. I only just got here late last summer but civilian life at Cal Tech is fine. I like the flowers, the green grass, the sunshine every day. I got to watch the Rose Parade up close and personal this year and it was terrific! So what do you know?"

"I know the only time the word *incorrectly* isn't spelled *incorrectly* is when it's spelled incorrectly. But seriously, how's your teaching job? Do you like it? Are you happy with your big switch in locations?"

"I've got great students in good classes and the opportunities for academic research are all around me here. The downside is that I don't attract as many girls since I'm out of uniform and don't have it to help me out.

"Before I left D.C., General Grimsley retired with his fourth star. He told me you had resigned your Army commission. He said he wouldn't miss me much but he wished you had stayed in. How is it with you and Gail? What are you up to now?"

"I'm still up to the same 5'8". Army life treated me well but God has given me a new vision. Gail and I bought land in Montana, which brings up why I called. You're a smart guy and the one with the brighter future out there with the other big brains at Cal Tech. There was good reason some of our country's best universities competed for you. But I've got a head scratcher for you so can you help me out with an astrophysics question?"

Wayne responded, "Go light, my friend. That's a joke, by the way. It's not very good but what can you expect from me at a moment's notice?"

"You still haven't found your touch," Gil said. "That's pathetic as ever but it's good to know you're still trying. Here's the question: If I assume that once upon a time our year was exactly and precisely three hundred and sixty days in duration, can you tell me what it would have taken for it to be changed to what it is now?"

Wayne said, "Sure, that's easy—if you let me assume you mean the tropical year. Kepler's third law of planetary motion says the cubes of the mean distances of the planets from the sun are proportional to the squares of their times of revolution around the sun."

Gil laughed out loud into the phone and said, "Easy for you to say! You tell better jokes when you're serious than when you're trying to be funny."

Wayne responded, "Okay, okay. You asked."

"I know. Really, I'm glad I've got friends like you. But can you translate that into kindergarten English for me? And while you're at it, you got me a little curious—does Mr. Kepler have a first and a second law?"

"Sure," Wayne said. "Kepler lived a long time ago. He was a good observer of the starry sky and concluded that our galaxy's planet's orbits were almost circles but not quite. They were squashed a little bit. You can think of them as ovals or racetracks but we egg-heads call them ellipses. That was and is his first law."

And Gil thought to himself, *Okay, I got that first part: the shape of a planet's orbit is close to but not quite a circle; it's an ellipse.*

Wayne continued, "Kepler's second law says that as planets get closer to the Sun they speed up and when they get farther from the Sun they slow down."

Gil thought, *Sure, when I was a kid I tied a string around my finger that had a ball at its end and twirled my finger. The ball sped up as the string wound up. I guess I could think of planets as being tied to the Sun. They speed up as they get nearer to it.*

It was as if Wayne read Gil's mind. He said, "Gravity is like a string tying planets to the Sun. Mercury is the closest planet and it travels faster around its complete orbit than Neptune does, which is the planet farthest from the Sun.

"Kepler's third law is a logical extension of his first two. It simply posits a connection between the size of a planet's orbit and the time it takes for the planet to go all the way around its orbit. In other words, the larger the average radius of a planet's orbit, the longer it takes to go once around the Sun. There is a mathematical relationship between the distance of a planet from the Sun and the time it requires to complete a full journey around the Sun."

And Gil thought, *Oh, boy, here it comes.*

"The equation for Kepler's third law has four inputs. To solve this equation you need to know three numbers to solve for the unknown, fourth number. You told me to assume Earth's orbital period 'once upon a time' in the past was precisely three hundred sixty days; our current tropical year is a tiny fraction less than 365.2422 days in duration. The distance between Earth and the Sun is approximately 92,960,000 miles; of course, this distance is measured at a specific time of year since Earth's orbit is not circular—it's elliptical, remember. Using those three inputs I can solve for the fourth, unknown number you've asked me about."

Gil couldn't help himself. He interrupted, "Whoa, whoa, whoa! Two things. First, I don't see how the solution to this equation will give me the answer to my question and, second, are you telling me we can measure the length of our solar year out to four decimal places?"

"Closer than that, actually, but we don't need greater precision to solve this equation. However, you bring up an interesting point. Our solar year is not precisely three hundred sixty-five-and-a-fourth days in length. Everybody knows about leap years because they've lived though one or more of them, but leap years don't always happen every fourth year."

"Wayne, come on, are you sure? Well, of course you are! But I don't know what you're talking about. Please explain."

"Sure. Every fourth year is a leap year *except* when the date is evenly divisible by one hundred but not by four hundred. So the year 2000 was a leap year because it's a number divisible by both one hundred and four hundred. But the year 1900 was not—it's a number evenly divisible by one hundred but *not* by four hundred so it was not a leap year. The same will be true in 2100. So, *you* have never experienced a 'fourth year' that was not a leap year but your lack of longevity has no effect on the mathematics. Fine-tuning adjustments are necessary because the length of our equatorial, or tropical year is not precisely three hundred sixty-five-and-a-fourth days in length."

Gil said, "Wayne, you've taught me something, which doesn't surprise me at all. But I don't think I can solve Kepler's equation without your help. And even then I'm not sure what it would tell me. I think you'll have to first solve the equation and then explain its relevance to my question—how did we go from three hundred sixty days in a year to three hundred sixty-five?"

"Alright, it will take only a few seconds. I have a small calculator here, which speeds the solution tremendously! Okay. Here. I have it. The equation's answer is 92,066,000 miles, rounded. Compare that with 92,960,000 miles I just told you is Earth's current distance from the Sun and you discover that to increase the length of our solar year by a fraction less than five-and-a-quarter days requires that the radius of Earth's orbit around the Sun on a specific day must have lengthened by 894,000 miles. So the answer to your question is that a catastrophic event must have occurred at some point in Earth's past history that shifted its orbit almost 900,000 miles further from our sun."

"Wow, all I can say is *wow*," Gil said. "I could never have figured that out by myself. I'm blown away! And it explains so many things for me."

"Glad to be of service. After all, what are friends for?" Wayne replied. "It's obvious you're up to something. I don't know what it is but it's obviously something. Let me know what this explained for you when you're ready."

"Thanks so much. I owe you a huge favor," Gil said. "You'll be the first to know."

"Good deal. Thanks for calling. I enjoyed visiting. Not everybody makes me feel as smart as you just did. The pleasure has been all mine. Give me a call again soon. I'd love to come see Maisie in Montana. If she looks like Gail and not you, she's a cutie. How old is she now?"

"She's a babe-in-arms and cute as a bug."

After Gil hung up he reflected on Wayne's words, "a catastrophic event must have occurred" and thought, *Noah's flood. What else could it be?*

CHAPTER 21

2006

T uo returned to his Army post in time to report for his normal duty rotation. Sue began researching livestock auctions and daydreaming of horses.

Gil made plans to host Teen Challenge representatives. Gail contacted officials about requirements for sponsorship of foreign nationals out of Lebanon's refugee camps.

"When pretty things get broken, we sigh and feel sad," Gil said at the end of one particularly long hard day when he, Gail, Sue and Sing were all sitting on the porch. "But I think we'd agree that when youth's beauty is scratched and becomes terribly marred, we must take action and do more than cluck our tongues, wag our heads and hope for the best. It's hard work but I just know this effort will be worth it."

Gil and Gail told Teen Challenge they wanted diversity in ethnicity and points of origin in their boys. Teen Challenge agreed. The deal was done and a partnership struck—except for one important caveat involving an obvious deficiency: the farmstead could barely accommodate a family of three. The house was as far from being a dormitory as one could imagine.

The young couple decided the problem could be solved by constructing one or more appropriate buildings, which they had already known they would have to do if they wished to proceed.

The farmstead was situated on a level, four-acre site with southeast-facing orientation a half-mile off the main road. The river with its low-land meadow was three-quarters of a mile away so sanitation regulations weren't an issue regarding expansion and new construction.

The spring of the year was the perfect time to begin construction in Montana, Gil thought. But what about planning? No thought had been given to planning for such a big project. Or had it? Just as Gil began to worry, the phone rang. Tuo was on the other end of the line. He said, "Dariush had been a civil engineer in Tehran, Iran and Mosul, Iraq in his previous life—before he fled as a refugee to Lebanon. Though there's an extreme need for his engineering expertise, he hasn't been able to function in his professional capacity here because we have no materials or political capital that are required before he can utilize his talent."

"Maybe Glasgow has an architect but, for sure, Great Falls will have one or more with good experience and reputation," Gil told him. "And Teen Challenge should know people from other projects they've done. Perhaps Jamie knows someone from Fort Benton who would be qualified for the job. Sing or Wyatt might have friends from the School of Architecture at Montana State they would recommend. If push comes to shove, Gail's father or Clyde could talk to somebody in a Des Moines office for us. We can *do* this!"

He hung up and turned around to face Gail, who was baking cookies with Maisie. "Tuo's phone call was a huge encouragement to me. It seems as if this project hasn't taken God by surprise. He might have already arranged for Dariush to be our perfect on-site engineer and construction manager."

Teen Challenge's experience was in dormitory-type structures but Gil and Gail vetoed that idea. Their vision was of a home environment, a family atmosphere. Much to their delight, they found an architect right there in Glasgow who got on board with their picture of single-story house-pods for seven to ten boys scattered at irregular but artistic intervals around a central dining and gathering facility, all of which would be incorporated into the existing farmstead. The pods themselves would have individual bedrooms arranged in pairs that shared bathrooms.

Sky Land's expansion would begin with one housing pod, the central kitchen and eating building, a heated chicken house, a small dairy barn and a large horse barn with stalls, tack room, supply room and indoor arena. Other pods and outbuildings would fit inside the vision and be constructed as the vision itself matured and unfolded. The pods would be wood frame construction and the dairy barn would be cement block while the horse barn would be pre-engineered steel. Pods would have muted color schemes except their front doors would be brightly painted and distinctive—red, green, blue, orange, purple. The central kitchen and housing pod would be built first in this initial phase of construction.

The boys began to arrive, eight of them. They were skinny, clever, practically shirtless—except Reuven, who was never without layers of clothing, and Johnny Ray, who had muscles on top of muscles.

Julio was an angry young Puerto Rican from a New York City barrio. He had been told he wasn't worth the air he breathed or the dirt on which he stood. Carlos was a Latino from Miami, Florida with a fierce love of baseball. He could have been a Rhodes scholar if it weren't for his grades. Jim Bob was a country boy from the northeastern hills of Oklahoma. He liked football—a lot. Johnny Ray was from the cotton fields deep in Alabama. His black parents had given up on sharecropping and relocated to the Birmingham projects when he was nine years old.

Jason was a coal miner's son from Appalachia. It was a toss-up as to whether Julio or Johnny Ray or Jason was the poorest. Terry was a cowboy from West Texas who liked to ride bulls almost as much as horses. Tomas hailed from Los Angeles and had been part of its gang-culture turf wars. Reuven was a cultural Jew, also from New York City. True to the stereotype, his parents were by far the richest of the group. He and Julio lived within three miles of each other but, in psychological and economic reality, they had lived worlds apart. While Julio was given to angry outbursts, Reuven was reticent in every regard.

Finally, Tuo escorted Farzad and his father, Dariush, from the refugee camp in Lebanon to Sky Land, Montana. It was arranged for Farzad to live in the horse barn's apartment with his father but he was to have daily contact with the eight other Teen Challenge kids. Dariush was glad to have a job as a ranch hand and on-site engineer. He showed himself to be an eager worker, willing to learn. Farzad assisted him in learning English.

Tuo was also able to arrange for Ali, an Afghani child who had been able to escape with his Christian mother from that country's repressive regime, to come to Sky Land. His father had been killed. Plans were made for his mother to be trained to work in the central kitchen and act as the "dorm mom" for all the boys in the first pod. Like Farzad, Ali would live with his parent and interact with the other boys every day. The primary language in Kabul and northwest Afghanistan is Dari. Dari and Farsi are different accents of the same language so Ali and his mother could communicate readily with Farzad and his father.

Ali is a common Afghani name that is pronounced '*Al Lee*' with the accent on the last syllable. The boys didn't regard his name as unusual, especially since the well-known heavyweight boxer from the late-1960s through the early nineties carried the same name. They didn't remember that his original name had been Cassius Clay before he had it legally changed to Muhammad Ali.

Ali was the youngest boy at eleven; Johnny Ray, at fifteen, was the oldest, biggest and strongest. The other boys were all either thirteen or fourteen years old. Some had experience with rural living, others had only known big city existence. In spite of the Teen Challenge referral, not every boy had been hooked on illicit drugs.

Sue had found a matched pair of two-year-old Belgian draft horses. Sing verified that they were in good health. Gil and Gail traveled to purchase the geldings. When Gail saw them, she exclaimed, "Wow! These guys must weigh a ton! And they're so much taller than other horses I've seen. They intimidate me."

Sue agreed. "Belgians typically weigh about two thousand pounds. Had they not been neutered, their behavior would have been unpredictable and, at times, aggressive. But as is, they're gentle as can be. They're gentle giants."

"Have they bonded with their trainers?" Gil asked when he saw them. "We've got children to worry about. Do these giants, gentle though they may be, pose a safety hazard for us?"

The sellers allayed their concerns but said children shouldn't be allowed to walk under them since they might be stepped on inadvertently. A primary person should be assigned to them for care and management. They likened the situation to a dog's having one master but being socialized by his trainer to be around many people. That set Gil's mind at ease so the transaction was finalized and transportation to Sky Land was arranged.

On their way home, Sue suggested that of all the boys, Terry was the logical one to have the primary responsibility for the Belgians since he had experience with horses. She said she couldn't be on the ranch every day but Terry would be. She could instruct Terry on use of the harness if he needed it. Gail agreed that Sue's comments made sense and Gil nodded his head. But he would keep watch and observe.

The horses were a big hit with the boys.

Sing was often close by just in case he was needed. Sue spoke with Terry, who said he was comfortable with them. Their names were Harry and David, after the mail-order guys. They liked to work, they liked to pull, they had been trained to drive, they knew all the commands: gee, haw, whoa, back, up, down.

Other boys decided they'd like to help Terry curry the big Belgians at the end of a workday—and even at the beginning, just before harnessing.

Gail remained a bit timid around them, but Sue's confidence encouraged Maisie to reach out and touch them when she was held up to them. But when Harry and David swung their heads around to get a good look at Maisie, their eyeballs were so huge and so close to her face that she turned away, hugged Sue and peed her pants. Sue calmly took a step back, comforted Maisie, touched the horses to show they weren't a threat—then handed her over to Gail, who took her inside for a fresh change of clothes.

Maisie and some of the boys preferred feeding the chickens and collecting their eggs to hanging with the horses. The hen house was an inviting shelter for them the same as it was for the chickens. And protecting chickens from predators needed to be done.

Maybe because of fond memories of Mollie, Gil wanted a few milk cows so he bought three heifers that were soon to calve and freshen. He explained to the boys who were assigned to that chore how difficult it was going to be to toughen their wrist muscles for hand milking. The good news was that the calves would take most of the milk at first. So they could more-or-less ease into the job. Gil gave these boys something to think about. "How can a black cow eat green grass and produce white milk that turns into yellow cheese?" Bless their hearts, they weren't quite sure if he was teasing or being serious with them.

Gil and Gail's most important task, though, was integrating the disparate boys, who were of different cultures and spoke various languages with a range of dialects and distinct accents. Jim Bob's drawl meshed with Johnny Ray's but not with Julio's machine-gun chatter. Jason's poor grammar assaulted Reuven's senses. Carlos and Farzad were shrill with their sibilants, which made Terry want to dampen their hisses. Some of the group were Christian; some were not. Some had been persecuted for the name of Christ; others hadn't heard the name of Jesus except as a curse word. Neither Gil nor Gail bore primary responsibility for the Teen Challenge boys but both had daily, significant contact with them.

"All work and no play makes Jack a dull boy," Gil often heard growing up, so after school work, farm chores, kitchen duty and cleaning their rooms, he encouraged the boys to play and rough-house. They engaged in all types of games, sports and activities—checkers to football, catch to cards, wrestling to reading. Julio liked to take his anger out on Johnny Ray, who was the only boy strong enough to handle it.

One day Johnny Ray, who almost always came out on top due to his age, reach and bulk, teased the young Latino. "Julio, dude, you've got to learn to pull your punches." They began to form an unlikely friendship as they boxed and wrestled.

Carlos and Tomas liked to play catch, sometimes with gloves, sometimes without. Tomas had the stronger arm in a game of burnout but Carlos had the better curveball.

Jim Bob liked to run. He would occasionally ask Farzad along. Gil liked to run with them when his schedule permitted. He wasn't a natural runner so the boys had to slow down and take it easy with him. Sing wanted part of the action; he schooled them pretty hard when he participated. Between breaths, they got it out of him that he had once been Montana's quarter-mile champion who attended college on a track scholarship. Gil cautioned, "Stay along the road until you get comfortable with the terrain. I don't want you to twist an ankle or get snake bit."

Ali would usually dribble a soccer ball by himself. Jason liked to shoot hoops and Reuven would rebound the ball back to him. The groups and the sports were fluid. The boys got acquainted quickly.

One day Gil, Gail and Sing met with them in their classroom with their resident teachers and counselors. After they were all assembled and attentive, Gil stood at the front of the classroom teacher-like and addressed the bunch seated like students in their desks lined up in rows. He said, "We work, play and eat together. We caravan to church as a unit. In this land of the big sky, we have ample opportunity for solitude but none of us is truly by himself. We have to live with that fact but we also are best served by rejoicing in it. We are not alone, speaking of which. . . .

"I was alone and lonely in my earliest years. My father was killed as a nomad in Lebanon's civil war. My mother was killed in Jordan as she wandered. I was adopted out of an orphanage at age twelve by missionary parents who loved me and raised me on a small farm in Iowa. They taught me about Jesus and I'm glad to say I grew up as a Christian. Mine is a story of redemption because I went from being a boy with no future to one who appreciates the opportunities he has.

"What God did for me, He can do for you. I'll be sharing this, my belief, with you on occasion. Other adults will do the same."

Sing, who had been standing on the side of the classroom, joined Gil at the front after his initial speech. He said, "Some of you boys will be working with me on our animals. You might discover you enjoy them. You probably haven't thought about what you'd like to do with the rest of your lives, but I'd like to help you consider options. Animals might be one of those options. I didn't know I wanted to be a veterinarian when I was your age. I was a child who hadn't thought about whether he wanted to be a brain surgeon or a freight train engineer or a baseball player, but the time came in my life when I realized some things appealed to me more than other things. God willing, I'll be here for you when you start thinking about what appeals to you, be it animals or baseball or freight trains."

Gail joined the two men next, chiming in. "An anthropologist is a person who studies ancient, human cultures and societies. Margaret Mead was a famous anthropologist who gave lectures about places she'd been and things she'd seen.

Sometimes she'd ask this question, 'What would you say is the earliest sign of civilization?' Some of the answers she would get were 'tools made of iron' or 'the first domesticated plant' or 'a clay pot.' Those were all good answers but not the one she was looking for. Do any of you have an answer?"

One of the braver boys held up his hand and said, "I saw a science fiction movie once about a man who had been captured by a superior race and put in a zoo with their other alien specimens. One day he captured a mouse and trained it as his pet. It wasn't until then that his captors understood he was more than an animal to be put on display. So is that a good answer—when you train and take care of a pet? When we as humans take care of animals the way Sing does?"

"That's a great answer and Sing does great work," Gail said. "But Margaret Mead would hold up a human femur, the largest bone in our leg, point to a thickened area where the bone had healed after a fracture and say,

'Here is my answer. Here we do not find violence, a rib pierced by an arrow, a skull crushed by a club. Here we find evidence of kindness. Someone must have cared for this injured person, hunted on his behalf, brought food to him, served him at personal cost, sacrificed for him. We humans measure civilization by how we respond to the most vulnerable, those in our midst who suffer.'"

Gil could see a few of the boys look down or away as if embarrassed that they were in this last group of human sufferers or had been a party to human suffering. A few squirmed in their seats even. He called for a five-minute bathroom and water break.

Some of them already have known too much suffering, he thought.

CHAPTER 22

2006

G il continued the teaching following the break. The boys jostled each other a bit but eventually settled down. They were energized but attentive.

"Kindness in the face of trouble is a quandary. A question that theologians like to debate is *what can man do or not do to overcome his in-born, corrupt nature?* They agree that man's heart has to be changed; every man's mind must be renewed and his spirit has to breathe new life to be able to withstand the searing light of God's holiness. How? Can man do it? Can any man? Is it possible?

"In the Bible, in the Book of Ezekiel, the prophet brings this great mystery, this dilemma, down to the level of our human intelligence. We'll study three passages in this prophet's book that should be read and considered together. By doing that, we can answer today's question with confidence. The outline for this exercise is 'Precept, Promise, Prayer.'

"The first text in Ezekiel is at Chapter 18 and verse 31, where this inward change is made the subject of a precept: *'Make you a new heart and a new spirit.'* A precept is like a command, as in 'Do such-and-such' or 'Do this-and-that' or 'Make you a new heart and a new spirit.' How is that possible? Johnny Ray, if I told you, 'Chop cotton,' that sounds like a command, like I'm telling you to do something, doesn't it? Could you obey, would you know how to go about it?"

"Mr. Webster, I know how to chop cotton. I've put in lots of time a-choppin' cotton. It's not too bad for five minutes but try bendin' over like that for ten hours after your blisters start a-bleedin'. But I could do it. Yes, sir, I could do it."

"Johnny Ray, for those who don't know, what is chopping cotton? These boys might wonder why you would chop up and destroy your cash crop."

"Oh, no, it's just the opposite. It means to get out there in the hot sun and hoe the weeds out of your cotton crop so those weeds don't suck up all the moisture. You're not choppin' the cotton, you're choppin' in the cotton to get the weeds out of it."

"Jason, how about you and digging coal?"

"I feel the same way—it's long, hard, dirty work. I'd rather not do more of it."

"Now, Johnny Ray, if I told you to make yourself a new heart, could you do it?"

"No, sir. I wouldn't know how to go about it. That's not possible for me to do."

"Jason, if I told you to make yourself a new spirit, could you do it?"

"Same answer. It's just not possible."

"Good answers, boys. And what's true for you is true for all of us. None of us can do that. So what does this precept mean for us? If we can't renew our minds, if we can't change our hearts, if it's impossible for us to breathe new life into our spirits—but if we *must* do all these things to be able to stand in God's presence, what does this mean for us? Johnny Ray? Jason?"

"I guess it means I'm in trouble," the big husky boy said nervously.

"It means I'm in deep, deep trouble." Jason fidgeted in his chair.

"Exactly. This command, this precept is to awaken in you a conviction of your helplessness to obey, to reveal to you your soul's danger. This precept is to be a sledgehammer on your natural conscience. But it can also be a useful challenge to prompt you to seek God, however slight your chance of success. Your effort may be feeble, imperfect and unpromising but it is laudable and even necessary for you to make the effort. We all should do it. We're told to do it.

"This effort will naturally cause us to think of our need. We think that perhaps, just maybe, our sad conditions can be fixed, and their ruin and death and helplessness and condemnation will be turned away. When our Lord ordered the paralytic man to take up his bed and walk, Jesus seemed to be telling him to do the impossible. By definition, a paralyzed man *can't* walk. And if that man had agreed—at that moment—with the definition, and had made no effort, the evil he was suffering would have remained. But along with the command there was an impulse in the mind of the man that the command was of God and that anything spoken by God must be possible. And it is precisely under this aspect that we are to view the command, 'Make you a new heart; make you a new spirit.'

"What am I talking about? For the answer, we need to read two portions of Scripture. Jim Bob, look up and read from John's gospel, Chapter 5, the first fifteen verses. Gail would be glad to help you find it, if you'd like. We'll pay special attention to verse 8. Julio, you do the same with Matthew 12:9–13."

Jim Bob read, *"One who was there had been an invalid for thirty-eight years. . . . Then Jesus said to him, 'Get up! Pick up your mat and walk.'"*

Julio read, *". . . a man with a shriveled hand was there. . . . Then [Jesus] said to the man, 'Stretch out your hand.'"*

Gil resumed his exhortation, "You say you cannot make a new heart or a new spirit for yourselves. Yes, except I say there is a sense in which you can, just as much as at the bidding of Christ a man was able to stretch forth a withered hand, as a crippled man was able to take up his mat and walk. A command from God eliminates all excuses. It assumes there is in every one of us a certain power of compliance. Reuven, read a Torah verse for us if you would, please."

"Yes, sir. Which one?"

"Deuteronomy 4:29. We won't pay attention to its immediate context—just this single verse for the point it makes."

Reuven was familiar with his Hebrew Bible so he turned to that Torah portion and read, *"But if you search there for the Lord your God, you will find Him, if only you seek Him with all your heart and soul."*

"Thank you. Now, Tomas, find and read Jeremiah Chapter 29, verse 13. While you're looking for it, I'll recite a famous verse that precedes it, verse 11, *'For I know the plans I have for you,'* declares the Lord, *'plans to prosper you and not to harm you, plans to give you hope and a future.'* I urge each of you boys to memorize this verse because it will encourage you when you're feeling down in the dumps."

Tomas had found verse 13 by this time, so he read, *"You will seek Me and find Me when you seek Me with all your heart."*

"Thank you. Finally, Carlos, read Second Chronicles Chapter 15, verses 1 and 2 for us. These two verses contain a few unfamiliar names but they're not too hard. You can handle them."

"The Spirit of God came upon Azariah, son of Obed. He went out to meet Asa and said to him, 'Listen to me, Asa and all Judah and Benjamin. The Lord is with you when you are with Him. If you seek Him, He will be found by you, but if you forsake Him, He will forsake you.'"

Gil continued, "These different references all make the point that effort on our part is rewarded. It's not futile. It's to our benefit that we expend energy to seek God. If we do, He says we will find Him. I believe that! This is a promise from God to us—to each and every one of us. It's as true for you as it was for me."

Sing took over teaching the next point in the outline. He said, "Ezekiel Chapter 11, verse 36 also makes a promise to us, *I will give you a new heart and put a new spirit in you; I will remove from you your heart of stone and give you a heart of flesh.'*

"This same Ezekiel who was instructed to call out to the house of Israel, *'Make you a new heart and a new spirit,'* also delivers God's kind assurance to the people, *'I will give you a new heart; I will give you a new spirit.'* The clear implication is that if we search, we shall find but if we don't search, we won't find. A blind man can see those words, a deaf man can hear them.

"Everything God does, whether in the material or moral world, is characterized by harmony, proportion, order, law. The old saying holds true, 'As our day, so our strength'; as the command to run, so the strength to run.

"Farzad, it can be hard to understand aphorisms. Do you 'get' the point of this saying? Can you apply it somehow in your life?" Sing asked the young boy.

"I think so. God wouldn't tell me to run unless He gave me strength to run. Of course, I can't keep up with you but I can run. And God wouldn't tell me to walk unless He gave me strength to walk. He wouldn't tell me to touch and brush our biggest horse unless He gave me courage to do it. It's like Mr. Webster said except the emphasis has changed from the telling, the command, the precept, to the promise. God promises to give me strength and courage to do what He tells me to do. He gave my mother strength when she had to have it, to die without renouncing her faith, and my father to live without losing his."

"Well said!" Sing smiled. "That's exactly right. When we tag this promise onto the precept, we see that God never exhorts us to do a thing without putting the means of compliance within our reach and power. Viewing these two Scriptures in juxtaposition with each other rids us of a host of speculative difficulties and objections. The precept doesn't stand alone; a promise stands alongside it.

"Harking back to Gail's comment about Margaret Mead and anthropology, God teaches us about His concern for the inherent dignity of the individual and the condition of the poor. The Chinese Academy of Social Sciences studied what distinguished Western civilization from other cultures. One of its members wrote: 'We were asked to look into what accounted for the preeminence of the West all over the world. We studied everything we could from the historical, political, economic, and cultural perspective. At first, we thought it was because you had more powerful guns . . . then we thought it was because you had the best political system. Next, we focused on your economic system. But . . . we have realized that the heart of your culture is your religion: Christianity. We don't have any doubt about this.'"

Gail finished the teaching, "We need a little break from being so serious. I've been working with some of the boys on a joke we think you'll enjoy. Take it away, fellas."

Johnny Ray grinned. It was obvious he'd rehearsed his lines. "Jesus was black and here's three good reasons why I know that: He called everybody 'brother,' He grooved to Gospel music and He didn't get a fair trial."

The crowd laughed. Reuven jumped in. "Oh, I don't think so. I think Jesus was Jewish and here's three good reasons for that: He lived at home 'til he was thirty, He was sure His mother was a virgin and His mother thought He was God."

"Huh-uh," corrected Tomas. "Jesus was a California dude and here's three good reasons why: first, He never cut His hair; second, He walked around barefoot all the time; and third, He started a new religion where they all wore robes."

Bashful Ali surprised the rest by raising his hands, waving them wildly in the air and saying, "No, I think Jesus was Italian and here's three good reasons why: He talked with His hands, had wine with all His meals and He used olive oil for a whole bunch of stuff."

Farzad said, much more quietly, "Dr. Siu's mother told me she was sure Jesus was Native American, most likely Sioux Indian and she gave me three good reasons why: He was at peace with nature, He ate a lot of fish and He communed with the Great Spirit."

Everyone laughed when Gail said, "I have the most compelling evidence of all that Jesus was a woman. Here are three sure-fire reasons why: He could feed big crowds at a moment's notice when the pantry was almost empty, He kept trying to get a message across to a bunch of men who just didn't get it, and even when He was dead, He had to get up because there was still work to do." The boys laughed, lightening the mood. They hadn't expected such a good joke like that from one of these adults.

"Alright," she continued, "Let's get back to business and finish this teaching. But first, we might need to review. Gil's outline was 'Precept, Promise, Prayer.' Ali, you're learning new words every day. Do you remember what we said a precept is?"

"Yes, it's a command. Somebody's telling us to do something."

"That's right. Very good. Terry, what is it we were told to do?"

"Make us a new heart, make us a new spirit."

"Exactly right. Again, very good. But we decided it's an impossible thing for us to do. So, what's the promise Sing told you about?"

Two or three of the boys piped up and said, "God will give us a new heart. He guarantees He will be found by us if we search for Him—if we search really hard for Him."

"Good job! I'm proud of all of you. You've listened really well. Our third text, Ezekiel Chapter 36, verse 37, adds prayer to this equation: *'I will yield to the plea of the house of Israel and do this for them.'* It's not just two points in our outline, but three that join together. The subject of a new heart and a new spirit is serious, one that calls for earnest prayer.

"Ezekiel's injunction, his precept, *'Make you a new heart,'* is followed by a word of consolation, a promise, *'I will give you a new heart.'* The first could lead to despair if it stood by itself. We might think, 'I can't do that; it's impossible; I could *never* do that'. The second could lead to presumption if it stood by itself. We would be tempted to say, 'I can do that; I don't need God; I can do that all by myself'. The third point in our outline, prayer, guards against despair just as it guards against presumption. The precept speaks of death, the promise points to life. The precept shows that we have work to do that is beyond our natural ability, the promise is that God will do it. The prayer is the guaranteed means whereby God shall do it for us. The precept is the will of God commanding; the promise is the goodness of God encouraging; the prayer is helplessness pleading at His footstool, with eyes fastened on the mercy seat because we are afraid to look upon His throne.

"In a word, they form, in combination, a holy, blessed, and glorious Trinity. For the precept is the Sovereign Father of the universe demanding obedience. The promise is the Son of His love pleading that the offender may be spared. The prayer is the indwelling Spirit within us waking up the heart to devotion and showing us how to both wrestle and prevail with God. Wherever and whenever—that you may be able to keep the precept, pray; that you may have part in the promise, pray; that you may have the spirit of effectual fervent prayer, pray. Keep the end in view—'a new heart and a new spirit,' an altered judgment and restored affections, a submitted will and a heavenly mind.

"Boys, this is good stuff. I'm so glad you listened well. Thank you for that." And Gail gave a little bow to them to honor their attentiveness as she sat down.

In closing, Gil stood and said, "But I want to leave you—all ten of you— with a final thought. It may be that our greatest challenge with you boys is to convince you that you have hope and a future, as I previously quoted to you from Jeremiah Chapter 29, verse 11. Let God's word speak for itself. Believe it! And decide—because if you don't decide for yourselves what you want from life, someone else will do it for you and you may not like the result. Think about it. I pray that your better selves will become your truest selves.

"I'm speaking of spiritual things, of course, but also of vocational careers and a secular mindset as well. Your spiritual worldview has powerful influence on your mental attitude. To illustrate, once upon a time, trained, thoughtful medical personnel believed it was impossible for a man to run a four-minute mile, that it would kill him. Roger Bannister finally did it in 1954. Six others did it in the next three weeks and John Landy ran 3:58 six weeks after the barrier had been broken. Jim Ryun accomplished the feat just ten years later in 1964 while still a high school junior in Wichita, Kansas. The moral of the story is that until athletes believed those things could happen, they could *not* happen. From a scientific viewpoint, from your viewpoint, perception is paramount. Don't limit your options. Believe God for the impossible. Then, in His time, do the impossible.

"There are men, learned men, who spend year after year sorting out butterflies, beetles and gnats. Others dig in the dirt looking for pottery shards or various orders of clamshells. They themselves are happy as clams in doing it because it was their career choice to do it. So I'll make you a promise.

"If you demonstrate to your teachers and counselors that you are college or trade school material, that you have gifts worthy of being developed, that you are motivated to put in the work to develop your talent, Gail and I will pay your college or trade school tuition. Reach out your hands and grasp this opportunity. The only caveat I put on this offer is that I can't guarantee the future. What I mean to say and say in a way we all can understand is this: I have money in the bank to back up my promise, but I can't guarantee that someone won't rob the bank. Other than that, do your part and I'll keep my promise to you.

"You have hope and a future. Because God loves you—He really does."

CHAPTER 23

2006

C lyde and Wyatt were faithful in visiting and keeping tabs on the ranch but they identified a full-time, on-site manager as a requirement. With Gil and Gail's approval, they hired the most qualified candidate. This decision freed Gil and Gail to concentrate their efforts on redeeming people while simultaneously being good stewards of the land.

Most of the field work was done with machinery because of the scale of the operation. Boys were trained to run this machinery as a part of their rehabilitation but doing so didn't mean it was their job. They helped with the work to learn job skills and employment discipline, but the ranch's productivity didn't depend on their labor.

Additional horses were acquired. A pair of Clydesdales arrived who were no taller than the Belgians but outweighed them by two hundred pounds. A team of Percherons was bigger yet. By this time, all ten of the boys were involved in caring for and working the animals. Maisie could toddle well enough now that her daily chore was joining with Ali in feeding chickens and gathering their eggs but, over time, she learned to touch the big horses and stare eyeball to eyeball with them. She was a trooper.

The boys seemed to be doing well. Occasional blow-ups weren't serious. Julio was still angry but boxing and wrestling with Johnny Ray gave him a healthy outlet for his rage. Still, most of the boys were either coming to believe in some type of faith or growing in it—except Julio. He had an anger about him that was constantly seething and bubbling just beneath the surface, which didn't leave much room for anything spiritual.

Ali and Farzad were committed to their Christian faith, in large part because they had already been persecuted for its defense. Reuven was religious but resistant to altering his views because he had been taught it meant abandoning his Jewish heritage.

The Teen Challenge officials recognized the need for and provided professional counselors trained to aid this age group. The psychologists who visited Sky Land looked forward to it and spent plenty of time there because its location so uplifted their tired bodies and souls that were so burdened with others' troubles.

Sing spoke with Gil privately one day as they took a look at the livestock together. "I'm concerned about Reuven."

"He's quiet, for sure. Reticent to the extreme." Gil replied.

"It's more than that, I'm afraid. Some people cast a shadow without being in a room. Reuven's the opposite. He's a man without a shadow. He's a walking sleeping pill. That spells danger."

"How so?"

"He walks around without a word. He doesn't wear black curls under a black hat but he might as well, for all the mixing he does with the other boys. They don't exclude him, he excludes himself from them. He hasn't accepted his heritage but neither has he rejected it. He doesn't know what, if anything, he believes. He has unresolved issues, many of which he is ignorant of.

"Julio explodes at least once a day, but like a volcano, he releases pressure so it doesn't build up. Reuven's got no release. Ten years from now, there might be a big explosion coming out of him that catches people unaware and is much more harmful."

Gil said, "Thank you for seeing that. I didn't. We surely don't want a big explosion ten years from now." He told Sing he would spend time with Reuven and talk with him.

Gil asked to meet with Reuven under one of the big oak trees that stood in the back of the farm a few days later. He began with a question, "What is *mikveh*?"

"A Hebrew word," Reuven answered absentmindedly. He was hunkered at the base of the tree, his back to its trunk, lost in thought—except he probably wasn't thinking.

"What does it mean?" Gil sat a few feet away, cross-legged in the grass.

"Mr. Webster, I'm not an expert."

"Do you have to be? I'm not trying to trick you. It's a simple question."

"Okay. A *mikveh* is a thing. It's in some houses but mostly it's in synagogues."

"You still haven't told me what it is. Did you have one in your house?"

"No."

"Reuven, I don't mean to be hard on you but you are proving a point with me. You're not a belligerent person so your lack of response leads me to think you hardly know what a *mikveh* is, let alone what it represents—that your belief is cultural indoctrination of which you know but little. After several minutes, you still haven't answered my simple question.

"But to clarify my point, I have personal definitions of three words, each of which is personal to you. Tell me whether you agree or if you've thought about them.

"The first word is *Hebrew*. You already used it less than a minute ago. I take it to refer to a certain bloodline, an ethnicity—as in, you are of Hebrew extraction while my biological parents were of Middle Eastern tribal origins.

"On the other hand, I am not Iranian or Iraqi or Lebanese, I am American. In the same way, you are not Israeli; you are American. Which brings up my second word, *Israeli*. I take it to refer to citizenship. I am not Turkish, for example, because I am not a citizen of Turkey. I lived there for a year when I was in the military and posted at Incirlik but I was an American citizen during that time. I was never a Turkish citizen. In the same way, you are American, not Israeli, because you are an American citizen, not an Israeli citizen. Does that make sense to you? Do you follow my reasoning?"

"Yes."

"The reason I parse these words so closely is because of the third word, *Jew*. In my experience, limited as it may be, I've found that many people, especially Jews, have trouble defining what a Jew is. So—here's my definition. The word is separate from 'Hebrew' and/or 'Israeli' and has its own, unique definition. Being Jewish has to do with an inner belief system. And in that sense, I'm Jewish and likely more so than you."

Gil continued, "I don't mean to offend you, but again in my limited experience, Hebrew people say things like, 'I'm Jewish so I can't be Christian. To become Christian would be to deny my Jewishness.' While I disagree with that statement on principle it seems absolute nonsense to me when those same persons can't define for me what it means to be Jewish."

Reuven looked at Gil, his dark eyes glimmering round and large, as if astonished.

"Okay, I'm getting a little carried away and too strong in my language so let's take a break. I'm giving you an assignment. Answer these two questions for me. Reuven, did your parents tell you that you can't be Christian because you're Jewish? If so, what does it mean to be Jewish? I'll see you again in three days after school and farm chores are done but before supper. Be prepared to answer those questions at that time, three days from now."

When the time came, Reuven didn't seek Gil; in fact, he had avoided Gil as best as he could during those three days. Gil didn't have to chase him down but he did have to corner him. They sat under the same oak tree, its branches swaying in the breeze, protecting them from the late afternoon sun which shone brightly in a blue cloudless sky.

Gil began by saying, "Okay, what are your answers to my questions?"

Reuven didn't want to make eye contact, as was typical for him. He fidgeted but finally responded, "No, my parents never told me I couldn't be a Christian. We didn't have those kinds of conversations. I don't suppose it ever occurred to them to say such a thing. And I don't know how they'd react if I became a Christian. They might be horrified, or they might just shrug their shoulders. I don't know.

"And, to answer your second question, I suppose to be Jewish means to be different. Nobody ever told me what it means to be Jewish so that's the best I can answer. But I think it means something more than bloodline or nationality."

Gil said, "Those are good answers. And I agree with you—to be Jewish means something more than bloodline or nationality. It's a belief system, which is why it's so important to know what you believe." He had brought with him a worn leather-bound bible and handed it to Reuven.

"Here, use my Bible. Turn to the first book in the newer Scriptures, Matthew, and take a close look at the genealogy in the first chapter. Jesus was in the bloodline of Abraham and David. He was a Hebrew, the same as you. He lived in Israel. He walked, talked and spent His life there. He should not be foreign to either you or your parents or your rabbi. He belongs more to you than He does to me in that regard.

"Ancient rabbis used to teach of two Messiahs. They had trouble reconciling the two because the two were so opposite to each other; however, as they studied Scripture, they saw prophecy of One to come who would suffer—they gave Him the label Messiah, Son of Joseph. They also saw prophecy of One to come who would rule and reign in triumph—they gave Him the label Messiah, Son of David. Are you familiar with Joseph and David?"

"Yes, we studied both during my few years in shul . . . uh, Hebrew school."

"So you know that both suffered before they ruled. The characterizations are memory devices, handles from which to hang a teaching: Joseph was sold into slavery and thrown into prison; David sat on a throne. The rabbis are not ignorant of the fact that Joseph also ruled in Egypt as second in command to Pharaoh or that David was also a fugitive for years, fleeing for his life from King Saul. Remember, these characterizations are not absolute, they're memory devices.

"Many so-called Christians don't know much about Christian doctrine just as many so-called Jews don't know much about Jewish belief, but I like to look at it this way: We have a lot in common. You are looking for the Messiah to come—as am I. The distinction is that you are looking for Him to come while I am looking for Him to come *again*—you for the first time, me for the second time.

"Reuven, for me to talk with you about becoming Christian is to talk with you about becoming more Jewish than you already are. In fact, given my definitions, I don't think you're very Jewish at all right now because it doesn't seem like you understand your heritage or know what you believe.

"I asked you to meet with me again in three days. This is the third day—so here we are.

"I can't go through the whole Bible with you in one sitting obviously, but I can take time with you to study the significance of the phrase *three days* in Scripture. Let's start with the newer Scriptures, then we'll go to the older Scriptures. Since we're thinking about the number 'three,' I'll ask you to look up and read three passages from the newer Scriptures. Use my Bible, turn to Luke 2:41–42 and read those verses."

Reuven already had Gil's Bible open to Matthew, so Gil helped him turn past Mark to the third gospel of Luke and read as instructed. *"Every year Jesus' parents went to Jerusalem for the Feast of the Passover. When He was twelve years old, they went up to the Feast, according to the custom."*

Gil said, "Take note that these Hebrew people, these observant Jews, were obeying Torah teaching. Now skip down to and read verse 46."

Reuven read, *"After three days, they found Him in the temple courts, sitting among the teachers, listening to them and asking them questions."*

"Now turn over two more books and read Acts 9:8–9 then skip to verses 17–19 and read them."

Reuven did as instructed and read,

"Saul got up from the ground, but when he opened his eyes he could see nothing. So they led him by the hand into Damascus. For three days he was blind and did not eat or drink anything . . . Then Ananias went to the house and entered it. Placing his hands on Saul, he said, 'Brother Saul, the Lord—Jesus, who appeared to you on the road as you were coming here—has sent me so that you may see again and be filled with the Holy Spirit.' Immediately, something like scales fell from Saul's eyes, and he could see again. He got up and was baptized, and after taking some food, he regained his strength."

Gil said, "It may be that Saul was immersed in a *mikveh*—a bath used for ritual purification since they were often in Hebrew communities. Be that as it may, turn back to Matthew and read Chapter 16, verse 21."

Reuven went back to the first gospel, the one with the genealogy, and read, *"From that time on Jesus began to explain to His disciples that He must go to Jerusalem and suffer many things at the hands of the elders, chief priests and teachers of the law, and that He must be killed and on the third day be raised to life."*

Gil explained, "The third day is an important theme throughout Scripture, both the older and the newer. And there are actually more references in the older than in the newer. Today, I've selected three for symmetry. You can study further at your leisure if you wish. But for now, turn in your Bible to Genesis 22:4–5 and read those verses. You're no doubt familiar with this Abraham and Isaac portion."

Reuven turned and read, *"On the third day Abraham looked up and saw the place from afar. Then Abraham said to his servants, 'You stay here with the ass. The boy and I will go up there; we will worship and we will return to you.'"*

Gil said, "You understand this refers to the sacrifice of Isaac, that Abraham's obedience also exhibited belief in resurrection. An important side note I'd like to bring to your attention involves the principle of first mention in Scripture. Verse 2 contains the first use of the word *love* in the Bible. Read it, please."

Reuven read, *"And God said, 'Take your son, your favored one, Isaac, whom you love, and go to the land of Moriah, and offer him there as a burnt offering on one of the heights that I will point out to you.'"*

Gil continued, "Now I'll read the word's first occurrence in the newer Scriptures as found in Matthew 3:16–17, *'As soon as Jesus was baptized, He went up out of the water. At that moment heaven was opened, and He saw the Spirit of God descending like a dove and lighting on Him. And a voice from heaven said, "This is My Son, whom I love; with Him I am well pleased."'*

"This trinitarian passage concerns the love of the Father for His Son, just as the Genesis passage you read concerns the love of a father for his son. Mark and Luke, the second and third gospels, use the same language to repeat this incident but allow me to recite John's, the fourth gospel's, first use of the word love. *'For God so loved the world, that He gave His only begotten Son, that whosoever believeth in Him should not perish, but have everlasting life. For God sent not His Son into the world to condemn the world; but that the world through Him might be saved.'* Those, of course, are the famous verses, John 3:16–17.

"The emotional impact of these references, as viewed from the angle of the principle of first mention, is staggering. This is not the love you have for cake and ice cream, the love of country or even the love of a girl and boy but the love of a father for his son. And not just any father, but *the* Father, and not just any son, but *the only begotten* Son. Then we're told that, in spite of that powerful love, both fathers sacrificed their sons—to save us and redeem us from our sins!

"But let's move on. Read Hosea 6:1–2 out of your Bible."

Reuven read, *"Come, let us turn back to the LORD: He attacked, and He can heal us; He wounded, and He can bind us up. In two days He will make us whole again; on the third day He will raise us up, And we shall be whole by His favor."*

Gil said, "For our third and final example, read Jonah Chapter 2, verses 1 and 11."

Reuven read, *"The LORD provided a huge fish to swallow Jonah; and Jonah remained in the fish's belly three days and three nights . . . The LORD commanded the fish, and it spewed Jonah out upon dry land."*

Gil added, "I'll read two passages, again from Matthew's gospel, to illustrate the importance of these Scriptures. First, from Chapter 12, verses 38–40:

'Then some of the Pharisees and teachers of the law said to [Jesus], "Teacher, we want to see a miraculous sign from You."

"He answered, 'A wicked and adulterous generation asks for a miraculous sign! But none will be given it except the sign of the prophet Jonah. For as Jonah was three days and three nights in the belly of a huge fish, so the Son of Man will be three days and three nights in the heart of the earth.'"

Gil then read the second and similar passage from Matthew 16:1–4,

"The Pharisees and Sadducees came to Jesus and tested Him by asking Him to show them a sign from heaven. He replied, 'When evening comes, you say, "It will be fair weather, for the sky is red." And in the morning, "Today it will be stormy, for the sky is red and overcast." You know how to interpret the appearance of the sky, but you cannot interpret the signs of the times. A wicked and adulterous generation looks for a miraculous sign, but none will be given it except the sign of Jonah.' Jesus then left them and went away."

Gil tied all these various references and his side comments together. He said, "Today is your metaphorical third day, Reuven. It is the day of salvation for you. It is the day your Hebrew blood becomes completed as you truly become Jewish. Today is the day you enhance what you were destined to be as one of those chosen by God. You're special to Him. Are my words true?"

"Yes, sir, they are. This is a deep revelation for me. I believe your words."

"Do you want to pray with me or bow before God alone by yourself?"

"If it's okay with you, I would rather be by myself for a while. If you would give my regards to Gail and her kitchen help, I would like to skip supper so I can fast and pray alone with God."

"That's fine. And—Reuven?"

"Yes?"

"Peace be to you. *Shalom.*"

"Thank you. And to you. *Shalom.*"

CHAPTER 24

2006

After gathering for worship, singing and praise in the classroom turned makeshift chapel, Gil stood to preach to the group of boys at a podium he had set up. He was dressed a little more formally than usual in a blazer, white Oxford shirt and black pants, although he wore his signature black leather boots—polished for church, not scuffed for the barn lot.

Gil began by saying, "I asked you to participate with me this morning with what I have chosen to call 'The Phrase Game.' I gave you assignments to prepare for this morning. Your assignments are silly in a way, but not if we understand what we're doing. Let me set our parameters.

"It's always serious when we open our Bibles and break spiritual bread together out of the Book of Life. This is God's Word—not to be taken lightly or trifled with. What I mean when I use the word *silly* is that we will be physically counting words in this particular exercise.

"But we're not going to be doing this exercise in a silly way; quite the opposite, we're going to be very serious. We do, after all, have to be on our guard against pointless nonsense in all areas of life, especially when dealing with God's Word.

"For example, no one knows for sure but some scholars have concluded that Shakespeare was forty-six years old when the King James Version of the Bible was completed and published. It so happens, and I invite you to turn to the King James Version and check it out for yourselves, that the forty-sixth word from the beginning in Psalm 46 in that translation is *shake* and the forty-sixth word from the ending in Psalm 46 in that translation of the Bible is *spear*. Is that profound? Does it mean anything? Of course not! To attribute any depth of meaning to that coincidence of finding *shake-spear* in Psalm 46 at word numbers forty-six when he was forty-six years old is true silliness. And this morning, we are *not* going to engage in that type of silly activity either. So let me explain further.

"None of the Bible's original languages were English so whenever we read the Bible in English, we are reading a translation from its original languages. We have many translations available to us. That's good since none of us are fluent in the Bible's original languages and different translations might give us different nuances of meaning. This is only to say that as we count words in English, our word counts will not correspond to the word counts in the original languages. Our word counts can also vary from one translation to another. But so what? Those variations won't affect the main point of our exercise.

"We are going to be counting down from twelve. After twelve, we shall consider a phrase that has eleven words, and so on and so on. I trust this will be fun as we count down from twelve through eleven and ten all the way to one—and, at the same time, be meaningful and rewarding.

"I asked Carlos to go first—to choose a phrase that is meaningful to him that contains twelve words—exactly twelve words. He will cite its reference and briefly comment on it from his personal perspective. I shall also participate at each word count. I will begin, Carlos will follow."

Gil then began the countdown with his twelve-word choice from the King James translation. "The Bible is filled with beautiful phrases, one of which is found in Psalm 51:1, '. . . *according unto the multitude of Thy tender mercies blot out my transgressions.*' David, the writer of this remorse-filled, guilty confession, had sinned—big time! He had ordered the death of a comrade with whom he had shared refugee status while sitting around campfires so he could steal that very same friend's wife. In other words, David was stealing from a friend who had proven his loyalty during years of hiding together in caves. What a horrible thing to do! He stole a friend's wife, then his life. Under conviction, in agony of soul, he wrote these words I just quoted.

"It goes without saying, but I need to say it anyway, I have also sinned. I know what it's like to make a mess of things.

"Good news; bad news; good news. God is good. He doesn't hold grudges. The bad news is, 'God doesn't forget' but the good news is, 'He can choose not to remember'—if we make true confession of our sin and repent of it.

"In spite of the fact that I'm a sinner; in spite of the fact that God hates sin; in spite of the fact He is holy and cannot tolerate sin in His presence, He loves me and is willing—more than willing, He is eager—to blot out my sins, my transgressions. He is filled with a multitude of tender mercies, not just mercies but 'tender mercies.' Praise His holy name."

Carlos came to the podium next and stood in front of the group. He stood up straight, his black hair combed, his thin lanky brown figure clad in pale green khaki pants and a light blue polo shirt, the best he had. He looked very "Miami Vice."

He cleared his throat, swallowed hard, cleared his throat again and began, "I used the New King James Version of the Bible as my translation and I think many of us did the same. It took me a long time to do this exercise because I would think of some phrase or other but when I counted the words it would usually turn out to be nine or fifteen or some number other than twelve, which frustrated me for a while. I began to wonder how much fun this so-called game was going to be.

"So I was glad when I finally found one that counted up to exactly twelve words. It is Luke 2:19, the whole verse: *But Mary kept all these things and pondered them in her heart.*' Somewhat to my surprise, this ended up being a good exercise for me, and as far as I'm concerned, God led me to the phrase that was perfect for me. It forced me to study God's word and think about it in a way I never had done before. Dare I say that it forced me to 'ponder?'

"I don't have things figured out. Of course I don't. Things have happened to me that took me by surprise or made me angry or confused or made me say, 'Whaaaat? What is this?'

"But I thought about this young girl, Mary, and what happened to her. A lot of people believe she was my age or even younger. She wasn't married. An angel told her she was going to get pregnant without having sex. First off, I've never had an angel appear to me, so if one did, I might jump out of my skin. Next and so far as I know, nobody before or since in the history of the world has ever gotten pregnant without having sex. If this vision had come to me in the middle of the night, I probably would have thought I was having a nightmare instead of a holy vision from God. Yet Mary, this young girl, didn't act like she was scared and it seems like she believed what the angel told her.

"And this wasn't the end of the story—it was just the beginning. In fact, there were a whole bunch more things that happened to her. She *had* to be, she just *had* to be, surprised. Really surprised. But I never read where she got angry, and though she couldn't possibly have understood it, I don't get the idea she was particularly confused or troubled. She trusted. She accepted that God had a plan for her life, and of course, that plan put her in a very special place throughout all the rest of history. Mary somehow kept all these things, all that happened to her, close to her heart and thought about them—she *pondered* them.

"That's a big lesson for me. I don't think I would have found this lesson if I hadn't been forced to look for it by counting words. This verse now means a lot to me. I'm glad I counted twelve words and found this verse. I'll try to keep certain things close to my heart and ponder them more from now on in a personal way in my life."

Gil took his turn with his phrase of eleven words, which had a similar theme to his earlier twelve-word phrase. He said, "Lamentations 3:22 reads, *'It is of the Lord's mercies that we are not consumed.'* Authorship of this short book of Lamentations is commonly attributed to Jeremiah, who is sometimes characterized as the weeping prophet. His is a book filled with, as you might guess, sadness and lamentation. These chapters are elegies.

"In the very center of this book of sadness, we find these words that refer, once again, to God's tender mercies. I am so very grateful that because God is merciful, I can have abundant life and not be consumed with bitterness in this life or in the fires of hell in the life to come. But I selected this phrase for another reason, as well.

"These chapters have been artistically constructed. The Hebrew language has twenty-two letters. Chapter 1 of Lamentations has twenty-two verses. Thus, there is a perfect one-to-one correlation between the number of verses in the chapter and the number of letters in the alphabet. Of course, we can't see it in

English, but each verse of Chapter 1 begins with the succeeding letter of the Hebrew language. In other words, it is an acrostic. To describe it as if it were in English, verse 1 begins with the letter *a* while verse 2 begins with the letter *b* and verse 3 begins with the letter *c*, clear on through to the alphabet's end at the last verse of the chapter. Each of the twenty-two verses is composed in three couplets of two lines each. The level of intricacy and detail in God's word is astounding, at least it is for me.

"But this intricacy doesn't stop with Chapter 1. Chapter 2 is also an acrostic. It has twenty-two verses, each of which begins with the succeeding letter of the Hebrew language. Each of Chapter 2's verses is composed in two couplets of two lines.

"Chapter 3 follows exactly the same pattern as Chapter 1 except it's even more intricate. The three couplets in each verse are themselves arranged as an acrostic such that the pattern is *aaa*, *bbb*, *ccc*, etc. As a result, its layout is Chapter 1's twenty-two verses times its three couplets for a total of sixty-six verses. You can look that up in a Hebrew Bible and see the arrangement for yourselves. You won't be able to read it but you'll be able to notice the three-fold repetition of the first letters. Reuven should be able to read it but you don't have to be able to read the Hebrew language to see this three-fold repetition.

"And all the verses make sense. And the over-all message of the Book of Lamentations makes sense. I couldn't do something like that if I tried during a month of Sundays. God's Word is awesome in every way, not only in its obvious, surface message but also in the intricacy of its hidden patterns." A murmur of appreciation went through most of the students as they shook their heads in awe of this profound pattern.

The next student, Julio, came forward. He began, "I chose Job 1:21, *'Naked I came from my mother's womb, naked shall I return.'* That's eleven words. So what? They don't mean nothin' to me 'cept I was born poor an' I'll die poor. So why try? What's the point of anything. I started with nothin', came from nothin' and I'll end with nothin'. That's what *I* got to look forward to—nothin'. Your own Bible says so right here. So there you go. I did what you told me to do. We good?" The young Latino gazed over at Gil with disdain and anger glittering in his dark eyes, which Gil understood was also partly empty bravado.

"No, Julio, not quite. You found eleven words but you missed the point of those eleven words. You spoke of a point, yet you completely missed the point. You're expressing nihilism, Job isn't. By the way, do you know what nihilism is?"

"You tell me. I'm sure you know all about it." Julio crossed his skinny brown arms in open defiance.

"I believe I shall. In spite of your lousy attitude, you might accidentally learn something. Nihilism views life as hopeless and meaningless. I don't agree with such a worldview nor does Job draw such a conclusion. Apparently, you do since you echo Macbeth's famous words that your life is 'a tale told by an idiot, full of sound and fury, signifying nothing.' You need to read some more and ponder what you read, as Carlos did.

"Job was not cursing God. Despite extreme loss, he was expressing complete reliance and total trust in God. He expressed hope for a future resurrection. Do you still have your Bible with you?"

"Yeah, shur."

"Listen to what Job, this same Job you say has no hope, says about his hope. Turn over a few pages to Chapter 19, verses 25 and 26. Read them for us and take note that Chapter 19 comes after Chapter 1."

"Well, duh, I guess I get that." Gil noticed some of the boys flinch at Julio's blatant sarcasm and disrespect but he ignored it for the time being. Julio reluctantly read the passage as instructed because he knew that the alternative would be jail time for him. "'*For I know that my Redeemer lives, And He shall stand at last on the earth; And after my skin is destroyed, this I know, that in my flesh I shall see God.*'"

"Job spoke these words after he had said he was born naked and would die naked. His first statement was spoken in the sadness of extreme loss but his second statement showed he had hope. Now, Julio, read aloud for me Matthew 6, verses 19–21, then verse 24. Use the Table of Contents to find it if you need to."

"Yeah, you're the boss." Then more quietly but still defiantly, "Whatever you say, Boss.

'*Do not lay up for yourselves treasures on earth, where moth and rust destroy and where thieves break in and steal; but lay up for yourselves treasures in heaven, where neither moth nor rust destroys and where thieves do not break in and steal. For where your treasure is, there your heart will be also . . . No one can serve two masters; for either he will hate the one and love the other, or else he will be loyal to the one and despise the other. You cannot serve God and mammon.'"*

"Thank you, Julio. Despite Job going through greater loss than you can imagine, he believed in life after death, or life after life, as one author cleverly put it. And Jesus always had two kingdoms in mind. He spoke here of two treasuries, two perspectives and two masters of two kingdoms. Each of these couplets presents two options that demand one choice. Many people—like yourself, I suspect—see the negative but miss the positive. They think Jesus is against success and the storing up of treasures when, in fact, He commanded us to store them up but to do it in the right way and put those treasures in the right place.

"Money won't stand the test of time, things won't stand the test of time. Even if they escape rust and thieves, they cannot escape the coming fire of God that will consume all material objects. The focus of these four verses isn't renunciation of earthly treasures but accumulation of heavenly treasures. Worldly wealth here will *definitely* be lost; heavenly wealth there will just as *definitely* be retained. Jesus doesn't speculate. Either things leave us while we live here on Earth or we leave them when we die. He knows and He speaks of certainties with the authority of one who has been in heaven in the Father's presence. Every day the person whose treasure is on earth is headed *away* from it but every day the person whose treasure is in heaven is headed *toward* it."

Julio glared at his feet, grimacing. He wanted to just tune Gil out but it was hard, standing in front of his peer group as he was.

"Julio, look at me when I'm talking to you. Don't stare down at the ground and scuff your boots on the floor. I don't like this passive-aggressive business. Put on your big-boy pants and suck it up!"

Gil approached the podium to Julio's side, leaned in a bit and got in his face so they were staring eyeball to eyeball barely a foot apart from each other. To the boys, it looked like it was going to be a fight for sure but Gil said quietly, almost in a whisper, "Julio, I'm not angry with you. You fancy yourself to be a smart guy. So wise up. There are treasures in heaven that are worth far more than a few bucks in your pocket or a gold chain around your neck today."

Gil then backed off and turned to face the group. "Here's a brief history lesson for all of you. Alfred Nobel was a Swedish chemist who made his fortune by inventing dynamite and other powerful explosives that governments bought to produce weapons of war. When his brother, Ludvig, died, a French newspaper accidentally printed Alfred's obituary instead of Ludvig's. Alfred was described as a man who became rich by enabling people to kill each other in unprecedented quantities. Reading his own obituary shook Alfred to his core. He didn't like what he read. He didn't want to be remembered that way.

"Alfred Nobel got a second chance. He changed his legacy. He invested nine million dollars to reward special accomplishments that benefitted humanity, including what we now know as the Nobel Peace Prize. Each of you also has a second chance. Your second chance is right here, right now. Julio, I'll be talking with you further about it, but for now, read Colossians Chapter 3, verse 2 out loud for me."

Julio stood straighter. His tone had lost its edge. "Yes, sir. *'Set your minds on things above, not on things on the earth.'*"

"Julio, God doesn't owe you anything, not a thing. But in His mercy and love for you, He offers an incentive, an investment guaranteed to pay off. He offers rewards with big dividends in the future or punishments that 'don't get no satisfaction' as the old Rolling Stones song says—heaven instead of hell, fulfillment instead of torment.

"I have faith you'll make the smart choice. And, Carlos, you might note that this verse, Colossians 3:2, has twelve words so there's something else for you to ponder."

Several of the boys were uncomfortable because of this confrontation, some were staring out the window at the horses wishing they were outside with them, others were looking sideways at Julio hoping he wouldn't say anything else and Ali was so nervous his knees were jiggling. He held up his hand and asked to be excused to use the restroom. Gil nodded his head and said, "Good idea. Let's take five."

CHAPTER 25

2006

Upon reconvening, Gil moved to the next step in The Phrase Game and recited the very first ten words of Scripture, Genesis 1:1, *'In the beginning God created the heavens and the earth.'* He said, "I attended church three times a week during my growing-up years on a small farm in Iowa and I continued that habit during college. I was taught to accept the Bible as God's Word. Let me just say that if you believe the first page of the Bible, you will have no trouble believing every other page of Scripture. As you get older, you'll study in greater depth, but for now, remember that God is our Creator."

"Carlos, let's lighten the mood. Will you come back to the microphone, please. I don't want to put you on the spot but here's a question especially for you. Does God have a favorite sport?"

Of course, Carlos looked nonplussed and everyone knew Gil had, in fact, deliberately put him on the spot for some reason. Carlos figured it must be some sort of joke so he played along and came up to the podium. "I don't know. Does God have a favorite sport?"

"Yes, baseball. I thought you'd be glad to know since it's your favorite sport. Look right here, the very first words God recorded for us in the Bible are *'in the big inning . . .'"* The boys laughed aloud, jabbing each other. Gil knew they were bonding despite their differences and said a quick prayer of thanks for the humorous inspiration.

"But seriously, you'll be coming into baseball season soon. As the batter steps into the box, he hopes to get a hit and not strike out. If a runner is on first base and tries to steal second, he hopes the umpire won't jerk his thumb and holler, 'You're *outta* here!' but, rather, will sweep his hands down and call, 'He's *in* there!' In junior high school, nearly all children hope to be part of the *in* crowd and not cast *out* as an object of ridicule. Soldiers are trained to march *in* step but they get hit over the head by the Drill Sergeant if they're *out* of step. During winters here in Montana, before our first snowfall, it's cold and dark *out*side but warm and light *in*side. I pray each of you young men come to be *in*cluded in God's family."

"Farzad, I asked you to find a good ten-word phrase so why don't you come up now and tell us what you found. So far as I know, you didn't play baseball in Iran but I'm sure Carlos can explain my little joke and play on words to you later if you'd like."

Farzad was the youngest one in the group. He was also a serious, quiet-spoken student who had suffered persecution, so he surprised everyone when he began in his halting English, "I have a joke, too. Who is the shortest man in the Bible?"

Gil looked out at the other students, smiled, then said, "I don't know. Who is the shortest man in the Bible?"

Farzad said, "I used to think it was Zacchaeus because the song the missionaries taught me says, he 'was a wee little man, a wee little man was he.' And the Bible says he climbed a tree so he could see over the crowd. So he must have been short, right? But then I came across 'Knee-High-my-ah' so *he's* got to be the shortest man in the Bible." Farzad smiled shyly.

"With that intro, I bet you found your ten-word phrase in the book of Nehemiah. Am I right?"

"Yes, sir. 'Knee-High-my-ah' 1:11 says, *'Let your servant prosper this day . . . and grant him mercy.'* Nehemiah was sad because he was a captive in a foreign land. He was a servant in the king's palace. The king noticed his sadness. Sadness couldn't have been his typical demeanor since the king noticed it. It had to be unusual. So Nehemiah told the king what was making him sad. Then he took a big risk and asked if he could visit his homeland. The king didn't cut his head off. The king granted permission to Nehemiah to lead a group back to Judah and rebuild Jerusalem. It was a miracle. The task was tough but the point is that God answered prayer—He prospered Nehemiah—he extended the royal scepter to him and granted mercy to him.

"I like this because it's an example of God answering prayer and of what can happen when He does. In closing, I've heard the joke, 'Be careful what you wish for because you might get it.' I don't mean to say that prayer is wishful thinking; I mean to say that God heard Nehemiah's prayer, granted him prosperity and showed mercy to him. Nehemiah got what he wished for."

Gil said, "Thank you, Farzad, for reminding us there is power in prayer. Julio, come back to the microphone with your Bible, please. Earlier, you read from the book of Job. Go back to it and read Job 2, verse 11 out loud for us."

"Okay," Julio said, returning to the microphone.

'Now when Job's three friends heard of all this adversity that had come upon him, each one came from his own place—Eliphaz the Temanite, Bildad the Shuhite, and Zophar the Naamathite. For they had made an appointment together to come and mourn with him, and to comfort him.'

"Thank you. Now, who do you think is the shortest man in the Bible, and do you think you can tell Farzad why you think Bildad is shorter than Nehemiah?"

"Well, now that you put it that way, 'Shoe Height' is shorter than 'Knee High.'" Julio had to laugh in spite of himself and his generally angry attitude lifted a bit. "Farzad, you and I are being taught new things today—we don't always have to be super-serious when we read the Bible. Point taken, Mr. Webster. I get it."

"Good, I'm glad. The devil has a plan for the lives of all of you. So does God. John Chapter 10, verse 10 records these words of Jesus, *'The thief does not come except to steal, and to kill, and to destroy. I have come that they may have life, and that they may have it more abundantly.'* Do you see the devil's plan? It's to steal from you, to kill you, and finally to destroy you totally. There's nothing good in or about the devil. Do you see God's plan? It's to blow fresh air into your chests so you can throw your shoulders back, breathe deeply and enjoy abundant life. There's nothing bad in or about God. The devil wants only bad things for you; God wants only good things for you."

Gil resumed the countdown, "I alluded to the truth of God as creator in my ten-word phrase. Now I would like to continue and expand the discussion of truth with four separate yet linked nine-word phrases. The first two are found in the famous verse John 14:6, *'I am the way, the truth, and the life. No man comes to the Father except through Me.'* Jesus Himself is truth, and in fact, John 18:37 declares that He came to 'testify to the truth.'

"Second Thessalonians 2:10–11 says many rejected His message since *'they did not receive the love of the truth.'* Some might shrug their shoulders and ask, 'So what?' But like it or not, decisions have consequences so *'for this reason God will send them strong delusion.'* For all who fail to recognize truth, who reject 'the truth,' delusion is their lot. Death is presumably far over the future's horizon for you young men but the inexorable fact of life is that every year each one of you will grow one year older. You won't stay young forever. Do you want to wake up someday at the end of your life only to realize you had wasted your life in a big delusion? I don't think so! No reasonable person would opt for that choice."

Gil called on Jim Bob, who strode up to the podium, his tobacco-stained teeth showing in his handsome, sun-tanned face as he grinned widely. "My choice is also a well-known nine-word phrase, perhaps the most well-known of all nine-word scriptural phrases. It's recited on many occasions, including funerals—even my own mother's funeral. The twenty-third Psalm begins with it: *'The Lord is my shepherd; I shall not want.'* And by the way, you brought up the subject of baseball, which is often described as America's sport. But I'm not so sure about that claim. I grew up in Oklahoma and a lot of us Okies think football's at the top of the list. And we know for a fact God has His favorite football team." Jim Bob flexed his muscles for emphasis.

"Good to know God likes football as well as baseball," Gil said. "I'll venture to guess his favorite football team is from somewhere in Oklahoma?"

"How did you know? God's favorite team is Oklahoma State. He's an excellent judge of quality, if I say so m'self. Oklahoma State had, among other things, probably the best tandem of running backs in the history of college football. For their 1986 and '87 seasons, they had Barry Sanders and Thurman Thomas. Both are now in the Pro Football Hall of Fame, Sanders with the Detroit Lions and Thomas with the Buffalo Bills. Thomas helped lead the Bills to four

Ali was Afghani and the smallest of the boys. He knew little of American history or Christian doctrine. He came forward and said, "My eight-word phrase is Psalm 96:9, *'worship the Lord in the beauty of holiness.'* I'm not sure exactly what to make of these words but there are eight of them. They tell me to worship God but not how to do it. I try but sometimes I worry I'm not doing it right."

Gil helped Ali by saying, "Let me talk for a minute about American history and Christian doctrine. Over two hundred years ago, when the United States was a nation in its infancy, a preacher and theologian named Jonathan Edwards wrote that beauty was maybe God's primary characteristic. Since then, others who have studied long and hard about God have written that perhaps holiness is His main characteristic. Who knows? But it's interesting because in certain ways, those two traits, beauty and holiness, are opposites of each other.

"Hebrews 12: 29 says *'our God is a consuming fire.'* A result of God's being totally holy is that He cannot allow unholy things to exist or profane people to stand in His presence. Ali, do you agree with me that you are not totally holy?"

"Oh, yes."

"So you would be consumed in the fire of His holiness if you tried to stand in His presence. How does that statement make you feel?"

"Frightened. Like running away. I don't want to get burned up."

"Exactly. Being burned by fire is one of the most painful things a human being can endure. And those who have been burned are scarred for life. But on the other hand, how do feel about beauty and beautiful things—flowers, horses, girls?"

"Well, I'm scared of our big horses—I'm more comfortable collecting eggs with Maisie from our chickens. I'm a little fascinated by girls." He gave a shy smile, "So far, I haven't run away from them."

"I understand. Girls can be scarier than our big horses. We all feel that way at one time or another. I'm not so old that I've forgotten those feelings. How about flowers, how do you feel about them?"

"I'm not afraid of them. Flowers won't hurt me—except some have thorns. They're pretty. I like to look at their colors. I've seen beautiful fields of bright yellow plants here in Montana. And some flowers smell really, really good."

"There you go. So you see, a consuming fire makes us want to run away from it while beauty makes us want to run closer to it. Is that fair to say?"

"Yes, I guess so. Both have their fascinations—but in opposite directions, as you said."

"Again, bingo. We'll speak more in future days and you'll learn more about God, but for now, let's say that God is fascinating. When we think about Him, some of our thoughts make us want to go 'hands off, stay away' while some of our thoughts make us want to go 'hands on, get close.' Both of those conflicting emotions are involved in worship and we need to recognize and honor both of them in our worship. God is both beautiful *and* holy. That's thought provoking. You made a good choice with your eight-word phrase. Good job, Ali."

Gil continued, "A book title from the 1960s is *Through Gates of Splendor*. Speaking that phrase—just by itself—can move me to tears. I recommend the book to you if you haven't read it. A seven-word phrase found in Hebrews 11:38 is kindred to it in poignant sentiment—'. . . *of whom the world was not worthy.*' Simply speaking it moves me toward tears.

"Hebrews 11 is known as the faith chapter in the Bible. After it speaks of heroes of the Christian faith like Noah, Abraham, Moses and David, it closes with reference to unnamed people who wandered homeless from cave to cave, clothed in goatskins, who were sawn asunder, stoned to death, slain with the sword. These died destitute. And these are they 'of whom the world was not worthy.' I want to weep for them—but I'm also inspired by their examples. I hope I can live my life in such a way that it can someday be said of me that I was better than this world, that I lived above it on a higher plain, that I loved and lived for God above all else, that I was in this world but not of it. And I pray that for each one of you, as well.

"Jason, you and others here know what it's like to be practically homeless, dirt poor. Please, come and share with us the results of your search."

Jason, like a couple others of the boys, was all knees and elbows. He was shy and had curly hair that was sometimes a tangled mess. He didn't square his shoulders or stand as straight or tall as he could have. He tended to hold his head down. In beginning, he admitted, "I am not a deep thinker. I'm not so good with words. I've always been poor because my West Virginia parents have been poor their whole lives. I mean, they don't hardly have no money a'tall.

"But I remember when I didn't know I was poor. Now—I knew when I was hungry. We didn't always have enough food to eat but neither did any other miner or tobacco sharecropper. None of us kids knew any different. We all dressed raggedy—pretty much the same. In a way, I was happier then. I'd kinda like to get back to feelin' that way—I mean, without feelin' hungry all the time.

"But God meets me at the point of my need. I have doubts—sometimes. I need reassurance—often. Soon enough, the time came when I knew I was poor." It took courage for Jason to continue with his personal story. "I got angry about it. I'm glad God sought me out when I was a lost sheep who wandered from the flock and was in danger of falling off a cliff in the darkness. Lost and lonely, that was me. But Jesus looked for me, found me, rescued me—bought me back at a price like you just said, Mr. Webster. He redeemed me. I'm still poor but I'm not so angry anymore.

"I take comfort that God knows my name and breathes His life into the events of my daily life in a personal, intimate way. So my seven words are found in Second Timothy 2:19, '. . . *the Lord knows them that are His.'* He knows who I am and what's in my heart. That's enough for me. That and some of these other wonderful phrases my friends selected like, *'The Lord is my shepherd, I shall not want.'*

"And I don't. I don't lack anything. I don't mean to brag but I'm satisfied that God knows my name. That's a lot. It's enough."

"Thank you, Jason. You have spoken of assurance. Assurance is a wonderful gift from God. He gives us the Holy Spirit who communicates with our spirits the assurance that God *'knows them that are His.'*

"Let me tell you the true story of Fannie J. Crosby who was born in New York a long time ago, in 1820. As a baby, she had an eye infection that a doctor treated improperly. Scars formed on and covered over her eyes such that she became blind for life. A few months later, her father got sick and died. Mercy Crosby, widowed at the young age of twenty-one, hired herself out as a maid while grandmother Eunice Crosby cared for little Fannie.

"Grandmother shouldered Fannie's education and became the girl's eyes, describing for her in vivid detail the physical world around her. Grandmother's careful teaching helped develop Fannie's descriptive abilities. But Grandmother also nurtured Fannie's spirit. She read and carefully explained the Bible to her and she always emphasized prayer's importance. When Fannie got depressed because she couldn't learn or see as other children did, Grandmother taught her to pray for special knowledge.

"When Fannie was fourteen, she learned of the New York Institute for the Blind and believed this was the answer to her prayers for additional education. She enrolled, graduated and stayed to teach there twenty-three years. She became something of a celebrity at the school and wrote poems for many different occasions.

"On March 5, 1858, just before her thirty-eighth birthday, Fannie married Alexander van Alstine, a former pupil at the Institute and one of the finest organists in the New York City area. One evening, Fannie's friend and composer Phoebe Palmer Knapp was visiting and played a tune for her on the piano. She asked Fannie what it sounded like. Fannie responded, 'Blessed assurance, Jesus is mine!' She then continued to sing the song and write those lyrics on the spot. Of course, that is the old hymn by the same title. It is still well known and sung in many places. I invite you to look it up in an old hymn book we might have laying around.

"Fanny went on to live a long life, dying in 1915 at ninety-five years of age. In her lifetime, she wrote more than eight thousand hymns and song lyrics. Jason, let Fanny's story inspire you as you give thanks to God for the blessed assurance that either is or can be yours."

Gil continued. "My six-word phrase is meant to encourage each of you young men who have potential to grow and excel in many ways: '. . . for such a time as this.' It's found in Esther 4:14 as Uncle Mordecai challenges his niece to accept a dangerous task, one that puts her life in danger. Read the story for yourselves. Suffice it to say, Esther accepted the challenge and rose to it. It was a watershed moment in her life, a time that defined the rest of her life, one that shaped her mind and thinking forever. We can't always recognize those critical times but sometimes we can, sometimes we know when one minute of insane courage is required of us. Esther seized her opportunity, albeit with trembling hands, and in so doing saved her people and gave them a lasting spiritual heritage. History sometimes turns on a dime and that dime is a defining decision for us. Be wise. Be discerning. *Carpe diem!* Seize the day that God intends to be your defining moment in time.

"We instructors here at the ranch do not agree with the paths some of you are stumbling down but we're pulling a better future out of you, by God's grace and with His help. It is *not* a foregone conclusion that you will grow up only to wear out Lazy Boy recliners on TV-soaked afternoons as you waste your lives in indolence and depravity. You can do and be better than that! Follow the scriptural example revealed to us time after time.

"Our job here, among other things, is to give you guidance and point you in the right direction. God gives to each of us talent and ability—some for one thing, some for another. First of all, He calls each of you to become His child. He wants to adopt you into His royal family. He is not willing that any should perish. Then, after adoption, to each of His children He provides 'hope and a future.' You need to prepare yourselves now for that future so when it knocks on your door you will be ready to answer the call and meet the challenge. Esther answered her call. She saved herself *and* her people from annihilation. She was in the right place at the right time to rise to her challenge. May it be so for you, as well."

Reuven came to the microphone next and said a bit sheepishly and timidly after Gil's oratory, "My six-word phrase is *'Blessed are the poor in spirit'* from Matthew 5:3. I didn't know what those words meant since I don't read your Bible. I studied what others said about them in some of the commentaries we have in our library here. It turns out that *poor* doesn't mean what I thought, at least in this verse and context. It means a person who doesn't think he's better than me, someone who doesn't want to kill me because I'm Jewish—excuse me, because I'm Hebrew; it means a humble man who knows he doesn't have anything to brag about when he compares himself to God."

Gil broke in, "It doesn't have anything to do with money, does it?"

"No, sir, it doesn't. If a guy's poor in the pocketbook he might have a hang-dog attitude but that's not what Jesus is speaking of nor is it the way He's saying we should act. This humble guy, who's poor in spirit, knows where he stands with God so he's not depressed or ashamed and can go around looking people in the eye with his head held high. He knows his spirit's more important than his pocketbook. He's blessed and he knows he's blessed. That's pretty cool."

He continued, "I'd like to be like this guy, blessed as he knows he is—ready to seize the day like you said, ready to do something and be somebody. Ready not only to be a child of God but also to have a personal relationship with Him."

Gil told Reuven it was possible, that he knew how it could be done. He reminded him of his phrase, though, that to be one of God's own, to be His child, meant walking in humility and being poor in spirit.

Then Gil moved on to the next phrase in the countdown, "My five-word phrase is *'Even so, come, Lord Jesus.'* That's found in the very back of the Bible at Revelation 22:20.

"A popular theme in movies is cataclysmic tragedy, be it hurricane, earthquake or ice age, atomic bomb blasts or tsunami waves. And such themes are not far-fetched because biblical prophecy contains images like the four horsemen of the apocalypse, who ride in on their horses bearing war, famine, disease and death with them. When I presented my seven-word phrase, *'. . . of whom the world was not worthy,'* I said it referenced unnamed, unknown people who wandered homeless from cave to cave, clothed in goatskins, who were sawn asunder, stoned to death, slain with the sword. Sadly, history is replete with gruesome examples like these of 'man's inhumanity to man,' and our own experiences teach us that self-same sad fact early in our lives.

"But the emphasis here is that the new earth and the new heaven are so wonderful, their glories so magnificent that we say, 'all the bad things pale and fade away in light of these good things that are promised in the world to come.'

"Scoffers like to scoff. That's what they do. They say, as they're poking fun at Christians, '. . . pie in the sky in the sweet by-and-by.' That's okay. Maybe the scoffers are jealous because they can't see good on the other side of bad. The fact is that things *are* going to get better for us. Now there are illnesses, accidents and tragedies that can kill us, yet Second Corinthians 4:17 describes them as *'light and momentary troubles [that] are achieving for us an eternal weight of glory that far outweighs them all.'*

"In the new earth and the new heaven, death will be no more. There won't be any more sorrow or sighing or sadness or tears or pain or suffering. Satan and his minions will be banished. Then the saints will behold God's glory and there shall be no need of the sun because of the strength and the brightness and the radiance of His glory. In short, there is so much to look forward to, that in spite of bad things that block our paths now and sometimes cause us to stumble, the day is fast approaching when all His saints shall proclaim, *'Come, Lord Jesus. Even so, come, Lord Jesus.'* Amen and amen!"

Gil continued, "Terry, come up and surprise us with your selection."

Terry walked up to the podium, head bowed. He was a serious student, some would say he was nerdy with his glasses, pale skin and bowl haircut. But he was intelligent and really good around animals. "My five-word phrase is *'Here am I! Send me'* from Isaiah 6:8.

"I wasn't born yet so I didn't experience the shock of the massacre of five missionaries by Auca Indians in Ecuador in 1956 but I remember my grandparents and others across West Texas telling me of their being shocked and stunned by it. Mr. Webster, you mentioned the book title *Through Gates of Splendor.* As I'm sure you know, that book was written by one of the widows, Elisabeth Elliot, of one of those five murdered missionaries, Jim Elliot. I've read it more than once, and like you, I recommend the book. It's not a real big book but it's a good one.

"The five reasons I chose this phrase are as follows," Terry said, reading each by number.

"One, it has five words. Two, my grandparents gave me what might be described as my going-away present before relocating me from the rodeo arena to here in Montana by taking me to see the movie *End of the Spear* during this last Christmas season. At the same time, watching that film updated their experience and memory of those murders. The movie continues the plot begun in the book *Through Gates of Splendor.*

"I was overwhelmed by the story told in the movie. Another of the five murdered missionaries was Nate Saint, the pilot for the group. He left a young son behind named Steve. Steve grew up to follow in his father's footsteps as a pilot and missionary to the same native Ecuadorian people. The movie tells the story of the relationship that has grown between Steve Saint and one of the now-elderly natives who killed his father, who actually took part in the doing of the deed. Unbelievable! It's an emotional story of forgiveness.

"Three: Revival broke out among those native Indians, but to my surprise, it didn't come about because of guilt over the murders. A widow of one of the murdered missionaries and a sister of another not only stayed in Ecuador—they also left the safety of their compound to go into the jungle and live with those very same primitive 'savages' who committed the murders, who, in cold blood, killed the husband of one and the brother of the other. These two brave women, by their actions, lit the spark for a revival's blaze to burn in that jungle. It's still there.

"Four: Another of the five murdered missionaries, Roger Youderian, was from Montana. He had been born and raised in Lewistown, which in Montana terms, is not far from where we're standing right now. I can't help but *ponder* God's hand in this.

"Five, and finally, the most important reason I selected this phrase, is that due to this set of circumstances, I am called to the mission field and have spoken Isaiah's words for myself. His words have become my words and so I say again, as I stand before God and hear Him ask, 'Who will go?' that I reply, *'Here am I! Send me.'*

Terry pulled a folded loose-leaf paper out of his jeans' pocket. "I'll close with a quote from a Christmas letter written by Nate Saint shortly before he was killed as he prepared for Operation Auca,

'. . . may we who know Christ hear the cry of the damned as they hurtle headlong into the Christless night without ever a chance. May we be moved with compassion as our Lord was. May we shed tears of repentance for those whom we failed to bring out of darkness . . . May God give us a new vision of His will concerning the Lost and our responsibility.'"

Gil was really proud of Terry but didn't want to embarrass him in a non-manly way so he refrained from hugging him and instead gave him a thumbs-up sign, then continued his line of thought. "It was fairly common in those days for missionaries to take their caskets with them to remote outposts because they knew they might need them and not return home. Their service often involved ultimate sacrifice—as in your jungle example, Terry."

Then Gil said, "My four-word phrase is *'Mercy triumphs over judgment.'* That's found in James 2:13. Though unplanned, the mercy of God is a theme that has emerged in this phrase game. You and I have presented and discussed several important theological doctrines once during the course of this game. Two examples: God is creator; He is redeemer. These doctrines mean we belong to God twice—once because He made us and again because He bought us by paying a high price. Examples of two other significant doctrines we have chosen are that God is holy but we can have assurance of salvation. We learned that holiness can be something of a scary thing but assurance is a comforting concept.

"But mercy has been mentioned over and over again. R. G. Lee, a famous preacher from years gone by, is known for the phrase, 'Pay day, some day.' That hints at both rewards and punishments; it speaks of a judgment day out there in the future for all of us. That could be another scary thought except we are here told that His mercy triumphs over His judgment. What a comforting promise! Yet I don't want to minimize the importance and seriousness of judgment; indeed, our gospel of mercy flows through judgment.

"Now, Johnny Ray, it's your turn to continue our count-down. Come up to the microphone, read your selection to us and say a few words about it."

Johnny Ray stood up, came forward and said, "My four-word phrase is *'Flee also youthful lusts.'"* The other boys snickered out loud and Julio actually threw a paper spit-wad at him. But Johnny Ray was brave as well as big so he persevered and said, "I know that sounds funny for a young man to say. I'm not a Bible scholar but Second Timothy 2:22 has exactly those words.

"I've heard tell that Scripture almost never tells us to run away from anything," Johnny Ray said, standing tall. "For example, David didn't run away from Goliath, he ran *toward* him and cut his head off. And Jesus didn't run away from the cross on Golgotha but He 'set his face like flint' to go up to Jerusalem. He pressed on and didn't flinch, though He made it clear He knew exactly the pain and agony of what was going to happen to Him there. And if you little fellas think I'm gonna run away from you we'll go out behind the woodshed and discuss it later. I'm not in the habit of tuckin' tail and neither was Jesus.

"So there must be something exceptional about young men and lust. A scriptural example that comes to mind is Joseph's running away from his master's wife when she tried to seduce him. Like Jim Bob said, I'm a simple guy and haven't had a lot of education but I don't have to be the brightest light bulb in the room to understand what it means when my parents tell me not to cross the busy street without looking both ways or not to touch a hot stove with my bare hands. I think this must be the same sort of a deal with sex and young men. Just like busy streets and hot stoves can be good in their place, they can also run you over and burn you bad.

"Here's the reason why I chose a phrase telling me to run away from lust. I grew up hunting and know that if I want to shoot a doe I can go out 'most any time and they'll behave the same way but if I want to shoot the big buck I have to catch him in rut when he's only got one thing on his mind and can't see straight or think about anything else other than that one thing. In other words, bucks go crazy certain times of the year and are apt to get killed during those times.

"There's a difference 'tween girls and boys the same as there's a difference 'tween does and bucks. I heard somebody say once, 'God invented sex so it has to be good.' Okay. That sounds right. But this four-word phrase tells me sex needs to be in the right place at the right time in the right way. Until I'm old enough to handle it in the right way I need to stay away from it—even if I have to run away from it."

"Thank you, Johnny Ray," Gil said. "You're wise. Simple commands are easy for any of us to understand. Since God is good and since He is filled with 'tender mercies,' we know it's for our own good if He tells us to stay away from something for a while. Of course, knowing and doing are two different things. That particular temptation is so big that it's better not to try to face it down but to run away from it.

"My three-word phrase is *'Remember Lot's wife.'* That's found in Luke 17:32. The narrative of Abraham, his nephew Lot and the destruction of Sodom and Gomorrah is found in the first book of the Bible, Genesis. Only Lot, his wife and his two unmarried daughters escaped that destruction. And they escaped only 'by the skin of their teeth.' The angels told them to hurry and not look back. Lot's wife disobeyed, looked back and was turned into a pillar of salt.

"Jesus used this narrative millennia later to remind his listeners of an important message. It's clear: do what you're told or pay the price, sometimes a heavy price. Sometimes the cost is your life if you disobey. Johnny Ray, this is why I said you were wise in your conclusion that you can't touch the hot stove and not get burned.

"Tomas, come on up and tell us your phrase."

"Yes, sir." He didn't mean anything by it but he approached the podium with obvious Los Angeles gang swagger.

Gil couldn't help but think, *Some people provoke a fight having no idea they did anything to provoke it. This poor kid might get shot someday just for walking down the street the way he does. And he's not a bad kid. He's not belligerent like Julio but a lot of people would think he was.*

Tomas said, "My three-word phrase is *'Seek My face'* from Psalm 27:8. All I did was search out a self-contained short phrase. But as I've listened to these other phrases, it dawned on me that my phrase fills a void. So I wonder if God may have guided my search without my being aware of it.

"I think most of the phrases presented here today have been comments on God's attributes and characteristics. Mr. Webster, you pointed out that several commented on God's mercy and you also described Him as Creator. Jason reassured us that God knows those who are His and Jim Bob reminded us the Lord is our shepherd so we don't need to worry. But my phrase requires positive action from us. Johnny Ray's phrase, for instance, requires action but of a negative sort: run away. So I think mine is unique: it tells us we have responsibility and must do more than sit back to relax while God does all the work. None of us boys are world-famous theologians, but as you've pointed out, we don't have to be to understand the Bible and what it tells us to do.

"The Bible tells me that I need salvation, that I can't save myself, that only God can accomplish His redemptive work of salvation in my heart. But having said that, I'm not a bump on a log and I have to seek His face. I must choose to love Him—or not; I must choose to embrace His grace—or not; I must choose to say 'Yes!' to Him—or not; I must choose to follow Him—or go my own way. I've got things to do, stuff I hafta do.

"My sister painted a picture for me that I brought along with me when I moved here. It's normally hanging in my room but I brought it over for this exercise today because it illustrates the emotion, from her point of view, of the phrase I chose. The words she wrote on it are from Isaiah 58: 9, '*Then you shall call and the Lord will answer; You shall cry and He will say, "Here I am."*' It may be that if we don't call, He won't answer—if we don't seek His face, He won't be found by us.

"So I need to call out, I need to cry out, I need to seek His face. I need to do those things."

"Well done, Tomas," Gil said. "God guided you in your search and therein lies a lesson for each of us. We might hear His voice boom down to us from heaven someday as the Apostle Paul did; it's possible we might call down fire from heaven as did Elijah the prophet long ago; we might see Jesus in transfigured glory as it was given Peter, James and John to behold—but it's more likely we shall hear Him in a much quieter way as we study the Bible. And there is evidence in each of our lives, I bet, that He has led us without our being aware of it at the time. Just like happened with you, Tomas. And while we're at it, turn to Saint Peter's last recorded words in Scripture and read them for us. You'll find them in Second Peter at Chapter 3 and verse 18."

"Okay, give me a second. Here it is. *'But grow in the grace and knowledge of our Lord and Savior Jesus Christ.'*"

"That makes your point," Gil said. "You're not permitted to be a bump on a log. You are told to seek His face. You're commanded to 'grow' in His grace and knowledge, aren't you?"

"Yes, sir, I am."

"Here's a humorous saying from Thomas Edison that fits right in with your verse, Tomas. 'Everything comes to him who hustles while he waits.' Edison was a famous inventor who invented things like the incandescent light bulb by working hard, having loads of determination and hustling while he waited."

Gil then cleared his throat to make a special announcement.

"And now, men, we're privileged to have a special guest with us. You've met our animal vet and some of you have worked alongside him during his visits with us here on the ranch. He asked to be included in this fun exercise and I was happy to oblige him. So—Dr. Liu, come take your turn. Since you're last, you'll be their favorite speaker today." Gil warmly shook his friend's hand as he reached the front of the classroom.

Sing had entered the room sometime earlier and stood behind the group unnoticed until now. His shirt sleeves were pulled up and he was a bit disheveled because he'd just finished wrestling a steer on a neighbor's ranch. He had intended to be there sooner but he couldn't always control his schedule. He took off his hat and chaps and mopped his brow with his red bandana. He began, "Sorry. I'm later than I wanted to be. I'd looked forward to hearing you boys and I'm glad I got to hear some of you. I got here as soon as I could but it's harder to lasso and corral a thousand-pound animal out in the open than it is a thirty-pound house pet in my office. This steer had horns, by the way. I had to be careful.

"My two-word phrase is *Jesus wept.*' This was a beginning memory verse for my children when they were pre-school because it is only two words long and was so easy for them to memorize. It's the shortest verse in the Bible and is John 11:35. It shows the humanity of Jesus.

"A life-shaking incident with friends of Jesus occurred shortly before Passion Week: the death of Lazarus. Emotions were intense. Jesus was setting his face 'like flint' to brave the specter of what He knew would be His torture and death on the cross on Golgotha. In spite of what was just over the horizon, Jesus took time with his friends and cried over their sadness and loss. He grieved with them. Even before He entered Jerusalem, He'd had an intense experience with his friends in their village of Bethany.

"This verse tells me He cares. Jesus cares what happens to me—and to you. Bad things happen to people, to all of us at one time or another. Sometimes we are innocent bystanders, sometimes we are born blind or with congenital heart defects. Sometimes we're sailing along in fair weather with clear skies and suddenly, out of nowhere, a storm rages down on us. The rug can be pulled out from under us through no fault of our own.

"You do not know all of my story or the story of my family's origins. Perhaps someday it will be appropriate for me to tell it and for you to hear it, but for now, let me just say that my grandfather saw his wife raped and killed in front of his eyes in China by Japanese invaders. Grandfather was tortured in a prison camp by Mao Zedong's communist soldiers. They broke his leg and smashed his hip. He barely survived and was crippled for the rest of his life. He was starved, lost his farm and had to flee for his life to this country with my father who was just a young boy. God didn't make any of those things happen. God didn't laugh as those bad things happened—He cried about those tragedies right along with Grandfather. It's not always easy for me to see the good in them but I don't blame God. I know He cares because *'Jesus wept.'*"

As Sing was returning to his seat, he bowed and said to the boys, "Thank you for listening." And to Gil, "You're very kind."

Gil wiped tears from his eyes. "Thank you for speaking, for sharing out of your life with us.

"Let's close in prayer." And with that, a wind burst across the room, a late-spring chinook whose source no one could see, as if it were the breath of God. It seemed to begin inside the room, inside the group of boys then to fan out through the windows into the open air to distant and busy places where people might stop and marvel that such a loud message could come from so quiet a countryside and so small a group of rag-tag boys. It seemed a harbinger of things to come in their lives.

CHAPTER 26

2006

B y now, all the boys except Julio had come to saving faith in Jesus as their Lord and Savior. He still exhibited anger issues so it surprised Gil when he came up to him one day and asked, "Mr. Webster, does the Bible talk about judgment?"

"Yes, in a hundred places—over and over."

"Where?" Julio held out his Bible to Gil.

"I'll give you two examples. The first is obvious, like most. It's at the end of Moses' life, at the conclusion of Torah, in Deuteronomy 31, verses 16 through 18." Gil handed the Bible back to Julio unopened. "But instead of my telling you, you turn to and read it, please. You'll find this passage at the end of the fifth book of the Bible."

Julio was surprisingly compliant. He nodded, "Okay, I'll look at the top of the page for a big long word. What did you say it was?"

"Deuteronomy. It means 'second law,' as in: God talked with Moses and gave him instruction then Moses repeated it for the people he led out of Egypt."

Julio read,

'*And the Lord said to Moses: "You are going to rest with your fathers, and these people will soon prostitute themselves to the foreign gods of the land they are entering. They will forsake me and break the covenant I made with them. On that day I will become angry with them and will forsake them; I will hide my face from them and they will be destroyed. Many disasters and difficulties will come upon them, and on that day they will ask, 'Have not these disasters come upon us because our God is not with us?' And I will certainly hide my face on that day because of all their wickedness in turning to other gods.'"*

Gil asked, "Do you understand what you are reading?"

"I think so. We had loads and loads of prostitutes in New York City. I know what they did for a living. I suppose *prostitute* means to sell your body. So, as these verses said, the people will 'forsake' God and 'break'—well, I guess I don't know what *covenant* means."

"Just think of it as they swore an oath of allegiance and made a solemn promise to God. It's similar to what you did with your gang back in the big city."

"Okay, I get it—except the judge told me I did a bad thing."

"Correct, but you misunderstand. Making a promise isn't a bad thing. The problem for you was that you made your promise to the wrong group of people and that's what got you into so much trouble. If you had made the same promise to God it would have been a good thing. Can you explain why to me?"

"I think I get it. Running with my gang got me in trouble because we broke the law. I like having friends but those friends got me into trouble. God is good. As you've told us over and over, He has our best interests at heart. He won't get me into trouble."

"Exactly. The point is that you need to be careful who you make promises to."

"Okay, so these people broke the promise they made to God and they got in trouble because they broke their promise."

"Correct. Nobody likes to be lied to, do they? If you make a promise to God, a covenant with Him, you must keep your promise. Disloyalty is a bad thing."

"Mr. Webster, you just confused me again. The judge, like, ordered me to be disloyal—to my gang. So—he ordered me to do a bad thing?"

"No, although I understand how confusing the whole mess is for you. The promise you made was bad because you made it to the wrong people. They got you in trouble. We're branching pretty far afield here but let's go with it. While not entirely accurate, just think of it as *breaking a bad promise is a good thing but breaking a good promise is a bad thing*. Fair enough?"

"I can roll with that, sure."

"Now, back to my question: Do you understand what you are reading?"

"These people did a bad thing because they broke a good promise. Breaking their good promise got them in trouble."

"Yes, heaps of trouble, a whole bunch of it. Now, I said I'd give you two examples of judgment in the Bible but why don't you ponder this first one for a day or two. The next time I gather you boys all together I'll give my second example to all of you as a group."

Gil gathered some of the Sky Land personnel together with the boys in the dining facility a few days later. Farzad sat by Dariush, his father, to help with translation. Gil began by saying, "The ladies have prepared hot apple crisp with ice cream for a special dessert after I say a few words about a question one of the boys asked me. I'll try not to be too serious or take too long.

"Speaking of food, studies have shown that Japanese who exercise moderately and avoid red meat in favor of fish suffer fewer heart attacks than Americans. Other studies have shown that Italians who enjoy wine with their meals also suffer fewer heart attacks than Americans. Dariush, what do you suppose this means?"

The poor fellow looked puzzled. His son translated. All he could do was shrug his shoulders.

Gil grinned at him and zoomed in with the punch line, "Speaking English will kill you."

Dariush was relieved that he wasn't in trouble. It felt good to be teased like one of the guys. He laughed and said, "It's getting the best of me, sometimes, I t'ink, for sure."

"Seriously, names given to babies used to have meaning, as often they still do. Maybe you're named after a family member. Some cultures, be they American Indian or aboriginal, use names such as White Cloud or Pretty Feather or Sitting Bull or Hunter. Can you give me some other examples?"

Reuven spoke up first, "I'm named after an important character in the Bible."

Ali said, "Mine is a family name."

Johnny Ray said, "Ray is my daddy's name. People call me Johnny Ray to tell us apart—so people know when they're talking about me and when they mean my daddy."

"Exactly. That's exactly the idea. Open your Bibles to Genesis, at the very front of it in the first few pages. Do you have it? Now go to Chapter 5. We'll look at the first ten names in the list as given there. What's the first name?"

That was easy so the students called out "Adam." The older men listened as they followed along with the boys' answers.

Gil said, "Right. That was easy. Everybody's heard of Adam and Eve, the first man and the first woman. Adam was a real man, but in Hebrew, the word can also be used in a general way as in 'mankind.' So, Carlos, write that down and remember it for the rest of us. What's the second name?"

It was another short name so the students called out "Seth."

"Again, correct. All these names are Hebrew. In that language, 'Seth' can mean and often does mean 'appointed' or 'is appointed.' Tomas, you write that down and remember it for us. What's the third?"

"Enosh."

"That means 'mortal' or 'mortality.' Farzad, you remember it. Fourth?"

"Kenan." Jim Bob couldn't resist so he said, "It means 'comedian.'" The group laughed since they understood the modern-day reference to Kenan Thompson, who was a long-standing comedian from "Saturday Night Live" on television.

Gil continued, "But Kenan actually is a real downer of a name. It means 'humiliation.' One can only hope his parents had a reason for this that was more than a slur and put-down for their boy."

Julio couldn't resist so he said, "Like the Johnny Cash song *A Boy Named Sue*. A drunk daddy gave that awful name to him so he'd learn to fistfight. Any boy named Susie is bound to get picked on real bad."

"That *is* what the song says. And I don't want to be too dogmatic about the derivations of some of these ancient Hebrew words. Some scholars think that Kenan means 'hymn singer' while others choose 'fixed' as the appropriate definition. But I'm going to stick with 'humiliation' so, Jim Bob, you're fond of it so you remember that word for us. What is next, the fifth name? Some of these ancient names are in use today, such as Adam, Seth and Kenan. The fifth isn't one of them, though."

It was a long name but finally Ali tried to say, "Mahalalel." He came as close to pronouncing it correctly as anyone else could have.

Gil said, "There's unanimity with the meaning of this name. It means 'the praise of God' or 'God be praised!' The *el*-ending almost always is a reference in Hebrew to God. Reuven, I'm sure you're familiar with that. Am I right?"

"Yes, sir."

"Ali, you were brave enough to try to pronounce it so you write it down and remember it for the rest of us. What's the sixth?"

"Jared."

"Another name we hear on occasion. Sometimes, it's a first name; other times, it's a last name. I've known one or two people who were named Jared. The root word here is 'to descend' so the meaning is 'one who prostrates himself' or 'one who bows down' or 'one who descends' or simply 'he shall descend.' You get the idea. Jason, you remember that name. What's the next?"

"Enoch," Reuven replied.

"It's looks like the third except it has a different ending. And the ending alters the meaning. Verse 24 says Enoch 'walked with God.' His years on this earth were fewer than for the others in this list so some people have imagined he was especially friendly with God. In their imaginations they say, *One day, after a long walk, God said to Enoch—we're closer to my house than yours so come home with me tonight.* That's just imagination but it paints a good picture. At any rate, the name means 'a dedicated man' so the illustration isn't far-fetched. Reuven, you hold onto that and remember it for us. What's the next name?"

Terry said, "Methuselah. I've heard of him."

"And how have you heard of him? What's he famous for?"

"He lived longer than anybody else—ever. Nine hundred sixty-nine years."

"That's right. We'll come back to him later. For now, Terry, you write down and remember that his name means 'when he dies, it comes' or 'when he dies, judgment.' Got that?"

Julio's ears perked up when he heard the word *judgment.* Terry said, "Yes, sir."

"There's two more names in this chapter. What's the next-to-last?"

"Lamech," a few boys called out, following in their Bibles now.

"That has to do with warring or winning or conquering. Johnny Ray, you take that one. Julio, what's the last name?"

"Noah."

"Everybody's heard that name, right? It has to do with 'comfort' and the name itself means 'rest.' Julio, you write that down and remember it. And I want you to notice we have biblical evidence with this name. The Bible itself gives us a good idea what this man's name means. Please read aloud for us verse 29."

Julio did. He read, "He named him Noah and said, *'He will comfort us in the labor and painful toil of our hands caused by the ground the Lord has cursed.'*"

Gil finished, "That's all the names in this chapter, ten of them. So, here's the thing. You boys read out, in order, from one to ten beginning with the first and ending with the last, the meanings of these ten names. Let's see if they make a sentence." The boys followed instructions, but the results were disjointed.

Gil said, "Good job. But if it's a sentence, it's hard to follow so I'll read it again and insert a few connecting words for clarity and to make the sentence smoother. See if this makes it easier for you to follow. 'Mankind is appointed [to] mortality, [which brings] humiliation [to us]. God be praised! He shall descend, a dedicated man [but] when he dies, judgment [comes]. [He will] conquer, [bringing] rest.' There you have it—for what it's worth.

All I'll say is that there might well be, and I believe there is, a hidden message, a gospel message, in these names. It's not overt or entirely clear, but from our perspective, we can see at least a strong hint of the gospel narrative—something like, 'Fallen, sinful mankind is destined to suffer the humiliation of death, but praise God, Jesus will come down to us, live with us and die a cruel death as a substitute for us. He will then conquer death and rise out of the grave, bringing salvation, rest and eternal life to all who believe in Him as the only begotten Son of God.'

"Now I'm going to give you an exercise in simple arithmetic that will lead us to an amazing discovery about Methuselah. You can do this with pencil on graph paper but most of you are probably more comfortable using your digital gadgets. Begin with a vertical line along your left-hand margin and label it at zero. That's our timeline. Then answer this question. How long did Adam live? Carlos, you wrote the meaning of Adam's name so I'll ask you. How long did Adam live?"

"One hundred thirty years."

"No, look again. Read further."

"Oh, I see. Verse 5 says that altogether he lived a really long time, nine hundred thirty years."

"Correct. The Bible says he lived eight hundred years after he had his first child at the age of one hundred thirty. Our biblical narrative says he had other children—we can assume lots of them. So along the bottom of your graph draw a horizontal line that represents Adam's life span. Mark the end of Adam's earthly life at nine hundred thirty years.

"Now, Tomas, how long did the next patriarch, the next person in this family tree, live? And when was he born?"

"The Bible says Seth had his first child when he was one hundred five years old. So that would have been in the year 105. His total life span was nine hundred twelve years."

"So he would have died in what year?"

"That would be 130 plus 912 or 1042."

"Yes. Does everybody understand the pattern, the arithmetic? Finish the exercise through these ten men whose names are listed in Chapter 5, and we'll discuss the results of our graphs tomorrow. Put your heads together, if you wish. You can work by yourself but you don't have to. Any questions? Good. See you tomorrow. Now it's time for dessert."

After reconvening the next day, Gil began, "I want you to make one more vertical line in your graphs. It will be more noticeable and easier to see if you draw it in red or make it a wavy line or somehow differentiate it from your other lines. It will represent the year of the catastrophe that is commonly referred to as Noah's Flood. You'll find the missing piece of information you need in order to solve this problem in Genesis 7:6. Figure it out and tell me the answer when you all agree on what it is."

It took several minutes and a lot of head-scratching. There was discussion as the boys initially came up with various answers but they ultimately reached a consensus. Julio spoke up with, "We got 1656."

"Good job. Johnny Ray, when did your man, Lamech, die? And, Terry, when did your man, Methuselah, die?"

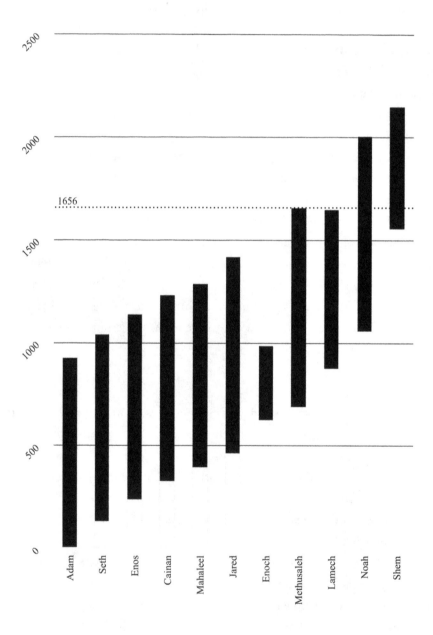

Johnny Ray looked at his notes and replied, "1651."

Terry did the same and said, "1656."

Gil asked, "So who lived longer according to the date on your calendar?"

They replied, "Methuselah."

"So the father out-lived his child. Is that right?"

Again, they both replied, "Yes. By five years."

"This question is for all of you but, Julio, I'll ask you to answer, "How does the year of Methuselah's death compare with the year of the flood?"

"They're the same."

"And what did his name mean?"

"When he dies, it comes."

"Boys, I put it to you there's a reason why Methuselah out-lived his son, why he lived longer than anyone else—ever—in history. It's because God waited as long as He could to bring judgment on the earth and its inhabitants. And Scripture has something else to say. Genesis Chapter 7, verse 7 says, 'Noah . . . entered the ark.' Verse 10 reads, 'And after the seven days the floodwaters came on the earth.'

"It's easy for me to believe that Methuselah understood the meaning of his name and that his long life was a sign to everyone who had eyes to see and ears to hear that when he died, judgment would slam down on rebellious heads. It's easy for me to think he helped Noah build the ark. It's easy for me to see in my mind's eye Noah at his grandfather Methuselah's gravesite, weeping for his elderly relative's death, then retreating to the big boat that was perhaps finished only the day before. Animals came into it and all was then ready. God shut Noah and his family in, locked the door and silence reigned during seven days of mourning over Methuselah's death before catastrophe hit. Violent judgment rained down, literally. When Methuselah died, the prophecy he carried inside his name was fulfilled. And who knows? Even now, that pattern might be on the verge of repeating itself. Some unknown, unnamed rock in outer space could be preparing to rain down judgment on rebellious heads.

"My message is, first, there's all kinds of information in Scripture—most of it is obvious but some is tucked into nooks, crannies and corners waiting to be dug out. Second, blessings are in store for all those who obey and honor a covenant with God while curses are in store for those who violate and dishonor promises to God. Third, God gives ample warning for rebels to repent—so don't wait until it's too late, until the door of escape is closed, shut tight and locked up. God's arms are open, He calls out to you. Run to Him while you can. Today is the day of salvation. God is not willing that any should perish. He takes no pleasure in the death of the wicked. If just one scoffing sinner had begged forgiveness, he would have found safety in the shelter of the ark of salvation."

The boys put their graph papers and electronic gadgets away, then took a snack break. Some of them were simply moving on to the next thing, the next item on their youthful schedule, but others, especially Julio, looked thoughtful, as it they'd gotten the main point of the exercise.

Gil watched Julio walk toward him. Anger seemed to have evaporated. "May I speak with you again, Mr. Webster?"

The fact that Julio was asking politely and almost timidly caught Gil's attention. He responded, "Of course. Let's go outside on the grass where we can be by ourselves and not get interrupted."

They sat on patio chairs. Julio fidgeted, his legs twitched and bounced, his Adam's apple bobbed as he gulped for air. It was obvious he wanted to say something. At last, he blurted out, "I understand about judgment. I get it." He tried not to cry out as he said, "I'm scared."

"Judgment's coming," Gil said, "but you can escape it. Did you catch that point in my teaching? The ark's door is open. You can enter into the ark of salvation."

Gil asked, "May I touch you, lay my hands on your head and pray over you?"

Julio was in the throes of a decision. Eventually, he nodded. Gil removed a vial of oil from his pocket and said, "This is anointing oil made from a Middle Eastern plant called hyssop. Psalm 51:7 says, *'Purge me with hyssop, and I shall be clean.'* This oil won't sting, burn or hurt you. I'll pour some of it on my hands, put my hands on your head and use this oil and my hands as physical symbols to purge the sin out of your life and replace it with the fresh, clean breath of the Holy Spirit as you confess to God. You must confess. You must repent of your sins, even if you don't understand it all. Are you ready?"

Julio gave a small nervous smile, took off his cap and nodded again. Gil rose, anointed Julio and prayed, "Father, purge Julio now as he confesses his sin. This is just between You and him. Hear his confession. I ask that You then wash him clean, make a new man out of Julio. Fill him with Your Holy Spirit, give him hope and a future. In Jesus' name. Amen."

Julio lips moved in silence. He sat quietly for a moment then he began to quiver and vibrate, his breath caught, he convulsed, his shoulders shook, he wailed and bent double, he slipped out of his chair and put his face in the grass as the dam broke. He went spread-eagle. The boys noticed but Julio was oblivious. Gil went to them and said, "We're fine. He's okay. This is what we've prayed for. Leave us alone. You pray and ask God to finish in Julio's life what is now begun."

Gil returned to sit near Julio, who was a long time prostrate before God. If Gil had to guess at the time he would have said it might have been more than a half-hour. When Julio stirred, Gil went to him and got on his knees beside him. He asked, "What did you see?"

"I saw how dirty I am. How much nothing I am. I saw how I can't compare."

"What made you see that?"

"I had a vision of God. I didn't know what clean was until I saw Him. I didn't understand holiness before then. I saw that I'm unclean, unholy compared to God."

"And did God condemn you? Did He treat you like other men have treated you?"

"No, He looked at me with love in His eyes. It was awesome. His look took my breath away. I've been starved for that all my life. He motioned for an angel or somebody to anoint my head with oil like you did. That angel did the same thing you had just done. Then He spoke this thought into my mind, *I'm giving you a new heart, a new mind, a fresh start, a new beginning. You are born again.*"

"Are you still angry? Are you still the guy who can start an argument in an empty house?"

"Not anymore. My spirit sings. I'm light as a feather." Julio flashed a smile to Gil and continued, "You maybe should hold me down or I may just float away."

After helping Julio to his feet, giving him a big hug and keeping his arm around him, Gil called the boys together and told them, "The universal church has two primary ordinances. The first is baptism; the second is communion. This next Sunday afternoon let's reconvene at the river's edge. We'll have a baptismal service so dress to get dunked if you've never been baptized and would like to be. I'll invite guests and ask each of you to give a personal testimony of God's working in your lives and making of you a new man with a new heart and a new spirit. If you 'wax eloquent,' as they say, the baptism might take several hours but if you simply declare your faith in Jesus and take a public stand for Him, it won't take long."

The boys were awed at what they'd just witnessed. Gil put his arm down to release Julio. The boys didn't know whether they could or should ask questions but they wanted to hang around Julio just in case he might say something or something else might happen.

A few of the boys were familiar with baptism. All of them asked questions. They read in their Bibles and made decisions about what they would do and say at their baptismal service.

Sing and Sue and her family members agreed to attend, saying they wouldn't miss it for the world. Gail, with Ali's mother and her kitchen help, planned a picnic meal to be followed by the communion ordinance. Would it be serious and formal like church or relaxed like a picnic? Ali's mother explained that serious things could also be relaxed so Carlos asked Gil if they'd be allowed to play baseball; Jim Bob asked if they could play football. Gil put their minds at ease. He said there wouldn't be enough people for full teams but, with Sing's and Sue's three boys and some of the ranch hands and other teachers, they looked forward to rousing and boisterous activity.

Sunday dawned bright and clear. After attending church in Glasgow, the troop drove back to Sky Land's riverside to gather for baptism. Carlos had his baseball, Jim Bob, his football. But game time came last. The boys changed into shorts and the crowd gathered by the water.

Nine boys stood in a line upriver but near shore, waiting their turn. Gil was assisted in the baptismal ordinance by Sing, one adult on each side, beginning with the tenth boy, Johnny Ray, who was the oldest and biggest. Gil smiled as he looked into Johnny Ray's dark eyes. "You ready?" he asked.

The big black boy grinned, his white teeth flashing. He spoke out to all those assembled, his voice booming across the water, "I testify that Jesus Christ is Lord of my life." He closed his eyes and mouth and folded his arms across his chest so he could hold his nose. Sing put one hand behind Johnny Ray's back while the other held his elbow. Gil did the same and proclaimed, "Johnny Ray, I baptize you in the name of the Father, Son and Holy Spirit . . . " The two men gave a little pressure on Johnny Ray's elbows and he fell backward into and under the flowing water, under its surface, fully submerged. Johnny Ray rose back up, drenched and still smiling broadly. Gil cried out, "Buried with Christ; raised to new life" and gave him a big wet hug. The other boys and the on-lookers clapped and cheered.

They progressed down the line in no particular order. Each testified. Ali and Farzad, the youngest and smallest, spoke of their joy at being delivered from almost certain death to life and liberty in America.

Tuo had flown halfway around the world from Incirlik, Turkey to be there. Sing bowed out so Tuo could assist with Ali and Farzad. Afterward, those two splashed out of the river water to their mother and father to share hugs and kisses.

When it was his turn, Julio testified. "My life and how I lived it was deeply flawed until a week ago. I was always angry. I'm thankful to Johnny Ray for letting me punch out my anger on him. I'm so glad he was man enough to take it. He could have pounded me into the ground any time but he never lost his temper and did it—not even once. Now I've invited Jesus into my life and the anger is gone. I'm so glad! Now I'm ready to go under the water, all the way under, and come up ready to live a new life."

The physical action of being submerged below living water in this formal ordinance gave each and every boy a "coat hook" to remember how they had publicly testified to their belief in Jesus as their Lord and Savior.

The cookout was a big success. Pies were served for dessert, along with ice cream. Then Gil explained communion. He said, "You may have noticed that the blond oak table at the front of the church sanctuary in Glasgow has engraved on it these words, 'This do in remembrance of Me.' Baptism is an action that will give you something to remember in your future days but what many people call "The Lord's Supper" is when we remember what Jesus has already done for us. Reuven, you'll be glad to know that this Christian ordinance is taken from the Hebrew Passover meal.

"As Jesus gathered with his disciples during Passover in Jerusalem, He broke bread with them. They ate a meal together, loosely similar to our eating together today. Your other teachers can go into greater detail with you boys at later times, but for now, all of us who are believers and who want to remember the sacrifice Jesus made to redeem us, are holding a wafer—a cracker or a type of bread made without yeast. It has some tiny holes in it and burn marks that look like stripes. They are to remind us that Jesus was beaten and pierced during His crucifixion. Gail will say a Hebrew blessing then, as we eat this morsel together, let's remember the trade Jesus made with us: He suffered punishment so we don't have to. Isaiah 53 has a verse I often cite, *'By His stripes we are healed.'*

Gail said in Hebrew and repeated in English, "Blessed art Thou, O Lord, King of the universe, who brings forth bread from the earth."

They ate the wafer and after a moment for silent reflection Gil said, "Jesus drank with His disciples as well as ate with them during His Last Supper. That's because the Passover celebration involves both eating and drinking.

"The Bible makes specific reference to drinking from the third cup that is lifted in the celebration after the meal has been consumed. That third cup represents redemption so it helps us remember that Jesus didn't die for nothing: His blood that was shed for us washes us clean from sin so that we can stand pure and holy in God's presence. We are now clothed in robes of righteousness."

Gail recited, "Blessed art Thou, O Lord, King of the universe, who creates the fruit of the vine."

All drank grape juice together after the blessing, rejoicing that the shed blood of Jesus was sufficient to cleanse them of the stain of sin. Their green cathedral, with dirt clods, baseball gloves and blankets spread on the ground, metamorphosed into a holy place and the bread and juice became for them, at that moment, memorial elements in a holy experience. Julio's face, dried of river water, was wet with tears.

CHAPTER 27

2018

Gil bought some turkeys for the farm, thinking they might be a profit opportunity at Thanksgiving. He figured newly hatched turkeys weren't that different from baby chicks at Easter . . . they needed to be constantly monitored that they didn't get too hot or cold or wet—but there was nothing new about that.

Gil read that turkeys could be fed to gain a pound a week and reach maturity and optimal weight in twenty-four weeks. It didn't occur to him, though, that there was no slaughterhouse or processing plant nearby—or anywhere in Montana, for that matter.

A late-summer thunderstorm swept across the prairie. Chickens knew enough to come in out of the wind and rain—but not those turkeys. They ran around helplessly and drowned by the hundreds. In a vain attempt to escape, several managed to fly up onto shed roofs. There was a desperate effort to save a few of the afflicted creatures by carrying them into the dry warmth of the dining hall but the only thing that happened was that they stunk up the place. The stench of wet, dead poultry that had to be disposed of suppressed appetites for days afterward.

Sing tried to console Gil—sort of. He had not been in favor of the enterprise from its inception so he said, "Turkey brains are small. Sometimes we wonder if they have brains at all but animals in general are wonders of God's creation. They offer such variety to us that we can't help but marvel.

"Blue whales are magnificent saltwater mammals. Their calves drink a hundred gallons of fat-rich milk a day. How can they even do that without sucking in harmful saltwater? Adult whale hearts weigh half a ton and their tongues weigh four times that! Their brains aren't anything to write home about but if you're tempted again toward turkeys, think about blue whales. They at least have brains. You'd be better off trying to raise whales in the desert than turkeys on these high plains."

Gil admitted ruefully, "Well, I guess one's about as impractical as the other. The next time I get a wild hair, please steer me toward honeybees or buffalo. Or just ask, 'Remember what five hundred wet, dead turkeys smelled like?' That'll jerk me back to reality."

Sing said, "Atta boy. Reality's good. Here's a quick test to help you with it. Let's see how you rate."

"Oh boy, I have a bad feeling, but okay. Let's give it a go. I'm game (a little pun, there)."

"Put your thinking cap on. The category is animals (because of your failure with turkeys). So here's four simple questions. First question. How do you put a giraffe into a refrigerator?"

"I don't know. I've never had to do that. How do you put a giraffe into a refrigerator?"

"Open the refrigerator, put the giraffe in, close the door. Don't complicate the issue. Use common sense. Second question. How do you put an elephant into a refrigerator?"

"Got it. Keep it simple. Don't over think it. Open the refrigerator, put the elephant in, close the door."

"No! Your refrigerator isn't big enough to hold both. Take the giraffe out, then put the elephant in. You've got to plan ahead and understand the implications of what you're doing. Third question. The lion king convened a convention. Attendance is mandatory. But not every animal attended. Who didn't come?"

"The giraffe and the elephant. They're in the refrigerator."

"Bingo. Good job. There's hope for you yet. Fourth and last question. The river is infested with crocodiles. How do you get across it?"

"Walk over on the bridge."

"No bridge. This is the jungle."

"Do I have a boat?"

"Not even a canoe."

"Do I have to cross the river?"

"Yes. You must cross the river."

"I give up. How?"

"Just swim across. All the crocodiles are at the convention."

Gil groaned as he slapped his forehead.

———

Gail and Gil had gotten a puppy for Maisie, the offspring of Jamie Ferguson's German shepherd male. One grew faster than the other but both were devoted to each other. Maisie could hardly go anywhere on Sky Land without her dog, Buddy.

Maisie confided in Sing, who visited and checked on Buddy but really came to see his favorite little "niece." Sing knew all of Maisie's secrets but he kept her confidence. She had once said, "Uncle Sing, you're the best teddy bear doctor in the whole world. And you know all about dogs, too. Nobody could take better care of Buddy for me than you. You're the best, Uncle Sing."

Buddy was the only pet on the farm. He was neither a stock dog nor a guard dog, though he was protective of the family.

Gil and Gail were responsible for Buddy in the early days. They would walk him for exercise and train him to be off-leash and on voice command. Buddy was intelligent and learned quickly. He also learned his natural order and where he fit in it because big tractors made lots of scary noise and the workhorses were huge. On occasions when he was a puppy, shaking with fright, Gil would pick him up, speak calmly to him and tuck him inside his jacket. Dogs are pack animals by nature so Buddy learned to trust Gil as his pack leader.

When Maisie was fairly young and Buddy was still in the puppy stage, Sing taught Maisie that one of her years was about like seven years to Buddy. He said, "Maisie, Buddy looks up to you now but the day will come when he is going to notice that he's grown more than you. He's not a lap dog, he's not a house dog.

His future isn't to be a pampered pet but a big, strong, outdoors guardian who will give his life for you, if need be.

"You need not be afraid but on that day when Buddy feels extra-specially big and strong, he will challenge you for place-in-the-pack supremacy in a way in which he will never challenge your father. When that happens, you'll need to meet his challenge and wrestle him down. Let's practice so you can be prepared for that day. Watch me and I'll show you what the 'submission position' for a dog looks like."

Sing played with Buddy then gently laid him on his side, put a knee over his stomach just above his hindquarters, and bent down with his forearms and chest over Buddy's upper torso. With that move, Maisie noticed that Buddy stopped his play, relaxed and lay very still. "See how quiet Buddy is? He knows my dominance over him. He knows he fits below me in the natural order of his things. It won't occur to him to challenge my authority now. All is peaceful and ordered in his simple world and he is comfortable with his place in it. He knows where he fits and he accepts it.

"Now you try. Buddy hasn't challenged you yet—and he won't for a long time, many months from now—so you can play with him the same as I did. Make it a habit to play with him and even rough-house out here in the yard. Today, at the end of your play, just for practice, lay Buddy on his side the same as I did. Don't hurt him. Be gentle. I'll coach you through it."

She did. Both Maisie and Buddy had fun but it was also good practice for that future day when the challenge would come. Maisie learned what it felt like when Buddy lay quietly in full submission to her. And he learned what it felt like when Maisie hugged and loved on him.

They grew together as best friends. Yet the human was above the animal in the pecking order, as God intended.

———

The years rolled by at Sky Land. Gail blinked, and just like that, Maisie was nearing school age. One day, while tending the horses, Sue grinned over at Gail and said, "Children like to get up, and make sure they get you up, too, at five a.m. until their second day of school."

Gail grinned back and responded, "She's growing fast. I think she's ready for her horizons to expand. If she's like me, she'll enjoy school from start to finish—and not just on the first day. I hope I'm as ready for it as she is."

Maisie graduated from collecting eggs to riding horses and herding cattle. She was young but only for a minute.

Gail blinked again and Maisie entered seventh grade as an experienced ranch hand and a smart young girl. Gail and Sue watched through the front window as Maisie and Buddy were playing tag, running and jumping, barking and laughing with each other one day.

Sue asked, "Who do you suppose is having more fun, the grown dog or the adolescent child?"

Parents aged and one set moved in. Duane had suffered a mild stroke, and while Ethel had nursed him back to health, they'd judged it better that he didn't drive anymore so they gave up their Iowa farm and relocated to Sky Land.

They seemed to be contented with their new stage in life. Ethel helped in the big kitchen, Duane was free to roam and help with the big horses, and both relished being a part of Maisie's growth and development.

Harvey was younger than Duane. He and Emma, long before, had turned over the daily operation of their farm to Clyde so they stayed in Iowa with Clyde's family. But all of them made regular trips to Sky Land.

Wyatt's friendship with Clyde flourished and their two farm families vacationed together. Both made sure Sky Land maintained agricultural excellence.

Sue's involvement with Sky Land also remained true. She trained the stable of draft horses not only to work but also to bring national recognition to the ranch for their beauty and quality.

They attended many state fairs and world-class shows, which provided wonderful experience to the boys in exposure, management, transportation logistics and working with animals. They polished harnesses, studied animal diets, curried the horses to help their coats shine and trimmed and polished hooves.

Sing ensured their excellent health—cattle, sheep, goats and chickens as well as horses. With his encouragement, Gil initiated a breeding program for the stock and shipped their offspring across the nation to enhance genetic diversity.

Boys came and went but most of them stayed through high school. Johnny Ray led Glasgow's high school football team in rushing yardage and was offered scholarships by several college programs. He came home to visit as his schedule allowed and regaled the boys with tall tales. His very presence spoke volumes to them and opened their minds to new worlds of possibilities.

He'd often said, "I think of Sky Land as my home away from home. I've met people who have second homes, vacation homes, motor homes and sometimes when I'm away from here, I feel homesick." Johnny Ray had told Gil that one of his favorite songs he played while traveling to away games was Paul Simon's song, "*Homeward Bound*" because the words tugged at his heart.

True to his word, Gil sponsored all the boys who applied themselves and wanted to continue their educations in colleges or trade schools. They were proud when Terry honored his commitment to God's calling and left home to serve as a missionary to Peruvian cowboys on the pampas.

Sing was especially pleased when Jim Bob decided he wanted to be a veterinarian. He was doing well in school and a plan was in place for him to graduate and return as a junior partner in Sing's clinic in Glasgow.

Teen Challenge brought new boys to the ranch each year such that their numbers swelled to fifty after fourteen years. They filled five pods scattered around the central kitchen facility.

Julio returned to the barrios in New York City. It was his burden but also his delight. The people there were his mission field. He was thankful to have Gil and Gail's support with Sky Land as a resource for other Puerto Rican toughs in need of escape from concrete and mean city streets. He addressed the boys during one of his trips. The boy he brought with him was dressed in gold chains and attitude.

Julio shared with the group, "After my father threw me away, I didn't have a hero, a man to look up to—until I came here and got knocked flat on my butt. Boys without heroes lack confidence. They stumble through life feeling like discarded mistakes. I stomped as I stumbled because I was so angry, but I found my hero here at Sky Land. He saved my life." Gil, forty-four years old now, his black hair beginning to gray at the temples, listened proudly as Julio spoke.

Another of Gil's pride-and-joys was Reuven, who also returned to New York—as a lawyer working for social justice, improving people's lives as he addressed the moral health of his country. Julio and Reuven had also forged bonds of Big Apple friendship with each other during their years at Sky Land that they maintained—for their good and that of the boys they served.

There were many success stories. Tuo had been promoted to brigadier general and was currently posted with the Joint Chiefs at the Pentagon but he continued to escort boys with their families each year to Sky Land. Some stayed in the United States; some returned to minister as educated, trained, responsible Christian adults in their native countries.

Gil invited Wayne Heifetz to visit. On his first trip to Sky Land, Wayne brought a gift and presented it to his hosts upon his arrival, together with an explanation. He said, "In 1990, as the Voyager I spacecraft was sailing away from the solar system, NASA commanded it to spin around and take a picture of Earth—from almost four billion miles away. In that image, Earth looks like a tiny dot, just a single lit-up pixel against a background of scattered sunlight in the darkness of space. As a housewarming present from one Army buddy to another, here is a framed image of that photograph, along with Carl Sagan's famous quote concerning it."

Gil accepted the gift and handed it to Gail, who unwrapped it and read the inscription, Sagan's quotation from *Tiny Blue Dot: A Vision of the Human Future*:

"That's here. That's home. That's us. On it, everyone you love, everyone you know, everyone you ever heard of, every human being who ever was, lived out their lives. The aggregate of our joy and suffering, thousands of confident religions, ideologies, and economic doctrines, every hunter and forager, every hero and coward, every creator and destroyer of civilization, every king and peasant, every young couple in love, every mother and father, hopeful child, inventor and explorer, every teacher of morals, every corrupt politician, every 'superstar,' every 'supreme leader,' every saint and sinner in the history of our species lived there—on a mote of dust suspended on a sunbeam."

Both recipients marveled at the beauty of the image and the poetic rhythm of Sagan's words. Gail said, "This is a wonderful gift. Thank you so very much. And how appropriate to receive this NASA photo from an astronomer! We'll think of you whenever we look at and marvel over this picture. Sagan wasn't Christian but his is a memorable quote, for sure. And what a beautiful blue dot it is that God's created for us. This image reinforces our belief that Earth is not an obscure place in an insignificant galaxy in a sea of nothingness. Earth is special to our Creator and fills a crucial role in a cosmic saga."

Gil and Gail were satisfied with how they were using the money with which God had gifted them. They were contented and fulfilled in their intergenerational ministry at Sky Land. They believed they were smack dab in the center of His will for their lives. At the same time, they knew more was to come.

One day as he swept the barn on a warm summer day, Gil said, "Things have been humming along smoothly but. . . ."

Gail smiled as she nodded, "Life could hardly be better but. . . ."

"But change is just over the horizon, just out of view, I think."

"I feel it, too. Something's coming."

Gil rubbed his hand along the top of his head and said, "You remember when I told you I didn't expect to die of old age?"

"Yes. At first, I thought those were the words of a man reveling in the strength of youth, but I've come to share that conviction with you. Something . . ." Gail gazed off into the distance.

That night Gil had a dream, Gail a premonition and Tuo, who was on the other side of the world, a vision. Since it was summer break at Cal Tech, Gil invited Wayne to enjoy a return visit at Sky Land at a date not too far in the future. He jumped at the opportunity. What he didn't know was that Gil was worried and wanted to pump his brain about what might be going on in the heavenly realms.

CHAPTER 28

2019

The next year, Tuo arranged to come and bring another new resident with him. He arrived with a boy named Micah, an orphan who could not speak. ISIS had invaded his village, killed both his parents and cut out his tongue as a warning to others who refused to recant their Christian faith. Micah was frail and undernourished but radiant in his faith and a vibrant witness to the other boys who saw with their own eyes that they didn't have it so bad after all. His silent witness convicted all in his presence they could *not* set a tepid Christianity in front of the world's boiling kettle of antagonistic paganism.

Gil could speak and communicate with Micah since the boy's hearing remained intact. He joined the younger children in their daily chores of feeding chickens and gathering their eggs. The feathered flock was healthy and quite large by now since they'd employed Sing's veterinary help.

Gail and the kitchen staff ministered to Micah by showering him with love and all the food he could eat. He thrived and seemed to smile all the time. His teeth weren't white and he needed dental work but that could be corrected.

While both Tuo and Wayne were visiting, Gail decided to declare a special occasion night. The adults—Gil and Gail, their two houseguests and Sing and Sue, who also had been invited for dinner—were gathered around the fireplace in the main house's living room. In this relaxed setting at this pleasant time in

216

the evening, Wayne again saw an obvious dissimilarity in body types between himself and the other three men. He said, "Wow. I'm the odd man out. You guys sure do look alike. Gil, how tall are you? How much do you weigh?"

"Holy mackerel, I'm glad we're such good friends—for you to ask me a question like that. Thanks to daily farm workouts, I'm still 5'8" and 170 pounds."

"Tuo, how tall are you? How much do you weigh?"

"Man, oh man. It seems like I've been through this series of questions once before in my life. Due to my military regimen, I'm still 5'8" and 168 pounds."

"Sing, how tall are you? How much do you weigh?"

He said, "Holy cow (a little veterinarian joke there), I didn't expect that question tonight. I'm long out of athletic track shape, but maybe because of wrestling steers in cattle chutes, I'm still 5'8" and 172 pounds."

Gail's mouth fell open. She said, "Exactly as I said fourteen years ago, you guys don't look anything alike yet you're triplets. I can't believe it. Triplets in my life again! I've been rubbing shoulders with you all this time, yet I hadn't seen it. What are the odds? After all these years . . . Sing, don't tell me you were born on the Fourth of July. Were you?"

"Well, as a matter of fact, yes. What made you guess that day?"

She was overcome with sudden emotion so Tuo said, "I was born on the Fifth of July and Gil was born on the Third. Our friend who was killed in Baghdad was 5'8", 172 pounds and he was born on the Fourth of July. I guess we lost a triplet and now we've gained him back."

Sue sucked in her breath as she looked over to Sing. "Our lives are intertwined with these lives in more ways than we could ever have guessed. God put us together thirteen years ago. I didn't doubt it but this 'God wink' sure cements the deal for me."

In this unity of spirit and destiny, they went on to discuss how Tuo's vision and Gail's premonition had both involved some sort of stellar explosion. They were very close to each other, so much so that Wayne was unsure how he fit into the mix.

Gil was sensitive to his friend's hesitation and uncertainty. He said, "Wayne, there was a time in our lives when God's plan for us required two influential men named General Grimsley and Colonel James. You don't know them but we could not have done what we did without them. I believe God put you in our lives in the same way—you're a piece in the puzzle of our lives without which our picture could not be completed. We're nothing special. God simply chose a peculiar set of circumstances to catch the attention of significant people around us. In both instances, we didn't see the connection. Colonel James did. You did. You're an integral part of our whatever-it-is. And don't you ever doubt it."

Tuo, now retired from active military duty and working full time in his refugee ministry, explained his vision as best he could to the others. "I don't know what to make of it but I saw stars in the sky, objects in space. Lightning flashed from sphere to sphere. Dynamism. Much movement. Nearby. It didn't seem like the celestial objects were way out there in unreachable space. It felt like I could almost reach out and touch them."

Gail echoed his description, "Yes, it's almost like we saw the same things in different ways. In my mind's eye, the bursts of light seemed close. And coming closer at incredible speed were big clusters of them—out of sight but just over the horizon."

Wayne beetled his brows in a frown and said, "It sounds like an 'event horizon.' Not one that involves a black hole, but nevertheless one that delineates a point of no return. Perhaps impending doom. You're describing dangerous things."

After a few moments of quiet reflection, Gil finally spoke. "Sometimes I worry that I don't have enough imagination, other times that I have too much. Sometimes I wish I could see the future and know what was going to happen; other times, that I have glimpsed it and wish I hadn't. I dreamed the same as you saw, that something wicked this way comes, to borrow Bradbury's book title—except I believe that these inanimate objects we're envisioning aren't wicked . . . they're God's judgment on man's wickedness. All of us have an inherent bent toward wickedness and I agree with Wayne's assessment. I think what we're seeing is judgment speeding through space to us in the form of big fiery rocks that are going to rain down on our heads."

Gil paused as the rest gazed at him quietly, all with anticipation in their eyes.

Gil asked suddenly, "Wayne, if we ask questions, can you add concrete specificity to our impressions? I think you are the one we can and should look to for answers. There's no way you're the odd man out in our group. As I said, we need you. God's supplied you for just such a time as this."

Wayne answered, "I'd be happy to—if I can. What's your first question? You might have more faith in me than I have in myself."

"Speed. We've mentioned our impression of speed. Talk to us about speed in space."

"Of course. Human sprinters moving at twenty-five miles per hour might be world champions in their sport but nevertheless, they would be classified as slow-moving when compared with horses or automobiles."

"I get that," said Tuo; Gil and Gail nodded in agreement.

"A baseball thrown at the extreme velocity of one hundred miles per hour might also be classified as slow-moving when compared to gunshots."

"Right."

"A bullet fired at a target is also slow-moving when compared to 'shooting stars.' The meteor that smashed into the Arizona plain centuries ago was moving at forty thousand miles per hour—fifty times faster than a speeding bullet or a jet fighter as it breaks through the sound barrier!

"High speeds are required in space because space is so big. Escape velocity from Earth's gravitational field is 25,000 miles per hour. NASA launched its Cassini spacecraft in October 1997. It made headlines just last month. After seven years, Cassini achieved orbit around Saturn. Though NASA's engineers accelerated it to almost three times escape velocity, space distances are so vast that Cassini still required seven years to get to Saturn.

"By the way, if we scaled the thickness of Saturn's famous rings to that of a DVD, the DVD would be twelve and one-half miles in diameter. Saturn's rings are very thin in comparison with their diameter. Scale is different in space than what we're used to on Earth."

"Okay. Sounds weird at first but I follow the comparison." Gil said. "A bullet on Earth is slower than almost anything in space."

Wayne continued, "Actually, we haven't gotten to the weird part yet. The weird part has to do with the definitions for low and high-speed impacts. Speed has consequences. Tuo, when you swing a hammer and it impacts a nail, the head of the hammer *impacts* the head of the nail and the hammer makes a sound as it whams into the nail. Gil, when a batter is successful and his bat hits the baseball, the same thing happens—the bat *impacts* its target and makes a sharp *crack* as the ball sails over the outfield fence. The hammer and the bat both touch their targets, they both impact their targets. And you recognize particular sounds that are produced by those impacts. That's what happens with low-speed impacts.

"But that's not what happens with high-speed impacts. In a high-speed event, there's not even an impact because there's no touching. The high-speed object never physically touches its target."

Gail couldn't contain herself. She interjected, "You're right, Wayne. Now you've gone from a little bit strange to really weird. I hesitate to say that you're talking nonsense but that's what it sounds like to me. If you hit your target, how can you not have touch?"

"I know, I know," Wayne responded. "The physics are entirely different when astrophysical high speeds are involved: prior to physical impact of one object with another, a nuclear explosion occurs such that these types of collisions involve immense explosions, not impacts. Explosion occurs first such that there is never impact in the way we think of it. Projectiles traveling at such high speeds contain so much compressive energy when they encounter atmospheric resistance that they disappear in a nuclear explosion before they physically touch their targets. It's the resulting nuclear blast wave that does damage, not physical touch or collision or *wham*, to use the farmers' technical terminology."

Gail jumped back in, "Okay, I understand your explanation." The rest nodded. "You're not talking total nonsense. But can you give us examples of these high speeds and so-called impacts that don't involve physical contact? I still don't *really* get it."

"I can, yes. Beringer Crater in northwest Arizona is the best-preserved impact crater we have. We don't know when it was formed since it happened before recorded history but it is circular, almost a mile in diameter and about two hundred feet deep. You may have seen photographs of it, some at ground level and some taken from high in the air. People searched years and years for the meteor itself but couldn't find any trace of it, which was quite a mystery for them at that time. The only thing we have is the crater and roughly thirty tons of beach-ball-sized fragments scattered around outside and beyond the crater's rim.

"Qualified experts have now determined and theorized that there was about 300,000 tons of material originally involved and the meteor was moving at more than 40,000 miles per hour as it neared Earth's surface. At that speed, it contained ten times more energy per pound than a stick of dynamite. Because of the heat build-up in our atmosphere, the stone exploded prior to impact and the circular crater was formed by the explosion. And that's why no large body of iron was ever found underneath the crater: the meteoritic rock had been vaporized in a nuclear explosion.

"And by the way, this process of nuclear explosion also explains why craters are uniformly circular, not elongated as would otherwise be anticipated if meteors penetrated Earth's atmosphere at oblique angles as they almost always do. An explosion is spherical so it produces circular craters while impacts that are at oblique angles produce stretched-out 'scratches' that gradually increase in depth. Before they had gained this understanding, scientists were extremely puzzled as to why craters they observed were always circular and not elongated.

"Nuclear bomb test explosions first produce a blinding, spherical shock wave and then a mushroom cloud. It is the shock wave that does most of the damage; it penetrates down into the ground but also goes up into the air as a mushroom cloud and sideways as a shock wave. So it isn't accurate to think of a meteorite as 'digging' a crater; instead, it compresses, fractures, pulverizes and melts the underlying rock layers by subjecting them to tremendous pressure waves with unbelievable amounts of heat involved."

Tuo exhaled loudly as he said, "I'm just a retired Army grunt. This is above my pay grade. May we take a break to let my brain cool down before it explodes?"

"Amen to that," Sing echoed.

"I'll get the coffee and doughnuts." Gail offered. "We've got regular, cake and jelly-filled. Or chocolate chip cookies, if you prefer."

Sue jumped up, eager to help. She needed a break from this astrophysics lesson, as well.

After a few minutes when they resumed, Wayne began by saying, "I've given hundreds of lectures but this is the first time I've had triplets in my class. I feel extremely honored by this unique turn of events. Thank you, Gil, for convincing me that my input is required to help you achieve that which has been prepared in advance for you triplets to achieve.

"I have a second example of a crater. It comes out of a sparsely populated area of Siberia near Tunguska, Russia. The event occurred on June 30, 1908 and is the most recent powerful so-called impact on Earth. Its explosion was a thousand times more powerful than the bombs we dropped on Hiroshima and Nagasaki in the 1940s. Eye witness accounts and first-hand reports confirm a blinding light with a loud blast of burnout in the sky at the end. Scientists believe that meteor was only fifty feet across and the explosion happened about five miles above Earth's surface. All the surrounding terrain was devastated by the fireball. Trees that were not incinerated were blown sideways by the blast wave. Again, this is a confirmed event in recent history and Gail, exactly like Beringer Crater in Arizona, there is no surviving meteorite to be found underneath the circular crater.

"We have discovered thousands of asteroids, over nine thousand of which are classified as near-Earth. They are larger, sometimes much larger, than the one that hit above Siberia. The good news is that none are projected to strike Earth in the next hundred years. You can just imagine the damage one of those big boys could do. The bad news is that we can't detect smaller asteroids until too late."

Gil asked, "Has Earth been struck only these two times? Do we know of other craters?"

"That's a good question. Scientists in the past had wanted to search for meteor craters but it was not until they observed and understood characteristics of craters from atomic bomb tests that they knew what to look for: unusual rocks. Rocks first, craters second. Once they found these particular rocks, they would then see if they could locate a crater. In other words, before the Manhattan Project clarified this for them they had been looking for the wrong thing in the wrong way in the wrong sequence."

"What unusual rocks?" Sing asked. "I would guess granite because of its density except that granite is everywhere and is not unusual at all. It's in all sorts of places."

"Good guess. And you are also correct as to why granite is not the right answer. These scientists needed to search out a mineral that was truly bizarre, one that is never or almost never found at Earth's surface because the atmospheric pressure is not nearly high enough to form it in typical circumstances. Diamond would have filled the bill since it requires that graphite be squeezed with a pressure of thirty thousand atmospheres; however, diamonds have been found in certain locations before and they are so valuable that, if found, scientists would immediately be shoved aside and crowded out of their discovery's location by profit seekers. A more satisfactory proof would be a mineral that had never been found, but at the same time, was not regarded as valuable.

"Coesite was just such a mineral: it had never been found outside a laboratory, it carried no value as a precious gem and it required that quartz be squeezed by twenty thousand atmospheric pressures—not as high as diamond but certainly far beyond the ordinary."

Tuo interjected, "You're right about one thing. I've never heard of coesite."

Wayne continued, "I said earlier that Beringer Crater in northwest Arizona is the best-preserved crater on Earth. It was the perfect place to begin the search. Two scientists, Eugene Shoemaker and Edward Chao, went there, and sure enough, in 1960 they found coesite outside the rim of that crater. Its discovery served as verification of their search process so it opened the floodgates and in the next ten years, forty-seven confirmed so-called impact craters on Earth had been found ranging in locations from Canada to South Africa. Proof was rapidly accumulating that big rocks can and do fall from the sky, rocks not merely the size of a baseball or a basketball or a house but also the size of a town or a city."

Gil said, "The first images of meteor craters that come to my mind are pictures of them on the Moon. I don't think of Earth at all."

"That's correct. We do think of Earth as a safe place," Wayne agreed. "It's comforting to think of our homes as safe places. But in fact, outer space and pictures taken in outer space illustrate that perhaps Earth is not so safe, after all. We not only find impact craters on the Moon but some scientists have concluded that the Moon itself was formed from the impact of a Mars-sized asteroid, that something, perhaps Mars itself, 'smashed' into Earth to form the Moon. Thinking about pictures we've seen leads to a very sobering conclusion.

"Now we have verified the existence of hundreds of meteor craters here on Earth. Most of them are small but space also has big things speeding around in it. For instance, the core of Halley's Comet is believed to weigh 100,000 million tons and measure five miles by nine miles. We know where and when to look for it, and so far as we know, it doesn't pose a threat to us but all we have to do, as you say, Gil, is look at the Moon to be reminded of what's out there."

After their discussion was over, after Sing and Sue left to spend the night at their home, after Gail left to help Maisie with her homework, Gil, Tuo and Wayne hung out, keeping the fire burning in the fireplace. Fascinated, Gil continued to ask Wayne about the Moon and planets in the solar system.

"Mountains on the Moon are typically around the edges of so-called impact craters," Wayne explained. "Mare Orientale is a basin, a perfectly circular plain that is surrounded by three concentric rings of mountains. Scientists understand this flat, circular basin to be an impact crater caused by a meteor. It is the size of Texas! The meteor that produced it was probably ninety miles in diameter.

"The Imbrian Basin is bigger and the Hellas Basin is bigger yet. It is about six miles deep and 1500 miles wide. I can hardly imagine how the Moon survived being pummeled by rocks of such gigantic size. Herschel Crater on Mimas, one of Saturn's moons, is one-fourth the diameter of Mimas. Another of Saturn's moons, Iapetus, has nine impact basins. Almost everywhere we look, we find craters upon craters upon craters. They're everywhere—on planets, moons and even larger asteroids. You might remember that twenty-five years ago, in 1994, Comet Shoemaker-Levy 9 was captured by Jupiter's gravity, broke apart into nine, mile-wide fragments and crashed into that gas giant, raising black clouds in their wakes, each of which was larger than Earth in size. Pictures of that event played over television and are still available for viewing on various internet sites. These same scientists have charted more than 150,000 asteroids near us in our solar system. *Near* is defined as much further than from here to town but close enough for them to locate and identify."

Gail had rejoined them at that point after Maisie went to bed. She said, "Wayne, you're scaring me. This sounds ominous."

Gil followed up as he said, "I heard a lecture by a creation scientist some years ago that stuck with me. He taught opposing world views: uniformitarianism versus catastrophism. The first is evolutionary; the second is creationist. The first is taught by the world and its secular educational establishments while the second is what the Bible says. I remember that because it made things so clear to me. I believe that God created all things from nothing in six days while evolution brainwashes our children in the lie that *all things continue* since who knows when. It's basically an old earth versus a young earth view. So, Wayne, this is scary stuff but I hear you arguing in favor of a young-earth position and, thus, catastrophism as a logical extension of creationism. I say, 'Amen!' to that because I believe the Bible teaches God as Creator."

Wayne gave his answer as, "Yes and no. I don't hold to a young-earth, creationist belief but evidence is conclusive when it comes to catastrophic events across our solar system. Astrophysicists have by now made so many unexpected discoveries that they have been forced to alter their original perspective. What they have found in space and on celestial bodies underscores the point that nature isn't immune to sudden, explosive catastrophe, and in fact, astrophysicists now posit and accept a cosmology built on catastrophe."

"Whoa!" Tuo held up his hand to signal stop. "My everyday vocabulary doesn't include a lot of big words. I'm with you on catastrophe but what's cosmology?"

"The study of beginnings—how things began. We accept catastrophism because we can no longer deny it."

Gail added, "I don't know these astronomical details but I agree with your bottom line. History is filled with catastrophes: wars, floods, earthquakes, etc. I'm old enough—barely—to have dim memories of people talking about Mount Saint Helens blowing its stack in 1980."

"Not to mention tsunamis produced by earthquakes," Gil said. "While we were at Incirlik, Turkey I saw news coverage of the tsunami that hit Japan and southeast Asia in December 2004. As I recall, more than 200,000 people were killed. Everything in that wave's path was absolutely leveled because it was traveling at 500 miles per hour. That catastrophe left nothing behind it except death and destruction."

Wayne stretched and yawned in tiredness at the end of an exciting day as he closed the discussion, "Catastrophic events occur with regularity. Some are just bigger than others, even global in scale. The sound produced during the eruption of Krakatoa in Indonesia between the islands of Sumatra and Java in 1883 was heard 2200 miles away in Australia and 3,000 miles away in Japan.

"We haven't been used to thinking of 'stars' falling out of the sky on our heads. But I guess we've seen or at least heard of exhibits of perfectly preserved woolly mammoths frozen solid in Arctic ice with grass still in their mouths. They don't live there now. Grass doesn't grow there now. There must have been a sudden, radical, almost instantaneous temperature change to catch and freeze large animals like that. The evidence is unavoidable: this solar system, perhaps the entire universe, exists under catastrophism. If catastrophic events are in our past and our present, it is reasonable and logical to anticipate they shall also be in our future. I hate to say it but your sense of foreboding is well placed.

"With that, I regret that I must say 'goodnight' to one and all. My body is so tired that my brain is addled. Tuo, you could beat the pants off me in a game of tic-tac-toe right now. I'll see you all in the morning."

Gail said, "Bright-eyed . . ."

Gil said, "Bushy-tailed . . ."

Tuo said, "And ready for a new day."

CHAPTER 29

2020

Wayne became a regular visitor and Tuo continued his mission of escorting Iraqi refugees to Sky Land, Montana. On various occasions, Gail reviewed their key Bible verse, Matthew 24:34, for their friends and Gil explained why they anticipated that Jesus might return and set foot on Earth on or before 2030 to 2048. They all were now familiar with the evidence for catastrophism.

On one of his visits to Sky Land, Gil asked Wayne if he remembered his phone call during which he had answered as to what it would have taken for a solar year to have lengthened by a bit more than five days.

"Yes, that was our 'first contact' after military life."

"It was on that phone call that you gave me the 900,000 number."

Gail explained that they had no idea whether what they called Noah's flood had been the triggering event or something else had precipitated Noah's flood. In either event, it seemed clear that a catastrophe of some type had pushed Earth 900,000 miles further from the Sun. She said, "We now think the triggering event was likely a celestial bombardment, and given our recent dreams, we believe the bombardment is soon to be repeated sometime in the future. It will shove Earth that same distance closer to the Sun, restoring it to its original orbit." They were finishing up dinner when the subject arose.

After dishes had been cleared, Gail brought out coffee and a cake she had baked that day. Gil got out his well-worn Bible, opened it and said, "After you gave me your 900,000-mile answer, I thanked you and said when the time came, you'd be the first to know. Now's the time." He read from the last book of the Bible, Revelation, at Chapter 8, verses 10 and 11a: *"The third angel sounded his trumpet, and a great star, blazing like a torch, fell from the sky on a third of the rivers and on the springs of water—the name of the star is Wormwood."*

Gail said, "So if you ever hear someone talk about a star named Wormwood, this is where they take their reference."

Gil followed up with more detail. "The very next page, at Chapter 11 and verse 3, equates forty-two months and 1,260 days—setting the requirement for 360-day years. At the very least, it's possible that Wormwood interacts with Earth in such a way as to tighten its orbit 900,000 miles, which would, in turn, shorten our solar year back to its original 360 days. Wayne, I know you have trouble accepting this, which emphasizes that if it happens you won't be ready for it. You come here to visit and relax. We won't press you. Just know that when the time comes and you're shaken to your core, when you're ready to hear what we have to say, give us a call. We'll be here."

Which is exactly what he did just a month later.

Over the phone, Wayne blurted out in a panic, "We've detected a swarm of meteors that is clustered around a Mars-sized object. All of them are on a collision course with Earth. Most are mere chips of rock that will burn up long before penetrating our atmosphere, several are the size of city blocks, but one is huge, so much so that my imagination makes me feel—already—its gravitational pull. It's inexorable. Terrifying in its mass. We have zero hope of deflecting or destroying it."

"Wayne, I'm stunned, jolted," Gil said over the phone. "Let me catch my breath. Gail and I were expecting this, or something like it but—similar to accidents—we know they exist and can happen to anyone, anytime, anywhere but we're surprised when they happen to us. Right now, I can't help but ask two obvious questions. How long have you known—you didn't know last month when you were here with us, did you? When will this swarm get here?"

"Let me answer your first question first. Not long, less than a month as you surmised. My colleagues from around the world have been working on suspicious data but we didn't know. Let me explain. Ever since Cassini entered orbit around

Saturn in June 2004 we had been using it for exploration. Shortly before we crashed it into Saturn on September 15, 2017, it found something we didn't know existed. It took us over a year to analyze the pictures and get over our initial disbelief. Then we needed more time to verify our observations, calculations and conclusions—but now we have no doubt. Astronomers around the world and astrophysicists like myself have been communicating with each other practically non-stop in the last three weeks.

"We're all super surprised. How could something of this magnitude jump out of Cassini's cameras at us like this? How could we have missed this before? It's like the mythical Planet X, the mystical Nibiru of conspiracy nuts, the biblical Wormwood you brought to my attention. It came out of nowhere. That's what makes me so angry, in spite of my fright—for the nuts and the prophets, for you and your Bible to be so right. No offense but I haven't believed any of this stuff! I don't know how I could have been so wrong but I have no other explanation."

Gil responded quietly, "I'm sorry. May I have your permission to pass this information on to Gail and Tuo?"

"Yes."

"Thank you. I'll speak to them but no others, then set a time for a conference call—the three of us with you, if that's alright. I promised you when the time came we would be here, available."

Later, during the call, Gail reminded the three men, "In other discussions we've had about the Bible and a few of its prophetic passages, we mentioned the possibility that Jesus might return by 2048 or perhaps earlier, say, 2030. We didn't just make up an outlandish statement out of thin air but we used Scripture to hypothesize a serious conclusion."

Gil followed, "We also believe the Bible speaks of a literal three-and-a-half-year *great* tribulation period that will happen before Jesus' return to Earth. Tribulation, by definition, involves catastrophe. It is possible, perhaps even likely, that catastrophe might include a huge meteor or some type of celestial body that slams into Earth, as early as, say, 2027. But we're surprised and almost speechless because there's a huge difference between the hypothetical or the theoretical and the physically real. Wayne, we were not emotionally ready for your news today. While we're here for you, at the same time, we're also shocked."

Tuo had a practical question, "You didn't swear us to secrecy before you laid this huge headline of impending catastrophe on us. Are we free to talk? Is this news ready to break? Or do we have to zip our lips?"

Wayne answered, "Hundreds already know. Heads of major states, including our President, are informed. I'm not sworn to secrecy. It's inevitable the news will get out before too many more months—or weeks or days. Since we don't have a solution for the problem, I think panic will mushroom as soon as people find out and the appointed time draws ever closer. If you, set up and expectant as you are, are surprised, imagine how millions of others will react. I don't see benefit to broadcasting this news, but on the other hand, I didn't swear you to secrecy before telling you. I guess I'm so desperate I'm breaking silence and begging you for help, for answers."

Gail reached over and touched her husband's hand. "How long do we have?"

"It required seven years for Cassini to get to Saturn," Wayne answered. "Using its cameras, we found Planet X, Nebiru, Wormwood or whatever you choose to call it. Our calculations tell us its arrival will be August of 2027 although its effects will be felt here before impact. You see, that's what makes this situation so unbelievable—how could we not have seen this swarm sooner? We should have been able to detect it. But we didn't!

"You predicted it long before we saw it. You even predicted the date of its arrival before I told you."

Gil said, "It's supernatural in every way. That's true. But we only suggested a plausible scenario. We didn't predict a date. We didn't know for sure and certain. We said, '. . . perhaps as early as . . .' Because it's prophesied in the Bible I doubt we can fight or avoid it. Most likely it will happen, ready or not."

———————

The news traveled like wildfire within their families. Gail called her mother Emma in Iowa, who called Gil's mother Ethel next door in Sky Land; both Ethel and Emma told their husbands; Harvey told Clyde; Gil called Sing, who told Sue and both of their parents; Sue called Wyatt who told his father; Tuo phoned his parents in Springfield, Missouri. Other astronomers and astrophysicists must have been equally as worried as Wayne because the evening news was full of it—in Asia, Africa, Europe, and every continent, even Antarctica. It dominated TV screens. Disbelief turned to shock; shock morphed into panic.

Duane accepted the news with equanimity, but the world and its residents panicked. As Wayne had observed, they were far less ready than Gil and Gail or Tuo or Sing.

Gail's first concern was her teenage daughter. She went to Maisie and found her sitting on her bed in her room. Mother sat by daughter. They hugged and wept. Maisie said, "Mom, I wanted to go to prom in a fancy dress with a corsage. I may live through high school but it looks like I won't live to be married. I wanted to kiss a boy, fall in love, get married and have a baby. I wanted to grow up, do so many things I won't get to do."

"I know, Honey. Heaven will be great but still . . . I wanted to grow old with your daddy. I wanted to watch you get married. I wanted to hold your babies, my grand-babies. We're all stunned. And I'm sorry—so sorry. This is a time of great shaking—for all of us."

They sat for a while. Gail touched her daughter's cheek then moved her hand to lift Maisie's face so they could look eye to eye. She bent forward until their foreheads touched. She said, "The shaking will come but don't you get shook."

"Okay, Mom. I won't. Thanks."

———

Gil gathered Sky Land's residents together. He said, "You've heard the news by now. Sometimes things happen that are harder on country folk and easier on city people; other times tragedies occur that are easier on country folk but harder on city people. This news fits neither category. Unlike anything anyone alive has experienced, this news affects all people in every nation, whether city or country, equally.

"You can and should be better prepared for news of this sort if you know God and live in His love but that is not to say you shall be spared. Planet X is headed our way here at Sky Land as surely as it is coming for everyone else."

Gil's mother had summed it up in her poetic way. "The holiest among us is not spared on account of his sanctity nor is the lowliest on account of his obscurity."

"Yes, Mother, both are impacted equally," Gil had agreed. "The Pope and the High Priest and the President—all wrapped in their fine garments—are impacted equally with the farmer in his bib overalls and the children at Sky Land."

Gil addressed the boys he had gathered one evening in their Bible study. "Boys, this news is life-altering so counseling is available here. Talk to us and each other when and as you wish, as you find it helpful or necessary. In the meantime, in the words of the ancient benediction, 'The LORD bless you and keep you; the LORD make His face shine upon you and be gracious to you; the LORD turn His face toward you and give you peace.'"

Reuven, back from his law practice in New York City with a troubled boy in tow, added softly and mostly to himself, "*Shalom.* Amen."

CHAPTER 30

2021

Wayne wrung his hands as he opined to his colleagues at Cal Tech, "I almost think it would have been better if we'd not had any warning. Now that the news is out, lawlessness and looting will strip away civilization's thin veneer of genteel society as Planet X flies ever closer. Bad things we're now faced with couldn't have happened with only a day's notice or, at the other extreme, with thirty to fifty years' advance warning." After their meeting concluded, he phoned his friends in Montana for words of assurance. He was desperate to hear voices of reason in the midst of his daily insanity.

Gail said, "I don't mean to pry but you hint at hopelessness as if there's no alternative. Initially, Gil spoke of our being surprised—and we were—but that's not to say we lack hope. *Au contraire*, we have buckets full of hope. We are investing our lives in sharing the good news of our hope with people in desperate need of it, as a matter of fact. We've got hope to spare! A verse in our Bible says, *'May the God of hope fill you with all joy and peace as you trust in Him, so that you may overflow with hope by the power of the Holy Spirit.'"*

Gil added, "Your warning is legitimate. Based on Scripture and what God has revealed to us in it, I agree with your analysis that we are powerless to deflect or destroy Wormwood. Looting and rioting are inevitable, given man's propensity toward angry lawlessness. We are in for hard times. "

Gail said. "That's why the prophets also call us to intercede for lost souls in serious, intense, powerful prayer. *'Put the trumpet to your lips,'* they say."

Wayne responded, "You and Gail are religious. Your explanation of your perspective made sense to me. But I haven't been religious and the concept of a God who is in control and reveals future events to people is foreign to my worldview. That's hard for me to swallow and I wouldn't give it a second thought except for the reality of what I've seen in my telescope. As I say, it's hard for me to admit I've been wrong, that my life's choices have been so seriously in error."

Tuo had flown another small group of refugees out of Lebanon to Sky Land and was in the kitchen when he overheard Wayne on the phone with Gil and Gail. He meandered into the living room and joined the conversation. "I hear you, brother. I was hardheaded at first, too, or, as the Bible puts it, I was slow of heart to believe. It took a friend's death to convince me how wrong I had been, to show me how empty my vain philosophy had been. My faith, so-called, had been like an assembly-line version of a machine that had been put together part by part only to fall apart under the pressure of real life."

Gil said, "You mentioned our 'perspective,' Wayne. I'm not sure you understand what it is. Our perspective is that humans are God's highest creation, that we are intended to live forever with Him as new men in a restored, perfect universe, that this brief life is to prepare us for real life in, as they say, the hereafter. Wormwood shall interact with Earth. Multitudes of people will surely die. We might die. But again, that's not to say we are without hope."

Tuo said, "These two dear friends offered hope to me years ago before I knew I needed it. Then the tragic time came when I saw my need and took advantage of the gospel's offer. In a way, you are more fortunate than I because you should be able to see your helplessness, your need, before tragedy strikes. My advice is to ask a lot of questions and make good use of the remaining time you have."

Gil said, "That's right. You may need time to question, process. If so, take time. I understand. We're here. We won't push. We'll answer the phone whenever you call but we won't push." Then he laughed, "At least, not yet. Maybe someday you'll need to buckle up for an onslaught of last-minute pushing on our part."

Gail added a last clarification, "You said we're religious. That's fine, but for some people, that word conjures up a negative emotion or memory. It's good if that's not true for you, but just in case, I suggest a better word: 'relationship.' God is personal and to know Him is to enter into relationship with Him. It's not like we have to put on special clothes, go to a special place and get His attention through rituals. We just enjoy having *relationship* with Him. Religion tends to say, 'I obey—so I'm accepted.' Relationship in Christianity says, 'Through Jesus I'm accepted—so I obey.' It changes our whole focus about rules and regulations."

Gil reached out for Gail's hand and smiled. "Wayne, my friend. I hesitated before committing my heart to Gail. I needed time. Despite my hesitation, the day came when we committed ourselves to each other and we've enjoyed relationship since then. It really is a miracle that Gail loves me like she does. I marvel at it. But it's true—she loves me. And it's beyond belief that God loves me, too. I marvel at that even more. But it's true—miracle of miracles, God loves me. As a friend told me once, 'We're not worthy but neither are we worthless.' The truth is that God desires relationship with all of us—that's what it's all about: relationship. Not religion.

"There are far too many instances in history of cruelty done in the name of religion. Such barbarisms, however, don't happen when relationship is the *modus operandi*. Religion isn't a bad word but it's possible to have religion and not know God; it's *not* possible to have relationship with God without knowing Him."

Wayne excused himself saying he had a lot to think about. As they said their telephone goodbyes Gil closed with, "Hey, Wayne, it's like the fella said who jumped off the top of a skyscraper, 'It wasn't the fall that killed me. It was the sudden stop!' Time is short and will come to a sudden stop but just because Wormwood is rushing through space to flatten you like a pancake doesn't mean you're out of time. Redeem it. Make good use of the time you have left."

Wayne's mood lightened as he retorted, "If I had known I wasn't going to die I might have enjoyed jumping from the world's tallest antenna—instead of screaming my head off like a baby. Gail, you've been cool as a cucumber since you found out about this coming swarm of big rocks in space. And I'm convinced you're not faking it. Gil gave me good practical advice. Can you give me guidance from your perspective? What do you plan on doing now?"

She answered, "We'll keep on keeping on. Opportunities for ministry, for acts of kindness, can only increase in the face of this worldwide challenge. People, old as well as young, will awaken from slumber as they confront their mortality. Some will retreat to drunkenness, for sure, and some to lawlessness, but many will ask questions and respond to the calm kindness and quiet goodness they see in Christians."

———————

After farm chores and over breakfast in the dining room the next morning, Gil stood in front of the boys and visitors whom he had called together one last time before some were set to depart. "The sobering news you've heard hasn't gone away. It's still here and it's still real. Pray. Read God's word. Process this news, but remember, it's not the end of the world. Almost—but not quite. Catastrophe but not annihilation. Go home to your families unless you feel safer here. We will, of course, provide as safe a haven as is possible here at Sky Land.

"We assumed—all of us, myself included—we had a future, which is not to say the place we're used to is the place we're meant to be, the place where we truly belong. Probably all of us thought our time here on this cool, green earth would be longer than a few more years. Maybe it will be. But likely it won't. Wormwood won't be the end of the world but it will certainly bring catastrophe. Our futures won't be what we had envisioned. They're going to be far different. It might seem like universal insanity is descending on Earth but it isn't. God's still in control.

"You boys have memorized Scripture. We've taught our daughter to do the same. All of us hold God's Word dear to our hearts. It's a comfort at all times, especially in times of crisis. Times like right now. So—tell me what the Bible, in Galatians, lists as the fruit of the Spirit."

Many answered in a sort of raggedy unison and recited Galatians 5:22–23, *"But the fruit of the Spirit is love, joy, peace, patience, kindness, goodness, faithfulness, gentleness and self-control. Against such things there is no law."*

Gil continued, "Jesus' marvelous qualities are framed in love. And we, as His people, are to exhibit selfless love. He said, *'A new commandment I give to you, that you love one another; as I have loved you, that you also love one another. By this all will know that you are My disciples, if you have love for one another.'*

"If you want people to be slack-jawed by your calm strength in witness, by the example you set in the shock of this time of crisis, love one another—but don't stop there: show love to your enemies, to those who don't love you, to those who have no intention to be nice to you. Be kind. Remember that no matter where you start in life, you're in charge of where you finish.

"Let me once again resort to a history lesson as a reminder of what we can do during these next months, to what you can be during this brief time. When the Pilgrims boarded their tiny ship, the *Mayflower*, to cross the Atlantic Ocean from Europe to the New World, they embarked with hope in their hearts. They found political freedom but also encountered deprivation, what their governor, William Bradford, described as 'the starving time.' He wrote,

'So as there died sometimes two or three of a day . . . [so] there was but six or seven sound persons, who to their great commendations, be it spoken, spared no pains night nor day, but with abundance of toil and hazard of their own health . . . made their [the sick and dying] beds, washed their loathsome clothes, clothed and unclothed them. In a word, did all the homely and necessary offices for them which dainty and queasy stomachs cannot endure to hear named; and all this willingly and cheerfully, without any grudging in the least, showing herein their true love unto their friends and brethren; a rare example and worthy to be remembered.'"

Gil spread his arms wide and said, "I urge you to follow this example and also to expand it as they did. Our time of trial can become a time of triumph. We can rise to the challenge. Governor Bradford also wrote of these early settlers,

'[The Pilgrims] yet aboard showed them [crew members on the *Mayflower*] what mercy they could, which made some of their hearts relent, as the boatswain who was a proud young man and would often curse and scoff at the passengers. But when he grew weak, they had compassion on him and helped him; then he confessed he did not deserve it at their hands, he had abused them in word and deed. "Oh!" (saith he) "you, I now see, show your love like Christians indeed one to another, but we let one another lie and die like dogs."'

"Notice that boatswain's language: heathen let their comrades 'lie and die like dogs.' He also took note that the Pilgrims didn't do that. Christians don't do that. We follow their example. We follow Jesus' example. We belong to their daring adventure for truth and to the story of their bravery, to that 'great cloud of witnesses' that's gone before us. We mimic the exquisite selflessness of Jesus as it is written in First Peter 2:21, *'To this you were called, because Christ suffered for you, leaving you an example, that you should follow in His steps.'*

"And now I'd like to call up my dear friend Dr. Sing Liu whose grandfather, now passed, was a true Christian witness in the face of many horrors, similar to what we may be about to face. His grandfather came through his trial the better for it, with his faith and hope intact."

Sing had quietly entered the classroom and was standing in the back. After Gil introduced him he just as quietly walked to the front podium and spoke. "A B-25 bombardier from long ago at the beginning of World War II who flew with Colonel Jimmy Doolittle as one of his Raiders was named Jacob DeShazer. He was captured, beaten and starved by the Japanese over three years and four months, with all but one-hundred-eighty-four days of that time spent in solitary confinement. As a result of his ill treatment in captivity, his appearance was stooped and gaunt, his face was pale, his cheeks were sunken and his eyes bulged. But his attitude and words were, 'Our country was the first to drop the atomic bomb. Now let us be the first to show mercy.'

"Jacob DeShazer, or Jake as he was known to his friends, attended college, married, and with his wife, returned to Japan in 1948 as a Christian missionary—to the place he had been tortured and the people who had tortured him. His first speaking engagement was on January 2, 1949. He told of his experiences to a full house with many press in attendance and closed by saying that he was glad they were no longer shooting at him and that he was no longer dropping bombs on them. Press and people alike loved his message and it became his model as he preached across the island country.

"In Jake's first two months back in Japan, he spoke in over two hundred places. His message enjoyed enthusiastic acceptance. Once, onstage at a theater in front of two thousand people, he was introduced to Captain Kato, who had been the head guard at the Nanking prison where Jake had been held prisoner. The crowd was hushed as the two men stood together. Jake smiled and reached out his hand to his former captor as he said, 'We meet today in the presence of the God who loves and offers forgiveness to all mankind.' Captain Kato nodded, then wiped a tear from his cheek.

"Jake was also introduced to and traveled with Captain Mitsuo Fuchida, the leader of the 360-plane squadron that bombed Pearl Harbor. Neither of them had been Christian during the war; both became Christian after it. Their message of Christian love and reconciliation resonated with crowds all across Japan. Perhaps never before in history has an entire group of people been so receptive to the gospel."

Sing wiped a tear from his cheek. "I know this story by heart because my grandfather lived it. He was a victim of cruelty in the aftermath of World War II. But he too learned to forgive and taught me how to do so as well."

Gail came up to stand by Gil and Sing. She said, "Probably nobody here will lead a squadron of airplanes into battle. It may also be true that no one of us will rot as a POW for almost four years in solitary confinement, starved and beaten. But let me follow our veterinarian friend by telling, as Paul Harvey used to say so famously, 'the rest of the story.'

"Peggy Covell's parents were Christian missionaries in Japan who fled for their lives to the Philippine Islands when World War II broke out. Japan captured those islands. Japanese soldiers then captured Peggy's parents, discovered a small radio among their meager possessions, accused them of communicating with the outside world, gave them a mock trial and beheaded them as foreign devils.

"Peggy knew her parents would want her to forgive so she moved, as an eighteen-year-old girl, near a POW camp in the United States on the Colorado/Utah border. She visited the camp every day and did all she could to help the camp's Japanese prisoners, who eventually asked her why she was so kind to them. She explained her Christian motivation that called for kindness. Her actions and her witness produced converts in that prison population.

"One of her converts was an ex-crew member of Mitsuo Fuchida that Sing just spoke about. At war's end, he found his former commander and relayed the story to him of Peggy's kindness, which played a huge part in Fuchida's conversion experience. And thousands were saved in Japan as a result as he witnessed about Jesus' love and forgiveness arm in arm with Jake DeShazer. Peggy's kindness bore tremendous fruit.

"Peggy lived a quiet life and died peacefully twenty-six years ago in 1995. Though her name is mostly lost to history, now you know the rest of the story. Her name is well known in heaven—as are yours."

Before they all sat down, Gil closed his comments. "We tend to forget speeches so I suspect you'll have trouble remembering what I said in my speech. But we remember powerful stories. You can easily remember and be inspired by these stories of the famous and not-so-famous and I'll summarize my speech for you in two words and have you repeat them. These two words are my exhortation for you: 'Be kind.' Repeat them."

"Be kind," The boys said in unison.

"What? Say it again."

"Be kind."

"Thank you. Boys, go in peace. Be kind. We all have time enough to be kind."

———————

Sue had been as shocked as anybody when she'd first heard the news. She'd checked in with Sing's father and mother, who had assured her they were fine. Then she had driven to Sky Land to do as she had done from childhood—find solace on horseback, rediscover her equilibrium in the balance of riding.

She found Maisie in the stables, with Buddy nearby. Together, they saddled up. The cadence of the horses' hoofbeats helped restore the accustomed rhythms of their lives. They found joy in this everyday activity. They remembered the biblical sequence of humble, holy, happy. They wanted to excel in the pursuit of happiness so they knew they were first called to humility and holiness, especially now—of all times.

They stayed out most of the afternoon. They returned when the shades of light were turning almost imperceptibly into early evening. That companionable hour came slowly, one shade of diminishing blue at a time until, in the sky to the west, it was pink, and the hills to the east glowed purple. To their delight, Gail had readied the kitchen and directed the ranch hands to light a bonfire in the corral for a hot dog cook-out. Following the easy, relaxed meal they enjoyed the smell of burnt marshmallows.

Sue said, "This reminds me of a moment from my childhood, an evening of innocent joy, untainted by guilt or regret, immortalized in my memory. Relish this smell, Maisie, these sounds, our afternoon on horseback. You never know, fifty years from now in the unlikely event we have fifty years on our cool, green Earth, this bonfire might come back to you as one of the sweetest evenings of your life—an interlude during a critical time."

The adolescent girl on the cusp of womanhood replied, "Thank you for sharing your time with me today, Sue. It meant a lot to my peace of mind. Someday I'll smell a burnt marshmallow and this memory will rise fresh in my mind."

CHAPTER 31

2021

Wayne contacted Gil and asked him to attend a symposium at Cal Tech as soon as possible. "Consternation reigns down here among the experts, myself included," he pleaded. "Please, your serenity and inner peace are sorely needed in our academic setting because we're at the end of our knowledge. We have no answers—none. I chair a committee and have secured permission for you to address our assembled group in plenary session tomorrow morning."

"Of course, I would be honored. When you said 'ASAP' you weren't kidding."

"How are things at the ranch?"

"Under control. I can travel today. I understand these are serious times."

"That's wonderful. Perfect. Thank you so much. I'm at my wit's end. Actually, I've taken the liberty of making airline reservations for you. With your permission, you depart Great Falls for Pasadena in five hours. Stay with me while you're here. I'll pick you up at LAX. I've arranged to introduce you. You'll have the opening hour. But I'll give you freedom to take as little or as much time as you please. It's up to your discretion. I'm sure the hall will be packed with our entire membership of seven hundred fifty because of the severity of our situation."

"Alright. I trust God shall give me the appropriate words. I'll get cracking. You do understand it will take me over three hours by car to get to the airport in Great Falls if I leave Sky Land right now—this moment."

"I do and I apologize. I tried not to do this to you but I've become convinced all my other plans have just been exercises in futility. I feel like a fool to put you in this position, but with all my heart I believe you should be at our podium—not me. I have nothing to say, pointless technical words but no words of wisdom. No words of appropriate attitude or action. We'll talk further after the fact. Right now, let me just say that my emptiness persuades me toward the truth of your beliefs. Your tank isn't empty, and for that, I'm truly grateful. It speaks volumes to me."

"I'll throw items in a carry-on and be on the road in less than ten minutes. And, Wayne, don't worry about it. This is my privilege. God will supply."

Gil had a question for Wayne later that day when they met at LAX and began their drive to Pasadena. As the car whizzed along under welcoming palm trees that lined both sides of the freeway, Gil marveled at how different the California landscape was from that of Montana.

He had lots of questions for the professor and a short amount of time to ask so he jumped right to it. "Wayne, what about the Giacobini-Zinner Comet? I think I remember somebody pointing it out to me once upon a time."

"Probably. They might have. It was discovered over a hundred years ago. Its period is six-point-six years. Its last two perihelions were in 2012 and 2018. An ICE mission gathered data from it in 1985."

"True to form, you lost me. What's perihelion? And is ICE an acronym?"

"Sorry. Perihelion is that point in a solar orbit closest to the Sun; period is the time between perihelions. ICE is an acronym for International Cometary Explorer. Giacobini-Zinner is known to us in the business as 21P. It's a small comet with a diameter of 1.24 miles. It's noticeable to the public because its fly-by is close to Earth—thirty-six million miles on its last pass in 2018. Its tail is easily visible."

"Wow, you guys process numbers on a different order of magnitude than the rest of us. Thirty-six million is a big number to me."

"It's a safe distance away from Earth, to be sure. When comets enter our inner solar system, their nuclei throw off sprays of water vapor, gas and rock into space that light up to leave tails behind. Because of their lit-up tails, comets become visible to neighborhood telescopes, sometimes even to the naked eye. They are easily identified because of these distinctive tails. Their debris streams sometimes result in meteor showers—shooting stars flashing across night skies."

"Ah, that's probably it. I probably remember hearing about or seeing a meteor shower this 21P, as you say, produced."

"Could be. In 1933, five hundred per minute were observed in Europe and in 1946 almost a hundred per minute were seen here in the States. An interesting factoid about the 1946 fly-by was that 21P passed within 131,000 miles of where Earth was eight days later. In astronomical terms, as you've already noted, eight days is quite short and 131,000 is a lot less than 36,000,000."

"Okay, now you've got me wondering—what if Earth had showed up eight days sooner?"

"Nothing would have happened."

"Are you sure?"

"Yes, except that the near-miss would have made the general public more aware of collision possibilities. On the one hand, it requires less than two hours for a comet to travel 131,000 miles, but on the other hand, 21P is so much smaller than the Moon that it wouldn't have affected ocean tides."

"How much smaller? How big is the Moon?"

"The size differential is roughly a factor of two thousand. The Moon's diameter is 2,159 miles compared to 21P's diameter of about a mile and a quarter."

"Okay, this helps bring your concerns into focus for me. The bottom line is that nothing like what we're faced with has ever happened before in the history of telescopes and modern astronomy—not even close. Is that it?"

"Yes. As you say, not even close. What we're looking at is unprecedented."

"You mentioned ocean tides. I don't know that I would have thought of them. Are they significant? How?"

"Ocean tides are produced by the action of the Sun, and to a larger extent, by the Moon. A body larger than the Moon or nearer to Earth would act with greater effect. A comet with a head as large as Earth, passing at a distance of four Earth diameters would raise ocean tides approximately three miles. As it is, the Bay of Fundy in Newfoundland has the tidal record at about thirty feet.

Compare thirty feet with three miles and you understand the devastation which would result."

"I don't need a micrometer to make that comparison. A blind man could see that three miles would flood the entire United States except for our inland high plains and isolated mountain peaks. So you're saying that in this example life would be drowned before collision would occur?"

"In a manner of speaking, yes. But it's doubtful collision would ever occur."

"How so?"

"At astronomical speeds, nuclear and gravitational forces come into play and seize the high ground, so to speak."

"Okay, that's right. You told us about the difference between low-speed and high-speed impacts during one of your visits to Sky Land. I remember being surprised that bullets flying at over a thousand feet per second are defined as producing a low-speed impact. Of course, I don't understand on other than the most rudimentary level what you're talking about, but I get the bottom-line of the concept."

Wayne said, "Immanuel Velikovsky wrote a book, *Worlds in Collision*, in the late 1940s that hypothesized a similar scenario in previous millennia to what we're now facing. In a nutshell, he talked about a large object interacting with Earth to produce a new planet, Venus, an alteration to an existing planet, Mars, and the formation of our Moon. He interviewed people and researched documents from cultures all around the world. He wrote about high tides, floods, thunder and lightning and cataclysms on a cosmic scale. He actually made quite an argument, but it's never progressed beyond the realm of the theoretical."

"Until now, perhaps."

Wayne agreed and finished, "Until now, perhaps."

Wayne's introduction the next morning was necessarily brief. He said, "Gil Webster served our country as an Army intelligence officer at the Pentagon. He is fluent in Arabic and served with distinction at a large NATO base on a covert operation, at the successful completion of which he was awarded special commendation. He interrogated prisoners and detainees in Iraq as part of our 'war on terror' and obtained actionable intelligence information at a greater rate than typical. For the last several years, he and his wife have owned and operated a ranch in Montana with the mission of rescuing adolescent, at-risk young men. They also have sponsored and lifted displaced refugees out of horrific conditions in Middle Eastern camps. They bank-rolled college educations for many of these same young people such that their lives have been transformed on every level: physical, moral, emotional, educational and spiritual. He has a delightful personality and a ready wit. He is learned and wise, but most of all, he is good of heart. I am proud to introduce to you my friend of many years, Gil Webster."

Gil acknowledged their subdued but polite applause. "Thank you. A third-grade teacher in a large city collected proverbs that were well known in past decades to country people. She gave each child in her class the first half of an American proverb and asked them to come up with its remainder. I have a few examples of responses she got back.

"Benjamin Franklin was famous for his inventions and common sense in the early days before the United States was the United States. He was politically active and at one time served as our ambassador to France. He operated a print shop in Philadelphia and published a newspaper. He also wrote and published *Poor Richard's Almanac,* in which he included many proverbs. Here's one, 'A penny saved is a penny earned.'

"In the 1700s people weren't concerned about inflation, but still believed that saving for 'a rainy day' was a good idea. A penny had value then but to third graders in our era, a penny saved is 'not much.' And that's what an inventive third-grader in this teacher's class wrote: 'A penny saved is . . . not much.'

"Here's another aphorism. I'll call out its beginning. If you know it's ending, call it out. 'You can lead a horse to water but . . .'"

Two or three at various locations in the audience called out, ". . . but you can't make it drink."

"Good. Our third grader's response was, as you might guess, inventive: 'You can lead a horse to water but—how?'" There was scattered laughter across the audience.

"How about this one? 'The pen is mightier than the . . .'"

". . . sword." Several knew that one.

"Good. The third grader's response was 'the pig.' The pen is mightier than 'the pig.' I guess that child had heard of pig pens and came up with his inventive response: The pen *is* mightier than the pig.

"Alright, one more. 'An idle mind is the . . .'" Silence. Nobody knew that one. "The third grader's response was 'An idle mind is . . . the best way to relax.' I can identify with that. Who among us hasn't wanted to, as we put it, 'veg out' in front of the TV at the end of a long day. It's a clever response. Inventive. And true to life.

"Men, more than women I'm sure, have an area of their brains labeled 'Nothing.' When my wife asks me at the end of a long day what I'm thinking about as I'm 'vegging out' in front of the TV it's hard for her to understand how literal I'm being when I respond, 'Nothing.' 'How can you think about nothing?' she asks. The concept eludes her, as it does many women, including my mother.

"My mother warned me against indolence when she thought I wasn't busy enough and needed a chore to keep me out of mischief. She would say, 'An idle mind is the devil's workshop.' You get the idea: being busy tends to keep us out of trouble while being lazy or bored tends to get us into trouble. Men, more than women, are prone to indulge in vacuousness and relax into nothingness. Usually that's alright but at some point, it becomes dangerous.

"My point with this exercise is to declare that we live in desperate times in which inventive responses are demanded. Indeed, we live in strange times in which poor people are fat and rich people are thin. At times, aided by deadlines and desperation, inventiveness with maturity sneaks in on even third graders. You, here, already have desperation. Now I challenge you to be inventive. Can you be as inventive as these third graders? Therein lies my challenge.

"I won't pretend to instruct you in astrophysics. But I remind you the distance between textbook theory and real life can be significant, as may well be the case in your current dilemma.

"While I'm not here to instruct you, I am here to declare three things to you. First, brace yourself. Earth will be," Gil held up air quotes with his fingers, "quote, unquote 'impacted'. Second, take heart. Earth won't be annihilated—it has a future. Third, do what you can to prepare for trauma. The impact will cause our orbit to be altered 900,000 miles closer to the Sun. Count on it!

"How, you ask? You know the answer. You already know the mechanism that shall alter Earth's orbit. But you don't know nor can you predict the effect this object shall have on Earth. I can. How? That's the question. How can *I* predict and quantify the effect of the impending impact? How can I be so bold as to tell you what's going to happen? What is the source material that allows *me* to be so confident?

"God's Word." Here, several in the audience groaned and others attempted to shout Gil off the podium with boos and hisses. But he had the microphone and pressed on. "It is said concerning the God of the Bible that He knows the end from the beginning. I want to shift that wording slightly this morning to say God knows both 'the end *and* the beginning.' He is above and outside of time. He knows all things. He's omniscient. He's not surprised by this situation that has surprised us.

"I draw your attention to a few words from the first book in the Bible, Genesis—the book of beginnings. I do the same from the Bible's last book, Revelation—the book of last things. Both Genesis and Revelation contain signs.

"Sadly, some preachers have lost the power of sign-making and focus their attention on sentence-making. Some, who should know better, fail to understand the 'signs of the times.' Some. Not all. Certainly not God who knows the end *and* the beginning." Here Gil shook a finger at his belligerent crowd. "Preachers or not, religious or not, God has sent a sign to those of you who can see it for what it is. This circumstance you cannot circumvent is a sign from God that is, in literal fashion, for your eyes only. You have been given a glimpse into the future. In that, you are frightened but fortunate. Your problem is also an opportunity." His voice rose. "See it for what it is. Don't waste it!"

Now that Gil had their attention, he continued, "My outline in my presentation for you this morning is straightforward. For clarity's sake, simple slides will illustrate it.

"First, the problem—one that was personal to me for many years. Two prophetic books in the Bible, Daniel and Revelation, speak of three-and-a-half years, forty-two months, and one-thousand-two-hundred-sixty days as if they shall be, sometime in the future from these old prophets' perspective, equal in duration. For the sake of time, my single reference this morning is Revelation

Chapter 11, verses 2b–3 that read, '*They will trample on the holy city for 42 months. And I will give power to My two witnesses, and they will prophecy for 1,260 days . . .*' Dividing 1,260 by 42 seems to posit a requirement that months shall be at some future point in time thirty days in duration. The logical extension is that years shall contain 360 days at that future snapshot of time. Of course, said requirement differs from current reality. Present-day reality is that we only have an occasional month of thirty days and our years are always longer than 360 days.

"I believe the Bible is God's infallible word. It presents reality—hence, the problem, a problem that was personal to me: these twin realities, one from Revelation and one from present-day observation, conflict with each other. Obviously, 360 days is not equal to *greater than* 360 days.

"Next, the second point in my outline is the problem's solution. My problem comes from the Bible so it is fitting that my answer also comes from the Bible. The first book in the Bible, Genesis, Chapter 7, verse 11, reads: '*In the six hundredth year of Noah's life, on the seventeenth day of the second month—on that day all the springs of the great deep burst forth, and the floodgates of the heavens were opened.*' Chapter 8, verses 3 and 4 read, '*The water receded steadily from the earth. At the end of the hundred and fifty days the water had gone down, and on the seventeenth day of the seventh month the ark came to rest on the mountains of Ararat.*'

"Chapter 7 says the flood began on the seventeenth day of the second month and Chapter 8 says the ark came to rest on the seventeenth day of the seventh month; in other words, the text tells us there was a difference of five months between the beginning and the ending of that worldwide, catastrophic flood event. Both Chapters 7 and 8 also define the precise time period another way: *one hundred and fifty days*. Basic arithmetic once again comes into play: 150 days divided by five months equals thirty days per month.

"Thus, the solution to my problem: months early in Earth's history were of thirty days' duration. In other words, the Bible predicts that 'that which once was, again shall be.'"

Gil's audience was drawn from people across the globe so they were tall and short, jet-lagged and semi-alert, caffeinated and on the edges of their seats, nodding in sympathy as they followed his logic or frowning and shaking their heads in emphatic disagreement. All were doing their best to be engaged, though, because of the crisis looming over their collective heads.

"The first book in the Bible deals with first things and the last book in the Bible deals with last things. Something happened in ancient history that altered Earth's orbit in such a way that its year was lengthened a bit more than five days. Something *shall* happen in future history to restore our planet's orbit to its original period or shorten its orbital period a bit more than five days. That which once was, again shall be.

"You may or may not share my belief system; in fact, chances are you don't. But I would be remiss if I failed to urge you to consider God and His message in the Bible. Whether you do or not is irrelevant to my brief presentation, however. My point is that you *do* believe what you *have* observed through *your* telescopes, which is the reason you are meeting here in plenary session with such urgency. You believe a large object is on a collision course with Earth. I can quantify for you, out of the Bible, the results of this impending collision.

"The impending collision that concerns you and all of us will not destroy Earth. In the Bible, Revelation's narrative does not conclude with Chapter 11. So you should prepare for extreme trauma but not final, total destruction. Earth's orbit will be altered but Earth won't be annihilated.

"You know better than I that Earth's orbit must be shortened approximately 900,000 miles for its solar year to be shortened a little over five days. So the question is, 'What can we do, what can you do to prepare for that event?' 'What can you do to prepare for an event that will tighten Earth's orbit by 900,000 miles?' I have no doubt but that you are in a unique position to benefit humanity by offering recommendations to prepare for trauma but not ultimate destruction.

"In closing, I say to you—take hope and be decisive. Be inventive, but above all, take action. As a college friend of mine used to say, 'Do something, even if it's wrong.' He was silly in saying that but I can and do urge you to linger not under a gray fog of indecision. The road of life is paved with flat squirrels who couldn't make a decision.

"Thank you for your attention. It has been my honor and privilege to address your august assemblage. I pray creativity to each of your keen minds as you tackle this problem that confronts you."

Gil yielded the podium to Wayne, who said, "Mr. Webster is modest. He has been succinct. At the same time, as you've witnessed, he is bravely eloquent and elegant. His words speak to me, as his Bible might say, as deep calls unto deep.

"He has not attempted to convert you, me, or any of us to his belief system but has restricted his remarks to the issue at hand as we have discovered and observed it. In that, his comments are directly relevant to our immediate concerns. Lest we become fatalistic, he has given us hope and urged us to action. My friend believes Earth is about to be relocated in its orbit approximately 900,000 miles closer to our sun and he knew it decades before we did. He discovered that by his reading of Scripture. You can easily verify the accuracy of his statement via Kepler's Laws. I appreciate that he let our own facts speak to us for themselves." A question-answer period consumed the balance of the hour.

The first questioner was polite and considerate. "I'm not familiar with your source material. You were quite clear in your presentation but I want to make double-sure I got your message. Am I correct in understanding you to say the first book in the Bible hints at an original orbital period for Earth of 360 days and the last book in the Bible predicts a return to its original orbital period? That such alterations necessarily involve catastrophic activity? Further, that we have historic precedent for that type of catastrophic activity?"

Gil answered, "Yes. That's one of the primary reasons I began, several years ago, expecting some sort of worldwide catastrophic event. I thought it most probable that it would be a large-scale impact event. Now, armed with your data, you are in a position to be of benefit to mankind in helping them prepare for it. Be inventive, creative in your work. That's an absolute requirement.

"Pay attention to the Bible. Study it, maybe with skepticism, but also give to it a generous amount of creditability. Because it's an anvil that has worn out many a hammer. It's been ridiculed and reviled yet it remains; it's been banned and burned but it is still beloved by multitudes as educated as yourself. Generations of pseudo-intellectuals have attempted to discredit it, dictators of every age have outlawed it and executed those who read it, yet fragments of it smuggled into solitary prison cells have transformed ruthless killers into gentle saints.

"Humanity has gained more from the Bible than from all other literature we have at hand. More of our law comes out of it than from William Blackstone.

More of our poetry is written by David than Homer; more of our inspiration is from Isaiah than Dante; more of our philosophy has its source in Saint Paul than Plato."

A floppy potato sack of a man stood. Gil's first impression was of the famous photograph of Albert Einstein because this second questioner's hair flew out from his head like a halo from a salt-and-pepper feather duster except it was thick and heavy instead of light and airy. This fellow had a caveman thing going on, Gil thought, with bushy eyebrows, black hair on the backs of his hands and a dark face with a permanent five-o'clock shadow. His voice was deep and powerful but he didn't exude virility or gorilla strength. The overall effect of his appearance was more sinister than comforting, more like Shelob, Frodo's giant cave-spider in a web, angling to sting, poison and add another trophy to his cocooned collection. He made no pretense of smiling as he addressed Gil with haughtiness in his voice. "You don't belong here. Your amateur presence is an intrusion and an insult in our academic midst. You lack professional qualifications. Why should I waste my time listening to you?"

Wayne's eyes pled with this floppy potato sack, this hairy caveman, to sit down and shut up. But this bullish mesomorph couldn't see Wayne's eyes or the pleading they held. Wayne was embarrassed by him in this situation but Gil decided to remain calm and show he wasn't riled by this impolite challenge. Some of the audience smiled in empathy as Gil responded, "Yours is a legitimate question. You raise a good point. Why, indeed? Sometimes my wife doesn't listen to me. Why should you?

"You belong to an exclusive club of which I am not a member. I respect that and I honor your credentials. The discipline belonging to you and your colleagues informs me of wondrous things like neutron stars compressed down to the size of a few square miles that are so dense they contain one-and-a-half solar masses. They fly in our galaxy at speeds greater than one hundred times that of our fastest rifle bullet. I wouldn't know of such things if left to my own ignorance. I'm an ignoramus when it comes to matters of astronomy. In fact, you might have preferred that your president introduced me that way."

The gorilla growled under his breath, "You're darn right."

Gil of course heard that so he said, "But using that logic and applying its unflattering terminology consistently, you're an ignoramus in theology and things having to do with God. While you can teach me out of your field of expertise, I can likewise teach you out of what I know. I'm teachable. Are you?

"You bear a heavy weight of responsibility because of your knowledge and the questions that flow out of it. For example, what would happen if one of these celestial neutron stars came into our solar system? Bad news. Very bad news! The gravity associated with such a thing would disrupt the orbits of our planets at a minimum and almost certainly make a huge mess of our solar system. And it looks like a variant on this hypothetical situation is soon to become reality for us—indeed, for all earth dwellers.

"Questions like these whirling in your head are sobering. Worrisome. You and your colleagues know, maybe more than most, that our civilization, our very existence as human beings, is only a thin veneer over the jagged edge of chaos. I bless you for carrying the weight of these staggering thoughts that are beyond me. But I urge you to carry this weight in humility, not haughtiness. And don't carry it by yourself. The collegiality within the membership of your club is valuable. I pledge not to penetrate or disrupt it. May you enjoy a partnership of effort in which no task is avoided for its difficulty or despised because of its unimportance. I wish the very best for you.

"But I also warn you against this strange ignorance you exhibit. Your bias is so strong it overwhelms any objectivity you might once have had. Beware of dissonance in your life and its non-cognitive noise that limits your options and stifles your creativity. Remember, *creativity* is the key word I set before you this morning. Open your mind to an objective study of principles that might be behind your own data set. The ideal academic in the ideal academic setting is knowledgeable without being narrow, prestigious without being pompous. You, as a fallen human being, are not as rational as you pretend. Never lose sight of how thin the veneer is that covers the jagged edge of cosmic chaos, or this veneer may collapse under the weight of your own incoherence. I urge you to reach for the ideal; don't stoop so low and settle for so little."

Gil's empathetic yet firm response encouraged more questions, even debate. A third questioner was an older woman whose bearing was dignified. Her voice trembled a bit from age, but the room grew silent as she began to speak. She said, "Over my many years I have struggled with and asked myself the question, 'What does Athens have to do with Jerusalem?' meaning, of course, what does reason have to do with faith? When I was younger, I understood that in our circles the implied and covertly snobbish answer was 'Nothing!' but I've come to realize that discoveries over the past fifty years require faith. Yet I continue to struggle with putting my hands on non-concrete objects I can't put them on. What are your thoughts?"

Gil answered, "Faith in the right Person is the key. Not faith in faith. Not blind faith. As I often tell the children around me, 'Be open-minded but not so much so that you let your brains fall out. Have faith but don't put your faith in a doorknob.' In other words, put your faith in a religious idea that can withstand rigorous, scientific scrutiny. By far the best religious idea is found in a man named Jesus. Logical symmetry tells us that whatever can be false can also be true, so let the evidence for Jesus speak for itself.

"Mature, substantive faith is practical. It reveals truth, enhances reason, elevates creativity, inspires inventiveness. It can give a person such as yourself a splendid audacity, a confidence in what you already know, deep down inside your soul—that there is more to life than physical materiality. The extreme danger for us, especially given today's crisis, is that the depth and strength of man's moral character hasn't grown to match the growth of his collective knowledge. His head has outgrown his heart.

"As you've already indicated, faith can involve a willingness to look foolish since it deals with unseen realms. A modern-day preacher said, 'Noah looked foolish building a boat in the middle of a desert. The Israelite army looked foolish marching around Jericho blowing trumpets. David, a shepherd boy, looked foolish charging a giant with a slingshot. The Magi looked foolish tracking a star to they-didn't-know-where. Peter looked foolish getting out of a boat in a storm in the middle of the Sea of Galilee. And Jesus looked foolish wearing a crown of thorns. But the results speak for themselves. Noah was saved from the flood;

Jericho's walls came tumbling down; David defeated Goliath; the Magi found the Messiah; Peter walked on water; and Jesus was crowned King of Kings.

"My answer for you is incomplete but perhaps adequate for this time and place. Are we okay or do you have a follow-up?" She shook her head, returned to her seat and sat down.

Gil wasn't sure what she intended by shaking her head, whether she agreed or disagreed, was satisfied or dissatisfied, but he continued, "We have time for one more question, I think."

A young man came to the microphone. His youth, gender and casual demeanor made him out to be the opposite in obvious ways to the previous questioner. His question had to do with catastrophism. He asked, "I get up every morning in sunny California and teach on a college campus 'where the livin' is easy.' My life has sailed smoothly along up until now. But these big rocks hurtling toward us have trouble written all over them. What do you have to say about that—besides 'get inventive, be creative?' It might be good advice but it doesn't help me very much."

Gil responded, "As has been pointed out already, I don't have an advanced degree in astrophysics. I can't tell you to sharpen the focus on your telescopes or add a few drops of barium to a solution of molten quartz. But I can say that only a few decades ago, the creation-evolution debate was philosophically framed as catastrophism versus uniformitarianism. Suffice it to say for this morning's brief presentation that catastrophism is now widely accepted. In your field of expertise, you observe impact craters on almost every object your telescopes reveal to your sight. You see craters on top of craters on top of craters, for example. Your recent discovery just makes the situation more immediate and personal.

"So here's a return question for your consideration, 'What if rocks reveal a catastrophe of such huge magnitude that it has apparently occurred only once in recorded history?' This premise is now accepted by many authorities in many different fields of study.

"My wife and I have been around the block a time or two. However, there are many places we haven't visited. That goes without saying for all of us. There are many wonders our eyes have not seen. But we don't have to see to believe, as I indicated to the previous, distinguished questioner. Neither my wife nor I have seen ten thousand feet of pure salt deposits. Yet we are informed that they exist below the Red Sea. We believe what we have been told. How can such a salt layer exist? I'm not sure but I accept that it does. And my experience also tells me such a thing is not normal! It speaks of catastrophe.

"I emphasize, there *are* places we have been and things we *have* seen. With our own eyes, we have seen coal seams in Wyoming that extend over thousands and thousands of square miles, deposits of up to two hundred feet in depth with fossilized trees standing vertical in the midst of their horizontal layers. Thousands of years' worth of supply. And how can Saudi Arabia have so much oil halfway around the world from Venezuela? Thousands of years' worth of supply. Only a catastrophe of epic proportions could have caused those formations that produced coal and oil. How can a dinosaur bone bed in eastern Montana be a half-mile wide and six miles long? Yet it exists—in dry sagebrush country. Its existence fairly screams of a huge catastrophe.

"So, again I close with the final question in my original outline, 'What can you do to prepare for an epic event that will alter Earth's orbit in such a way that it will be tightened by 900,000 miles and our solar year shortened five days?' Because it will happen. It's a matter of belief—but not belief only. It's also a matter of observation. I've just quantified for you what you already discovered with your own eyes and your own telescopes and your own calculations. You believe it as much as I do because you've observed it. And yes, it's going to involve huge catastrophe. Your smooth sailing on the sea of life is over. This huge rock in space is bringing death for multitudes of people. Truly, it's bad news. I don't believe death can be averted, which gets to the heart of your question.

"Here's my final word. The Bible says, *God is . . . not willing that any should perish but that all should come to repentance.'* That's good news. The bad news you've seen through your telescopes is that many will perish. In the final analysis, you're right. Creativity isn't enough. Repentance is required. I'm sorry but there it is. Are you ready to repent? Because, as you've discovered, judgment day is on its way. And, young man, that rock in space may have your name written on it."

He paused, "I'll be available and around for the rest of the day if you would like to speak with me further." Gil's audience sat stunned by how he ended his presentation. There was no applause.

Gil had the rest of the day off so he sat in the back of various lecture halls to listen to other speakers and be with Wayne. He learned some things but most of the discussions and all the mathematics were outside his knowledge base and vocabulary. When he needed to stir his blood and get some exercise at mid-afternoon, he took a break for a campus tour and appreciated Cal Tech's unique architecture and beauty. He laughed when he noticed a student in a T-shirt that read, "You're unique—just like everyone else." It seemed obvious that despite the brainpower of the student body, college students were college students the world over.

That evening Wayne apologized for the single rude questioner as he kept his attention on traffic while driving to the restaurant he had selected for dinner.

Gil responded, "That's alright. We both know that when someone says he doesn't mean to be rude, he really means he's going to be."

So Wayne began, "I don't mean to be rude but . . ." And they both laughed, then Wayne continued, "He's a good man—as troubled men go."

"And as troubled men go he certainly went," Gil said.

"You got me thinking, for sure. It's obvious you've spent a lot of time thinking about things I've not spent much time thinking about. I hope you realize—no, let me rephrase this—Do you realize that so much of what you presented flies in the face of all I've been taught over my entire life? Frankly, I didn't expect you to end by telling me I had to repent. It reminded me of unkempt guys in sandwich boards on street corners."

"I'm sympathetic toward your predicament." Gil looked out the car window at the traffic whizzing by. "I didn't plan to end that way, either." He swallowed, "You know, you could have a fatal car wreck a minute from now. Neither of us considers that very likely; however, Wormwood will arrive by your calculations on August 2027. So whether in a minute or a few years, here is a question of paramount importance for you, not some unknown, rude questioner: 'Am I ready for what comes next?' You need to ponder it today, right now, while you can."

"You don't let up, do you?" Wayne's smile turned into a concerned frown.

"I don't mean to be rude . . ." Gil smiled, ". . . but this is a moment pregnant with possibility. This might be your hour of decision. It would be irresponsible of me to let it pass you by without calling it to your attention."

They had arrived at their destination by this time. It was a converted house on a street on which commercial development had encroached. It had limited on-site parking and a small entry but its reputation for quiet dining was well deserved. Wayne had selected it in hopes of finding a respite from the hubbub and tension of the day. He had made reservations and they were escorted up to the second level to what had likely once been the master bedroom suite. They ordered and enjoyed a leisurely meal. As they ate, Gil said, "In answering the last questioner this morning, I used the phrase 'creation versus evolution' as an introduction to the broader concepts of catastrophism versus uniformitarianism. Between the two of us, let me give you a few hints of creationist evidence available to you or anyone—the rude questioner, for that matter. Dust depth on the Moon. Salt content of our oceans. Blue stars, double stars, spiral galaxies. Blood clotting. Irreducible complexity."

Wayne interrupted on that last one and said, "What's that? You stumped me at 'irreducible complexity.' That almost sounds like an oxymoron. I've heard that NASA, back in the 1960s, engineered big pads on the feet of the lunar lander because they were concerned it might disappear down into several feet of accumulated dust on that first moon landing. I remember they didn't know what to make of it when lunar dust turned out to be less than an inch in depth. I understand the implications this has for recent creation but what is 'irreducible complexity?'"

Gil answered, "That concept comes out of biology, primarily. As even laymen know, body parts integrate into systems that function together. Some body parts vary while still allowing the larger system to work. One example out of many is human legs. Some legs are short and thick while others are long and thin but short, stout people can walk as easily as tall, skinny people. But the imaginary process of transforming fish fins into human legs would leave any hypothetical in-between creature able to neither swim nor walk. In that state, it wouldn't be viable. It would die. Take enough of a fish's fins away on its supposed journey to land life and it loses its ability to track down dinner before it becomes dinner.

Also at some point, gills would have to be replaced with lungs, leaving our poor hypothetical creature unable to breathe. I've over-simplified but these are good illustrations.

"The bombardier beetle is another in an army of amazing creatures. It has two chambers of inert chemicals in its abdomen. When threatened, it ejects them into a mixing chamber and expels them from its body toward the threat. As they mix, they burn and turn into flame. Again, the biology and chemistry are over-simplified but evolution can't explain how or why one chamber with one chemical would form without the other. Both chambers and both chemicals must come into simultaneous existence for the system to work; otherwise, the beetle would explode and incinerate itself. The beetle's parts can only function as a system.

"Or the octopus in the ocean depths. Or the eagle soaring in the sky, using its exceptional eyesight to spot mice far below in the grass. Animals ranging from the towering giraffe to the lowly ant."

"What about the giraffe? Explain what you mean?"

"Check valves in the necks of leaf-eating giraffes allow them to lower their heads fourteen feet to get a drink of water without damage from increased blood pressure. Think about it. Their heads would explode if they didn't have check valves in their necks, which couldn't have developed or appeared slowly or the giraffes all would have died of thirst."

Later, as they relaxed over dessert, Gil asked, "Have you fed hummingbirds or had occasion to watch them?"

Wayne said, "As a matter of fact, yes. My mother had flowers and feeders on our deck when I was growing up. One of my jobs was to refill the feeders while she tended the flowers. We enjoyed spending time watching those little birds speeding around and fighting with each other. I remember astonishing statistics that their hearts could beat a thousand times a minute and their wings at eighty times per second. I can verify their wings whirred so fast I couldn't see them."

"I asked about them because they're another example of crucial parts working together to allow an animal to function and stay alive," Gil said. "Researchers today use high-speed cameras to film hummingbirds as they eat. Conventional wisdom used to be that capillary action drew the nectar up during feeding but that has been proven wrong. Capillary action has upper speed limits, and as you just said, speed limits don't work well with hummingbirds. Everything about them is fast!

"They have long, forked tongues, each with a groove in it. This tongue unrolls when inserted into the flower and nectar is pumped up its grooves at up to twenty times a second. Each part of the hummingbirds' beaks, tongues, grooves, *et cetera* must function together for the system to work and there is no reason for any of the individual parts to exist apart from the whole."

Wayne said, "Wow. Another almost unbelievable statistic. Twenty times a second! Actually, I'd wondered about that as a child. How was it a hummingbird could approach a flower or a feeder, hover as it inserted its beak for only a second into the food source *and* get nectar? A second wasn't long enough to drink. Or so it seemed to me. I guess it turns out it was long enough for them to take twenty drinks. Who knew?" He then called for the check.

It was mostly quiet on the drive to Wayne's home but Gil broke the silence. "My point is that the creationist position requires a Creator, an intelligent Designer.

"You mentioned statistics in reference to animals. Probably everyone has marveled from time to time on that topic. Here's another couple of my favorites. Researchers have attached geolocators to arctic terns as they began migrations and discovered they flew an average of 56,000 miles on an S-shaped route over the Atlantic Ocean from the Arctic region to Antarctica and back. This is the longest animal migration known to man. These tiny, three-and-a-half ounce birds take advantage of prevailing wind patterns and, since they experience summers at both poles, they see more daylight than any other creature. That example is more a statistic, a factoid, than anything else. But it illustrates the breadth of God's creation.

"Equally amazing and on the other end of the size scale, frigate birds have six-foot wingspans and can fly without landing for as long as two months. They sleep while aloft by shutting down half their brain, entering into what is called unihemispheric, slow-wave sleep alternating one eye open for a while and then the other. How could such advanced brain activity like that have developed in a species with such a small brain?"

Companionable silence returned as Wayne drove. Gil enjoyed the one-day change in scenery from Montana's wide-open spaces to Pasadena's tree-lined boulevards. The cool, sweet evening air had none of the afternoon's humid languor.

***

Gil's flight the next day was mid-afternoon. Wayne met with colleagues at Cal Tech while Gil toured Pasadena's famous City Hall. They rendezvoused on campus at the main cafeteria for lunch.

Later, Wayne waited with Gil at LAX for his flight to board. They sat. Gil shifted his carry-on between his feet. "Is your group moving toward consensus? Did you make forward progress today? Were my yesterday's comments helpful? Or did your colleagues look cross-wise at you because they resented my closing remarks?"

Wayne shook his head and answered, "It's too early. Some things are falling into place but most are falling down around my ears. We formed various task forces. Their reports will trickle in. Our one consensus is that we appreciated your presentation's perspective. You gave us guidance on how to deal with evidence we already have. You quantified what we only knew qualitatively. It had never occurred to us to think about 'nine hundred thousand miles.' Whether the membership accepts your conclusion is up for grabs, but it gives us a starting point for focused study and research."

"What's your opinion? Do you accept my conclusion? Particularly the repentance part?" Gil gazed at Wayne's stoic Army commander face for a clue.

"Yes to your first questions, because I know you and remember your original phone call on the topic. The Bible, the source for your conclusion, is mostly foreign to me but I don't have any problem with you nor can I question your conclusion itself because I trust you and the truth of your testimony. I'm not so sure about your requirement for repentance, though."

"It's God's requirement, not mine." Gil paused a second. "I've worked on you pretty hard these past two or three days. I suspect you thought you were being hard on me when you asked me to come down from Sky Land at a moment's notice. In a way, I need to apologize to you since I think the opposite is closer to the mark: I've been harder on you than you anticipated. It's just that I'm burdened for you and want you to come to spiritual truth. Wayne, with all my heart I want you to be saved from pain, death and destruction."

"When I called I admitted to you my tank was empty. I asked you to speak truth. I just didn't expect you would make me drink from a fire hose."

Gil said, "Touché." He smiled sadly. "Unrepentant people will die. I pray that you and all your colleagues will realize that 'now is the day of salvation.' You may or may not be able to save the world but you can take action to save yourselves. I plead with you, as a personal friend, to read the entire last book of the Bible, Revelation, to get an overall sense of its message. Don't take it lightly. Take note of Chapter 6 that finishes,

'Then the kings of the earth, the princes, the generals, the rich, the mighty, and every slave and every free man hid in caves and among the rocks of the mountains. They called to the mountains and the rocks, "Fall on us and hide us from the face of Him who sits on the throne and from the wrath of the Lamb! For the great day of their wrath has come, and who can stand?"'

"That sentiment is elsewhere in Scripture. Hosea, an earlier prophet, uttered similar words. Time is short. Judgment is coming. Wayne, you even know the month of its arrival.

"The briefest of summaries of the Bible's message is 'God is love.' A clever one-panel cartoon I saw years ago was of a couple of guys near mid-field in a football stadium. They noticed another guy in the stands behind the goal posts who had a big sign reading, 'John 3:16.' One said to the other, 'Who's John?' His friend replied, 'I don't know but he sure is a big boy!'"

Gil smiled and Wayne laughed because he hadn't seen that punch line coming. Gil continued, "You no doubt know that John isn't a football player but that John 3:16–19 are Bible verses. They read,

'For God so loved the world, that He gave His only begotten Son, that whosoever believeth in Him should not perish, but have everlasting life. For God sent not His Son into the world to condemn the world; but that the world through Him might be saved. He that believeth on Him is not condemned: but he that believeth not is

condemned already, because he hath not believed in the name of the only begotten Son of God. And this is the condemnation, that light is come into the world, and men loved darkness rather than light, because their deeds were evil.'

"Emotional experience is an important part of personal Christianity, which typically begins with repentance from sin. But the Greek word for 'repent' means 'to change your mind.' A component of the Christian *experience* that sometimes receives short shrift is the mental, academic, 'mind' part of the equation. It may be that God opens your mind and softens your heart gradually, like the dew, which ever so quietly comes in the night. In fact, I pray it is so for you.

"Dew uses no force, makes no noise, shows no sign, but does great work. Its translucent gems, with life's moisture in them, are laid into each uplifted hand of grass, leaf, bud or flower. We witness the result but not the operation. Meadow and mountain are baptized but no one sees the finger from which the dew drop fell. The foot that bore the blessing leaves no print. God might come to your soul, as He does to His field— quietly. We may mark no motion of the miracle that is being done but you *shall* be born again. Alive in your spirit with the Holy Spirit. A new creation in Christ. I believe and prophesy that blessing for you."

"You're quite the preacher," Wayne said. "I had no idea."

"Gail has accused me on occasion of poetic eloquence. Sometimes the words spring up before I know they're there. Dew is distilled beneath serene heavens. It isn't deposited on tempestuous nights. So act now, my friend, before the storm arrives." Gil looked up and saw his plane was boarding. He turned to his friend to give him one last piece of advice. "I'll leave you with an inspirational true-life illustration. In November 2008, ten Pakistani terrorists bombed the Taj Mahal Palace and Oberoi hotels in Mumbai, India and killed one hundred sixty-four guests and visitors. This is the testimony of a survivor of that attack. He says, 'The murderer was coming toward us with his machine gun. He'd gunned everybody down. I was on the pile of those bodies, and I knew the barrel of the gun was above me because his footsteps were so close. I didn't move. And he walked away.'

"This was during an interview a few days later after the attack. The interviewer asked, 'Why do you think he didn't kill you?' The survivor said, 'The only thing I can think of is that I was so covered with others' blood that he took me for dead and walked away.'

"Wayne, my friend, the application I make for you out of this illustration is that Jesus bled and died to save us. It is only after we are covered by His blood that we find life.

"The Bible's narrative can withstand any scrutiny you care to apply to it. It's true: from beginning to end, from top to bottom. One of the things it says is found in John 18:37 where Jesus says, *'I was born and came into the world for this reason: to testify to the truth.'* That's what you asked me to do when you asked me to come down here. I have testified truth, absolute truth. The Bible is God's word and God's word is true."

They parted company. Wayne promised to consider Gil's words as he wished him a safe journey.

Gil gave him a big bear hug. "Not to worry. This is the safest jet in the world. It'll just barely kill me if we crash."

EPILOGUE

My name is Sing Liu and I am third-generation Chinese in America. I was born here. I met God here. I met my wife here. My children were born here. It looks like I'm going to die here. Soon. Maybe.

I'm okay with it, either way—living or dying. Sort of. My emotions are jumbled. Philippians 1:21 is a short Bible verse that reads, *"For to me, living means living for Christ, and dying is even better."* Okay. Still, I'm in shock from current events.

Jesus poses a question in John's gospel. *"I am the resurrection and the life. He who believes in Me, though he may die, he shall live. And whoever lives and believes in Me shall never die. Do you believe this?"* I respond that, with all my heart, I do believe the message of the good news of the gospel in Jesus Christ. That's why I answer that I'm okay either way. Living or dying, I'll be with Jesus and enjoy life with Him forever. But I'm human and I'm shocked.

Don't get me wrong. I don't have a death wish. Grandfather lived many years here on Earth. He was blessed. Length of years is a blessing from God.

Not long ago, my wife Sue said, "You're serious-minded—and that's fine. I love you for you. But there's a change in you. You're more Mr. Sober Sides than normal. If I don't mind saying so, you've got the best wife in the world. You've got four wonderful children. You've got it good but you're not acting like you're on top of the world. Something's wrong. What is it? Talk to me."

I answered her, "This world's not much to be on top of but I'm already missing it. At the same time, I miss heaven. I feel stuck in-between. It's like

265

Glasgow and my vet clinic are gone but heaven's not here. I'm grieving but I don't quite know how to cry. Don't get me wrong. I don't grieve as one who has no hope but . . ."

Bless her heart, Sue understood. She's such a comfort to me. I can hardly imagine the almost-despair Grandfather must have felt all those lonely years without his wife in partnership at his side. My wife, my partner, my soul mate, my lover and confidant said to me, "While this world is not enough, it's all we've ever known. It's familiar. I don't want to depart this cool, green earth before my time any more than you do but I thought my time would be another twenty or thirty or forty years. It's shocking to be told my time—our time—is so short. Heaven may get here first or it may be coming hard on the heels of Wormwood, but you're right—both are coming but neither is here. Wormwood may arrive first with all its trauma, tragedy, destruction and heartache. It's unfamiliar. The thought of it is foreboding. Like you, I look forward to the time when our hope is realized, when the 'not yet' will be the 'here and now.' But the transition may hurt—bad."

She continued, "May I wax philosophic?"

I smiled and said, "Please, by all means, karate kid. Wax on."

"Our deep thinkers assure us that joy is best mixed with a tinge of melancholy for it to be exquisite gladness. We must indulge light and shadow, allow them to have their interplay and judge not by the one or the other."

I teased her. "By deep thinkers, you mean persons with more horsepower in their brains than Scarecrow after the Wizard of Oz bestowed a diploma on him?"

"Yes, but you're right. We can never be too careful when dealing with these so-called deep thinkers. Sometimes they're just wandering deep in the weeds, pretending to be a wizard with all the answers."

My wife's personality is more upbeat and outgoing than mine, but she too yearned for heaven. Her paraphrased words of Scripture comforted me. "The human condition is to hunger after wholeness. Grandfather now lives in an eternity that never grieves. Neither of us is afraid to join Grandfather in his place of wholeness. The Bible says if all we get out of Christ is a little inspiration for a few short years, we're a pretty sorry lot. The truth is that Christ *has* been raised up and became the first in a long legacy of those who are going to leave the cemeteries. There is a nice symmetry in this—that death initially came by a man, and resurrection from death came by a man. Everybody dies in Adam and everybody comes alive in Christ. As Eugene Peterson paraphrased Scripture:

'Death is swallowed by triumphant Life!
Who got the last word, oh, Death?
Oh, Death, who's afraid of you now?'"

Sue smiled and I smiled back, suddenly feeling much better.

"Well then, Honey, in light of our current situation, how do you want to be remembered—if there's anybody left here to remember us?" Sue asked. "Not what do you want on your tombstone. How do you want to be remembered?"

This was a serious conversation so I took my time and thought before replying. "As a Christian husband and father who had a good wife, provided for his family and helped lead his children to saving faith in God. Since you can't chisel all those letters into granite just say, 'He made a difference.'"

I took her by the hand. "You're the life of the party. I'm blessed, so fortunate to be loved—so lucky you love me—but we both know that the next world is going to be a whole lot better even than this one. The real party is there, not here.

"I'm not sad anymore—just impatient to get *there*. And it would be great if the trauma of getting *there* didn't hurt too much. As the old joke puts it, I want to die in my sleep like Uncle George—not screaming in terror like all the passengers in the car riding with him."

She interrupted to mimic a child strapped in the back seat of a car on a trip—shaking its hands and stamping its feet, "Are we there yet? Are we there yet?!"

I gave a quiet laugh and said, "That's it exactly. I try not to stamp my feet, but I wish heaven and its party time would hurry up!"

"I think it is," she replied. "August 2027 is almost here. As they say on racetracks and airstrips, it's coming in 'fast and hot.'"

Glasgow and its rugged surroundings have been great. I love them. But they're not without their weeds, insects and frigid temperatures. Creation, even in the most idyllic places, is marred, fallen. Our natural bent is not holiness, but depravity. We can't save ourselves. Our best works are insufficient. They're not good enough. The best of men are only men at best. All of us have sinned; all of us fall short of the glory of God.

Jesus is the only way to the Father. That's the good news. There is a way out. It's narrow but it's there. And that narrow door is open for all to enter.

The bad news is that it takes a certain amount of bending, stooping and even breaking to crawl on our knees through that down-low, narrow door. Humility doesn't come naturally to prideful people.

Japanese culture interacted with Grandfather in the cruelest possible way. Its interaction with him was evil. No question about it. But, like all cultures, it also contained instructive elements.

An ancient Japanese art form called Kintsugi is the art of repairing and restoring broken pottery using lacquer mixed with powdered gold or other precious metal dust. The pieces are meticulously put back together and the cracks are filled with the gold lacquer. The emphasis of this process focuses on the beauty of the repaired cracks; the scars of what happened are highlighted, not disguised. The end result exhibits beauty that surpasses the unbroken original.

As a philosophy, Kintsugi uses the repaired cracks as the focal point of the object rather than something to keep hidden. Japanese culture values the artfully repaired object as better, stronger, more beautiful and of far greater character than before it was broken. This principle, when applied to a person instead of an object, can have a dramatic and positive effect on someone who feels broken.

The concept that a person's brokenness can result in greater strength—a new level of appreciation of life, better relationships, new possibilities and, at times, a spiritual change—becomes exciting and can be quite beautiful. There is even scientific data to back up the claim that individuals who have accepted the damage they have endured come out on the other end of their experiences stronger and wiser than they were before the trauma occurred.

Such applies to Grandfather and his story. Exactly. Directly and precisely.

The irony of the human situation is that most, if not all, of us are going to be surprised. Whether individuals or nations, the righteous ones are going to exclaim at the final judgment, "When were we good? When did we please You?" and the unrighteous ones are going to exclaim, "When were we bad? When did we displease You?" Both will be surprised.

So beware and be warned. Life in the hereafter will either be worse or better than you ever thought it could be. Your worst nightmare might be worse than you dreamed, or your best dream will be better than you imagined.

The meteor swarm approaches. Wormwood is on its hot, explosive way to us. Judgment is coming. Who shall escape? Not you. Surely not you. Not me. Especially not me. Except I'm not afraid. Shocked, yes. Shocked and stunned. Unsettled. But not afraid. Are you? Are you more than shocked? Are you more than unsettled? Judgment is in the air as well as in space. As my children and the kids I've worked with at Gil and Gail's Sky Land Ranch might say, "You should be freaked out!" I agree. If you haven't gotten down on your knees and crawled through that narrow door you should be freaked out.

But think of it this way. You still have time. You still have a couple of years before the giant rocks in space fall on you. Maybe. If you're lucky. Do you feel lucky?

AFTERWORD

John Birch was a true, unsung hero whose exploits helped turn the tide of World War II in the Pacific theater of operations. Following is an excerpt from an essay he wrote in early 1945 (the year he was killed) that he titled, "The War Weary Farmer."

"I want to own some fields and hills, woodlands and streams I can call my own. I want to spend my strength in making fields green, and the cattle fat, so that I may give sustenance to my loved ones, and aid to those neighbors who suffer misfortune. I do not want a life of monotonous paper-shuffling or of trafficking with money-mad traders.

"I do not want a hectic hurrying from place to place on whizzing machines or busy streets. I do not want an elbowing through crowds of impatient strangers who have time neither to think their own thoughts nor to know real friendship. I want to live slowly, to relax with my family before a glowing fireplace, to welcome the visits of my neighbors, to worship God, to enjoy a book, to lay on a shaded grassy bank and watch the clouds sail across the blue.

"I want to love a wife who prefers rural peace to urban excitement, one who would rather climb a hilltop to watch a sunset with me than to take a taxi to any Broadway play. I want a woman who is not afraid of bearing children, and who is able to rear them with a love for home and the soil and the fear of God.

"I want of Government only protection against the violence and injustices of evil or selfish men.

"I want to reach the sunset of life sound in body and mind, flanked by strong sons and grandsons, enjoying the friendship and respect of neighbors, surrounded by fertile fields and sleek cattle, and retaining my boyhood faith in Him who promised a life to come."

ABOUT THE AUTHOR

Don McBurney was a U.S. Air Force pilot, flying an EC-121 in radar recon and combat air patrol over Vietnam. He also patrolled Korea's DMZ on TDY assignments. After his military service, Don graduated from Oral Roberts University with a master's degree in theology. He retired as one of Montana's senior real estate appraisers. Don and his wife of fifty-two years are active in their local church and are proud parents of five children and (so far) nine grandchildren. He was honored to publish in the national *Appraisal Journal*. His previous novel is *The Triplet*. Don resides in Whitefish, Montana.

A free ebook edition is available with the purchase of this book.

To claim your free ebook edition:

Visit MorganJamesBOGO.com
Sign your name CLEARLY in the space
Complete the form and submit a photo of
the entire copyright page
You or your friend can download the ebook
to your preferred device

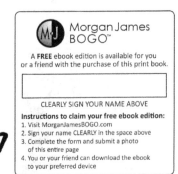

Morgan James BOGO™

A **FREE** ebook edition is available for you
or a friend with the purchase of this print book.

CLEARLY SIGN YOUR NAME ABOVE

Instructions to claim your free ebook edition:
1. Visit MorganJamesBOGO.com
2. Sign your name CLEARLY in the space above
3. Complete the form and submit a photo
   of this entire page
4. You or your friend can download the ebook
   to your preferred device

Print & Digital Together Forever.

Snap a photo   Free ebook   Read anywhere

CPSIA information can be obtained
at www.ICGtesting.com
Printed in the USA
JSHW021603240122
22227JS00001B/80